MURDER
AT THE
BREAKERS

A Gilded Newport Mystery

MURDER
AT THE
BREAKERS

ALYSSA MAXWELL

KENSINGTON BOOKS
www.kensingtonbooks.com

KENSINGTON BOOKS are published by

Kensington Publishing Corp.
119 West 40th Street
New York, NY 10018

All Kensington titles, imprints, and distributed lines are available at special quantity discounts for bulk purchases for sales promotion, premiums, fund-raising, educational, or institutional use.

Special book excerpts or customized printings can also be created to fit specific needs. For details, write or phone the office of the Kensington Special Sales Manager: Kensington Publishing Corp., 119 West 40th Street, New York, NY 10018. Attn. Special Sales Department. Phone: 1-800-221-2647.

Kensington and the K logo Reg. U.S. Pat. & TM Off.

ISBN-13: 978-0-7582-9082-3
ISBN-10: 0-7582-9082-9
First Kensington Trade Paperback Printing: April 2014

eISBN-13: 978-0-7582-9083-0
eISBN-10: 0-7582-9083-7
First Kensington Electronic Edition: April 2014

10 9 8 7 6 5 4 3

Printed in the United States of America

*To my Newport family, all of you, and most especially
my best friend and wonderful husband, Paul.
And to my mother-in-law, Norma,
who was with us for far too short a time.*

*And to Evan Marshall, who has believed in me,
encouraged me, and helped brainstorm
the idea for this series. Thank you!*

Acknowledgments

Many thanks to John Scognamiglio for bringing this project to life, and to Kristine Mills-Noble and Steve Gardner for the beautiful cover design and artwork, respectively.

My deepest appreciation, also, to Nancy J. Cohen, for helping me learn to think like a mystery writer.

Chapter 1

Newport, Rhode Island, August 1895

She awoke that morning to an angry sea battering the edges of the promontory, and gusting winds that kicked up a spray to rattle against her bedroom windows. She might simply have rolled over, closed her eyes again, and sunk pleasantly back into sleep, if not for the—

Here the nib of my pen ran dry and scratched across the paper, threatening to leave a tear. If not for the *what?* I knew what I wanted to say; this was to be a novel of mystery and danger, but I was having a dickens of a time that morning finding the right words.

As I pondered, my gaze drifted to another page I'd shoved aside last night. Sitting on my desktop inches from my elbow, the words I'd hastily scrawled before going to bed mocked me with their insipidness. "*Mrs. Astor Plants a Rose Garden,*" the title read. Who could possibly care, I wondered. Yet people apparently did care, or I wouldn't have been sent by my employer, Mr. Millford of the Newport *Observer*, to cover the auspicious event. Not that Mrs. Astor actually wielded anything resembling a garden tool, mind you, or chanced pricking her tender fingers on a thorn. No, she'd barked brisk orders at her groundskeepers until the placement of the bushes suited her taste, and then ushered her dozen or so guests onto the terrace for tea.

I sighed, looking up from my desk to stare out my bedroom window. The scene outside perfectly matched the mysterious one I'd just described: a glowering, blustery day that promised intermittent rains and salty winds. The inclement weather heralded ominous tidings for my protagonist, not to mention wreaking real-life havoc on the tightest of coiffeurs.

No matter, I had no plans to stray from home until much later in the evening. I dipped my pen in the inkwell and was about to try again when from behind me a hand descended on my shoulder.

With a yelp I sprang from my chair, shoving it away with the backs of my knees. I sucked in a breath and prepared to cry out in earnest, but before I could utter a sound, a second hand clamped my mouth.

"Shush! For crying out loud, Em, don't scream. I thought you heard me. Ouch!"

I'd instinctively bitten one of the fingers pressed against my lips, even as recognition of the familiar voice poured through me and sent my fear draining from my limbs. Still, I had no intention of apologizing. Wrenching from his grip, I turned and slapped my brother's hands away.

"Blast it, Brady! What are you doing here? Neither Katie nor Nanny would have let you upstairs without asking me first."

"The front door was unlocked. I called out, but when no one answered I let myself in." A flick of his head sent a shank of damp, sandy blond hair off his forehead—and assured me he was lying. That particular gesture had accompanied Brady's fibs for as long as I could remember. The only truth to his statement was that he'd let himself in.

"You sneaked in, didn't you?" I folded my arms in front of me. "Why?"

"I need your help, Em."

"Oh, Brady, what now?" My arms fell to my sides, and with a sigh that melted into a yawn, I walked to the foot of my bed and reached for my robe. "I suppose you must be in real trouble again, or you'd never be out and about this early."

"Are you going to The Breakers tonight?" He referred to the ball our relatives were holding that evening.

"Of course. But—"

"I need you to do something for me." He threw himself into the chintz overstuffed chair beside the hearth. I remained standing, glaring down at him, braced for the inevitable. "I, uh . . . I did something I shouldn't have. . . ."

"Really? What else is new?" Several scenarios sprang to mind. A brawl. A drunken tirade. Cheating at cards. An affair with yet another wife of an irate husband bent on revenge. One simply never knew what antics my half brother, Stuart Braden Gale IV, might stir up on any given day. Or night. Despite hailing from two of Newport's oldest and most respected families—on both our mother's and his father's sides—Brady had seen the inside of the Newport jail nearly as often as the town's most unsavory rapscallions. And on many a morning, I'd paid the bailiff on his behalf more times than I, or my purse, cared to count.

"I want to make it right," he hurried on. "The Breakers will be mobbed later and I'll be able to sneak in, but I'll need your help."

"I don't like the sound of this one bit, Brady. Whatever it is, you know you should just come clean. You can't hide from Uncle Cornelius for long."

Before he could reply, a pounding echoed from the hall

below. I heard a tread on the staircase and moments later there came a rap at my bedroom door. With an imploring look, Brady shook his head and put a finger to his lips. He jumped up from the chair and moved to the corner of the room where my armoire would hide him from view. A sense of foreboding had me dragging my feet as I went to the door.

"Good mornin', Miss Emma." Katie, my young housemaid, peered in at me and tucked an errant red curl under the cap she'd obviously donned in haste. Her soft brogue plunged to a murmur. "Sorry to disturb you so early, miss, but Mr. Neily's below. Shall I tell him you ain't receivin' yet?"

"Neily?" A burst of wind rattled the windows, sending a chill down my back. "On a morning like this?" My maid didn't answer, and I managed to refrain from angling a glance into the shadows cloaking my brother. "Thank you, Katie. Tell him I'll be down in a few minutes. Show him into the morning room, please, and bring in coffee."

"Aye, miss." The girl hesitated and then bobbed an awkward curtsy.

I closed the door.

"You won't tell him I'm here, will you, Em?"

With pursed lips I met my brother's eager blue gaze. "He's looking for you, is he?"

"One would assume."

Going to my dressing table, I pinned my braided hair into a coil at my nape, secured the sash of my robe into a knot, and slipped my feet into a pair of tattered satin slippers. In the bathroom my great aunt Sadie had installed before she died, I turned the creaky faucet and splashed cold water onto my face. Ordinarily I wouldn't dream of greeting company in such a state of dishabille, but this was my cousin Neily, here on a blustery August morning hours before he typically showed his face beyond the gates of his family's summer home.

Would I keep my brother's secret? Blindly lend him the help he asked for?

I sighed once more. Didn't I always?

When I stepped back into the bedroom, Brady was nowhere to be seen, though I thought I heard the telltale click of the attic door closing.

Downstairs, I paused in the morning-room doorway. A coffeepot and two cups waited on the table; fruit, muffins, and a tureen of steaming oatmeal occupied the sideboard. Under any other circumstances, my stomach would have rumbled. Not today.

It didn't appear as if my cousin had brought an appetite either, as he hadn't helped himself to any of the repast. I pasted on a smile and stepped into the room. "Good morning, Neily. What brings you here so early, and in such weather? Not that it isn't always good to see you." Could he hear the hesitation in my tone? "Will you join me in some coffee?"

He had been standing with his broad back to me, staring out at the ocean, his dark hair boyishly tousled in the way that had become fashionable among the sporting young gentlemen here for the summer season. He turned, his somber expression framed by the tossing gray waves and the ragged clouds scuttling past like ripped, wind-born sheets.

"Good morning, Emmaline," he said curtly, a civility to be gotten over quickly so he could come to the point of his visit. He held his black bowler between his hands. "Is Brady here?"

I blinked and clutched the ruffled neckline of my robe. For once I didn't bother correcting Neily on my name. I preferred Emma, but my more illustrious relatives insisted on using my full name, as they did with all the girls in the family. "Brady," I repeated. I paused, hating to lie, but for now I'd do what I could to protect my brother, at least until I knew more.

I discreetly crossed two fingers. "You know Brady's never up this early. Is something wrong?"

"He's up today and, yes, something's wrong." His overcoat billowing behind him, he came toward me so quickly I almost backed up a step, but managed to hold my ground. "If I were to look around, are you sure I wouldn't find him?"

Only if you look in the attic. But please don't. Then again, by now Brady might be somewhere on the first floor, perhaps in the adjoining service hallway, listening to every word.

Aloud, I said, "Look all you like." I was sure Neily could hear my heart pounding. "Did you check around town?"

"He's not at his digs, and he's not sleeping it off at any of his usual haunts. This is important, Emmaline, and I need your help. So does Brady, as a matter of fact."

Good heavens, did he think I hadn't figured that out for myself? But I raised my eyebrows in a show of ignorance.

Neily's grip on his hat tightened, leaving fingerprints on the rain-dampened felt. "If you happen to see him, if he shows up here . . ."

"Yes, I'll tell him you're looking for him. Now, about that coffee . . ." I started toward the table, but Neily's next words stopped me cold.

"No, don't tell Brady anything. Call the house. Immediately. Ask for me. Tell no one else anything. No one. Not even Father."

That reference to Cornelius Vanderbilt II held just enough emphasis to send a lump of dread sinking to the pit of my belly. "You're scaring me, Neily. What exactly has Brady done?"

In a rare occurrence, Cornelius Vanderbilt III, heir to a fortune that had surpassed the $200 million mark a generation ago, shifted both his feet and his gaze, obviously no longer able to meet my eye. "I . . . I don't like to say, Emmaline, not just now. It could all just be a . . . a misunderstanding."

I strode closer to him. Realizing I was clutching my robe again, I dropped my hands to my sides and squared my shoulders. "What could be a misunderstanding, Neily? Stop being mysterious. If Brady's in trouble, I have a right to know."

"It's railroad business." A faint blush stained those prominent cheekbones of his, raising my curiosity tenfold and making me wonder, Brady's present crisis aside, what business machinations the family had gotten up to now. "Please, Emmaline, that's all I can tell you."

I knew I wouldn't get any more from him. "All right. If I see Brady or hear from him, I'll call. He was invited for tonight, wasn't he?"

Tonight's ball was to be both a coming-out party for my cousin Gertrude and a housewarming event for Alice and Cornelius Vanderbilt's newly rebuilt summer "cottage"—an affair that promised to be the most extravagant Newport had ever seen.

"He's invited, but it's doubtful he'll show." Neily started past me, then hesitated, staring down at the patent leather toecaps of his costly boots. "I couldn't help but notice that . . . that Katie isn't . . ."

Ah. Early that spring, a few weeks after the family had come up from New York to supervise the final touches on The Breakers, a young maid in their employ had shown up at my door, distraught and with nowhere else to turn. Katie Dillon had told me little more than what was obvious, but I'd surmised the rest. I'd been furious with Neily, and vastly disappointed with the cousin I'd known all my life and had come to admire.

"No, Katie *isn't*," I said coldly. I tugged my robe tighter around me and pushed away images of that awful night of blood and pain and tears. Katie had been in her third month, had hardly begun to show yet. "Not any longer. The child died and nearly took Katie with it."

For the briefest moment Neily hung his head, quite a show of remorse for a Vanderbilt. "But she is . . . she's . . ."

"Fine now, thank you for inquiring." My tone rang of dismissal. I had far more important concerns than soothing his conscience.

Neily lingered a moment longer as if searching for words. Then he was gone, leaving me staring past the foggy windows to the waves pluming over the rocks that marked the end of the spit of land on which my house, Gull Manor, perched boldly above the Atlantic Ocean.

A half an hour earlier I'd been imagining mysterious happenings, but suddenly I'd entered a very real mystery of my own. Who was the villain? Who the victim?

A step behind me broke my troubled trance. I didn't bother turning around. I knew my brother's skulking footsteps when I heard them. "Right now Neily only suspects I did what I did," he said softly. "If I undo it, there'll be nothing to hide. All I need for you to do is be my lookout later."

I walked to the window and reached out, pressing my palm to the cool pane. "Brady, I don't see why I should help you if you won't trust me enough to tell me what you did."

"Of course I trust you. But it's better you don't know too much. I don't want you implicated."

I whirled, true fear for Brady knotting my throat. His clothes and hair had dried, but his rumpled appearance lent him a vulnerable, lost air that tugged at my heartstrings. "Oh, Brady. If you don't change your ways, someday you'll be beyond anyone's help."

He held up a hand, palm up. "Just keep an eye on the old man, Em. That's all. Right before midnight. Everyone should be in that cavernous hall of theirs toasting cousin Gertrude before the midnight supper. But if you see Uncle Cornelius edging toward the staircase at any time between eleven forty-five and midnight, do something, anything, to stop him. All right, Em? Can you do that for me?"

I regarded his trim, compact frame, his fine, even features, and the smudges of sleeplessness beneath his eyes. Brady was my elder brother by four years. Our parents were alive and well, but living in Paris among all the other expatriated artists searching for inspiration, many of whom had once, in a simpler time, called Newport home. Arthur Cross, my father, was a painter and, yes, a Vanderbilt, but a poor one, descended from one of the daughters of the first Cornelius. Brady wasn't a Vanderbilt at all but Mother's son from her first marriage. His father had died before he was born, a Newport dandy with a penchant for spending rather than earning and who had been presumed dead in a yachting accident, though his body was never found.

With no available parents, somehow I had become the guiding force in Brady's life. Even at twenty-one I was the steadier of the two of us, the more practical, the one who remembered that food and clothing and a roof over one's head couldn't be won at poker or dicing. But when I couldn't guide him, I picked him up, dusted him off, gave him a lecture, and fed him honey cakes and tea. Why that last? Because despite his many failings—and they were numerous—there remained some endearing quality about Brady that brought out my motherly instincts. What can I say? I loved my brother. And I would do what I could to keep him on the straight and narrow.

"Promise me your intentions are honorable," I demanded in a whisper.

"I swear it, Em."

With a nod and an audible breath, I agreed to help him. I just prayed I wouldn't regret it.

At a little after nine that evening, I turned my buggy onto Victoria Avenue and drove the short distance to the end of Ochre Point. Half-stone walls topped by gleaming, curling wrought-iron fences and backed by immaculately trimmed hedges marked the perimeter of The Breakers property along Ochre Point Avenue. Flanked by two pairs of massive stone pillars, the soaring iron gates stood open to the long sweep of drive leading up to the house's hulking outlines, illuminated against the night sky by the interior lights and countless gas lanterns.

Shipley, the gatekeeper, stood ready to turn away anyone who didn't hold up one of Alice Vanderbilt's gilded foolscap invitations. He hailed when he recognized me and waved me on through the gates, chuckling only slightly. He knew as well as I that I'd raise eyebrows driving my own carriage, especially after Aunt Alice offered to have one of her drivers collect me. I hoped I could pass my horse and vehicle off to a footman before either of the elder Vanderbilts saw me and tsked at my "outlandish behavior."

I maneuvered carefully past the stylish black victorias and sleek broughams lining the drive and occupying the open pavement in front of the grand porte cochere. With so many footmen and drivers milling about in their colorful livery, the area had taken on the festive atmosphere of a midsummer fair. A footman in the Vanderbilts' distinctive maroon livery came running to help me down.

"Good evening, Miss Emmaline. Beautiful night, isn't it? You're looking mighty fine, if you don't mind my saying."

Such was my rapport with many of the servants here; after all, I was closer in circumstances to most of them than to my well-heeled relatives. I thanked him heartily and made my way beneath the arched portico that jutted from the ornate marble façade of the four-story, seventy-room "summer cottage." The Venetian-style villa easily dwarfed its Bellevue Avenue neighbors, even the stately Marble House, built two years earlier by yet another branch of the Vanderbilt family.

The absence of one servant in particular was enough to make me stop just inside the door. "Bateman," I said to the head footman, "where is Mr. Mason tonight? Surely he isn't ill?"

I could think of no other reason that would prompt the Vanderbilts' long-time butler, Theodore Mason, to miss such an important event.

The good-looking, fair-haired young man cast a glance over his shoulder at the bustling entrance hall, then leaned closer to me. "He's been dismissed, Miss Emmaline. For stealing. Mr. Goddard caught him at it."

I gasped in disbelief. But before I could ask questions, more guests entered behind me, forcing me to continue on down the marbled hallway, through a set of wrought-iron doors, and to the steps of the Great Hall, where the family waited to greet their pre-ball dinner guests.

There, Aunt Alice stood at the head of the informal receiving line. "Why, Emmaline, how enchanting you look, my dear." She gave my sash a tug and smoothed her plump hands over my gown's newly refurbished sleeves as if she could somehow fuss my attire into a more fashionable state. A thoughtful gleam entered her eye, and if she was remembering my pale green gown from last year's midsummer cotillion at Rough Point, well, she would be correct.

"Thank you for inviting me for dinner, Aunt Alice."

The actual fête wouldn't begin for another two hours. I and about thirty other "close family and friends" had been invited to a pre-ball meal.

"Yes, yes, of course, dear," she said heartily. Her gaze dropped to my right hand; she, of course, knew better than to wonder if I'd brought along a lady's maid. "No valise?" she observed.

"No, Aunt. I won't be changing for the ball." No, I'd been hard put to come up with one dress appropriate enough for a night at The Breakers. Meanwhile, I longed to ask her about Mr. Mason, but I knew tonight would be the wrong time to raise the subject. Instead, I leaned down to kiss her round cheek.

She gave my shoulders an affectionate squeeze. "You know, Emmaline, our nice Mr. Goddard has been eager for your arrival. I've seated him beside you for dinner. Be pleasant with him. I do believe he wishes to ask you to dance later."

I mumbled something noncommittal, but Aunt Alice heard what she wished.

"Oh, good, he'll be so pleased. Cornelius, here is our lovely Emmaline.... Ah, Mr. and Mrs. Greerson ... and Mrs. Astor, how very good of you to come...." With practiced finesse, Aunt Alice handed me off down the receiving line.

Uncle Cornelius tweaked my cheek. Of average height and build, with graying hair and the sloping posture of an accounting clerk who spent long hours poring over ledgers, the fifty-three-year-old head of the Vanderbilt family would hardly have turned heads on a busy sidewalk. Until, of course, one met his gaze; those dark eyes seared and skewered and gave no quarter. And yet for me, he very nearly beamed with one of his rare smiles.

"You're looking robust, Emmaline. Comes from breathing the sea air year-round, I expect. How are your parents?"

"They write that they're well, Uncle, thank you for asking."

"Your father sell any paintings lately?"

"Yes, just last month," I was happy to be able to tell him.

"Make a good margin on it?"

I hadn't the vaguest idea what Father made on his paintings. Occasionally my parents wired me a few dollars to help with the running of Gull Manor, but otherwise I made due with the small annuity Aunt Sadie had left me along with the house, and what wages I earned on my own. But I smiled and said, "I believe so, yes, Uncle."

"Good. Though for the life of me I'll never understand why he didn't want the position I offered him at New York Central. Artists—bah!"

There was little I could say to that, so I merely smiled. Strictly speaking, Cornelius Vanderbilt wasn't my uncle. We were second cousins twice or thrice removed, but addressing that steadfast, imposing old gentleman by merely his first name—or his equally formidable wife, for that matter—was a notion more daunting than even my stout heart could rise to.

His attention, too, passed to the Greersons and Mrs. Astor, and I moved on to greet the rest of the family. Neily kissed the air near my cheek and mumbled a stiff good evening. Gertrude, the star of the evening and a good head taller than I, hugged me enthusiastically. We paused to admire each other's gowns, hers a feminine confection of white chiffon, mine a flounced watered silk that had seen the better part of a decade. At least the mossy color set off my hazel eyes nicely.

"Nanny did a splendid job," she whispered with a genuine smile, knowing full well my gown had been turned more than once, with new sleeves, fresh lace, and a beaded sash recently added in an attempt to bring the frock up to date.

"They won't let me stay up for the ball," Gladys, the youngest Vanderbilt, complained in my ear when I bent down to hug her.

"I'll try to sneak up later to keep you company," I whispered back. "And you can help me write my article about the ball for the society page."

She giggled and kissed my cheek. "Don't forget."

I promised I wouldn't and moved up the wide, carpeted steps into the Great Hall. I'd been in the house a handful of times since its unofficial reopening in the spring, but the breadth and depth and soaring height of this room, with its ornate gilding and carved Italian marble, still forced the air from my lungs in a giddy rush. I glanced up at the faraway ceiling, painted to give the illusion of the sky poised above an open courtyard.

The original house had been a larger version of my own Gull Manor—timbered and shingled, with gabled rooftops and sprawling wings. But when that house burned to the ground three years ago, Cornelius and Alice had commissioned a stone and marble gargantuan to be built in its place, insisting it be the grandest, most sumptuous mansion New England had ever seen. I couldn't imagine one more majestic.

Or more ostentatious. But that was an opinion I kept to myself.

The moment our intimate dinner ended the servants rushed into the dining room to set up for the 300-odd guests who would be supping there at midnight. I ran upstairs to a guest room to freshen up, and by the time I descended the grand staircase the festivities were in full swing.

Although much of the house had been fitted out with electricity, Aunt Alice favored the richer glow of traditional illumination, especially for an event such as this. I couldn't say which glittered brighter, the gaslight and candlelight shimmering on the myriad treasures and artwork that filled my view, or the guests who had spent small fortunes on tuxedos and ball gowns and rummaged deep into the family vaults for their finest jewelry. I fingered the cameo pinned to the ribbon at my throat—a gift from Aunt Sadie—and nearly felt ashamed of the tiny teardrop diamonds hanging from my ears.

Then again, when I considered how many disgraced maids I could help with the kind of money these people tossed blithely away on an average afternoon, well . . .

A lively Strauss waltz filled the air. As I made my way through the hall, greeting acquaintances, I wondered what Brady might be doing. Was he here already, maybe somewhere below stairs waiting for his chance to sneak . . . where? I still didn't know what he planned to do tonight.

"Good evening, Emma."

I looked up into the handsome face of Jack Parsons, a bachelor friend of my father's from his university days. They had been roommates at Yale, but where Father had studied the fine arts, Mr. Parsons had prepared himself for business and finance. Word had it he'd made millions following Uncle Cornelius's lead in the railroad industry.

"How are you, Mr. Parsons?" I managed without blushing, even as I took in the features that if anything had gained more appeal with the advent of fine wrinkles around the eyes and mouth. I admit I'd once entertained a bit of a schoolgirl fascination with the distinguished yet rakish Mr. Parsons. I suppose I must admit, too, that it hadn't been all that long ago.

"I'm fine, Emma, just fine," he said in that easy way he had. "I had a letter from your father last week. Thinking of paying him a visit in Paris this fall."

"Oh, he'd like that. . . ."

We chatted until a hail drew my attention.

"Emmaline Cross! Emma, over here!"

Through the crowd I spotted a familiar face. And while that face hadn't always brought me pleasure during our childhood, tonight Adelaide Peabody Halstock's slightly crooked smile summoned a grin of my own. I excused myself from Mr. Parsons.

"Oh, it took forever to make my way in," my old schoolmate said as she took both my hands in her own. Her satin evening gloves spanned her forearms like liquid pearl, making my own gloves appear thin and yellowed in comparison. We both pretended not to notice the difference. "Did you know the family has practically set up court in the Music Room to greet all the guests? I declare, Gertrude and Alice are sitting on gilt and velvet thrones."

I had to look up a bit to meet her gaze. "Aunt Alice means to make an impression tonight."

"She has certainly done that." Adelaide swept the room with an appreciative glance.

The beadwork on her gown clattered lightly as she leaned to kiss my cheeks, and suddenly even Nanny's efforts on my own gown seemed sadly inadequate. This, too, we pretended to ignore. "We must steal somewhere quiet later and catch up," she said. My hands ached slightly in her grip; Adelaide had been athletic in school, a champion in tennis and archery, even cricket. "But first I'd like for you to meet my husband. I was so disappointed you couldn't make it down to the city for our wedding. It was a splendid affair."

It didn't slip my notice that, after marrying a New York shipping and railroad magnate, Adelaide had picked up the habit of referring to New York City as "the city," as if no other metropolis were of any account.

"I'm certain it was and I'm terribly sorry, Adelaide, I just couldn't get away last summer." I didn't bring up the reason, didn't say the word deemed so unspeakable in mixed company, but I saw the knowledge of it in the flash in Adelaide's green eyes.

I *worked,* and it had been the need for wages that had kept me from leaving Newport during the high Season of ninety-four to attend her wedding. Even tonight, though I was a relative and an invited guest, I should have been working, making careful mental notes of all in attendance—what was worn, what was served, what was said, all of it to be included in a society page article for this week's Newport *Observer.*

I say I should have been, because that night all I could think about was Brady.

Adelaide tossed the blond curls I'd always envied. "Come meet Rupert. Now, where is he?" Releasing my hands, she linked her arm through mine and we wove a path across the dance floor. "He hasn't been well recently, so I'm doubly delighted he could be here tonight."

I hid a smirk. Phrases like *doubly delighted* would scarcely have been in the vocabulary of the former Adelaide Peabody, who, like Brady, hailed from a staunch old Newport family—at one time a wealthy family who had owned several of the city's most popular hotels. But then times changed and rich summer tourists began building their "cottages" rather than staying in hotels. That happened a generation ago, and Adelaide's family sank into hard times.

The memory raised my sympathies for her, as well as for her husband. Politely, I said, "I'm sorry to hear Mr. Halstock has been poorly."

"His heart," Adelaide whispered in my ear, and I remembered hearing, probably from Gertrude last summer, that Rupert Halstock was more than thirty years older than his new wife. "His doctor has strictly forbidden him his port, cigars, and poring over stocks and dividends for more than two hours a day. Believe you me, Emma, it's been no picnic policing his daily activities. But well worth it. The dear man is growing as sturdy as a goat."

The man she pointed out stood in a group of older gentlemen before the open piazza doors that overlooked the rear gardens. Beyond the straggly whiskers sprouting beneath his chin, I hardly detected anything "goat-like" about Rupert Halstock. Far from the picture of returning health, his pallor alarmed me and left me shuddering at how he must have looked while in the throes of his disease. I shuddered, too, to envision the vivacious Adelaide with this much older man.

The group shifted and Alvin Goddard, Uncle Cornelius's financial secretary, honed in on me with a predatory smile. With his sloping shoulders and grizzled hair, he resembled Uncle Cornelius in a superficial way, but where Cornelius Vanderbilt wore his heart, conscience, and intentions on his sleeve, Alvin Goddard was more reticent, at times secretive. I thought of poor Theodore Mason, an out-of-work butler because of this man's accusations—accusations I couldn't bring myself to believe. My own smile threatened to slip as he came toward me, his hand extended.

"Miss Vanderbilt, it was my understanding we were supposed to be seated next to each other at the dinner table. What happened?"

Yes, I had managed to circumvent Aunt Alice's seating plan by following the younger Vanderbilts to the lower end of the table. But I smiled and let Alvin Goddard raise my hand to his lips. "It's Miss Cross and you know it, sir."

"Miss Vanderbilt-Cross," he said with emphasis. "You should be proud of your heritage, of being the Commodore's great-great-granddaughter. Shouldn't she, Mrs. Halstock?"

"Oh, indeed she should, Mr. Goddard."

"Is that what I am?" Gently extracting my hand from his when it seemed he would never release it, I did my best imitation of one of Adelaide's curl-tossing shrugs. "I never can remember how many greats there are between my illustrious ancestor and myself. I do, however, remember exactly how much inheritance passed down the line from him to me. None."

And Alvin Goddard would do well to remember that. He was decades older than me, shared none of my interests, and I had no intention of encouraging him. I kept hoping he'd realize that with me he might have a Vanderbilt, but not a penny of the Vanderbilt fortune, and he'd move on to greener pastures. But perhaps he believed marrying me would cement his place in Uncle Cornelius's employ. After all, it was because of me that Brady had been offered a place in the family business, albeit his duties were mostly clerical.

I sighed. How much longer would Brady hold his position?

I had yet to meet Adelaide's husband, who just then cupped a hand to his ear and yelled to his companions to speak louder. But Aunt Alice caught my eye from nearby and beckoned me to her.

"Excuse me one moment, Adelaide."

She squeezed my wrist before she let me go. "Come by Redwing Cottage tomorrow for luncheon and we'll talk then."

When I reached Aunt Alice, she drew me to her side. "Emmaline, dear, might I ask a favor of you?"

"Of course. Anything." I expected her to partner me for the next set with either Mr. Goddard or someone's younger son.

Aunt Alice was always on the lookout for a potential husband for me. Not a great magnate or his primary heir, mind you, for I could never aim so high, but someone with a modest trust fund and a respectable family. Never mind that I wasn't in the market for a husband.

But that wasn't what she had in mind. "Neily met a girl in Paris last year, Grace Wilson, and she's here tonight. Over that way—no, don't look yet! All right, now."

I followed her gaze to the dance floor where Neily spun a young redhead about in his arms. She wore rose taffeta in the latest Parisian fashion that slimmed and elongated an already flawless figure. Her features were striking and she danced with skill, but she might have been any one of dozens of beautiful young debutantes here tonight. It was Neily's over-the-moon expression that provided me with instant information and explained Aunt Alice's scowl.

"Her father made his fortune blockade running during the Civil War," she whispered as though imparting the blackest of sins. "Now she's set her cap for Neily and I won't have it." Her voice turned as hard as a steel rail. "I don't care how much money her family has, she is altogether fast, that girl, and a fortune hunter. Not to mention that she is years older than my son."

Not to mention, also, that her brother had married Carrie Astor, whose mother was among Aunt Alice's most vehement social rivals.

I didn't like the turn in the conversation, but against my better judgment, I asked, "What do you want me to do?"

"Keep an eye on them for me, and don't let them sneak off alone."

Aunt Alice flounced away and I blew out a breath.

"Evening, Em."

I very nearly gasped, thinking the greeting from behind me came from Brady. But as I whirled to see a more youthful face than my brother's, I remembered that my youngest male Vanderbilt cousin liked to use my pet name as well. "Hello, Reggie. You weren't at dinner."

"Had other things to do."

I wondered what that meant, but let it go. "I'm glad to see your parents let you attend tonight."

"I'm sixteen now, after all." He smoothed strands of dark hair off his brow in a gesture surely meant to look suave. Reginald was a younger version of Neily and promised to be handsome someday. Their dashing looks must have skipped a generation because they certainly hadn't gotten them from either of their stocky, ordinary-looking parents.

"Yes, and good heavens," I replied, raising my chin. "I have to look up to meet your eye now, don't I? I don't remember having to do that back in the spring."

He grinned and held out a hand. "Dance, Em?"

I laughed. "Why not?"

From the dance floor I could keep a closer eye on Neily and Grace Wilson, and I had nearly an hour before I needed to make sure Uncle Cornelius didn't venture upstairs. Reggie proved a more skilled dancer than I would have guessed, displaying none of the awkwardness one would expect of a sixteen-year-old. As I drew a breath I noticed something else unexpected.

"Reggie, have you been drinking? And I don't mean champagne punch."

He gave a cavalier shrug. "It's a party, Em."

"And while your father's head is turned, you raid his liquor cabinet. Reggie, trust me, it isn't a good idea."

"What can happen?"

I could point to a host of things that could go wrong and make Reggie's life difficult at best, tragic at worst. At the same time I wondered at which end of the spectrum my brother's intrigue lay tonight.

"So tell me," Reggie said, breaking in on my sober thoughts, "how's Katie?"

Something in his voice nearly caused me to trip over my own feet. Holding Reggie's hand, my other hand resting on his shoulder, I went utterly still and studied his smooth features—the gentle bow of his lips, the dark brows arched over darker eyes that held . . . a touch of challenge and a hint of irony that had no rightful place in the visage of a sixteen-year-old boy.

I stepped back. "Reggie . . ." I found I couldn't say it. Could barely think it.

Katie . . . Had I been grossly unfair to Neily? Could the boy before me be so much less a child than I could have imagined? My temples began to throb. At that moment, the music ended and the couples on the dance floor drifted apart for a breath of air, a sip of champagne, and the requisite reshuffling of partners before the orchestra took up a new number.

When I glanced back at Reggie, that disquieting look had vanished and he was once again the mischievous boy who sneaked sips of whisky when no one was looking. "Nice dancing with you, Em. See you later."

In the next half hour I danced, chatted, kept a watchful eye on Neily and Grace, and pondered all that Katie Dillon had inferred to me last spring, and all she hadn't. What I knew for certain was that the man who had briefly fathered a child on her hadn't given her a choice in the matter. Good gracious, Reggie? Had Neily let me believe it had been him in order to shield his younger brother's indiscretion?

No. Everything in me shouted that it wasn't possible. Maybe Reggie had only asked after a girl who used to work for his family, and maybe that look in his eye had merely meant he'd eavesdropped and heard the matter discussed.

But the gnawing in my belly persisted . . . and grew as midnight approached. At twenty minutes to twelve, liveried footmen and hired waiters began moving like a silent army through the Great Hall, wielding trays filled with glasses of Uncle Cornelius's finest champagne. In the confusion, I lost sight of

Neily. I spotted Grace's rich, bejeweled coif across the room, but only briefly. Then she, too, disappeared from view, though she might merely have been obscured by the crowd. If the two were up to something, Aunt Alice would have to catch them at it herself. I had more pressing concerns.

Aunt Alice herself fueled my unease when she appeared at my shoulder. "We're nearly ready to toast Gertrude and I can't find Cornelius anywhere. Did you see which way he went?"

Oh, no. I'd been so concerned with Neily, Reggie, and Katie, I'd let Uncle Cornelius slip away. With less than twenty minutes now before midnight, surely he'd return any moment. But if he didn't . . .

Brady might just then be making his way up one of the service staircases. Should I try to warn him that Uncle Cornelius was nowhere to be found? But how could I do that when I had no idea which room marked Brady's destination? I thought back to what he'd told me that morning. He wished to return something he'd taken . . . borrowed . . . stolen . . . something to do with railroad business. Then it had to have come from either of two places: Uncle Cornelius's office, or his bedroom, both on the second floor.

I might have gone running up the grand staircase to search for Brady, but the second-floor rooms all opened onto a gallery that looked down over the Great Hall. I couldn't risk being seen and followed, especially by a family member.

Aunt Alice gave me the perfect excuse to leave the Great Hall and devise a plan. "Emmaline, be an angel and check the billiard room. Tell that husband of mine if he doesn't come at once he'll spoil Gertrude's night."

I set off at nearly a run, my haste raising numerous eyebrows. Several men occupied the billiard room, but Uncle Cornelius wasn't one of them. Instead of seeking him elsewhere on the first floor, I slipped quickly out through the double doors onto the rear piazza and then down the steps onto the lawn.

The day's rain had left the grass sodden, and moisture instantly soaked through my embroidered dancing slippers. They'd be ruined, but I hadn't time to lament the fact. Toes squelching, I circled the side of the house, looking up as I neared the front. The second story was dark except . . . there! A beam of light passed across the windows of Uncle Cornelius's bedroom. Brady must be inside.

I was about to hoist my skirts, scamper around to the front door, steal inside and up the service stairs when the light suddenly went out. I waited, staring into the darkness, my ears pricked. "Brady," I whispered—stupidly, for at that distance and through the closed balcony door he could not have heard me. A minute or two passed. I decided my best course was indeed to run inside, but just then a sharp thwack from above rooted me to the spot. Two or three more clunks followed. Moments later, the balcony door swung open and sounds of a scuffle burst from inside the room.

"What? You!" a man's voice exclaimed.

"Brady?" I cried out hoarsely, too frightened now for discretion.

There came a grunt, more scuffling, another thwack—louder and sharper now, like a gunshot piercing the quiet—and then the thud of something or someone hitting the stone balustrade. My heart pounding, I scrambled backward to get a better view, and as I looked up again, a dark silhouette tumbled over the railing and plummeted to the ground at my feet.

Chapter 2

I cried out, then pressed both hands to my mouth. My heart pummeled inside my chest, and I stood motionless, breathless, staring down at the black heap before me, my brain thrashing to make sense of what had just happened.

With trembling fingers I lifted my hems from the wet ground and tiptoed closer, afraid to look, unable to turn away. The night closed around me like a fist, blocking out the house, the lawns, the nearby drive crowded with sleek horses and posh carriages. The music and lively hum of voices drifting from the piazza doorway faded. The crickets were silenced. I heard only the distant rumble of the ocean striking the cliffs at the base of the property.

A haze swam before my eyes, and through it I could make out scant details about the figure sprawled facedown on the ground: the formal tailcoat and tapering black trousers, the buffed dress shoes, the dark but graying hair. A notion rose like bile to choke me.

"Uncle Cornelius? Oh, God. Oh, no . . ."

My hands fisted in my hair. Then, needing to be sure, I

leaned down closer, reached out, and laid my fingertips on one shoulder. I gave a shake, waited . . . and hoped for some response. When none came, I sucked in a breath and with both hands pushed to roll the figure over. The eyes that gazed unseeingly, grotesquely up into mine sent me scrambling backward, puddles splashing up onto my legs, my heart crashing against my stays.

The face staring up at the sky was not Uncle Cornelius's. "Mr. Goddard!"

Relief that my relative had been spared mingled with my horror. I don't know how many seconds passed while I simply stood and stared, dumbfounded. Then my feet were in motion, bringing me around to the front door. The footman manning the vestibule eyed me with alarm, but I rushed past him. In the wide entryway of the Great Hall I stopped, halted by the insanely normal scene that greeted me. The music had ceased and the guests stood several deep in a circle spanning the entire room. I began threading my way through with entreaties of *please*, and *step aside*, and *let me pass.*

Then I drew up short. At the center of a circle, Uncle Cornelius stood with a beaming Aunt Alice beside him. At his other side stood Gertrude, hunching slightly in her frilly white dress, looking awkward at finding herself the recipient of all that attention. Reggie and Alfred were there as well, hovering behind their sister. As the room blurred slightly around me, glasses of champagne were held high and Uncle Cornelius spoke words my mind could not then decipher. A resounding chorus filled the hall and thundered in my ears, drowning out my racing thoughts.

I needed to find help, but I also needed to avoid panicking the guests. There were so many of them, nearly three hundred . . . fear could cause a stampede. Who would help me—help Mr. Goddard? Though in truth my instincts told me the man was beyond earthly aid.

Another uncertainty pounded through me. Where was Brady? Did he have anything to do with Mr. Goddard's fall?

Oh, God, what had Brady done?

The crowd broke apart. With Uncle Cornelius and Aunt Alice leading them, the party streamed past me toward the dining room. I found myself engulfed in a milling kaleidoscope of color and echoing voices. Dizziness threatened to overtake me, but I staggered forward, searching for a face I could trust. Neily... Adelaide... my father's old friend, Jack Parsons... I saw none of them.

"Emmaline? Are you all right?"

From behind me, fingertips touched lightly on my shoulder. I turned around, relief sweeping through me. "Neily..."

"Good God, Emmaline! What happened to you?"

Only then did I realize how I must have looked, with my hair straggling from its pins, my gown soaked at the knees and hems, and the wild, desperate look in my eyes. I swayed, and my cousin's arm swept around my shoulders. As fast as my legs would allow, he walked me into the nearby music room and on into the library. He sat me down on a sofa, moved away, and shortly returned to press a snifter to my lips.

I dutifully drank, then coughed and sputtered as the brandy lit my throat on fire. Neily crouched in front of me and took my hand.

"Em... tell me what happened."

"I... outside... a man... Mr. Goddard..."

Ruddy color suffused his face and his hand tightened around mine. "That fiend! Why, when I get my hands on him, I'll—"

"No, Neily," I said quickly. "Mr. Goddard didn't hurt me. He... oh, God." I shook my head to clear it, to stop the roaring in my ears. "There's been a... a horrible accident. I think... oh, Neily, I think there's been a death at The Breakers."

* * *

"Wait here," Neily said after I hastily explained what I'd witnessed.

I jumped up from the settee. "No, I'm coming with you."

He didn't like it, but I refused to stay put. Quietly we stole out the piazza doors so none of the guests now supping in the dining room would see us and take it into their heads to follow. Outside, Neily held an oil lantern beside Mr. Goddard's face.

"It's Goddard, all right," he confirmed, though there hadn't been a doubt in my mind. He pressed his fingertips to the man's neck where the pulse should be, then held his hand in front of Mr. Goddard's nose, feeling for a breath. With another sigh, Neily sat back on his heels, the tails of his evening coat hanging in the wet grass. "He's a goner, I'm afraid. I think his neck broke in the fall. God . . . poor Alvin . . ." He glanced up at the balcony. "It may only be the second floor, but the ceilings in this house are so high the distance is certainly great enough to kill a person. But how the hell did he fall?"

I shook my head. My thumping pulse rapped out a possibility, but I wasn't about to incriminate my brother until I learned more. All I knew was that I needed to find Brady; talk to Brady.

My cousin set the lantern down on the grass and came to his feet. From beneath him the light angled over his face to cast ghoulish shadows that emphasized his frown lines, the hollows of his eyes, the grim set of his mouth. "Tell me what happened. What were you doing out here?"

"I'd . . . just wandered outside for some air," I lied, not meeting his eyes.

A *damn* slid past his lips. "The police have to be called."

My stomach turned over, but I knew he was right.

In the next minutes Neily covered poor Mr. Goddard with a sheet, ordered a footman to keep watch, and discreetly used the telephone in the servants' hallway to make the necessary call. With him occupied, I stole the opportunity to race upstairs to Uncle Cornelius's bedroom.

"Brady," I whispered into the darkness. "Brady, are you in here?"

Silence and the light creaking of the still-open balcony door greeted me, gave me chills. I waited another moment, my eyes straining to see into the shadows of the expansive bedroom. All lay silent, and I could make out no one hiding in any of the corners. But why would Brady still be here, if indeed he had been here at all? I'd been foolish not to hurry upstairs sooner instead of going outside with Neily to examine the body. Obviously, I hadn't been thinking clearly.

I returned to the library, where I sat hugging an arm around my middle and, yes, sipping more brandy while I waited for Neily. Surrounded by the soothing influence of walnut paneling and Spanish leather, I found myself staring at the inscription carved above the marble fireplace:

I CARE NOT FOR RICHES, AND DO NOT MISS THEM
SINCE ONLY CLEVERNESS PREVAILS IN THE END.

Slowly, shock receded, leaving bleakness to settle over me. It's true I hadn't liked Alvin Goddard much, but now I could hardly remember the reasons. Uncle Cornelius had certainly trusted him, and even Brady had esteemed him as a sharp-witted wolf of a businessman who never missed a detail to his employer's benefit. Yet, despite the claim inscribed in stone in front of me, Mr. Goddard certainly hadn't prevailed tonight. A few hours ago he had kissed my hand and now *this*—it was simply too horrible to comprehend.

"I just told Father what happened," Neily said as he strode into the room. "He and Uncle William are outside. They . . . they saw the body and now they're waiting for the police. Mother and the guests don't know anything yet." He stood a moment on the balls of his feet, then seemed to reach a decision. "I'm going upstairs to have a look. Do you want to come with me?"

Avoiding his eye again, I stood.

"I suppose we shouldn't disturb anything," I whispered moments later as Neily pushed open the door to his father's bedroom suite.

"No, the police will want to see the room exactly as it was at time of . . ." He left the sentence unfinished.

Would they find a clue linking Brady to the accident? A breeze blew in from the balcony, and a slight tinge of liquor wafted on the air—something I hadn't noticed upon entering the room before. Still clutching my middle, I walked in a few strides and stared into the darkness while Neily turned up the gas and lit a sconce.

I blinked as the room burst into light, and gasped. On the floor, sticking out from the far corner of the bed, lay a pair of feet, toes pointing upward. A moment's dread held me immobile. Then I hurried across the room. This time, I made no mistake in the individual's identity. I'd have known him anywhere, in any position, in any state of consciousness.

"Brady!"

I was about to go to his side, but Neily grabbed my arm from behind. "Wait, Emmaline."

"What do you mean, 'wait'?" I struggled to break free, but he held me fast. "He could be—"

"He's breathing. But look at him. Look at everything around him. The papers, the bottle, the fallen candelabrum . . ."

I stopped struggling and saw what Neily was trying to point out. Brady didn't appear to have been attacked. He appeared to have fallen in a state of drunkenness and passed out. A bottle of Tennessee bourbon lay on its side just beyond his head. And those papers fanning away from beneath his hand . . . I could see the words *New Haven-Hartford-Providence* emblazoned across the top of the first page, and beneath them, figures, first in mileage, then in dollars.

"The stolen plans," Neily said softly at my shoulder.

"What?"

"The railroad business," he clarified. Then he pointed. In the corner of the room, the waist-high steel and brass safe my uncle always traveled with stood like a sentinel, its door appearing to be sealed tight.

I whirled to face Neily. "He was bringing them back. I swear it. He meant to make it right."

"But Alvin caught him at it . . ."

"Don't say it, Neily. Don't even think it. Brady wouldn't . . ."

His gaze swung sharply up from Brady's prone form. "You knew about the documents?"

"No." I shook my head briskly. "At least, not until this morning. And even then I didn't know much. Brady came to see me, he said—"

"Why didn't you tell me?" He grabbed my shoulders, almost hurting me. "Emmaline, you promised to call me if you heard from him."

Brady stirred and let out a groan. At the same time, I became aware of voices and footsteps coming up the stairs. Brady sat partway up and groaned again. Reaching out, he grabbed a fistful of coverlet and groped into a semi-upright sitting position, only to double over as a fit of coughing overtook him. Then, moaning, he pressed a hand to the back of his head. Uncle Cornelius, his brother William, and two policemen barreled into the room.

Red-faced and puffing, Uncle Cornelius drew up short. "What in hell is going on here?"

In the next minutes, Neily and I helped Brady up off the floor and into a chair. Cornelius and William stood by scowling while all the lights were lit. One of the officers gathered up the fallen papers and the other picked up the silver candelabrum that lay on the floor on its side, its two tapers having rolled beneath the bed. I noticed wax and scorch marks on the rug— thank goodness nothing had ignited. The main structure might be fireproof, but the furnishings were not.

Through the open balcony door, the sounds of commotion drifted from below. The shrieks of whistles and the deep-toned barking of orders told me more policemen were securing the area and inspecting the body. Officer Jesse Whyte approached my brother. "Good evening, Brady."

Running a hand up the back of his tousled blond hair, Brady gave a nod and a low groan that resulted in Officer Whyte wrinkling his short, thin nose and pulling back. "Been nipping a bit tonight, eh, Brady?"

"No . . . I haven't been, actually. . . ."

"Uh-huh."

This was not Brady's first encounter with Jesse Whyte; far from it. Nor mine, for that matter. A lean man in his early thirties with large ears and deceptively youthful features, Jesse lived in the same house he'd grown up, a white clapboard colonial just down the street from our own family home on the Point section of Newport. We were old neighbors, old family friends.

As a cop on a beat, Jesse had apprehended Brady on countless occasions over the years, though only rarely had charges been brought. Typically, Jesse would bed Brady down for the night in an unlocked cell to let him sleep it off, and call me in the morning.

Now a plainclothes detective, his taut expression overrode the initial relief I'd felt when he strode through the bedroom door. "You want to tell me what happened, then, Brady?"

My brother's pale eyebrows drew together. He squinted, suggesting unconsciousness had left his brain fuzzy. I thought of the empty bottle of bourbon, but when Brady's gaze swerved to mine, his eyes were sharp. I shrugged and shook my head slightly to indicate that I hadn't told the police officers anything—yet.

When he hesitated in answering, Jesse's partner held up the documents we'd found littering the floor. "We take it these aren't yours, are they, Mr. Gale?"

"What the blazes are those?" Standing several feet away, Uncle Cornelius craned his neck to see. "Is that my seal at the top of the page? Those should be locked up in my safe, damn it!"

Brady's face turned ruddy. "I've never seen them before."

My pulse lurched at the bald-faced lie.

"What the hell were you doing in my bedroom, Brady? How'd you get those documents?"

I flinched at Uncle Cornelius's booming voice; everyone flinched, actually.

"We'll ask the questions." The second officer was a humorless bully of a man named Anthony Dobbs who'd once given Brady a black eye. He angled a warning look at Uncle Cornelius, who simply glared back, thoroughly unintimidated.

Uncle Cornelius murmured some words to his younger brother, William, who left the room, I assumed, to answer any questions that might arise downstairs and keep the guests calm. My uncle settled into a wing chair by the fireplace and pinned a stern gaze on Brady. Neily moved to lean in the balcony doorway, his shoulder even with a dent in the door frame that momentarily captured my attention. The house was brand new and perfect in every way. . . .

Jesse, meanwhile, walked unhurriedly to the dressing table, dragged the cane bottomed armchair across the rug, and set it in front of Brady's. He sat with the same leisurely manner, taking a moment to unbutton his coat and settle comfortably before leaning forward with his elbows on his knees. "Brady, were you stealing those documents from Mr. Vanderbilt's safe?"

"No!" Staring down at his feet, Brady shrugged. "That is, I did, but that was the day before yesterday, Jesse. I had a change of heart about using them. I was about to replace them in the safe when—"

"When Alvin Goddard caught you!" With a sneer, Officer Dobbs made a notation in a notepad he'd produced from an inner pocket of his tweed coat.

Uncle Cornelius jumped to his feet and seemed about to storm across the room. Neily stepped into his path. "I'll explain in due course, Father, but let the officers finish their questioning."

Uncle Cornelius fumed, but retreated to his wing chair.

Jesse continued with the interrogation. "Did Alvin Goddard confront you?"

"No, I never saw him. I was moving toward the safe, and then . . ." His eyes closing, Brady shook his head. "Then I woke up . . . and Neily and Em were leaning over me."

"That's all you remember?"

"That's what happened."

"And you never saw anyone else in this room?"

"Think, Brady," I piped up from across the broad mahogany bedstead. "Did you hear anything at all?"

"I . . ." Brady pressed the heels of his hands to his temples. "Wait!" His hands fell away. "I did hear something. I remember now. I was making for the safe when I heard a creaking behind me, like a light footstep. I started to turn . . . and then my head felt like it was going to explode."

"He's lying." Officer Dobbs scowled as he scribbled in his notepad.

Jesse ignored the comment. "You're saying someone attacked you, Brady?"

"I think so, yes."

Dobbs let out a huff. Jesse, however, leaned closer to Brady, reached out, and ran his fingers over the back of Brady's head. He winced at the same time Brady did. "Size of a walnut," Jesse murmured. "Hurt?"

"Hell yes." Brady lifted his own hand to his head as Jesse pulled away.

"Can you remember anything else that might help identify your attacker?"

Brady hesitated, then shook his head. "Damn, but I wish I could."

With both hands I clutched the bed's curving footboard. "But obviously there *was* someone else in this room. A third person who knocked Brady out."

"Why do you say that, Miss Cross?" Officer Dobbs rounded on me, his pad and pencil held aloft. "The other person might merely have been Alvin Goddard, catching your brother red-handed. The two struggled. Your brother threw Goddard over the balcony. Drunk as he obviously was, he stumbled back inside, hit his head, and passed out."

"Over the balcony?" Brady sprang up from his chair, sending the piece tumbling over backward. "I may be a thief, a cheat, and a drunkard, but I'm no murderer!"

It took some minutes and a substantial dose of cognac to calm Brady down. Through Neily's and my combined efforts, we resettled him in his chair and persuaded him to repeat, calmly, the events as he remembered them.

Jesse turned to Uncle Cornelius. "Sir, why would Alvin Goddard have entered your bedroom tonight?"

Uncle Cornelius stared at the other man as if he didn't understand the question. Then he dropped his face into his hands. "Dear God, he's really gone, isn't he?"

No one said anything. Neily shuffled his feet as if about to move to his father's side, but then seemed to change his mind and stood staring down at the carpet. Officer Dobbs, meanwhile, inspected the fallen candelabrum for traces of blood, but declared the item perfectly clean except for the smudges left by Brady's fingers.

After a moment, Uncle Cornelius pulled himself together with a lift of his shoulders. "I sent Alvin in. Before toasting my daughter, I conducted a bit of business in my office. I sent Alvin here afterward to return the paperwork to my safe." His eyes narrowed on my brother. "What were *you* doing here, Brady? What papers did you steal?"

When Brady pulled a sheepish expression, Neily lifted his chin and spoke up. "He swiped the plans for the New Haven-Hartford-Providence line." He gestured to the bed where Jesse had deposited the documents. "My guess is he copied them and wanted to return them before anyone noticed they were missing. Thing is, I'd already noticed. Sorry, Brady old boy, but your nasty little secret is out."

Uncle Cornelius stood, his features blacker than I'd ever seen them. I cringed as he crossed the room, snatched up the documents and glowered at them, then snapped them down again. He lurched as if to hurl himself on Brady. Only Officer Dobbs's quick reflexes stopped him, and for once I was glad for the boorish man's presence. The policeman's beefy hands closed around Uncle Cornelius's upper arms from behind, or I believe my uncle might have gone for Brady's throat.

"Damn it, Brady, I gave you employment for Emmaline's sake, so she wouldn't have to worry about her elder brother. And this is how you repay me? Theft? Disloyalty? You're a swine!" He struggled in the policeman's grip. I cried out for him to be reasonable, but he seemed not to hear. "No one crosses me like this! No one! I want to know who you sold me out to!"

The blood drained from my face and I tightened my grip on the footboard for fear my legs would collapse beneath me. Officer Dobbs noticed my distress. "I think it'd be best if you left now, Miss Cross. And as for you, Mr. Vanderbilt," he said with a warning tug on Uncle Cornelius's arms, "I'll let you go if you promise to calm down."

I'd no intention of going anywhere, but even if I had, Jesse had other ideas. "Indeed, Mr. Vanderbilt, you're not helping matters. But, Emma, don't you go anywhere. According to what your cousin told me over the telephone, you were a witness to Mr. Goddard's death. Is that true?"

All eyes turned toward me.

"I . . . um . . . well . . ." Oh, how I suddenly wished I'd curbed my tongue when I sought help from Neily earlier, at least until I'd had the chance to talk to Brady. Was I about to implicate my brother? "It was dark and I couldn't really see anything. . . ."

Officer Dobbs released Uncle Cornelius and took a stride closer to me, his bulk looming over me in a manner obviously meant to frighten. "Where were you when Mr. Goddard fell from the balcony?"

"Easy, Tony." Jesse stood up from his chair and eased past his fellow policeman. "Emma, please just answer the question. Tell us exactly where you were and what you saw."

His courteous manner won him a thin smile of gratitude, but it faded as I realized I had no choice but to reveal what I had witnessed. "I was outside the library."

"Just below the balcony, then."

I nodded in response to Officer Dobbs's gruff observation. "Yes, I saw a light pass across the windows. . . ."

"Candlelight?" Jesse's gaze flicked to the candelabrum he'd picked up from the floor and set on a side table.

"It must have been. It went out and a couple of moments later, the balcony door swung open."

"What happened after that?"

Every instinct urged me to lie, to pretend I saw and heard nothing until poor Mr. Goddard hit the ground. I wanted to protect Brady, but if I lied and the truth came out, it might only make matters worse for him. I drew a breath. "I heard scuffling sounds, and someone said, 'What? You.' It was Mr. Goddard's voice, I believe. And then he fell." A shudder went through me at the memory.

"Did you see a second individual?"

"I couldn't see anything beyond the balcony railing. It was too dark."

"Were you alone at the time?"

"Yes."

"What were you doing outside?"

I bristled at Officer Dobbs's accusing tone, but Jesse gently patted my shoulder. "Just tell the truth."

"I was . . ." I walked to the side of the bed, sank onto the edge, and let my head sag between my shoulders. The night had taken its toll on my nerves, my spirit, and my reserves of energy. I wished nothing more than to awaken from this horrendous dream, to run and tell dear Nanny O'Neal all about it, feel her supportive arm around my shoulders, and hear her calm, sweet voice suggest a cup of strong tea with a wee bit of brandy.

"It's all right, Em," Brady said very low, though the resignation in his voice announced that *it* was nowhere near to being all right. "You might as well go ahead and tell them."

My head felt impossibly heavy as I raised my face and met Jesse's sympathetic gaze. "I was outside trying to figure out which room Brady would enter, so I could warn him that I'd lost track of . . . of Uncle Cornelius."

Dobbs narrowed his pouchy, bulldog eyes. "You mean your brother had persuaded you to help him."

"Oh, Emmaline." The admonishment rode the crest of a gusty sigh, and I felt the weight of Uncle Cornelius's censure bearing down on my shoulders. "To become mixed up in your brother's chicanery . . . I'd have expected better of you."

"I'm sorry, Uncle," I said quickly. "Brady assured me he wanted to make things right by returning what he'd taken. By helping him, I hoped to avoid trouble for everyone."

That was partly true, though I admit my foremost concern had been Brady all along. I had always refused to give up on him, but now I was beginning to fear he'd betrayed me—tossed me in front of a proverbial speeding train.

"Let me get my facts straight." Jesse moved away from me and began pacing back and forth across the priceless Persian rug. "Brady, yesterday you stole important documents from Mr. Vanderbilt—from the safe?"

Uncle Cornelius made an ominous rumbling sound as Brady nodded.

"You had the combination?"

Brady nodded again.

Jesse ticked that fact off on one finger and then held up a second. "Mr. Vanderbilt the younger," he said with a nod at Neily, "discovered the theft and . . ."

"And I went searching for Brady this morning," he supplied. "Including inquiring at Emmaline's house. She claimed she didn't know where Brady was at the time."

I couldn't look at him. "I'm sorry, Neily, but he is my brother."

Jesse held up a third finger. "Brady told you what he'd done."

"Not precisely. N-not specifically," I stammered.

Jesse looked perplexed. "Can we safely assume he asked for your help in returning the documents tonight?"

I looked down at my feet. "I didn't know what he'd taken, but yes."

A fourth finger sprang up. "We know Brady entered this room sometime before midnight. You were holding the candelabrum?" he asked Brady, who nodded. "And then Alvin Goddard entered the room. Standing below, Emma heard a commotion. Someone who she believes was Mr. Goddard said, 'What? You.' Which suggests he recognized whoever was in the room with him." A fifth and final finger ticked off the last in the series of events. "And then Mr. Goddard fell or was pushed to his death."

"Wait," I protested. "What about Brady being attacked? Someone obviously knocked him out before Mr. Goddard even arrived."

"Or as I already said . . ." Officer Dobbs's thick lip curled in another of his nasty sneers. "Your brother had been drinking. Even so, he managed to overcome Goddard, who caught him in the act of replacing the documents and threatened to expose him to Mr. Vanderbilt. Mr. Gale pushed Goddard over the railing, staggered back into the room, and promptly passed out from booze and the exertion of the struggle. Probably hit his head on the bedpost as he went down."

"That's ridiculous." Coming to my feet, I went to stand behind Brady and set my hands on his shoulders in as much of a show of solidarity as my flagging hopes could muster. "My brother wouldn't harm a fly, much less another human being."

Officer Dobbs snorted. "Does your brother not overimbibe on a regular basis, Miss Cross?"

I scowled and looked away from him.

"And does he as often as not get into brawls when he's been drinking?" Dobbs persisted.

Again, I didn't wish to answer the question, but I didn't need to. The knowledge was written on the faces of all present, even Brady's, I'm quite sure, though I couldn't see his expression.

"You'll all need to be available for questioning in the morning," Dobbs said. "Mr. Vanderbilt, once the officers downstairs have finished their inspection of the crime scene and have a list of all present here tonight, you can let your guests leave." Triumph gleamed in Dobbs's beady eyes. "We have our culprit."

"No!" I shouted.

"Sorry, Miss Cross. It's time you accepted the fact that your brother has always been a good-for-nothing—"

Jesse cut off his partner with a wave. "That's enough." Then his voice gentled. "Brady, do you have anything more to add? Anything in your defense?"

"Only . . . that I don't think I killed anyone, Jesse. I honestly don't."

"I'm sorry, Brady. I truly am. But I don't see that I have any other choice."

With a resigned nod, Brady stood. The word *no* shot from my mouth countless more times, but no one listened, not even Brady.

Officer Dobbs produced a pair of handcuffs. "Stuart Braden Gale, you are under arrest for the murder of Alvin Goddard. . . ."

My brain formed denials until I realized I was actually shouting the words. The officers began walking Brady out of the room, and Neily's arms came around me, holding me still when I might have gone hurtling after my brother.

In the doorway, Brady stopped and turned partly around. "It'll be all right, Em. I've done some rotten things in my life, but I didn't do this. At least . . ." He paused, his brow furrowing, teeth catching at his bottom lip. "I don't think I did. . . ."

His uncertainty cut through my horror, tugging my heartstrings while at the same time jolting me back to practical matters. "Make sure he's seen by a doctor," I called out. "Do you hear me, Jesse? My brother received a wound to the head. He needs a doctor."

Jesse nodded, and then they were gone.

My eyes sprang open and I bolted upright. Several seconds passed before I remembered I was home in bed, and that the incessant roaring in my ears was only the tide against the promontory. As I sat shivering and clutching the sheets, the night's horrors paraded through my brain. A vague sensation nagged that a detail of the utmost importance had invaded my dream and thrust me from sleep.

Though I'd have preferred to retreat back into quieter dreams and forget all that had happened, I forced myself to review the night as though examining pictures in a catalogue. The images were jumbled, indistinct, so I climbed out of bed and made my way in the dark to my desk. By the struggling light of a cloud-choked moon, I found a clean sheet of paper, uncorked my ink, and began writing at a furious pace. The voices, the struggle, the body . . . Brady on the floor, the fallen candelabrum, the bourbon . . .

Suddenly, I jumped up and hurried barefoot down the hall toward the only source of comfort I could rely on. Without knocking—with hardly a notion of what time it could be—I opened Nanny O'Neal's door and sprinted inside.

"Nanny! Nanny, wake up."

The broad figure beneath the blankets stirred. Then Nanny came fully awake, just as she always had when I was a child and had come seeking solace after a nightmare. She had been my nurse years ago, and now she cooked and kept house for me here at Gull Manor. But she was so much more than that. My friend, my confidant, my grandmotherly source of wisdom.

Her hand groped on the bedside table for her spectacles, and she wiggled her bulky frame into a sitting position. Through the darkness she peered at me, her chubby arm coming around my shoulders. "Too upset to sleep, sweetie?"

I shook my head. "Brady's been framed. I know it."

"I believe it, too, Emma. Brady might be irresponsible and rash, but underneath he has a good heart. You have to keep believing in him."

"No, Nanny, you don't understand. I have proof there was someone else in that bedroom tonight. Someone else is involved."

She grasped my shoulders and set me at arm's length. "What proof, Emma?"

"The bourbon," I said conclusively.

Chapter 3

The next day brought more rain, a drizzly, blustery morning that felt more like September than mid-August. After several hours of fitful dreams that left me distraught and anxious to see Brady, I gave up on sleep just after dawn. As early as it was, I found Nanny already awake and the morning room filled with the welcoming aromas of a hearty breakfast. I headed for the coffee urn.

Nanny sat at the table with the morning edition of the Newport *Daily News* open before her, a bowl of oatmeal half-finished at her elbow. "I knew you'd be up with the sun today, if not sooner."

"Still reading the enemy?" I indicated the newspaper. I wrote my society page articles for the much smaller Newport *Observer.*

"The letters to the editor are livelier in the *News*. Sit. Eat."

I sighed. "It smells wonderful, but as hollow as I'm feeling this morning, I'm afraid I'm not very hungry. Coffee will do."

Her spectacles flashed briefly in my direction. Then she calmly hoisted her stout body out of the spindle-back Windsor chair. "You'd be surprised."

With that simple statement, she padded to the sideboard and promptly loaded a plate with plump sausages, scrambled eggs, and slices of toast whose russet coating hinted at a generous sprinkling of cinnamon. Nanny had set out to tempt me this morning. Next, she ladled oatmeal into a bowl, and as she brought both plate and bowl to the table, she winked. "Maple and brown sugar. Your favorite. Starving yourself won't help Brady."

"Neither will gorging myself."

She sat back down, picked up her spoon, and poked it at the air toward me. "Eat."

After a lifetime of learning one could never successfully argue with Nanny, I did as I was told, grudgingly at first, then with growing enthusiasm. I had to admit, filling my belly with warm, rich food renewed my strength, my outlook, and my re-solve to see my brother exonerated for a crime I knew, in my bones and in my heart, he could not have committed.

Within the hour I was dressed in my sturdy blue carriage dress—the one of Aunt Sadie's that Nanny had freshened with black velvet braid and new jet buttons. Outside, Katie helped me hitch Barney up to the buggy, both of which also had be-longed to Aunt Sadie.

The rain had abated to a light mist that silvered the promon-tory and lent a shine to our faces. Barney, a sweet roan gelding who was willing to go out in any weather as long as he didn't have to proceed at too hasty a pace, gave my shoulder an affec-tionate nibble as I tightened his harness and secured it to the traces. Katie stood back as I did so, and another of last night's revelations bubbled up through the muddle of my thoughts.

I pondered how best to broach the delicate subject, then de-cided there was no good way except to dive right in. "Katie," I said, "I've been wondering about . . . well . . . about when you first came to stay with me last spring."

A wave of crimson flooded her face, her freckles standing out golden in comparison. "I'm ever so grateful to you, Miss

Emma, and I try my hardest to pull my weight, truly I do. I suppose I shouldn't have presumed. It's just that I'd heard tell of your aunt always lending a hand to any girl in need and I . . . I hadn't anywhere else to go. . . ."

I didn't think it was possible for such a ruddy blush to deepen, but Katie's did. She clutched her apron and began twisting the hem around her index finger.

"I know, Katie. It's quite all right. Aunt Sadie provided a much-needed service here in Newport, and I'm only too happy to continue in her footsteps." My great aunt Sadie, who'd lived a spinster's life by choice and quite proudly, had rescued countless disgraced and dismissed maids over the years, opening her home, her finances, and her arms to them when no one else would. I'd inherited her house; it was only right I inherited her good works as well.

I secured the last buckle on Barney's harness. Scratching behind his ears, I turned to face Katie. "What I'm wondering is whether I understood the facts of what brought you here."

"I was in the family way, miss," she murmured so low I had to strain to hear her over the shush of the breeze and the hiss of the ocean.

"Yes, Katie, of course. But . . . the man . . ." Before I could continue she turned away with a cry.

"Oh, please, miss! Don't make me talk about it." She drew her apron up over her face.

"But I need to know," I persisted. "Was it Mr. Neily? Or was it Reg—"

She let out a wail. "Don't make me think about . . . about my poor babe . . . and . . ." Her words dissolved into sobs.

"All right, Katie. There, there, now." I went to her and patted her back, then slipped an arm around her shoulders. "We won't discuss it just now. Someday, though, when you're ready."

With a trembling breath, she lowered the apron, wiping her

eyes with it before letting the starched linen fall back in place against her skirts. "Thank you, miss. And now I should see to . . . to the laundry."

"In this weather? Where would you hang it to dry?"

"The dusting, then." The wind blew and she shivered.

I realized she was hoping to escape accompanying me into town, perhaps fearing that in the closeness of the carriage seat I'd return to the subject she so wished to avoid. I set her at ease. "You go on inside and have a cup of tea first. And more of Nanny's porridge."

As I watched her trudge back up through the kitchen garden, I pondered cousin Reggie's newfound attempts to play the grownup. Whisky was part of that game. Did it also include forcing himself on helpless maids in his father's employ? The notion sickened me.

And what did it say about the society we lived in that poor girls like Katie were dismissed without references while the men who disgraced them received pats on the back and the discreet applause of their fellows?

Climbing into the seat, I flapped the reins and set Barney to a walk. If it didn't rain too hard, the oiled canvas roof should keep me fairly dry. I was just circling to the front of the house when a larger and more solid vehicle turned off Ocean Avenue and rumbled toward me.

Oh, dear. I should have planned for this and left earlier.

"Emmaline, where do you think you're going in that weather-beaten contraption?" my uncle's voice boomed even before the brougham had stopped. The rear door swung open and Uncle Cornelius leaned his grizzled head out of the carriage.

"Into town, of course, to see Brady and talk to Officer Whyte."

"Not alone, you're not. Jakes!" he called out. "Take Miss Cross's buggy back to her stable and unhitch the horse." The footman sitting beside the driver jumped down from the box. My uncle's face angled back in my direction. "Emmaline, you're coming with us."

"Thank you, Uncle, but I'll need my own carriage today. I have other errands to run. Jakes, turn around."

The footman came to a standstill, looking from his employer to me and back again. I settled the debate with a "Giddup, Barney," that started the buggy moving. "I'll see you in town," I called as I maneuvered around my uncle's carriage and continued onto Ocean Avenue.

"We have the preliminary report from the coroner," Jesse Whyte said once Uncle Cornelius, Neily, and I had settled ourselves in front of his desk at the police station. I was relieved that Officer Dobbs was nowhere in sight. Elbows propped on the desktop, Jesse tented his fingers beneath his chin. "I'm afraid it doesn't look good for Brady."

"Nothing looks good for Brady." My uncle scowled. "He was caught red-handed."

I bristled, but turned my attention back to Jesse. "What did the coroner say?"

"Bruising indicates the victim was struck on the shoulders, head, and the back of the neck before he fell."

"Or was pushed," Uncle Cornelius muttered.

Neily leaned forward, hands on his knees. "It couldn't have happened in the fall?"

Jesse shook his head. "He might have struck one of those areas on the balustrade, but all three? And since he fell onto grass, it isn't likely he acquired the bruises as he hit the ground. Besides, the blood had time to clot and cause discoloration before death occurred."

"I don't understand."

It was Neily who turned to me to explain. "When someone

dies, their blood stops pumping. That means no bleeding beneath the skin, and therefore no bruising."

"That fits with my theory of a third person in that room. Someone who knocked Brady out and then attacked poor Mr. Goddard." I stopped short. "Jesse, please don't sit there shaking your head."

But he did just that. "Sorry, Emma, but we found the candelabrum beside your brother. He's already admitted to using it to see his way into the room." He sent me an apologetic look. "I can't ignore the facts. Brady had motive, opportunity, and the very weapon used to incapacitate Goddard before he was pushed to his death."

"But . . ." My stomach sank as I realized this time he'd used *pushed* instead of *fell*. But I wasn't about to give up. "There's something else we're all forgetting. Something no one thought about last night, not even Brady." I gripped the arms of my chair. "The bourbon. Brady doesn't drink bourbon. Ever. It's champagne, cognac, dark ale, or Scotch whisky. Nothing else."

"Oh, come now, Emmaline." Uncle Cornelius patted my hand where I continued to clutch the chair's arm. "Bourbon, whisky . . . obviously Brady grabbed the first bottle within reach when he snuck into the house last night. The butler's pantry was well-stocked, and I seriously doubt he's all that particular."

"But he is, Uncle." I slipped my hand out from under his. "He's particular about little else, but adamant about that. He always says bourbon turns him green."

"She's right, Father," Neily said with a mirthless grin. "And it's because of the time he and Alfred and I stayed up all night in the playhouse drinking your best Tennessee bourbon—" He broke off, then added with a rueful nod, "Yes, the stuff the president of Vanderbilt University sends you every Christmas. And we smoked cigars we pinched from your billiard room. We were all three sick as dogs the next morning."

Uncle Cornelius shot him a reproving glare and rumbled something about young delinquents needing the proper restraint.

Neily shrugged. "It was years ago."

"So you see," I said eagerly, "someone tried to set Brady up. But they didn't do a very good job of it. You need to let him go and continue the investigation."

"We'll continue the investigation, Emma." Jesse patted the leather folder sitting on the desk in front of him. "We'll consider all avenues. But I can't release Brady. Not based on whisky versus bourbon."

"But—"

"Now, if any of you can name someone else who might have had reason to do Mr. Goddard in," he interrupted, "speak up. It could help Brady's case."

Uncle Cornelius began shaking his head. "Alvin was a good man. An excellent financial secretary and an ace businessman in his own right. Didn't have an enemy that I knew of."

My mouth fell. Rich and influential men always made enemies, always inspired envy and resentment. But I just as quickly closed my lips. I wanted to talk to Brady before I offered up any further theories. "Can I see my brother now?"

"Neily, go with her," my uncle said before Jesse could respond.

I dug in my heels and raised my chin. "I'd rather see him alone."

Jesse nodded. "I'll take you to him."

I promised myself I'd be strong for Brady's sake. But seeing him in that cell, behind bars that were quite locked this time, undermined my resolve. The fact that he actually looked better than he usually did whenever I'd come to bail him out—less bloodshot, less pallid, less disheveled—only made matters worse. Because despite his more chipper appearance, for the first time I could remember, the devil-may-care light had faded from his eyes.

"Aw, don't cry, Em."

I held a handkerchief to my nose and tried to blink away my tears. "Can't help it, Brady. They won't let you go home with me this time."

He wrapped his hands around two bars and brought his face closer. "Didn't think they would, at least not yet."

"But I have some new evidence. That bourbon bottle. Someone else had to have put it there. You didn't drink any of it, did you?"

"Ordinarily I'd shudder and say no. But to tell the truth, I can't remember much about what I did last night."

I wanted to stamp my foot in frustration. Instead, I asked, "How's your head? That's also proof someone else was in that room. Did a doctor take a look at it?"

"Still tender and, yes, they brought in Dr. Kennison last night." He raised a hand to the back of his head and winced. "But for all I know, Em, I knocked it against the bureau or the bedpost as Alvin and I struggled."

"Don't say that, Brady!" I stepped closer and lowered my voice to a whisper. "Especially where someone might overhear. You did not push Alvin Goddard to his death, so don't go saying incriminating things and putting ideas into people's heads. I'm going to get you out of here, Brady. I swear I will."

"No, Emmaline. You can't get mixed up in this mess. Leave it to the police. Let Jesse handle it." His brow furrowed with worry. "Has Uncle Cornelius hired me a lawyer?"

"No, and . . . I don't think he's going to," I said as gently as I could.

"He thinks I'm guilty." His lips thinned. "Can't say as I blame him."

"Oh, Brady, why did you steal those documents?"

He met my gaze, his blue eyes frightened and sad and something more . . . regretful at having disappointed me, I thought. "The old man's been quietly buying shares in an existing New England line—"

"New Haven-Hartford-Providence," I supplied.

He nodded. "He's planning a buyout. Wants to expand into New England. There are a lot of original investors who don't like the idea of Cornelius Vanderbilt controlling a railroad monopoly that encompasses the entire Northeast."

"But what did you intend to do?"

"Head him off. Beat him at his own game. By bringing those plans to a few key investors, we could pool resources and stop the buyout before Cornelius accumulated the controlling shares." He blew out a long sigh. "I'd have been paving my way to my own riches, Em."

"So what changed your mind?"

"A couple of things," he said with a shrug. "For one, I realized the New Haven-Hartford-Providence line has been losing money. Lots of it, through mismanagement and skimming off the top. The corruption is rampant. It might not be such a bad idea to scrap it and start over, and a shark like Cornelius Vanderbilt would be just the man for the job."

"You said a couple of things. What's the other?"

A corner of his mouth lifted and he rolled his eyes. "Don't laugh, but I just couldn't blindside the old man like that. Call me sentimental. A lot of good that does me, though, if he's still ready to lead me to the scaffold."

"Don't say things like that!" I slapped my purse against the bars, sending Brady back a step. I moved closer to the cell and again lowered my voice. "What can you tell me about Alvin Goddard? Did he have enemies that you knew of?"

"You mean besides me?"

"Be serious!" I raised my purse in warning, as if I could slap sense into my brother through the bars.

He shook his head and shrugged. "Everyone has enemies of some sort. I suppose Goddard was no different."

A notion had me pulling back and studying him through a narrowed gaze. "Were there allies, Brady?"

"Sure, he had friends, business associates, all kinds of lucrative connections."

"No, I mean you. Were you alone in deciding to steal those documents, or did someone put you up to it? One of the investors?"

He did that little sideways bob of the head he'd always given our mother whenever she asked a question he didn't want to answer. The cot springs whined as he lowered himself onto the edge of the mattress. "There was no one else involved. I came up with the harebrained idea all on my own."

"You sure?"

He swung his face toward me. "Of course I'm sure. Look, Em, I'm tired. Didn't get much sleep last night, as I'm sure you can imagine."

The anger in his voice said he was shutting me out, which meant two things: There was something he didn't want to tell me, and I wouldn't likely get much more out of him today. "Just one more question, then." When his gaze softened, I smiled apologetically. "How did you ever manage to get the combination to Cornelius's safe?"

He chuckled softly. "It was months ago, at the New York offices. Right in front of me one day he turned around and opened the safe. Guess he didn't think I could see over his shoulder." He shrugged. "He must've still thought of me as Arthur Cross's naïve little stepson."

"More fool he," I muttered. "I don't suppose you'll tell me the combination?"

"Oh, no." He came to his feet and strode toward me as if to grasp my shoulders and shake me, though he stopped a foot short of the cell door. "No way, Em. I won't have you playing at intrigue on my account. See where it got me? You don't need Cornelius Vanderbilt as an enemy. Now, go home, little sister, and stay there."

"First, I'm going to send a telegram to Mother and Father." Brady's eyebrows quirked; he clearly didn't expect much help from that quarter. I hesitated another moment. "Do you need anything?"

"They feed me pretty well in here, and Jesse looks in on me when he can." He smiled, though his eyes remained bleak. "Don't suppose you'd bring me some cigarettes?"

"I would, but I don't suppose they'd let you have them."

He nodded and looked away. I blew him a kiss and left him, along with a generous portion of my heart.

I got as far as the sidewalk before the image of Brady holding on to those bars and putting on a brave face turned me about and sent me back inside.

"I'd like to see Officer Whyte again, please."

"You'll have to wait, Miss Cross," the sergeant manning the front desk replied. "He's busy."

Then wait I would. Surely I could convince Jesse to release my brother into my custody. He'd known us both all our lives, and he was Brady's friend. Besides, we lived on an island with only one way off: by boat. It wasn't as if Brady could simply run off in the night.

From where I stood in the lobby I had a clear view into the main room. Officer Dobbs had returned and sat tapping away at one of the typewriters, pausing now and again to squint down at a paper while uttering what must have been oaths beneath his breath, judging from his expression. Was he typing up the report on Brady?

A few feet away from him, Jesse was on his feet talking to a man in street clothes—dark blue suit and gray overcoat. Smartly tailored, but not extravagant, his attire marked him a professional, if not quite wealthy. He was no one I recognized, which immediately made him interesting—everyone in Newport knew everyone—yet that wasn't the only reason I found myself staring. Framed by thick dark hair that curled slightly at the ends, his square jaw, straight nose, and strong brow caught my fascination, as did the broadness of his shoulders, the tapering lines of his figure beneath his coat.

"This Mr. Gale is being charged?"

Hearing Brady's name, I pricked my ears.

"Looks like it," Jesse said. "He was found at the scene of the crime. And there appears to have been a motive."

For a moment I thought to admonish him for discussing Brady with a stranger; then I remembered he was merely revealing what was already on public record.

"What about the other guests? From what I understand, some three hundred of the Four Hundred were in attendance last night. Fish, Goelet, Oelrich, Astor, Halstock . . ."

My curiosity piqued, I moved into the wide doorway that separated the lobby from the main station. The gentleman referred to the very cream of society's upper crust, determined, rumor had it, by how many people could comfortably fit in *the* Mrs. Astor's New York ballroom: 400. Was someone finally agreeing with me that any number of people at the ball might have had reason for wanting Alvin Goddard out of the way?

Jesse shrugged, shook his head, and spoke some words I couldn't hear over the typing—drat that Dobbs. I started to move closer, then stopped and pressed tight to the doorway as the gentleman glanced my way. His gaze skimmed past me into the lobby, slowly slid back, lingered until my face heated, and finally returned to Jesse.

Those dark eyes left me unsettled . . . tingling, as if I'd been touched. Left me speculating, too. Was this man a reporter, or had Uncle Cornelius hired a private detective to investigate the crime? If so, to help Brady or to seal his fate?

Either way, I wouldn't be asking Jesse for any favors in that man's hearing, because if I identified myself as the alleged culprit's sister to either a reporter or a private detective, I wouldn't have another moment's peace.

Outside, I made my way to the telegraph office on nearby Franklin Street. I penned a quick message, scratched it out, and then tried again to convey in a few short sentences the seriousness of Brady's situation without sending my parents into a panic. There was little they could do all the way from Paris, but I hoped they'd be able to send funds to help with Brady's legal fees. I also hoped Mother, if not both of them, would board the next America-bound ship.

My errand completed, I picked a direction at random and started walking, my stride so brisk several pedestrians sidestepped anxiously out of my way. Never mind that the evidence against Brady was shaky at best, and anyone with an astute mind and open eyes should see that. The only people who mattered believed him to be guilty: the police and Uncle Cornelius. The drizzle had let up for the moment, but I shivered nonetheless. If Cornelius Vanderbilt decided to pressure the courts into convicting my brother, he would be convicted. Plain and simple.

I needed a plan to prove Brady's innocence without a doubt. With each step I took names paraded through my brain—potentially 300 of them. How would I ever sort through all those people and discover which of them might have held enough of a grudge to commit murder? Where would I start?

The answer, I realized, was to start at the beginning. For that I needed to get back to my carriage. With a start I realized I'd drifted up to Spring Street and had covered quite a distance in the opposite direction from Washington Square and, just beyond on Marlborough Street, my waiting buggy. I turned around to start back, but a sight about a half a block away stopped me cold.

It was the man from the police station.

Had Jesse told him who I was? I could hardly imagine him doing anything of the sort. But maybe it hadn't been too hard to guess the identity of the one woman visiting the police station today.

Our gazes locked for an instant. Quickly, I schooled my features to reveal no hint of recognition and darted a look at the building fronts beside me and across the street, pretending I was looking for an address. Molly's Dress Shop stood two doors down. I headed there and darted inside.

"Good morning, Emma! How nice to see you," the proprietress, Molly herself, exclaimed upon spotting me hurrying into the shop. She looked about to say something more, the knowledge of what everyone in Newport had already learned this morning written plainly on her features.

Molly had been my mother's favorite seamstress here in town, and I'd known the woman forever. Like my mother, she was tall and trim and youthful despite her forty-plus years. Unlike my mother, she dressed modestly in a white shirtwaist with leg-a-mutton sleeves and slim charcoal skirt. When I walked in she was helping a customer, a Mrs. Peterson, and bolts of colorful muslin lay unrolled across the cutting table. "Are you . . . er . . . looking for something in particular today?" Molly asked. Sympathy tinged with uncertainty flickered in her eyes.

"I'm . . . ah . . . just passing through today, if you don't mind," I said a little breathlessly. "Hello, Mrs. Peterson," I hastily added, wishing I could have avoided the prying eyes of one of the town's biggest gossips. But it couldn't be helped. "Molly, would it be all right if I ducked out the back?"

Mrs. Peterson raised her silver eyebrows in comprehension. "Avoiding someone, Miss Cross?"

"Uh, well, you might say that." I pointed toward the back room. "Molly, may I?"

"Of course. Back door's unlocked. It's trash day, though, so don't trip over the bins in the alley."

With Mrs. Peterson's inquisitive gaze burning into my back, I hurried on. I exited through the alley without any trash-bin mishaps and came out onto Mary Street. Another quick rounding of a corner brought me onto Clarke. I hastened northward, past the old Artillery Company, and then back across Washington Square, where in my preoccupation I nearly collided with the oncoming trolley rumbling its way toward Long Wharf. A shout of "Watch yourself!" from an unseen female pedestrian somewhere behind me virtually saved my life.

By the time I reached Marlborough Street I was huffing for breath and tugging at my collar. I'd left Barney and my rig in the carriage shed behind St. Paul's Church, whose steeple cast a thin shadow across the front of the police station. A glance over my shoulder revealed no well-dressed stranger in pursuit.

"You're in a hurry, Miss Emma. Everything all right with your brother?"

I didn't stop to ask Mr. Weatherby, St. Paul's sexton, how much he had heard about last night's ordeal. Yes, in a town like Newport, news traveled fast and rumors spread like weeds. I assured him Brady's involvement was a misunderstanding, thanked him for brushing Barney down, and promised I'd see him at Sunday morning services.

Did I see a flash of gray overcoat as I swung the buggy back onto Marlborough Street? I might have, but I didn't linger to be sure. Was I overreacting? Maybe, but as garish headlines ran through my mind, I didn't think so. This man might poke around as much as he liked. I had my own information to gather. My next stop was The Breakers.

Chapter 4

The skies opened up as I drove through The Breakers' main gates. Parker, the young footman on duty at the front door during the day, ran out from the porte cochere with an umbrella at the ready. A lot of good it did. I was already wet from the ride in my open-sided carriage, and in the nearly sideways rain poor Parker became fairly drenched as well.

Inside, he quickly handed me off to the acting head butler, Bateman, and excused himself to change into a dry uniform. Bateman hurried me into the ladies' parlor off the marbled entry hall. Within minutes my carriage jacket had been whisked away by a maid for drying, and I sat wrapped in a thick shawl, sipping strong tea. I was grateful Bateman hadn't brought me into the library, where the memories of last night would have replayed over and over in my mind.

"Is there anything else I can bring you, Miss Emmaline?"

Russell Bateman wasn't much older than Brady, which was far younger than the typical head butler. With his wheat-colored hair and freckled complexion, he appeared greener than the most inexperienced under footman, yet I knew him to be capable of assuming an authoritative role when necessary—as was the case now. Mason, as I'd learned last night, had been recently let go, supposedly caught stealing by Alvin Goddard.

I wondered about that.

"Thank you, Bateman, I'm fine now. Has my uncle returned from town yet?"

"He's been in and gone again, miss. None of the family is presently at home."

"None of them?" This surprised me. I'd hoped that if nothing else I might probe Aunt Alice with a few strategic questions. "They've all gone out in this weather?"

"The events of last night have left the family unsettled, miss. I believe Mr. Alfred suggested an afternoon at the Casino and then dinner at the country club."

"Probably a good idea," I murmured. If I shrank from the idea of having tea in the library, I could only imagine how the rest of them felt inhabiting a house where a man well-known to them all had died less than twenty-four hours ago.

Seeming unsure what to do with me, Bateman hovered near the table as I sipped my tea. It might not have been very sporting of me, but I decided the family's being away provided me with a rare opportunity. Setting my cup in its saucer with a light clink, I caught his eye. "Bateman, you're aware of the circumstances surrounding Mason's dismissal, yes?"

"He was accused of stealing valuables from the family."

"Like what?"

"Well . . . I believe some rare bronze figurines of Mrs. Vanderbilt's were taken. Chinese, I think, and priceless."

"But he's worked for them for years with never a mishap. When did the items go missing?"

"In the spring, it seems. No one noticed right away, though, what with all the refurbishing going on." He lifted the porcelain teapot. "More tea, miss?"

"Thank you." I held out my cup. "Did he admit to the theft?"

"Not at all, miss. Mr. Mason insists he's innocent."

"I imagine the family wishes to press charges."

Bateman shrugged a shoulder. "That's doubtful. Nothing was ever found, so there's no proof Mason did it."

"Were his room and all his possessions searched?"

"Of course, miss. But if he did take anything, he'd already disposed of it. Probably pawned the bunch of it up in Providence."

"Then what made Mr. Goddard so certain it was Mason?"

"Opportunity, miss. No one had as much free rein in the house as Mason. And—" He broke off, shuffling his feet.

"What?" Quickly surmising the reasons someone suddenly took to stealing, I played a hunch. "Did Mason have financial troubles?"

"He, ah . . ." Bateman threw a glance over his shoulder at the doorway. "Seems he'd taken to gambling on his free time. Horses, mostly. Oh, and greyhounds."

"Oh, dear." Bateman was fidgeting now, eager to be away, but I had another question for him. "Was he very upset to be dismissed?"

The man's gaze sharpened. I could see his mind working, trying to divine my meaning. "He was furious, miss. But that doesn't mean . . ."

Doesn't mean he was driven to murder? Possibly not—probably not—but as easy as it had been for Brady to sneak in last night, who was to say the Vanderbilts' head butler, who knew the house better than the family themselves, couldn't have done likewise? I'd always liked Mason, but as Jesse had implied, all avenues needed exploring.

"No, of course it doesn't," I conceded, wondering where Mason could be found, if he was still in town. I lifted my teacup in both hands to warm my palms against the nearly translucent porcelain. "I suppose I'm trying to prove a point, at least in my own mind. And it's that opportunity does not necessarily a criminal make."

Our gazes met for an instant before his angled away. Obviously I wasn't just talking about Mason. Bateman probably believed Brady was guilty, but it was never proper for a servant to express an opinion, especially of a personal nature. It was time to let the man resume his duties.

"If it's all right, Bateman, I need to run upstairs. I believe I lost something last night . . . in all the commotion. One of my earrings. They were a present from my parents and I'd surely hate to lose it."

"I'll send Lucy up with you to help you search."

I didn't bother objecting. It didn't matter if I had an audience or not, or that my earring would not be found in Uncle Cornelius's bedroom—that it was, in fact, safe at home in my jewelry box.

A few minutes later, as Lucy got down on her hands and knees and began combing the bedroom floor, she apologized nonstop for the rug having been thoroughly swept and scrubbed that morning.

"We were awfully intent on cleaning up the spilled spirits and candle wax. If your earring had been here, miss, there's a good chance it was swept up into one of our dustpans and tossed in the garbage."

"I'm sure not, Lucy. One of you would have noticed it." I felt a tad guilty, because while the eager girl focused her attention downward, I looked upward, studying the dent in the frame of the balcony door. That was why I had come, to examine that depression in the wood and compare it in size and shape with the candelabrum Brady had used to see his way across the room. I placed my hand up against it. My palm fit easily inside, and I judged the depth to be about a quarter inch, suggesting a good, strong swing against the frame. But with what?

The base of the candelabrum might easily span four or so inches, but not the main shaft, nor the slender branches. If

someone swung the piece by those branches and struck the
wood hard enough to make that dent, wouldn't the delicate,
curving silver have snapped? And if someone had held the candelabrum farther down, they could not have gotten enough
momentum for the base to have made such a defined depression in the wood.

"Miss Emmaline, did you step out onto the balcony last
night? Should we search there, too?"

I whisked my hand to my side and turned to find Lucy still
on all fours, staring up at me curiously. "Uh, no. I was just
checking the floor where the rug ends." I swept my foot back
and forth several times. "Don't see it anywhere."

Lucy nodded and returned to raking her fingers through the
Persian rug's thick nap. Pretending to stare down at the nearest
chair cushion, I once again set my hand in the dent and smoothed
my palm up and down, my fingers spread. The rough edges
abrading my skin and a crackling paint chip told me the hollow
had been recently made.

I wondered how long before Uncle Cornelius made it disappear, and whether I could convince Jesse to come out here with
the candelabrum before that happened.

"I give up, Lucy. It's possible my earring fell off downstairs,
or even on my way home."

"Have you checked outside, miss? You know, in the grass,
where . . ." Her voice trailed off. She rose to her feet.

"I guess I'll come back when the rain stops. Or maybe when I
return home my housekeeper will have miraculously found it.
Would you please find my carriage jacket so I can be on my way?"

"Of course, miss."

Downstairs, she helped me on with my overgarment and ran
to open the front door for me. "Will you give Katie my regards,
miss? Tell her I say hello?"

I remembered then that Katie and Lucy had been roommates
up in the third floor servants' quarters, both here and in the

New York mansion. None of her former coworkers had contacted Katie all summer; maybe they were afraid to involve
themselves in her troubles, fearing their jobs would be at risk. I
offered Lucy a smile. "I'd be happy to, and Katie will be glad to
hear it. She'd be happier still if you paid her a visit sometime.
Gull Manor isn't far from here."

"I'll . . . uh . . . I'll try, miss, when I have some time off. Do
you want Parker to walk you out with the umbrella?"

I turned my collar up. "No, thanks. I'll just make a dash."

Nanny fussed over me when I arrived home, scolding me
halfheartedly for traipsing about in the rain. I only half listened
to her lecture while I considered all I had learned on my travels.

"Theodore Mason had as much or more reason as Brady to
want Alvin Goddard dead," I said as Nanny removed the pins
from my hair and tossed a towel over my head.

"I've known Teddy Mason for forty years," she said mildly.
"He didn't kill anyone."

"Oh, I believe you. But the point is that he could have just as
easily as Brady. The evidence against both men is purely coincidental . . . or what do they call it? Oh, yes. Circumstantial."
But the last word became gibberish as Nanny moved behind
my chair and rubbed my hair with the towel none too gently,
wobbling my head this way and that.

"Circum-who?" She released the towel so that it flopped
over my face, and stooped to pick up my dripping half boots
from the floor beside me.

"Circum*stantial*, Nanny." I peeked out from a corner of the
damp fabric. "I'll wager you can find him—find where Mason
has gone. Couldn't you, Nanny? I didn't want to ask anyone at
The Breakers. Too obvious."

She set my boots before the drawing room fire. "I suppose I
could inquire with a friend or two."

"Humph. Word spreads along the servants' gossip route

faster than a speeding locomotive, and no one is better connected than you. I wouldn't be surprised if you discovered who
killed Alvin Goddard before suppertime."

"Well, if I do, you'll be the first to know. In the meantime,
I'll make some honey cakes to take to Brady tomorrow."

The next morning brought clear skies, and Nanny and I set
out together to the Point, to Brady's third-floor flat in the colonial that had been our childhood home. My parents still owned
the house, but rented out the two lower stories to a retired
sailor and a pair of widowed sisters, respectively. In Brady's un-
tidy digs, Nanny and I collected clothes, toiletries, and a few
magazines. I hesitated over Brady's tobacco pouch and papers,
but left them where they lay. The police wouldn't let him have
them, though I didn't doubt Jesse provided Brady with the occasional discreet puff.

His eyes lit up at the sight of Nanny's honey cakes. I asked
him if he had remembered anything new, and when he merely
shrugged with a mouthful of crumbs, I left Nanny to chat with
him for a few minutes and headed into the main station searching for Jesse.

I found him at his desk, hunched over a stack of familiar documents.

"The New Haven-Hartford-Providence Line," I said in way
of greeting.

He flinched and glanced up. "Emma, I didn't see you come in."

"No, you were engrossed in those railroad plans. I hadn't
known my uncle delivered them to you."

To my frustration, he tucked the papers into the leather
folder I'd seen yesterday and set them aside. "A bit reluctantly."

"I can imagine. You must have had to threaten him."

Jesse extended a hand to give my gloved one a shake. Then
he gestured me into the chair facing his desk. "What brings you

back today? I mean, besides seeing Brady." Did a glimmer of resignation enter his eye? I believe it did, and I couldn't blame him. He must have thought I'd come to plead Brady's case again.

Which, of course, I had. But this time I left my emotions at the door. I glanced longingly at that closed folder, wondering what revelations the documents might contain, then calmly met Jesse's gaze. "I discovered something of significance yesterday at my uncle's house."

He folded his hands over the documents in that pensive way he had. "Now, Emma, don't you think this investigation is best left to the professionals?"

From anyone else the question would have been condescending . . . and infuriating. From Jesse Whyte, it was fraught with sympathy. I shook my head. "I can't sit by and watch my brother wrongly accused. And surely you can't sit by and ignore pertinent evidence."

Without a word, he leaned back in his hard-backed swivel chair and raised his palm, cuing me to continue.

"You might not have noticed the other night, but there is a dent in the balcony door frame. I went back yesterday to inspect this dent and realized it's highly unlikely the candelabrum found next to Brady could have caused it."

"How do you know that dent wasn't caused by the carpenters when they rebuilt the house?"

"Jesse, you've met my aunt Alice, yes?"

Looking puzzled, he nodded.

"She was involved in every stage of the rebuilding. She inspected every detail down to the nails used in the paneling. Do you truly believe she would not have noticed such an imperfection in her husband's bedroom, or that she wouldn't have demanded it be fixed immediately?"

"I see what you mean. Still, one of the cleaning maids could have done it, or . . ."

"Jesse, all I ask is that you return to the house with the candelabrum and compare it to the indentation in the molding. It might just prove that another object caused the bruises on poor Mr. Goddard's body and on the back of Brady's head. As a professional," I said, throwing his own word back at him, "you must at least entertain the possibility."

His gaze bored into me. "Is this like the bourbon?"

"Jesse, please, I am not grasping at straws. You know me better than that." Indeed, he did. Jesse's parents, and now he, owned a house on the Point only a few doors down from my childhood home. He had often joined us for supper, had sat in our back garden and talked long into the night with both my father and Brady. I leaned closer to him across the desk. "The bourbon, that dent—these are clues that don't quite add up to the picture of Brady as a murderer. If there's a chance in hell of clearing his name, then I'll ride into hell and back. Who will help him if you and I don't?"

He thought for a moment, teeth working at a corner of his lips. "Tell me this. How would someone manage to bring a weapon into the house and then sneak it back out?"

"Easy," I replied with a snap of my fingers. "Every guest that night brought a valise at the very least. Some of the ladies brought small trunks carrying their dancing slippers, ribbons, extra petticoats, hair accessories . . . you name it. They all wished to be flawless for the ball, and wrinkles from riding in a coach would not have been acceptable. As the guests arrived they were ushered directly upstairs with their valets and maids to perfect their appearance before being announced in the ballroom. So you see, anyone might have secreted a weapon in their baggage and gotten it out of the house in the same manner."

"All right. All right, I'll go look at this dent of yours." He blew out a lengthy breath that told me he'd decided to humor me, though he still had his reservations. "But I'll have to use the candelabrum's measurements. The real thing has been entered into evidence and can't be removed from the station yet."

I rewarded him with my brightest, widest smile and came to my feet. "Thank you. In the meantime—"

"In the meantime, Emma, you should return to your normal routine. If anything else occurs to you, by all means bring it to my attention. Until then, visit friends, help plan the Vanderbilts' next soirée, write your articles. I'll take care of Brady."

That was advice I didn't plan to follow, but he did remind me of another stop I needed to make. After collecting Nanny and bidding Brady good-bye until tomorrow, I drove the rig to lower Thames Street, stopping in front of the offices of the Newport *Observer*. I had three typewritten pages in the portfolio I'd brought from home. It was time to see which ones I'd end up delivering.

"These are fine work, Emma, just fine." Mr. Millford, owner and editor-in-chief of the *Observer*, held two of the articles, one in each hand, and scanned them for a second time. "Yes, indeed, fine work," he repeated, but in a tone that sent my hopes drifting downward like leaves falling from a tree. He sealed my fate by placing one of the articles back in my hand. "I'll take the article on the ball, and, of course, your write-up on Mrs. Astor's new rose garden. It'll make a nice addition to the Fancies and Fashions page."

"But, Mr. Millford . . ." I rattled the paper he'd handed back to me. "This is an exact account of what happened the night of Alvin Goddard's death. I was an eyewitness." I didn't add that my article gave a fair description of the facts without condemning my brother. That much was obvious. "I'd have had it for you yesterday, but . . ."

"Yes, Emma, I know you had enough on your mind yesterday. And this is a *fine* account." I wished he'd stop using that word. "But the article on Goddard's death has already been written up and approved for Sunday's edition."

"But . . . written up by whom?" My back went ramrod straight and my chin shot up. The image of the man I'd seen in the police station yesterday sprang to mind. A reporter, hired without my knowing about it? Not that Mr. Millford needed my approval for new employees. But . . .

"Ed."

Flames might have shot out of my mouth, I was so instantly angry. Ed Billings. I might have known. Ed covered all the significant news stories, not because he was an ace reporter, but because he was a man. And I was a woman, which relegated me to parties and fashion and wedding announcements. I gritted my teeth.

"Ed wasn't there that night. I was." Fury added a tremor to my voice. "I'd have had the story to you yesterday, but . . . well . . . I had one or two other concerns, as you can well imagine. Can't you un-approve his article and approve mine?"

My employer was already shaking his head. "First off, you're too close to the incident. You know you are, Emma, and it's likely to compromise your objectivity. Second, why would you want to dirty your hands in such sordid details? Why, your account of who attended the ball and what all the ladies wore is charming. First-rate. Just what our female subscribers love to read when they sit down to their afternoon tea." He tapped the article with the backs of his fingers. "You're darned good at what you do, Emma. Don't try to change."

My article stuffed back inside my portfolio, I dragged myself outside. Nanny sighed the moment she glimpsed my expression.

"He didn't take it, eh?"

I climbed up beside her. "Ed beat me to it."

"Well, you had a lot on your mind yesterday." She patted my arm.

"It wouldn't have made a difference if I'd been quicker. I'd still have been patted on the head and put in my place." I flapped the reins. "Giddup, Barney. Let's go home."

"Don't be discouraged, sweetie. You helped Brady today. Jesse will be going back to The Breakers to look at that dent."

"Yes, but will he go with an open mind?"

I dropped Nanny at home, changed into a fresh day gown, and climbed back into the buggy. I'd forgotten all about an invitation for luncheon yesterday; understandable, of course, but an oversight all the same. Adelaide didn't have a telephone as her husband didn't believe in them. I decided to drive over there, apologize, and see if she was free today. Just as Nanny had her connections among Newport's servants, so did Adelaide have her close ties with Newport's wealthiest summer citizens. I hoped she might have heard, oh, anything, some wisp of rumor or scandal that might help Brady's case.

The Halstocks' summer home, Redwing Cottage, faced Bellevue Avenue on the ocean side of the street. The house was in the Queen Anne style with a wraparound veranda, turret, oriel windows, and copious amounts of gingerbread dripping from the eaves. Despite the quaint design, the house was no cottage, but a three-story mansion not far from The Breakers, with a similar cliff-top ocean view.

When I turned onto the circular drive, I had to stop Barney a dozen yards shy of the entryway. A freight wagon stood in front of the house, and two men I recognized were just then loading a crate into the bed.

"Good afternoon, Mr. Manuel and Mr. Manuel," I hailed as I climbed to the ground. The brothers set down the crate.

"Well, if it isn't Miss Cross." They settled their burden in the wagon and Edwin, the elder and taller of the two, tipped his hat at me. Like Jesse Whyte, the Manuel family had lived near us on the Point. The brothers, along with members of their extended family, ran the island's main moving company. "Here to visit Miss Peabody?"

"It's Mrs. Halstock now and, yes, if she's home."

"It's hard to get used to that," Elton, the shorter and stockier brother, said with a laugh. He gestured for me to go inside. "But she's here."

I lingered, considering the contents of the wagon. There were a number of crates, assorted furnishings, and, leaning against the side of the wagon, several flattish items draped in cloth and secured with twine that must have been paintings. "The Halstocks aren't moving out, are they?"

Edwin shrugged. "We're paid to move it, not to know why."

I bid them a pleasant afternoon and wandered inside. When no footman or maid met me, I simply called out, "Adelaide?"

My voice echoed through the central foyer, bouncing against the high, carved ceiling and reverberating down the mahogany-paneled walls. A broad archway opened to my left, and through it I glimpsed the curve of a grand piano. Straight ahead, another doorway framed a dining room dominated by a marble-topped table surrounded by a dozen or so shield-back chairs. To my right, a wide staircase marched away to the upper story, the wide half landing bathed in a rainbow of light from a stained-glass window.

As I wondered which way to turn, the red velvet curtains draping an alcove just beyond the bottom of the stairs fluttered. An elderly man shuffled out, his shoulders hunched, head down, his balding pate aimed toward me. He was dressed in country attire of linen trousers, striped frockcoat, and a loosely tied ascot. The clothes hung limply on his frame as though fashioned for a much larger man.

I took a step toward him. "Excuse me?"

With a gasp, he drew back, one frail hand arcing to his chest, palm pressing his heart. For a moment all he did was stare across the way at me as if attempting to make sense of an apparition that had appeared out of thin air. Though I recognized him from two nights ago, the change in him took me aback.

"Mr. Halstock. Good afternoon, sir. I'm Emmaline Cross. I hope I'm not intruding, but I've come to visit your wife. She and I were good friends as children." Well, that might have been overstating the case. Adelaide and I had been friends in the way children are when they live near each other, attend the same schools and church, and know all the same people. We had always been convenient friends, if not especially close ones.

His brow rumpled, bringing attention to discolorations in his skin, those tiny brown spots that come with age, as well as a mottled hue that suggested shock or surprise or unease. "Adelaide . . . ?" He lifted the hand from his heart and raised it to his temple. "The young one . . . She's upstairs, I think . . ."

I walked closer to him. "Sir, I think you had better sit down." He stiffened at my approach, but let me grasp his arm lightly and lead him to a brocade side chair set against the wall. "Is there someone I can call? Your valet?"

Nodding, he stared down at his knees. "Suzanne. You can call Suzanne. She'll come."

"Who's Suzanne?" I crouched lower to hear his feeble whisper. "A maid? Your housekeeper?"

"Mr. Halstock is referring to Mrs. Rockport, his sister in Providence."

I straightened as a second man stepped out from the alcove, this one in the formalwear of a butler or valet. In contrast to his employer, he stood straight and tall, and walked with confidence. His keen blue eyes angled from me to the man sitting beside me.

"Are you all right, sir? You should have waited for me," he gently admonished. "I'd only gone into the kitchen to check on your lunch. I did say I'd be back momentarily."

"Yes, yes . . . I came out for something. . . . Can't remember what it was." A whine entered Rupert Halstock's unsteady voice. He began looking about him in obvious distress.

"It's all right, sir. Why don't we return to the morning room now. You'll have your lunch, and then you'll remember what it was you wanted."

"A capital idea, that." Mr. Halstock leaned heavily on my arm as he struggled to his feet. His manservant came to his other side, but the old gentleman refused any help but mine. I might have found that amusing if it hadn't occurred to me that Rupert Halstock wasn't nearly as old as he appeared. In fact, he and Uncle Cornelius were close in age, but where the heartiness had yet to abandon the latter, the former seemed prematurely poised just this side of the grave.

He managed to straighten just as faltering footsteps echoed in the vestibule.

"Careful now, don't bang it into the corner. . . ."

The Manuel brothers made their way into the hall half carrying, half dragging a crate that stood nearly as tall as a man. "We're ready to pack the spinet and take it out, Mr. Halstock," Edwin said. "The rest is loaded."

"Take the spinet? The hell you will." The sudden strength in Rupert's voice surprised me. His fingers trembled violently around my forearm. "It belongs to my wife, a wedding present from me! She plays it every evening after supper. Do you think I'd let you take Gloria's beloved spinet? Get out! Get out of my house this instant! Aimes, show these insolent fools to the door!"

The brothers exchanged astonished looks, then looked to the servant for help. Aimes shook his head slightly and made a subtle gesture with his fingers that sent them backing out of the hall and out of the house.

"They're gone, Mr. Halstock. Why don't we go have that lunch now, sir?" The servant held out the crook of his arm.

Rupert Halstock nodded and docilely leaned on the other

man's sturdy forearm. Before they could take a step, the elder man turned back to me. His frown returned. "He's taking the train, miss."

I blinked. "Who is?"

"We mustn't let him take the train."

"Oh, uh . . ." I flicked a glance Aimes, half hoping for an explanation; he merely held his features politely steady. "No, sir, don't you worry. We won't let him take the train."

"Good . . . good." Rupert reached out and touched a withered, fluttering finger to my cheek. "There's a good girl. My Gloria's going to take quite a shine to you. She's upstairs in her sitting room. You go on up and introduce yourself."

"Thank you, Mr. Halstock. I will."

But first I watched the wealthy and powerful shipping magnate shuffle across the hall on the arm of his servant until they disappeared behind the crimson curtain. Only then did I turn to mount the staircase. Above me, at the half landing, Adelaide stood pale and trembling, one hand clutching the banister, the other poised at her throat.

"Oh, God, Emma . . . what am I to do?"

Chapter 5

Upstairs, Adelaide led me across an open, rectangular hall into a room directly opposite the top landing. A fragrant, ocean-tinged breeze flowed through the open windows; the bright yellow walls, festive florals, delicate watercolors, and light, wicker furnishings marked this very much a lady's day parlor. An embroidery frame sat tilted in front of an overstuffed chair, the needle stuck into the landscape design giving hint to what had occupied Adelaide before she'd heard the commotion in the hall below.

Despite the cheerfulness of the scene, a heavy silence hung over us both. At first we stood, both obviously ill at ease and at a loss. Then Adelaide dragged her feet to a pretty little camel-back sofa and patted the cushion beside her. When I settled next to her, she grasped my hands, her inner struggle evident in her tightening features.

"Oh, Emma, he'd seemed so much better recently. I don't know what could have caused this relapse."

"Maybe he's just tired today," I lamely offered, needing to say something.

"Do you think it could be a result of the ball? The exertion and then . . . all that happened that night. It's all Rupert could talk about yesterday. Oh, I never should have suggested we attend. It's just that it had been so long since we'd socialized. . . ." She gave a little sniffle.

"You mustn't blame yourself, Adelaide. And, no, I don't think the ball could have caused your husband to fall ill again. I know what happened was a terrible shock to everyone, but Mr. Halstock wasn't directly involved. I doubt it caused him the kind of emotional pain that could make a person ill."

"You really believe it isn't my fault?"

"Be assured on that account."

She sank back against the cushions. "He doesn't recognize me when he gets this way. That's why I didn't come down . . . in case you were wondering. It only would have upset him more."

"Oh . . . no, I wasn't wondering about that." And yet, it did seem strange that she hadn't come rushing down at the first sign of her husband's distress. Then again, he'd spoken of his first wife as though she were still alive. I could only imagine how distressing that was for Adelaide.

"I'm sorry you had to witness that scene."

Here I felt a wave of remorse. "I shouldn't have stopped by without sending ahead first. It's just that you don't have a telephone or I would have called."

"Rupert doesn't like telephones." Adelaide smiled fondly at what she must have considered her husband's eccentricity.

"I saw the Manuels as I arrived," I said to take her mind off more gloomy matters. "You're not returning to New York already, are you?"

A light blush stained her cheeks, but she shook her head. "Manhattan in August? Goodness no. We're just easing some of our clutter here, moving things from one house to the other."

"I see. Do you miss it, though? The city, I mean."

"I don't know." Turning her head to stare out the window at the swaying branches of a lush maple, she considered. "It's exciting and Lord knows, there is no end of amusements in New York. But I must confess that Newport is home. It always will be, I suppose."

I grinned. "You can take the girl off the island . . ."

"But you never take the island out of the girl. So very true." Her smile faded. "But here I am running on about my own troubles, when you must be beside yourself about Brady. How is he, Emma? You know I don't believe a word about his guilt."

"Thank you, Adelaide." I meant it. Her words warmed me and very nearly sent a tear trickling from the corner of my eye. I quickly blinked it away and seized the opportunity she'd provided me with. "Since you brought it up . . . I've been wondering, Adelaide, if you might have heard any rumors or indication that someone wished harm on Alvin Goddard."

"Me?" Her eyes filled with surprise; her hand rose to her bosom.

"Yes, someone he might have been doing business with. Surely a woman in your social position hears all sorts of things."

"Well, that is true." She plucked at the corner of an embroidered sofa pillow. "But Mr. Goddard worked solely for your uncle. Most of his business dealings were through Mr. Vanderbilt." She tapped a finger against her chin. "Of course, there is . . ."

"Yes?"

"I really don't like to say. And it's more of a personal matter than business." She twisted the ring on her middle finger, a diamond the size of a marble.

"I promise anything you tell me will stay between us." I didn't stop to ponder the truth of that statement, but encouraged her with a pat to her forearm.

"Well . . . it has to do with your cousin Neily. And that woman."

"You mean Grace Wilson?"

"The very same. Did you know your aunt and uncle gravely disapprove of their association?"

"Aunt Alice did mention something about it, yes. But exactly what are you suggesting? What did Neily and Grace Wilson have to do with Mr. Goddard?"

Adelaide shot a sideways glance at the doorway and lowered her voice. "I overheard Rupert and Cornelius talking one night a couple of months ago. They were in Rupert's smoking room in our Fifth Avenue house, and while, of course, I'd never dream of eavesdropping, I happened to be walking by and . . ."

Her hesitation spurred my impatience, as well as a sudden memory: During the ball, I'd lost track of Neily. Even after Alvin Goddard fell and I went looking for help, Neily was nowhere to be seen in the ballroom. Why hadn't he been in the center of the room with his family, toasting his sister? Then, as everyone had paraded into the dining room, Neily had come up behind me, from which direction I couldn't say. Where had he been . . . ?

"Please, go on," I urged her. "This is important. What did your husband and my uncle say about Neily?"

"Well, they were discussing how Neily had met Miss Wilson in Paris last year, and how he seemed to be utterly infatuated with her. Your aunt is certain the woman is a fortune seeker, so your uncle gave Alvin Goddard the task of having Neily followed, to determine just how involved the two of them had become."

I frowned. "But that doesn't make sense. Mr. Goddard was my uncle's financial secretary. Why would he be charged with a task like that?"

Adelaide laid a hand against my cheek. "Oh, my dear Emma, how naïve you are despite your illustrious connections. Mr. Goddard was a wizard at financial matters. Do you believe his talents were merely due to his business acumen? Or simple luck?" She shook her head, a knowing gleam entering her eyes. "Such men must be versed in all manner of espionage."

"Espionage! Adelaide, you must be reading detective novels."

"Not at all. A man like Mr. Goddard must know what is going to happen in financial matters well before they happen, in order to circumvent disasters before they take hold. Such a man has connections everywhere, even in the darkest corners where most people wouldn't dare tread."

"Are you saying . . ." I paused, thinking about the man who had subtly and unsuccessfully attempted to court me, and the distaste I'd felt in response. ". . . that Alvin Goddard was dishonest?"

Adelaide smiled sweetly and shook her head. "Emma, darling, in our world, the distinction between an honest businessman and a dishonest one is exceedingly scant, and rarely discussed."

"In *your* world, maybe," I murmured. But this revelation certainly put an entirely new spin on events. If Alvin Goddard had been less than forthright in his dealings, he might have angered any number of businessmen, both associates and rivals.

Where did that leave Uncle Cornelius? We had been discussing Neily, though, and for now I returned our focus to that subject. "So Mr. Goddard used his resources to spy on Neily?"

"That's what I gathered."

"I wonder if Neily knew? And if he did . . ."

"He'd have been furious, no doubt." Adelaide raised a perfect, golden eyebrow. "Not to mention eager to prevent Mr. Goddard from revealing his findings to his parents."

"But to suggest he might have . . ." A chill washed through me, and even as I denied the possibility of Neily having killed anyone, I asked myself again: Where had he disappeared to during the ball?

"Emma, do forgive my manners. I'll ring to have some lunch brought up."

The thought of food only tightened the knots already forming in my stomach. My thoughts raced and the faces of potential suspects flashed dizzily in my mind. Theodore Mason . . . Neily . . . Brady . . . and everyone with whom Alvin Goddard had ever conducted business with, for, or against. Except, of course, it had to have been someone in Newport who had access to The Breakers two nights ago.

I came to my feet. "I'm sorry, Adelaide, but not today. You've given me lots to think about. And there's something I need to do."

I was going to confront Neily, simply tell him what I'd learned and ask him point-blank if he'd known Alvin Goddard had had him followed. And then I was going to ask him where he'd been when Mr. Goddard died. I didn't believe Neily was guilty, but the questions needed to be asked, and I believed that after nearly a lifetime of knowing him I'd be able to sense if he was lying.

I turned my buggy onto Bellevue Avenue, but came to an immediate stop. Between the two entrances of the Halstocks' circular drive stood a man with his feet braced well apart and his square chin raised so he could see over the shrubbery-lined iron fence that bordered the property. The sight of that strong profile sent my pulse for a lurch. I eased Barney forward until the carriage came even with the individual. He turned around to face me.

"Good afternoon."

"Who are you?" I demanded.

He was tall and well-formed, broad at the shoulders, with a torso that narrowed to a trim waist and hips. His hair was a trifle on the longish side, midnight dark, and curling slightly at the ends. His equally dark eyes bored into me. "I'm sorry?"

"You heard me," I snapped at him from my perch. I studied

him a moment, intrigued by his handsome features, his masculine air. "Who are you and why have you been following me?"

He removed his hat and bobbed an elegant little bow. "I wasn't aware that I had been. I'm merely a summer tourist enjoying the sight of Newport's cottages, as they call them."

"No, you aren't. I saw you at the police station yesterday, heard you asking questions, and when I left, you followed me to Spring Street." At my angry tone, Barney stamped and twitched. I adjusted the reins and leaned down closer to the man, then wished I hadn't when he flashed me a smile—a charming one that made my breath hitch. With an effort, I held on to my frown. "Are you a reporter? A detective? An opportunist? What?"

His smile never slipping, he bobbed his head again. "All right, you have me. You guessed right the first time. I'm Derrick Anderson, reporter with the Providence *Sun.*"

"And?"

"And I'm here doing an article on America's wealthy industrialists and most powerful men. Rupert Halstock is one of those men. So you see, I wasn't following you. Merely seeing the man's house for myself."

"What about yesterday? Do you deny following me from the police station?"

A twinge of fear had me bracing when he moved toward me, but he kept going until he stood beside Barney's head. Reaching up, he scratched behind Barney's ears, just where the gelding liked to be rubbed. "I'll admit I was rather curious about you yesterday. If you'll remember correctly, it was you who stopped to listen to my conversation with Officer Whyte. Don't deny it; I caught you staring."

"I . . ." Oh, dear, that was right. I did, and he had. But . . . "You were asking questions about my brother's case."

A mistake. His eyes flashed at the information I'd just given him; until that moment, he hadn't known my identity.

"You're Emmaline Cross, then."

"It's Emma," I said automatically, impulsively. Another mistake, but somehow the man had undermined my composure.

"Glad to make your acquaintance, Emma. You can call me Derrick."

"Certainly not. And you may call me Miss Cross." I lifted the reins to move on, but Mr. Anderson held on to Barney's harness.

"I don't suppose you'd answer a couple of questions about the Halstocks? For my article. It's obvious you're a friend of theirs."

"I'm a friend of Mrs. Halstock's." I considered a sharp flap of the reins against this man's knuckles and moving on, but a protective instinct toward my childhood friend raised my curiosity and prompted me to ask, "What kinds of questions?"

"Well, for instance, it's common knowledge Rupert Halstock hasn't been well in recent months. How is that affecting Halstock Industries? And how is his young wife coping with the stress of his illness?"

I hesitated, pondering Mr. Derrick Anderson of the Providence *Sun*. He had the cockiness one would expect of a reporter. Yet, there was a deeper confidence that bordered on cavalier, along with an elegance that simply didn't fit. His manner left me unsettled, suspicious. And not a little fascinated.

I raised my nose in the air. "Please unhand my horse, Mr. Anderson. I must be moving on."

With a chuckle that angered me for no good reason, he stepped back onto the sidewalk. "Have a pleasant afternoon, Miss Cross."

"Good day to you, sir."

I was still thinking about Mr. Anderson when I arrived at The Breakers a few minutes later. Uncle Cornelius, I was told, was in his office with his lawyer, newly arrived from New York. Bateman escorted me upstairs to the loggia, where I found Aunt Alice tucked against the pillows of a chaise lounge, staring out at the bright blue vista of sky and sea beyond the property. Below her on the wide sweep of the rear lawns, her youngest daughter, Gladys, frolicked with her governess and a furry, caramel-colored dog that resembled a tiny fox. Its piercing yips blended jarringly with Gladys's and the governess's shrieks of laughter as they ran about in circles and took turns tossing a ball to the animal.

Aunt Alice snapped from her reverie at the sound of my step. She smiled, seeming happy to see me, and invited me to pull up a chair close beside her. "Good of you to call, Emmaline. I'm sorry we weren't at home yesterday. You understand. Did you find your . . . What was it you were looking for?"

"My earring. And, yes," I lied with a stab of guilt, "I found it on the seat of my buggy."

"I'm happy to hear it. Fancy driving yourself around as you do, though," she said half fondly, half in censure. "I'm not sure it's at all proper, dear."

The last thing I wanted was to remind her that neither my annuity from Aunt Sadie nor my wages from the Newport *Observer* allowed me to hire a driver. If I'd mentioned anything of the sort, she'd have hired me a fellow by sundown, and my illustrious relatives did enough for me already.

I told her the simple truth. "I enjoy driving myself, Aunt Alice. I like the independence."

She cast me a shrewd look. "You see, right there. That's why you have no serious suitors. If you'd just let me throw you a coming-out party—"

I help up a hand. "Thank you, Aunt Alice, truly. But again, I like my independence."

"Really, Emmaline, you can't stay single forever."

Couldn't I? Aunt Sadie had, with nary a regret. Aloud, I

said, "Well, after the other night, I believe we've all had enough of coming-out parties for a good long time."

"Yes, I suppose you're right." She sighed. "Poor Gertrude."

Poor Gertrude? What about poor Mr. Goddard? His death might have cast a shadow over the evening, perhaps even over the summer Season, but Gertrude would live on to marry—gloriously, I was sure—have children, and grow old. Mr. Goddard, on the other hand . . .

Wanting to divert Aunt Alice from thoughts of marriage, I almost mentioned that Jesse Whyte would be coming out to inspect the dent in the door frame of the balcony, but I thought better of it. The less my Vanderbilt relatives knew of my involvement in the murder investigation, the better. They'd never approve, and with a telephone call or two they would see to it I didn't learn another thing about that awful night.

At that moment Gladys looked up, waved, and called out a hello. I waved back, at the same time casually asking, "By the way, is Neily at home?"

"I haven't seen him since yesterday afternoon." Aunt Alice scowled in that way she had, a gesture that could send servants scurrying and lesser mortals cowering in corners.

"Didn't he have dinner with you at the country club?"

"No, though he was supposed to. We spent the afternoon at the Casino. Neily played several rounds of tennis with John Astor, and then the two of them left, supposedly to freshen up and join us for dinner. John arrived later with his wife, but that was the last we saw of Neily."

"Aren't you worried?"

"He'll turn up. He always does." She smiled as, below, Gladys coaxed her little dog to dance several jerky steps on its hind legs. "Do you want to leave a message for him?"

"No, it's nothing." But my mind began working at a furious pace. Had harm come to my cousin? Or was this an act of rebellion, Neily's way of telling his family he didn't appreciate their attempts to control his life? Or was he hiding somewhere, for reasons that went beyond a young man's bid for freedom? "I was just wondering how he's been since . . . the other night."

Aunt Alice nodded but, apparently having no insight to offer me, looked out toward the ocean once more. I would have to track Neily down later.

My thoughts then drifted to Mr. Derrick Anderson. The fluttering that arose in my stomach I ignored, or attributed to hunger, but I wondered about the coincidence that had brought the man to Redwing Cottage today. His excuse of writing an article about America's wealthiest industrialists didn't ring true, not after he had asked questions about Brady yesterday and then followed me along Spring Street.

Had he heard about Rupert Halstock's illness . . . his confusion? The incapacitation of a businessman like Rupert Halstock could send speculation skyrocketing and stocks plummeting. Perhaps Mr. Anderson was here to do an exposé on the next American industrial crisis.

And Mr. Halstock was hardly in a position to defend his business acumen. Why, the poor man couldn't even keep his wives straight; he'd spoken of his first wife as if she were still alive and of Adelaide as though he hardly knew her. Wishful thinking brought on by his malady?

"Aunt Alice," I said, "were you acquainted with the first Mrs. Halstock?"

"Gloria? A good, steady woman she was, never given to dramatics of any sort. I liked her very much." The emphasis she placed on *her* made me suspect Aunt Alice didn't think very highly of Adelaide. "A pity they never had children."

"Didn't they?"

"No, poor Gloria couldn't carry to term. So tragic. I suppose that's why Rupert chose such a young woman the second time around." The lift of an eyebrow confirmed my suspicion about Aunt Alice's sentiments toward Adelaide.

"He does have family, though, doesn't he? While I was there he mentioned a sister."

"That would be Mrs. Rockport. Suzanne. She was always devoted to Rupert. But she won't set foot in the house now that—" She broke off and began playing with the scalloped lace cuff of her sleeve.

I didn't envy Adelaide having to contend with both her husband's ailment and a disapproving in-law. "But if he cares for the second Mrs. Halstock, if she makes him happy, isn't that all that matters?"

"Oh, I suppose. She does seem devoted. She hardly lets him out of her sight."

And yet something in her tone implied this wasn't a good thing. "He's been ill, so of course Adelaide is sticking close by him."

"Hmm . . ." Aunt Alice lush eyebrows converged. "Even before that, though . . ."

I didn't ask her to finish her cynical thought, but resolved instead to keep a protective watch on my old friend and her ailing husband. I wasn't about to allow any reporter from Providence to make their life together any more difficult than it already was.

Besides, at the moment I had my own family difficulties to contend with. I still needed to talk to Mr. Mason and Neily. I had Nanny working on finding Mason's whereabouts, but how would I find my cousin if he didn't wish to be found? Then I remembered what Neily had done when he set out looking for Brady on that first rainy morning. I'd have to search out Neily's haunts.

Chapter 6

I spent the remainder of the afternoon hurrying from place to place: the Newport Casino, the Yacht Club, the restaurants along Bellevue Avenue, the shops along Spring Street. I even strolled the waterfront in hopes I might spot him leaping onto or off of one of Newport's countless summer pleasure craft. Not only did I find no sign of Neily, but could glean no information about him from any mutual acquaintances. But I was not without luck, for I ran into someone of nearly equal importance, quite by coincidence.

Having given up, I circled back to Molly's Dress Shop to apologize for my hasty dash through her store the day before, and to see what new trimmings I could have Nanny add to old gowns. As the bell above the door jangled, Molly looked up from her cutting table. Her customer glanced around, too, and I recognized the stunning redhead Aunt Alice had pointed out to me at the ball.

Molly set down her shears and crossed to me. "Emma, you're back. Or are you running through again?"

"No, and sorry about that, Molly, but you saved me from a

reporter I suspect would have hounded me with questions about Brady."

At that Grace Wilson pricked her ears and studied me more intently.

Molly grasped my hands. "How is he? No one I've talked to believes a word about the charges against him. You can tell him that as sure as the sky is blue."

"Thanks, Molly. Oh, but don't let me keep you from your customer." I peered over her shoulder. Miss Wilson's striking red hair and green eyes were set off to perfection by a walking ensemble of lime green silk with a smart peplum jacket that frothed with lace at the collar and cuffs. A matching purse and parasol completed the impeccably tailored outfit. Hardly able to take my eyes off her myself, I understood why Neily was so taken with her—if indeed what Adelaide had told me proved correct.

I schooled my features to show a proper degree of recognition. "You look so familiar. Have we met?"

"I don't . . ." She paused, her expression a blank. Then her eyebrows rose. "Weren't you at The Breakers, at Miss Vanderbilt's coming-out ball?"

I experienced a moment of doubt. Had she realized I'd been spying on her and Neily that night? There was nothing for it but to play my hand. "Why, yes. I'm Emma Cross." I strode toward her, a hand extended. "I'm a cousin of the Vanderbilts, on my father's side."

We chatted for the next few minutes while she purchased several yards of a breathtaking poppy blue silk. Then, while she and Molly discussed the pattern for the dress Miss Wilson wanted, I picked out some pleated chiffon Nanny could use to brighten up an evening gown of mine. I purchased an extra yard of the fabric for a day dress of Nanny's that could use a lift as well. I made sure I lingered long enough to exit the shop at the same time as Miss Wilson.

"Good afternoon, Molly, and thanks," I called to the propri-etress, tucking my little bundle beneath my arm. Then, holding the door for Miss Wilson, I suggested refreshments at the tea shop across the street. "Unless you're in a hurry to be off. I wouldn't dream of detaining you."

She studied me an instant, the faintest of blushes tinting her cheeks. "No, I'm in no hurry."

I was glad she agreed for two reasons. I hoped I'd learn some new information from her, true. But as we stepped into the tea-room, furnished in lightly painted woods and decorated with bright, floral chintzes, the warm scents of freshly baked rolls and tea biscuits curled beneath my nose, and my stomach rum-bled. It was nearly four o'clock and I'd never eaten lunch. We sat facing each other across a little marble-topped table near the window overlooking the street.

We engaged in the usual small talk during which I learned she was in town with her mother, renting a Bellevue Avenue house a few doors down from Adelaide's, and that their father was expected to join them later that week. She listened with in-terest as I explained my connection to the Vanderbilts. Over a treacle bun and peppermint tea, I decided to come to the point.

"I remember you danced with Neily at the ball," I said lightly. "He's quite a fine dancer, isn't he?"

She agreed and brought up a ball she'd attended at the As-tors' New York mansion last spring, an obvious attempt to change the subject. I didn't let her. "Have you and Neily known each other long?"

"We met for the first time in Paris last summer," she said somewhat defensively. "I haven't seen your cousin much since."

"No? I had the impression you were rather well ac-quainted."

"Not at all. I can't imagine what gave you that impression."

"Seeing you together on the dance floor, I suppose. Horrible, what happened that night, wasn't it?"

She blinked, obviously taken aback by my line of questioning—intentionally meant to trip her off her guard. She took momentary refuge in a sip of tea, then said, "Especially horrible for you, Miss Cross, having witnessed the incident. And with your brother the main suspect and the victim your suitor, well . . ."

"My suitor?" My turn to be taken aback, I pressed a palm to my breastbone. "Who on earth told you that?"

"I believe Mr. Vanderbilt mentioned it in passing that night."

"Uncle Cornelius?"

She smiled, her even features taking on the feline grace of a Siamese cat. "Mr. Vanderbilt the younger."

"Oh . . . Neily." I waved my hand at the notion. "He knew better than that. If Mr. Goddard had any intentions toward me, I assure you they were completely one-sided."

Miss Wilson nodded slowly, and I realized she had intentionally turned the tables on me, leaving me flustered and no longer in control of the conversation. She obviously hadn't liked my inquiries about her and Neily.

Well, I'd just have to turn the tables again.

"I looked for Neily immediately after the incident, Miss Wilson. Oddly, I couldn't find him anywhere in the ballroom, though the rest of the family and all the guests were toasting Gertrude. And no one has seen him since yesterday afternoon."

Her eyes widened as I spoke; her back stiffened. "What are you saying?"

"Only that Neily's whereabouts at the time of the murder, and now, are in question."

"Surely you're not accusing your own cousin?"

"I'm not accusing anyone. But my own brother has been charged with the crime, wrongly I'm convinced, so no question can go unasked."

"Neily didn't kill that man," she blurted, then clamped her full, bow-shaped lips together.

"Of course not," I agreed in a soothing tone. "But if the police should ask him where he was at the time—"

"He was with me."

I feigned surprise while privately wondering if she was telling the truth. Either way, her claim spoke volumes about the nature of her and Neily's relationship.

"We went below stairs together, to the butler's office." With a perfectly manicured hand she gripped the edge of the table and leaned closer toward me. "Look, Miss Cross, Neily and I just wanted a few minutes to ourselves, beyond the disapproving eye of his mother. The Vanderbilts don't approve of me. They think I'm some kind of fortune hunter, which is ridiculous considering my father is richer than Midas. I couldn't give a fig about Neily's inheritance. His father can cut him off completely for all I care."

She certainly seemed impassioned, and sincere, too. I played with my teaspoon, tapping it lightly against my cup. "Is he threatening to?"

"Cornelius? He's dropped some hints to that effect. And he had that awful Mr. Goddard—"

Follow us. She didn't have to say it. What Adelaide had told me, then, was the truth.

Miss Wilson bit back her words and blushed furiously, her eyes fever bright in comparison. I took pity on her. "I believe you about your feelings toward my cousin. And I don't for a minute believe that Neily had anything to do with Mr. Goddard's death." I reached across the table and patted her wrist. "He and I have always been good friends, and I want him to be happy. If you see him, will you please tell him to call me on the telephone or to come out to Gull Manor to see me as soon as possible? Oh, and that he should put in an appearance at home before they begin to worry."

She nodded, as good as a verbal admission that she would, in fact, be seeing Neily in the near future. We left the teahouse and went our separate ways. I briefly considered following her, then discarded the idea. But I wondered, as I headed back to my buggy, if I believed my own assertion of Neily's innocence.

"Good news," Nanny said when I arrived home. She hadn't waited for me to come in the house but had bundled out to meet me in the barn. I had unharnessed Barney and was using a hoof pick to dislodge chunks of dirt and pebbles from his hooves. Nanny sidled in front of the gelding and held up the carrot she'd brought with her. "I know where the Vanderbilts' butler is."

I released Barney's left rear hoof and straightened. "That's former butler, but that was quick."

"I'll have you know it took me all afternoon," she replied with an indignant huff, but her eyes smiled at me from over Barney's head. "Actually, Irene from over at the Astors' place ran into Teddy Mason in front of the Brick Market two days ago. He's taken a room in the Harbor Hill Boarding House. It's on Broadway."

"I think I know it. Two days ago," I mused, more to myself. "That was the morning of the ball. If it weren't already so late and if I hadn't driven Barney to town twice today, I'd go there now."

"You'll go tomorrow, but not alone, young lady. I'm coming with you."

My automatic protest died on my lips. "That might not be a bad idea. He knows you, and he might be more willing to talk to you than me. He'd probably worry that I'd run telling tales to Uncle Cornelius."

"Finish up with Barney," Nanny ordered me. "I've got a pot roast in the oven that should be done right about now, and we don't want shoe leather for supper, do we?"

"I brought some pleated chiffon home from Molly's," I called to her retreating back. "Enough for both of us."

"I hope it's blue, to match my eyes," she called back gaily.

Glad I'd chosen correctly, I smiled and began running the brush through Barney's coat.

"Herr Mason? Yah, he took a room here. He's very quiet and I almost never see him. But I think he's not in at the moment."

The Harbor Hill, situated on Broadway about a half mile beyond the west end of Washington Square, was a three-story Victorian that could have done well with a coat of fresh paint and some cheerful flowers in its gaping window boxes. But the landlady proved to be a pleasant woman with a light German accent and wisps of brown hair pulled up into a bun at the crown of her head. To add legitimacy to our visit, Nanny had wrapped up some of last night's leftover pot roast and potatoes, along with a generous slice of peach pie. Nanny held out the linen-covered basket.

"May we leave these for him?"

"Oh, smells heavenly. I'm sure he'll be delighted. Who shall I say called?"

"Mrs. Mary O'Neal," Nanny replied, and then with a twinkle added, "we were old school chums, Mr. Mason and I, and sweethearts for a short while."

"You never told me that," I whispered as we walked back to the rig I'd parked at the curb.

"A girl can have her secrets, can't she?"

I couldn't argue with that.

We drove back into town to deliver another basket of leftovers, this time to Brady. We had to wait in the main station while an officer first rifled through the parcel—searching for files or crowbars, one supposes—and then brought the bundle back to Brady. His cell door was locked up tight when Nanny and I were finally allowed back there, and he was sitting hunched on his cot with the basket on his knees.

Looking decidedly glum, he placed it on the mattress beside him and came to his feet. "Thanks, ladies. Appreciate it."

"Pot roast and potatoes with glazed carrots, Brady. Your favorites," I said, trying to raise his enthusiasm.

He shrugged and nodded.

"Are you catching a cold?" Nanny pushed her half-moon spectacles higher on her nose and peered at him through the bars. "Open your mouth and say '*ahhhh.*' "

"I'm not ill, Nanny."

"Then what's wrong?" I felt immediately stupid; since we were standing in the city jail, the answer was obvious. Yet on my previous two visits, he hadn't seemed nearly so . . . defeated.

He leaned his forehead against the bars. "I don't think they're going to let me out, Em."

"Oh, Brady," I said, incredulous. "Did you really think they were going to?"

"Yeah, actually, I did. I thought after a day or two Jesse would come let me out, tell me it was all a big mistake. But . . . they really believe I did it, don't they?"

"Well, we don't," Nanny said with an imperious lift of her double chin.

"No, we don't," I seconded. "And I've convinced Jesse to return to The Breakers to inspect a dent in the door frame that might just prove the candelabrum wasn't used against Mr. Goddard. In the meantime, can you think of anything else that might help your case? Anything to do with those railroad plans, maybe?"

"Such as what?" he asked warily.

"Such as whatever you're hiding," I snapped. His mouth thinned and he started to back away from the bars. I gentled my tone. "I'm sorry. I'm only trying to help. What about the investors? Who were you going to approach with the plans?"

"I've already given the police that information."

"What?" My voice became sharp again, and with an effort I held on to the last of my patience. "Brady, the police think you're guilty. Jesse wants to believe in you, but even he has his doubts based on the evidence. I am the only one fighting to exonerate you. So tell me, who did you approach with those plans?"

"No one who would have murdered Alvin Goddard." Just as I despaired of ever getting a straight answer from my brother, the stubborn gleam in his eye faded. "Jack."

I frowned. "Mr. Parsons?" My father's handsome, dashing friend from his college days? When Brady nodded, my pulse rattled in my wrists. "He's an investor?"

"Sure, along with every other speculator summering in Newport, most of whom were at the ball and easily could have followed me into Uncle Cornelius's bedroom, knocked me out, and shoved Alvin off the balcony. There's no reason to think Jack . . ."

"No, of course not," I agreed, yet my mind went hurtling over possibilities. If Alvin Goddard had drawn up the plans that would set investors scrambling, one of them might have stopped at nothing to halt those plans.

Oh, but not Jack Parsons. He was one of my father's oldest friends, had often taken my family sailing on his yacht, had sent yearly birthday gifts for Brady and me, and taken me on the front of his saddle when I was small and urged his horse to a careful canter, much to my delight. Besides, if someone were angry enough to murder over Uncle Cornelius's planned buyout of the New Haven-Hartford-Providence line, wouldn't they have gone, not after the administrator, but the mastermind of the project?

Uncle Cornelius. For the first time I wondered if the murderer hadn't made a mistake in that dark room. . . .

"Stop it, Em."

I snapped out of my reverie to be confronted by Brady's scowl.

"This is exactly why I didn't mention Jack in the first place. I can all but smell the smoke coming off your brain as the wheels grind. As much as I want out of here, I'm not about to incriminate an innocent man."

"Neither am I," I promised. "But Jack may know something. He may have heard something significant, even without realizing it. We should at least speak with him." I purposely used *we*, hoping to distract Brady from the fact that I alone would continue the investigation. "Where is he staying?"

His expression told me I hadn't fooled him. "He leased a house on Lakeview Avenue."

"Good. That's not far from The Breakers."

Leaving Brady with strict orders to enjoy his leftovers and not to worry—too much—Nanny and I returned to Gull Manor. I needed to think, and the lull of the waves and the bracing scents of the sea always helped steady my mind.

I discovered an unexpected visitor waiting for me at home.

A clearly nervous Katie ran out from the kitchen as I pulled the carriage round back. "Mr. Neily is here, miss. He arrived about a quarter hour ago. I offered him tea, but he wasn't wantin' any."

"Thank you, Katie. Where is he?"

"Right here." Looking impossibly tall in our kitchen doorway, he stepped out to the yard. Something in his expression prompted me to steel my nerves with a deep breath before leading him back into the house and to the sunroom that stretched alongside the kitchen garden, forming an L with the main part of the house. Battered sofas and worn tabletops vied for space with potted plants, oriental vases, and a bronze statue of some

Tibetan garden goddess whose name I didn't know. Aunt Sadie had had a taste for all things exotic. Beyond the wide bay windows overlooking the ocean, whitecaps and wispy clouds mirrored each other. Closer to the house, Katie climbed into the carriage and steered Barney into the barn.

"This is a surprise, Neily," I said with a breeziness I didn't feel. "What brings you here? Oh, have you seen your parents yet? They've been worried. Wondering where you've been."

"I can handle my parents." He moved past me to the center of the room and stopped, removed his hat, planted his feet, and blatantly ignored my gesture that he take a seat. "What are you doing, Emmaline?"

To pretend I didn't know what he meant would have been to insult his intelligence. "Miss Wilson and I ran into each other at the dressmaker's shop. Afterward, we had tea together."

"And discussed the murder, and me."

"Yes," I said quietly. "Brady is innocent, Neily, and I intend to get to the bottom of things."

"By frightening my fiancée?"

I sucked in a quick breath. "You're engaged? She didn't mention that. Only that your parents didn't approve of her."

"Unofficially engaged, and, no, they don't. Not that it matters."

"Doesn't it? She told me they'd hinted at cutting you off, and that your father put Mr. Goddard in charge of having you watched."

Neily snorted. "Do you think either would stop me?"

I walked to the windows, then turned back around to face him. Now, with the light behind me and shining directly on him, I could read his features more clearly. "If you're disinherited . . . how will you live?" He opened his mouth, but I held up a hand. "Don't tell me Grace's dowry is enough. I know you, Neily, and I can't imagine you living off your wife's money."

"I can work, Emmaline. I was practically raised in Father's

offices. I know the railroad business inside and out, and if I have to go looking for employment, I will. Someone would hire me, if only to stick it to Father."

"Then you weren't furious with Alvin Goddard?"

A muscle worked in his cheek. "Furious? Yes. But not with Goddard. He is—was—only Father's lackey."

Goose bumps erupted on my arms as those words brought back my earlier question. Had Uncle Cornelius and not Mr. Goddard been the intended victim? I schooled my features. "Then you won't mind answering a question about that night."

He held out his hands, waiting.

"After Mr. Goddard fell—or was pushed—I went running back to the ballroom. Yours was one of the faces I searched for, but I didn't see you anywhere even though the rest of the family was toasting Gertrude. Where were you?"

"Below stairs."

That's what Miss Wilson had told me. "Alone?"

His eyes sparked. "No."

"Neily . . ."

"I can't believe you're accusing me of murder, Emmaline. You've known me all your life."

Yes, but when I finally found Neily that night, he'd come up behind me, not from the service stairs, but from the direction of one of the Great Hall's two staircases, both of which led to the second floor. Or had he come up the service stairs, entered from the service hallway, and made a circuit of the room first, swept up in the tide of guests streaming into the dining room? Just then I had no way of knowing.

"I'm trying to get at the truth," I said. "I've known Brady all my life, too, and I know he didn't commit the murder either."

"I'm sorry, but I can't help you." He slapped his hat back on his head, a gesture of finality. Helplessness filled me as I watched him stride to the doorway. In all honesty, I couldn't believe he was any more guilty than Brady, but at the same time

I felt him withholding . . . something. An idea suddenly occurred to me. "Neily, wait."

He stopped and turned, his expression setting strict limits on how much time he'd allow me.

"There is something you can do to help. Can you open your father's safe?"

His expression sharpened. When he started to shake his head, I plowed on. "If Brady didn't do it, and you didn't, then it might have been one of the investors in the New Haven-Hartford-Providence line."

"The police have those documents."

"Yes, as evidence against Brady. But are you going to tell me there aren't copies?" His silence gave me my answer. "I'll also need to see the guest list for Gertrude's ball so I can compare the two."

"Emmaline, don't you think the police have already done that?"

"Maybe. Maybe not. They believe Brady's guilty. Even Jesse Whyte has his doubts; I can see it in his eyes. Any further investigating is for appearance's sake only." I pinned him with my sternest gaze. "You know as well as I that Brady makes a convenient scapegoat for a social circle that protects its own."

"Surely you don't believe men like my father would try to protect a murderer."

I went on staring; it was my turn to let the silence speak for itself. Men of my uncle's caliber protected each other for the simple reason that they each harbored secrets not even their families could imagine. Release even the slightest hint of one of those secrets, and the whole of their carefully erected empires could come crashing down. So, yes, to safeguard those empires, I believed they'd even protect a murderer.

The murmur of the waves and the cries of the gulls, present all along, seemed to fill the room with their oppressive echoes. Neily dropped his gaze, contemplating the floor tiles. Slowly, he nodded and very softly said, "You're right. And if the Four Hundred have decided Brady must go down for this crime, then down Brady will go."

My heart thumped a painful beat. "Then you'll help me?"

Neily didn't answer. He simply turned and left, leaving me to stew for the rest of the afternoon. At about ten o'clock the next morning my telephone jangled, nearly causing me to spill coffee down the front of my dress. My nerves buzzing, I ran to the alcove beneath the stairs to pick up.

"Father's playing golf at the country club," Neily said in a rush that was barely audible through the ear trumpet. "Mother and Gladys have gone down to Bailey's Beach, and Gertrude is in town shopping with Esther Hunt. I'd say you have at least an hour and a half before anyone returns home."

"What about Reggie and Alfred?" I whispered into the mouthpiece. I didn't want Nanny to overhear that I was about to cross a line with my investigation, and with my conscience.

"Alfred left about ten minutes ago. He was dressed for tennis." An apologetic note worked its way through the staticky wires. "It's not that they're taking the murder and Brady's arrest lightly, Emmaline. It's just that no one really has the stomach to hang about this house right now. Not all day, at any rate."

"I don't blame them. What about Reggie?"

"He's somewhere on the property, but don't worry about him. He's been sulking lately, keeping to himself."

I immediately thought of Reggie on the night of the ball. He hadn't been sulking then . . . but he had been drinking, secretly. Concern prickled across my shoulders. Reggie had always been a mischievous child, but also an engaging one. The thought of him drinking on the sly and withdrawing from his family was a troubling one, and I wondered if I could manage both to search

Uncle Cornelius's safe and have a word with my younger cousin before the family returned home.

Neily snapped me back to priorities with a terse, "Hurry, Emmaline. I won't be extending this offer again."

I was calling for Katie before I'd even replaced the ear trumpet to its cradle. We harnessed Barney in record time and, without bothering to change into a suitable carriage gown, I set out. From Ocean Avenue I turned onto Hazard Road to avoid driving past Bailey's Beach, where Aunt Alice and cousin Gladys might happen to see me. From Hazard I headed east on Ruggles Avenue, which cut over to The Breakers. As I was about to cross Bellevue, however, a carriage traversed my path and a voice called my name.

The open curricle stopped directly in front of me, blocking my way across the avenue. From the passenger seat behind the driver, Adelaide smiled and waved. "Good morning, Emma. Visiting the relatives?"

Oh, dear. What if she happened to run into Gertrude and her friend Esther in town? Would she mention she'd seen me on my way to "visit family" in an almost empty house? I'd much rather no one but Neily knew of my errand today.

"I . . . uh . . ." I couldn't come up with anything believable, so I said, "How is your husband feeling today?"

"Noticeably better, thank you." Despite the optimistic words, she looked decidedly uneasy as she darted a gaze over her shoulder. Then she turned back to me. "If you're not visiting family today, why not come into town with me? You could leave your rig at Redwing Cottage."

Sighing, I clucked to Barney and steered him onto Bellevue so that my carriage came up alongside Adelaide's, albeit on the wrong side of the street, so now we were blocking the street in both directions. This was my old friend, after all, and we local Newport girls stuck together. "Can you keep a secret?" I whispered as I leaned out across the space between us. She nodded eagerly, and I continued. "I have an errand today, one that has to do with Brady, and I need to get to The Breakers as soon as possible."

She cast a quick glance up at her driver's straight back. "A *secret* errand?"

"It is. And that's why I must ask you not to mention that you saw me here. Can you do that for me, Adelaide? For old time's sake?"

"Of course, Emma." She reached over and clasped my gloved hand, giving a firm squeeze. "You can always depend on me. If there's anything I can do to help . . ."

"Just that. Mum's the word, yes?"

She released my hand and raised her own to her mouth, making a motion as if securing a button. We bid each other good-bye and she moved on. I continued down Ruggles. Soon I was passing through the vast iron gates and up the curving drive. Conveniently, Shipley, the gatekeeper, was nowhere in sight, and I could only guess that Neily had given him a task somewhere else on the grounds.

Neily met me outside. "Hurry. There's no one upstairs right now. The bedrooms have already been tidied and the maids are occupied below stairs."

Taking me by the hand, he hurried me inside and up the closest set of stairs to the upper gallery. As this overlooked the Great Hall, we dashed across the landing and ducked quickly into his father's suite. There he released me, shut the door, and wasted no time crossing the room. The safe, I saw, had already been unlocked: He swung it open and gestured me over.

"I've already looked through," he murmured, "and I didn't find any copies of the investor list. He probably left the original in New York. But I knew you'd want to see for yourself, so go ahead. I'll go listen at the bedroom door. If I hear anyone coming, we'll slip outside onto the balcony."

The notion sent a chill up my back when I considered what

had transpired between the last two people to set foot on that balcony. I shook the notion off. I was here with Neily. I was safe.

Right?

Another thought struck me. Had Neily removed anything from the safe before I arrived?

Chapter 7

With both hands I began sifting through the papers in the safe. There were two shelves inside plus the floor of the safe, though the bottom section was taken up by some half-dozen small boxes, some wood, others covered in leather or velvet. To satisfy my curiosity, I opened each one and peeked inside at items such as jewelry, both Uncle Cornelius's and Aunt Alice's, keys, and several gadgets and gages whose use eluded me, but which I assumed were train related.

Quickly, I turned my attention to the upper shelves, pulling out binders, ledgers, and sheaves of paper. The notebooks contained little besides numbers—schedules, mileage, timetables. The papers included stock statistics, real-estate records, and references to the various lines of Uncle Cornelius's New York Central. But I found nothing mentioning the New Haven-Hartford-Providence Line or its investors.

Just as Neily had told me.

"Are you finished?" he hissed from across the room.

Over my shoulder I gazed up at him, pinned him really, with a look of suspicion.

"What?"

"You looked through before I got here," I said evenly.

"And?" He paused as his expression went from puzzled to defensive to outraged. "Come now. Surely you don't believe I'd invite you over here if I intended to hide anything from you. I could have just refused to open the safe."

I supposed that made sense. I stared at him another moment, thinking about the Neily I'd known all my life: the Neily who possessed little guile, who tended to wear his heart on his sleeve. "Sorry," I said, and turned back to the safe.

"You'd better finish up, Emmaline."

"One more minute." For a good portion of that minute I sat back on my heels and stared into the blackened innards of the safe. I returned my focus to the jewelry cases as the image of an etched letter formed in my mind, something I'd seen while opening the boxes but paid no heed to. . . .

I pulled a case from the middle of the stack and opened it. There, at the very top of the glittering pile sat a pocket watch with the letter *P* engraved at the center of a medallion on its cover. By the thickness of the chain, and the weight and warmth of the metal against my palm, I judged the piece to be solid gold, probably twenty-four karat.

My heart raced as I pondered whom that *P* could belong to. Not Cornelius Vanderbilt, nor his father, William Henry, nor *his* father, the first Cornelius. I thought of Aunt Alice's side of the family, but her father's name was Abraham Gwynne. I could think of no relative with the initial *P.*

What would Uncle Cornelius be doing with a valuable watch that obviously wasn't his? The answer seemed simple: Someone had given it to him. But not as a present. A present wouldn't bear the wrong initial. This had to be collateral on a loan, or the payment of a debt—from someone whose name, either first or last, began with *P.*

My mind snatched at a possibility: Parsons.

Jack Parsons.

"I found something." I held up the pocket watch for Neily to see. He left his position at the door and came closer. "Have you ever seen this before?"

He bent over me, frowning as he regarded the design. "No, never."

"See the initial?"

"*P.* So?"

"So why would your father have such an item locked in his safe?"

"I couldn't say. Put it back and let's get out of here."

Twisting, I glanced up at him. "I don't suppose I could—"

"Have you gone mad? Of course you can't. Put it back now."

"It might be a clue."

"Look here, Emmaline." He straightened and set his hands on his hips. "You came for a list of investors. You didn't find it, so let's go."

I'd never heard him sound so much like his father before. Reluctantly, I set the watch in with the rest of the jewelry and slipped the case back into its rightful place between the others. As I stood, the sound of carriage wheels crunched on the drive. Neily grabbed my arm.

"Come on!"

Knowing it would be futile to outrace whoever had just arrived home, we made no attempt to run down to the library or one of the parlors, but instead headed out onto the second-floor loggia. I threw myself onto a chaise lounge and tucked my skirts neatly around my legs. Neily took up position at the balustrade, one hand in his trouser pocket, the other shoulder leaning against one of the pillars that supported the loggia's six impressive arches.

"Act natural," he ordered. "Talk about something." His face was flushed, his chest rising and falling with each labored breath. I hadn't realized how unsettled he'd been while I conducted my search.

"I . . . um . . ." Footsteps sounded on the stairs. I glanced out to sea and pointed. "Oh, look, those two yachts appear to be racing."

"Yes, that's good." He turned to face the ocean. "My money's on the sail with the red crest. How about you, Emmaline?"

"Hello, you two. Gambling again, eh, Neily? You know you shouldn't corrupt our cousin."

I relaxed immediately. It wasn't Aunt Alice or Uncle Cornelius, but Gertrude and her good friend Esther Hunt. Esther's father had designed The Breakers, as well as many of Newport's other summer cottages, and it was partly because of that, because her father had in essence "worked" for the Vanderbilts, that Aunt Alice didn't approve of the girls' friendship. Poor Richard Hunt passed away last spring, and not even the whispers attributing his demise to Aunt Alice's excessive demands on his creative genius had convinced her to soften her attitude toward his daughter.

But Gertrude was twenty now and eager to assert her independence before she became some man's wife. And, unlike Neily, she felt no compulsion to hide the friendship she had no intention of abandoning.

"Oh, Emmaline, I'm so sorry." Gertrude's smile faded and her green eyes became all the more vivid by the heavy brows gathering above them. "I shouldn't be making jokes, not with Brady . . ." She sent me an apologetic and equally sympathetic look. "How is he?"

"He's all right. Holding up as best as can be expected."

"I think he's innocent," Esther Hunt announced, as if making a statement to be recorded in the newspapers.

I smiled and thanked them both, and to change the subject asked if they enjoyed their shopping. They immediately launched into a summary of the treasures they'd discovered in town. I listened indulgently, enjoying their enthusiasm and the short respite from what had come to occupy my every waking moment, and most of my dreams as well.

I liked Esther; something in her bearing never failed to put me at ease. Pretty in an unassuming way with her blue eyes and golden brown hair, she had a breezy, natural way about her, a propensity to laugh, and a constant readiness to speak her mind. She'd coaxed Gertrude out of her natural shyness so that, at least when they were together, the awkwardness drained from my cousin's long limbs and left a willowy confidence in its place. Esther taught Gertrude to enjoy her life and value her own opinions. Aunt Alice, of course, disapproved of all that. But I knew Esther was good for Gertrude, who hailed from a home where self-expression was never encouraged.

"Phew. It's warm today." Gertrude slid the pin from her wide flowered hat and freed the dark curls that had been tucked up beneath the brim. She tossed her head back and gave it a shake, then rubbed a hand across her nape. "The footmen are bringing our packages up now. Care to see them, Emmaline?"

Before I could answer, Esther perched beside my feet at the end of my chaise. "We saw your old chum Mrs. Halstock while we were in town."

"Shopping?" I asked casually, hoping Adelaide hadn't mentioned to them that she'd seen me on my way to The Breakers.

"No, her carriage was stuck behind a bakery wagon and a draft cart that had had a bit of a collision." Gertrude dragged a cushioned, wrought-iron chair closer to my chaise. "My, the things that came out of her mouth. I suspect she thought no one could hear."

"Practically worthy of a dockworker." Esther chuckled. "She cut off quick enough when I called to her from the sidewalk. A bit high-strung, that one."

"I'll say." Gertrude leaned back and loosened the high collar of her walking dress. "We tried to be civil and ask after her husband, and she just brushed us off and ordered her driver to move on the moment the way was clear."

"Adelaide always was caught up in her own little world," I said. "Probably wanted to do her errands and get home before Mr. Halstock missed her." I swung my legs to the side of the lounge and came to my feet, realizing with relief that it didn't matter now if Adelaide had mentioned my visit here; I'd already been found out. Now I hoped to leave and escape questions. "Well, if you'll all excuse me . . ."

"Won't you stay to tea? Mother and Gladys should be home soon." Gertrude's brows converged above her nose again. "What brought you over today?"

"Oh, I . . . I was hoping your father might have heard something new about the case," I improvised. "Something the police might not share with me."

Gertrude and Esther exchanged a glance; then Gertrude shot a glare at Neily, who stood with his back to us, pretending to watch the progression of the yachts sailing past the property. "Father doesn't talk about it," Gertrude finally said. I thought she was about to add more, but she pressed her lips together, emphasizing her slight underbite.

"Has Officer Whyte been out again?" I asked.

Again, looks were exchanged.

"What is it you all don't want to tell me?"

Neily turned around but looked somewhere over my head rather than at me. "He came early this morning to measure something in Father's room. But he said he didn't think it had anything to do with the crime. And he said the less mentioned about it to you, the better."

My jaw fell, though I couldn't have said which bit of information dismayed me more. How could Jesse dismiss the dent in the door frame as irrelevant to Brady's case? And why would he deem the matter none of my business?

Those questions accompanied me down the stairs and out to the drive, where my carriage waited. Parker, the entryway footman, followed me outside to help me up, but I paused, suddenly realizing I hadn't heard a peep from Reggie the entire time I'd been there.

"I thought Master Reggie was home, Parker, but I didn't see him. Would you happen to know where he is?"

"I believe he strolled out that way about an hour ago, Miss Emmaline." He gestured down the service driveway, where the roof of the old playhouse poked through a gap in the trees.

"I won't be leaving just yet, then. I'd like to go say hello."

"As you wish, miss."

I followed the driveway that veered to the right away from the front of the house. About halfway down, a quaint, shingle-style cottage sat nestled in oak and red maple trees. I climbed the steps onto the covered front porch, for some reason averting my gaze from the four childlike figures carved into the posts, and knocked on the door. No one answered, so I opened the door and walked in.

"Reggie?" I called softly. The parlor area was empty, but a dark blue necktie lay tossed over the back of the little settee. A telltale shuffle drew my attention to the kitchen area.

My cousin sat hunched over the oaken kitchen table. He clutched a glass in one hand, and the distinctive color of the contents left little question as to what he was presently imbibing, even if the label of the bottle near his elbow hadn't proclaimed the contents to be some of his father's Tennessee bourbon.

For a moment Reggie didn't move, his profile sharp, almost gaunt against the brightness of the window behind him. He looked decades older than his sixteen years; it was like glimpsing a future fraught with troubles, disappointments, and defeats. My heart squeezed, and for an instant I actually grieved for the lost potential of the Commodore's great grandson.

Then I snapped myself back to the present. Reggie was behaving like so many wealthy young men his age—rebellious and spoiled, cavalier and self-absorbed. Surely he'd grow out of it in time.

But when he turned toward me and I looked into those bleary eyes, sunken in shadows and surrounded by bloated skin, I did something I probably shouldn't have. I shook my head sadly. "Oh, Reggie. You've got to stop this. At least don't sneak off to drink alone."

"No? Then tell me, Em, who should I drink with?" He laughed, an unpleasant sound.

I pulled out a chair and sat across from him. "You shouldn't drink at all at your age. Can you tell me why you do?"

"Why are you here, Em?"

I blew out a breath and crossed my arms on the tabletop. "I was wondering . . . Were you here when Officer Whyte came this morning."

He nodded. "I saw him."

"Did you hear him talk about the case against Brady?"

"Sure." He smiled and a knowing gleam entered his eyes. "I hear a lot of things I'm not supposed to. People around here seem to think I never pay attention."

I let that pass. "He mentioned me, didn't he?"

"He told Father you needed to let the police handle the investigation, and that we should discourage you from asking questions."

"And what did your father say?"

"Oh, he agreed. He wants the police to finish up, and Brady to be indicted and moved up to Providence."

My blood ran cold. "He said that?"

"Well, not in so many words. I mean, he didn't mention Brady by name. He said 'the guilty party.' " Reggie ran his finger around the rim of his glass. Then he picked the glass up and tossed back the remaining contents. His lips pinched tight as a shudder ran across his shoulders, but he picked up the bottle and splashed in another two or three fingers' worth.

"And did your father agree with Officer Whyte that I should stop asking questions?"

"What do you think? He doesn't like it that you write that

column for the newspaper. Says if it were anything else but the society page, he'd put his foot down and make you stop. A matter of respectability and family pride, he says. He thinks you need a husband, and quick. Mother agrees."

"And what do you think?" I asked in a low voice that trembled slightly with anger. His revelations didn't surprise me much, but it unsettled me to know I was discussed when I wasn't here.

"I think you should do as you damn well please." He raised his glass as if to toast me. My gaze drifted to the bottle, almost half-empty now. He held his booze rather well, I noted. Too well; it meant he drank often. He noticed me staring. "Want some?"

"No, thanks." Yet my eyes remained riveted to that bottle . . . a bottle identical to the one that had been found beside Brady after the murder. True enough, Uncle Cornelius always kept plenty on hand. But . . .

"Reggie, when Alvin Goddard died . . . where were you? I mean, did you see or hear anything unusual?" I added quickly to avoid sounding like I was accusing him.

But was I? Could Reggie have had time to push Alvin Goddard from the balcony and return downstairs in time for Gertrude's toast? But then again, anyone might have gotten hold of that bottle and placed it near Brady. Well, anyone who knew where to look, that is.

"Oh, I'd snuck off to the butler's pantry for more of this," Reggie said in reply to my question. He lifted the bottle and tilted it in my direction before setting it down again.

"Did you go upstairs at all?"

"I was up and down all night. You don't think I could stand being in the middle of that crowd without a breather now and again, do you?"

"I suppose not. And when you were upstairs, did you see anyone? Brady, for instance? Or Mr. Goddard?"

"Is this more of your investigation, Em?"

"Humor me."

"All right, I will, if for no the other reason than because Father wouldn't. Yes, I saw Alvin. He was going into a meeting with Father and a few other men."

"Do you remember who the others were?"

"Well ... let's see ..." He drummed his fingertips on the table. "Uncle William was there, of course, and John Astor, William Wetmore, Stuyvesant Fish ... um ... I think old man Halstock ... and ... that friend of your father's, the one Father used to call 'that eager pup'—Parsons."

Jack Parsons. It was one name that kept coming up.

He slanted an eyebrow at me. "Any more questions?"

"Only this. Did you see any of those men enter Uncle Cornelius's room that night?"

"Sorry, Em. I wish I had. I wish I could get Brady off the hook. I like him, you know." He leaned further over the table, bringing with him a sharp whiff of spirits. "He understands me."

Yes, all too well.

"Don't drink any more today, Reggie," I said as matter-of-factly as I could. "Go back to the house. Gertrude and Esther are back, and your mother and Gladys should be home soon, too. They'll wonder where you are and someone might come looking for you. You don't want them to see you ..." I trailed off and gestured at the bottle and once-more empty glass. As I did so, I thought of Brady and where he sat at that moment. And I thought of what often became of charming young men who turned to the bottle whenever life challenged them.

Sunday dawned bright and clear, and just hot enough to make me uncomfortable beneath my layers of muslin and linen. Nanny, Katie, and I piled into the buggy and drove into town to attend church. Not where my Vanderbilt relatives and most of their acquaintances worshipped, at beautiful Trinity Church with its soaring white steeple, but at the much smaller and more modest St. Paul's, where I had attended with Aunt Sadie during the last decade of her life; where she had played the organ almost every Sunday since before I was born.

A small crowd nearly filled the sanctuary by the time we arrived; we found seats together near the back. I thought I'd find respite here, an hour or so of peace, but on the contrary. As the summer heat closed around me, augmented by so many tightly packed bodies, my mind drifted from the usual platitudes intoned from the altar.

Using my little hymnal to fan my face, I pondered what Aunt Sadie would have done if faced with my dilemmas. With her fiercely independent spirit and refusal to accept any terms but her own, how would she have set about vindicating Brady? So far I'd hit a dead end at every turn; Officer Whyte, Uncle Cornelius, Neily, and even Brady himself seemed intent on hiding the truth—or, at least, hiding it from me. Was each trying to protect me, or did each have a reason to prevent the truth from coming out?

Yet, even I could hardly put stock into the list of suspects I'd compiled so far: Theodore Mason, Jack Parsons . . . and Neily? It all seemed absurd, beyond the scope of possibility.

Or was it? Theodore Mason had been accused of theft by Alvin Goddard and sacked without a reference. Jack Parsons . . . I sighed. If he owned the watch I'd found in Uncle Cornelius's safe, it could mean he was in financial straits. It was possible he owed Uncle Cornelius money—a great deal. People killed because of money all the time, didn't they? And then there was Neily, carrying on a courtship with a woman his parents disapproved of. Mr. Goddard had been spying on him and reporting back to Uncle Cornelius. . . .

Another name whispered through my mind, along with a remembered aroma so pungent my throat began to close. It was the sickly stink of bourbon, and the name . . . was Reggie. Again, it seemed impossible, but why? Because he was a boy?

Because his father was the richest man in America? Those, I realized, were only the reasons he'd never likely be suspected . . . or charged. But something was clearly eating away at Reggie, something with the power to destroy him. Could that something have led him to commit murder?

I went rigid, my hymnal slipping from my fingers and thwacking to the floor. Heads turned in my direction. I smiled my apologies even as my heart thrashed with a possibility I hadn't considered previously. Uncle Cornelius seemed content to let Brady take the blame for Alvin Goddard's murder.

Was it because he believed one of his sons had killed the man?

Neily, Reggie . . . and there was Alfred, too, although the middle Vanderbilt brother spent most of his time at Yale lately, and was never one to defy his parents. He wasn't a drinker or a gambler or a ladies' man, not someone with anything to hide. No, I couldn't imagine Uncle Cornelius suspecting Alfred, but as for the other two . . . perhaps I wasn't the only one with questions about my cousins. And if Uncle Cornelius believed one of them to be guilty, wouldn't he use his considerable resources to prevent his own son from being accused, much less charged?

It wouldn't be the first time a man in his position interfered with the law.

Nanny nudged my shoulder. "Almost time to go."

Indeed, the congregation was on its feet, singing the final hymn. I could barely remember the words, I was so impatient to be gone. The time for tact, politeness, and propriety had passed. It was time instead to confront my suspects with direct questions and let their replies bear witness to their guilt or innocence.

Perhaps attending church reaped its benefits that morning, for the angels sent me a minor blessing. Upon stepping outside, we ran into one of Nanny's countless acquaintances, elderly

Mrs. Bronson who was only too happy to bring Nanny and Katie home. That left the next hours wide open for me. I headed back up to Broadway, to the Harbor Hill Boarding House.

"I'd like to see Mr. Mason, please, if he's in," I boldly told the proprietress when she opened the door. Her eyes widened slightly, and no wonder; here I was, a lone young woman seeking a private audience with a man at his home. Most improper, but would that have stopped Aunt Sadie?

I think not.

"Ah, I remember you," the landlady said in her breezy German accent. "You came the other day with the older lady. Pot roast and potatoes."

"Yes, that's right."

"I get your basket." I tried to stop her, but she disappeared into the gloom of the house. A few moments later she returned and handed me the basket Nanny and I had left for Mr. Mason, now empty. "I'm sorry, but the gentleman is not here anymore."

The determination that had brought me here began to flag. "Mr. Mason moved out?"

"Not exactly. He still pays for room—for *his* room," she corrected herself, "but for now he lives elsewhere."

"Can you tell me where?"

Her eyebrow rose, disappearing beneath wisps of brown hair. "He did not say. He checks for mail sometimes. I tell him you called . . . again, yah?"

"No." I blew out a breath. "No need to tell him I called. Thank you, and sorry to disturb you."

But she wasn't listening to me. She was retreating into the house, closing the door, and saying, "Yah, I will tell him."

I didn't wonder what Aunt Sadie would do now, but I tended not to use strong language, even when there was no one around to hear. Without having formed a plan, I climbed back into my carriage and headed back into town. By the time I reached Spring Street, I knew where my next destination would be: Lakeview Avenue, in the hopes I would be able to identify Jack Parson's rented house. He was next on my list, and I had questions for him, the first being whether or not a certain pocket watch belonged to him.

I made the mistake of turning my rig onto Spring Street to cut across town. When I reached the corner of Spring and Church streets, the roadway jammed as Trinity Church let out. Fine carriages vied for space with single riders and pedestrians attempting to cross. With an impatient scowl I settled in to wait until two familiar faces near the corner caught my attention.

Adelaide saw me the same time I spotted her and we each raised a hand to wave. She stood at her husband's side, one arm hooked through his. Rupert Halstock appeared distracted by the surrounding crowd, his lined features pulled into an expression of childlike confusion. The manservant I'd encountered at their home flanked Mr. Halstock's other side, and with one arm extended, the valet made sweeping gestures in front of his employer to keep people from treading too close.

Adelaide turned to them and spoke some words. Her husband seemed not to hear her, but the servant nodded and stepped protectively closer to the ailing gentleman at his side. The next thing I knew, Adelaide was holding her skirts clear of the dusty street and making her way in and out of the slow-moving vehicles . . . to mine.

"Good morning, Emma, how fortunate to run into you like this." She stretched a gloved hand toward me, and what could I do but grasp it and help her up onto the seat next to me? "You don't mind driving me home, do you?"

"Good morning, Adelaide. Er . . ." I yearned to make my excuses. Drat this mire of Sunday traffic, or I'd have been halfway to Jack Parson's house by now. At my hesitation a desperate plea filled Adelaide's eyes, and I knew she had made no light request. "What about Mr. Halstock?" I asked.

Her gaze skittered to the sidewalk, where a gleaming

brougham inched to a halt in front of her husband and his valet. A footman hopped down from the back to open the door. "Please, Emma, just drive on. He won't miss me."

Within minutes the way began to clear and Barney was able to achieve a steady walk. As we drove in silence for another minute I felt the tension drain from Adelaide's posture. "Is he worse?" I asked softly.

"He's taken to accusing me of taking things. *Stealing* things from the house." She faced straight ahead, the brim of her silk hat hiding her face, but I heard the tears tightening her throat.

"What kinds of things? Is it that he's misplacing them and blaming you?"

"It's mostly the things we moved down to our New York house. Rupert seems to have forgotten, and so he accuses me of stealing paintings and statues and such. Oh, Emma, it's become so wearying. So distressful. The doctor says he's better of late, but I'm afraid I don't much see it." She pulled a lace handkerchief from her purse and dabbed at her eyes.

"I'm so sorry, Adelaide. I wish there was something I could do to help." I held the reins with one hand and patted her wrist.

"Oh, but there is." She lowered her hanky and turned toward me, her eyes surprisingly bright and clear. "You can cheer me up. That's why I hailed you. Just talk to me, Emma. I've so few friends. . . ."

"What do you mean?" I maneuvered Barney around a mud puddle as I turned toward Bellevue Avenue. "You were always so popular in our schooldays."

"Oh, but I no longer associate with many of our old school friends. My marriage has moved me above them, Emma, yet so many of the wives of Rupert's peers refuse to accept me. Your aunt Alice Vanderbilt included."

"Oh . . ." What could I say? While Adelaide judged me worthy of her association because of my Vanderbilt relatives, many of those same relatives judged her beneath their notice. It didn't surprise me. It took more than a rich husband to gain acceptance into Aunt Alice's social circle. As she always said, *breeding* was what mattered, while money was merely window dressing. Which, I suppose, is why they accepted poor, penny-pinching me into their club.

"What would you like to talk about?" I asked Adelaide brightly, hoping to raise her spirits.

"Anything but illness. How is Brady's case going? Are you still investigating?" She asked the latter question in an undertone brimming with eagerness and intrigue.

I bristled. Did she think it was any easier for me to discuss my brother's troubles than it was for her to discuss her husband's illness? Good heavens, should Brady be convicted, he might very well face execution.

But Adelaide never had been particularly good at empathy, at seeing past her own difficulties long enough to consider those of others. If I had to name a character flaw, that was hers, but if she had always been a bit self-absorbed, I'd never known her to be vindictive. In this instance, she was being curious, not hard-hearted, so I buried my anger and answered her matter-of-factly. "It's not going at all well, I'm afraid. There are questions whose answers could prove Brady's innocence, but the police don't seem inclined to ask them."

"And so you are, aren't you, Emma?"

"I'm trying to, but sometimes it's like banging my head against a wall."

She emitted a little chortle. "Do you have any other suspects?"

Her enthusiasm raised my ire again. "This isn't a detective novel, Adelaide."

"But surely you must suspect . . . someone," she insisted, perhaps not noticing how my lips had thinned.

"All right, yes. There are several people who I believe had motive and opportunity, but I won't tell you who." She looked about to object, so I added, "I won't tell anyone until I have more proof. I wouldn't want to accuse an innocent person. That would be as wrong and as damaging as the accusations against Brady."

"I suppose you're right. And you must have a care, Emma." Her sudden earnestness surprised me. "Not only for those who might be wrongly accused, but for yourself. You're right—this isn't a detective novel, and the guilty party won't appreciate your snooping around in his business."

Those words sent a chill down my back, but I snapped my face toward hers and met her gaze head-on. "I'm not afraid of anyone, Adelaide. No one is going to stop me from uncovering the truth. Not the murderer, not the police, not Uncle Cornelius."

We passed the Newport Casino, and soon the storefronts gave way to summer-lush trees and the hedge-lined walls of Bellevue Avenue's mansions. We were nearing my destination, and I longed to find a way to politely free myself of Adelaide's company.

Her long lashes narrowed around her lovely eyes. "You're quite determined, aren't you? You're frightening me a little, Emma. I don't believe I've ever seen this side of you before. It's as if, by living in your aunt's house and driving her rig, you've gained something of her stubbornness."

I couldn't help grinning. "You might just be right about that. Whoever decided to frame my brother didn't take the spirit of Aunt Sadie into account. She never backed down from anyone or anything in her life, and neither will I."

Chapter 8

I might have a portion of Aunt Sadie's spirit, but not her devil-may-care attitude when it came to polite society. She had never worried about whom she insulted or who disapproved of her "brazen ways." But when Adelaide implored me to stay and have lunch with her, I couldn't find it within me to say no. Especially not when she grasped my hand in both of hers, thanked me for being "such a dear," and even apologized for not being as good a friend to me as she should have when we were younger.

I truly couldn't resist her entreaties when her husband arrived home with his valet, hobbled past us grumbling about a missing Ming vase, made his way into the library, and slammed the door.

Poor Adelaide, fate had granted her fondest wishes, but with a cruel twist. My old friend was hurting and feeling very much alone, and no amount of riches could offer the comfort she sought. Only her husband's restored health and judgment could do that, or, in the interim, an hour or two of my company. And so I followed her up to her second-floor sitting

room with its light wicker furnishings, pretty watercolor paintings, and expansive views onto the rear gardens and the glittering ocean beyond. She talked while I mostly listened, and we
nibbled on crabmeat and watercress sandwiches, strawberries
with heavenly Grand Marnier sauce, and airy almond puffs.

Shadows fell across the east-facing gardens by the time I finally
worked up the wherewithal to excuse myself, but I couldn't help
patting myself on the back for a deed well done. She walked me
down to the front door, and there it occurred to me to ask a favor.

"Adelaide, I have another stop to make before going home.
It's close by. Would it be all right if I left Barney and the carriage here for a little while?"

"As long as you like, dear friend. Shall I accompany you?"

"No," I said, perhaps a tad too quickly. I tried to cover by
implying she surely had better things to do, but she saw
through my ruse.

"More detective work?" Her lips pursed and she set a hand
on my shoulder. "You won't do anything ill-advised, will you?"

"I promise I won't, Adelaide. Just a friendly chat with an old
friend of the family." I tried to convince myself as well as her,
but secretly I wondered how Jack Parsons would react to my
questions about the watch I'd discovered in Uncle Cornelius's
safe.

But first, of course, I had to figure out which house on
nearby Lakeview Avenue was his, and I'd realized this might be
easier done on foot. I could walk slowly, watch the houses,
double back if I needed to, without attracting undo attention.

A sight that greeted me as I turned from Bellevue onto Lakeview prompted me to grasp my skirts and speed my steps. A
man dressed in a plain but well-tailored black suit presently
strode up a front walkway toward a large gabled, shingle-style
house.

"Mr. Mason!"

He stopped and turned, his figure tall and straight, his silver
hair impeccably groomed and only slightly thinning for a man

of his years. "Miss Emmaline?" A frown deepened the lines scoring his forehead, and the glance he flicked toward the house's paneled front door indicated a wish for escape.

Civility, however, dictated he wait as I approached him. "What a surprise, Mr. Mason. Are you . . ." I paused and regarded the deep hunter green trim around the windows and outlining the steep gables of the house. Only one explanation could account for the man's presence here. "Are you working here now?"

"I am, Miss Emmaline. Mr. Parsons, with whom I believe you are well-acquainted, was good enough to offer me temporary employment for the length of his stay in town."

"This is Mr. Parsons's house?" Could I be so lucky? I felt an inner burst of success.

"Indeed, it is." A look of pain entered his eyes, swiftly followed by a flicker of embarrassment. The circumstances under which he'd been dismissed from The Breakers hung in the awkward silence.

With a mental shake, I remembered why I'd come. "I'm glad, Mr. Mason. I wonder . . . did the landlady from the Harbor Hill tell you that Mrs. O'Neal and I had come to visit you?"

"Oh, I . . . I . . ." He ran a hand lightly over his neatly slicked hair. "I'm terribly sorry. I meant to send a thank-you note, but then this position came up and I hurried to accept. Mary—uh, Mrs. O'Neal's—pot roast is unequalled."

"Indeed, it is. Is Mr. Parsons at home?"

"Not presently, Miss Emmaline."

"Oh. Um . . . might I come in anyway? Just for a moment."

He surveyed me with puzzlement that bordered on suspicion, but he could hardly refuse my request—and we both knew it. "After you, miss."

He brought me to an informal parlor at the back of the house and offered me tea. I accepted, even though I'd consumed more than ample refreshments at Redwing Cottage. Anything to prolong my stay in the hopes Mr. Parsons would soon return.

Mason returned with a pot of tea and a platter of fruit and biscuits. My stomach groaned rather than growled, but I dutifully plunked treats onto my plate and pretended to nibble. He seemed about to bow out of the room, but I gestured him to the chair on the other side of the sofa table.

"Please stay, Mr. Mason. There's something I'd like to ask you."

"It's hardly proper, Miss Emmaline."

"Nevertheless. You know my brother has been accused of murdering Alvin Goddard the night of Miss Gertrude's coming-out ball."

Nodding gravely, he perched somewhat stiffly on the edge of his chair. "You and Mr. Gale have my sympathies. I'm certain he'll be exonerated."

"Thank you." I knew I must proceed with caution, for my next question would all but accuse Mason of the crime. Vaguely I wondered if there was anyone else in the house—someone close enough to hear me should I need assistance. . . .

"Mr. Mason, please understand that I'm only trying to get at all the facts. I've learned that it was Mr. Goddard who accused you of stealing from your employers."

A muscle in his cheek bounced. "He had little on which to base that accusation, miss, other than the circumstantial evidence that I had unlimited access to the entire house, whereas other staff does not." He drew himself up as he spoke, his chin outthrust with wounded dignity.

"Yet despite a lack of any truly damning evidence, you lost your position."

"Unfortunately, yes. It very much surprised me that Mr. Vanderbilt didn't show more faith in me."

"You were happy in your position with the family, weren't you?"

"For a good many years, miss, as well you know. I watched the children grow into adults. I presided over every important family event as well as saw to their everyday needs. It saddened me to leave them."

"It must have angered you as well."

After a brief hesitation, he said, "I won't deny that it did."

I sipped my tea, but from over the cup I scrutinized every muscle in his face. "Was your anger directed toward Mr. Goddard?"

"Why, Emma, are you accusing my new butler of murder?"

The voice made both Mr. Mason and me flinch. Jack Parsons stood in the doorway, a newspaper tucked beneath his arm, the grin spreading across his handsome face mocking us ever so slightly. His blond hair, disheveled by the wind, fell with roguish appeal across his brow. It never failed to surprise me that a man my father's age could appear so hale, so full of youthful vigor. Jack Parsons was timeless, and sometimes I wondered what devil's bargain he might have made to stay that way.

After a beat he sauntered toward us and settled into the leather chair to my right, tossing his newspaper onto the table. At the same time, Mr. Mason jumped to his feet. Mr. Parson's grin persisted. "Sit, Mason. Go ahead and answer Miss Cross's question."

Mason once again settled uneasily onto the chair's edge. His gaze veered from his new employer to practically impale me against the back of the velvet sofa. "Yes, I was angry at Mr. Goddard. One doesn't simply walk into a head butler's position, especially not in a household of such magnitude as the Vanderbilts'. It took years to work my way up—years of hard work, dedication, unerring loyalty. . . ." He broke off, clutching his hands together in his lap so hard they shook. A deep breath calmed him only marginally. "Because of Mr. Goddard, my future is no longer secure. Who wouldn't be angry?"

I had no answer for him. Any normal person in his circumstances would express similar emotions. But the question remained: Was I staring into the troubled eyes of a normal person, or of a murderer?

"Your turn, Emma." Mr. Parsons took no pains to hide his

amusement. "Why don't you ask Mason where he was on the night of the crime? Perhaps he has an alibi."

"Mr. Mason?" I said.

"I was in my room at the Harbor Hill."

"Can any witnesses substantiate that claim?" This again came from Jack Parsons. I almost scowled at him but kept my attention on the butler instead. However entertaining this all might be to Mr. Parsons, it was deadly serious business to me, and to Mr. Mason, judging by his grim expression and trembling fingertips.

"Unfortunately not." He shook his head and added a shrug for good measure. "I spent the night alone. Reading."

"What book?" I asked automatically.

Mr. Parsons chuckled his approval, no doubt of my quick thinking and clever attempt to trip the butler in his story.

But Mr. Mason gave his answer readily enough. "Dickens. *Great Expectations.* It seemed both appropriate and ironic."

"David is a likable protagonist," I said, watching him intently.

"The main character is called Pip," he corrected me. "You're thinking of *David Copperfield.*"

It proved nothing. I'd read Dickens in school; most people had. And as the Vanderbilts' butler, Mason would have access to their extensive library over the years.

Still, I found myself wanting to believe him. I remembered how kind he'd always been to my cousins and me, greeting our antics with a patient smile and keeping our confidences, even lending his services as butler when the bunch of us played at being adults in the playhouse.

"Any other questions, miss?"

"No, Mr. Mason. And thank you. I hope you understand."

He came to his feet. "I wish Mr. Gale all the best."

But not, his tone implied, at his own expense.

Not quite able to look Mr. Parsons in the eye yet, I directed my gaze at the newspaper he'd dropped on the table. The headline emblazoned across the top of the page stole my breath:

STUART BRADEN GALE IV ACCUSED OF COLD-BLOODED MURDER

Abandoning my tea and plate of barely touched biscuits, I snatched up the paper.

> Lifelong Newport resident Stuart Braden Gale IV was arrested at The Breakers early Thursday morning on charges of brutally beating Alvin Goddard, financial secretary to Cornelius Vanderbilt II, and pushing the defenseless man to his death from a balcony poised some twenty feet in the air. Though Mr. Gale denies the charges, all evidence points in his direction. . . .

With a cry of disgust I slapped the paper to my lap. I didn't need to read the byline; I knew who wrote the sensationalist piece: Ed Billings, my fellow reporter at the *Observer*, a man possessing few scruples when it came to getting "the scoop."

"He wasn't anywhere near The Breakers that night. Mr. Shipley, the gatekeeper, would not have let him in," I complained bitterly, remembering the much more accurate and tempered article I'd written. The one Mr. Millford had turned down with a proverbial pat on my head.

"Who wasn't at The Breakers that night, Emma?"

"My nemesis, Ed Billings. It doesn't take many powers of observation to see he got his information secondhand or even thirdhand and then exaggerated, embellished, and dramatized the facts."

"I'd say thirdhand," Mr. Parsons said. "No one at the ball would have deigned to speak to a reporter, unless it was one of the servants."

"And that's hardly likely after Mr. Mason's dismissal. They all must be terrified for their jobs."

"So what are you doing here, Emma?"

A lie very nearly sprang from my tongue, something about being out walking and happening upon Mr. Mason. But perhaps Aunt Sadie gave me a nudge from beyond, because I remembered her courage and my own vow to take the direct approach.

"I came to see you," I said evenly. "Brady told me you'd leased a house on Lakeview, so I decided to try my luck in finding you. Mr. Mason happened to be outside as I rounded the corner."

"Fortunate. What can I do for you?" Concern entered his expression. "Do you need money? For Brady's case?"

"No, nothing like that," I said quickly and dismissively. "Although this does have to do with Brady. Mr. Parsons—"

"Emma," he interrupted with a flick of his hand, "you're all grown up and I'm an old family friend. Don't you think it's time you started calling me Jack?"

"Oh, I . . ." His deep brown eyes held mine, and something in their dark depths flustered me and made me stumble over my reply. Suddenly his chiseled, patrician features held me immobile while the mingled scents of hair tonic and shaving soap burrowed like fine brandy inside me.

Apparently, certain elements of that old schoolgirl fascination lingered to muddle my senses. I clasped my hands, bit down on the insides of my cheeks, and refused to succumb another moment to Mr. Parson's—Jack's—charms.

Good heavens, a man old enough to be my father.

"All right, if you insist. Jack . . ." The sound of it on my lips sent heat to prickle my cheeks, but I plowed on. "Brady tells me you're an investor in the New Haven-Hartford-Providence line Uncle Cornelius has been secretly planning to purchase."

Jack's sensual charisma drained away as his gaze flared with surprise. "So much for secrets, not with you around. Does your uncle know you're aware of his business dealings?"

"What my uncle knows isn't the point. It's who else knew, and did that person set my brother up?"

"How so?"

"Jack," I said more easily this time, "I know Brady went to you with the idea of stealing Uncle Cornelius's plans for the line and attempting to outbuy his buyout."

"And you think what, Emma?" His voice had hardened to that of a stranger's. "I told Brady it was a lousy idea."

"I'm not accusing you of anything." Yet, I refused to back down. "You met with Uncle Cornelius and Mr. Goddard during the ball."

"Your uncle often mixes business with pleasure. There was a small group of us who met in his office that night. So what?"

"Did tempers flare at that meeting?"

"Not that I remember. But we weren't there to discuss the New Haven-Hartford-Providence line—" He broke off, frowning.

"What? Do you remember something that might be significant?"

He compressed his lips a moment. Then, "I'm not sure if it's significant, but Halstock was fuming about something. Wasn't about the buyout, though. I think it had to do with his Hudson shipping routes."

"What about them?"

"He and Cornelius were arguing in whispers when I entered the office. I could only make out a few words and I could be wrong, but it seemed Halstock was accusing Cornelius of stirring up competition among the smaller, local shippers. Maybe they've been cutting into Halstock Industries' revenues."

For an instant I seized upon the notion of another suspect. Then I remembered Rupert Halstock's condition. "Or it could be that Mr. Halstock is confused," I said sadly, "and doesn't realize what he's saying."

"Could be . . . although that night he seemed more himself than he'd been in weeks."

Had he? Or did Jack want me to believe it? A wave of mistrust washed over me as I considered that Jack might be attempting to cast suspicion onto Rupert Halstock . . . and away from himself.

"Can I ask you one more question?" When he showed me a half smile of consent, I drew a breath and dove in. "Uncle Cornelius is in possession of a pocket watch etched with the initial *P.* A very costly watch. Is it yours?"

"Why on earth would Cornelius Vanderbilt have a watch that belonged to me?"

Answering a question with a question usually signified evasion. I leaned forward. "Many reasons. It might be collateral on a loan or an out-and-out payment for . . . who knows?"

"You are a suspicious one, Emma," he said with a laugh. Reaching into his vest pocket, he withdrew a timepiece every bit as expensive looking as the one in Uncle Cornelius's safe. "As you can see, my own watch is right here. I'm not quite sure what you're getting at, but really, Emma, if it weren't Brady's life at stake here, I'd be deeply hurt by the implications of these questions. But if I can do anything to help you or Brady, I'm only too willing."

"I'm sorry, Jack. But as you say, it's my brother's life at stake." I came to my feet. "I'll be going now. Thank you for putting up with me. Thank you for understanding."

He walked me to the door, bending to deposit a kiss on my cheek before bidding me a good day. It was only as I made my way back to Adelaide's house to collect Barney and the rig that I realized he'd never answered my question of whether the watch belonged to him.

Chapter 9

Adelaide must have been watching out her windows for me, because when I returned to collect my buggy, she came scurrying out to meet me on the drive.

Her cheeks were slightly flushed, her eyes agleam. "Well?"

Not for the first time, I tried to hide my impatience with her. "Well what?"

"Was your mission a success? Did you learn anything useful?"

"Really, Adelaide, you've got to stop reading those adventure stories."

She took hold of my arm. "Come inside. Stay for supper."

"Thank you, but no. I really should be getting home. Nanny might worry what's become of me, and since you don't have a telephone here . . ."

"Oh, bother Nanny. Surely you don't answer to your servants, Emma."

I slid my arm free and dug in my heels. "Nanny is much more than a servant. She's like a grandmother to me and—"

"Oh, forgive me, do. But I won't take no for an answer. I'll just send one of the footmen over to Gull Manor with a message to let her know." She reclaimed my arm, linking her elbow through mine and steering me toward the front door. "Now tell me as much as you can, without divulging the most secret details, of course. . . ."

I spent the remainder of the afternoon and early evening with my old friend. Her questions about my investigation continued, making me sorely regret ever confiding in her. Not that I could blame her, really. Her chatter and her short, nervous motions as we sat down together for an early supper—without her husband—were all too telling when it came to Adelaide's emotional state. I sensed her balancing on a narrow and fragile precipice, and securing my company for supper had been her attempt to latch on to security and steadiness, if only temporarily.

Dusk was settling over Bellevue Avenue by the time I drove Barney out through the gates of Redwing Cottage. With the long shadows of the mansions and the overhead branches plunging the road into an artificial twilight, I was glad I'd lit my carriage lanterns, and glad, too, that Barney never hurried above a walk even on the brightest afternoon, much less in the growing darkness where he might miss his footing and stumble. I didn't take any shortcuts along less inhabited and darker streets, but kept to Bellevue Avenue until it ended and Ocean Avenue curved along the sea.

By now Bailey's Beach was deserted, the tide dragging ribbons of foam high onto the sand, the windows of the bath houses shuttered. Just past Hazard Road I heard the grind of a carriage pulling up behind me. I thought little of it until the approaching rumble built to a rolling thunder accompanied by the staccato beat of hooves. Someone was certainly in a hurry, and I attempted to hug the roadside as closely as possible to let them pass.

They didn't pass, but instead pulled up until their horse practically nudged my rear bumper. I cast a quick glance over my shoulder, and through the opening between my canvas roof and the back of my seat I saw that the animal wore blinders. Of the driver I saw little; he sat deep beneath his own canvas roof, bundled in a hooded cloak.

That struck me as odd on a night as balmy as that one, but maybe the individual sought to keep the briny air from settling into his hair and clothes. I turned around again and tried to signal him, but Barney stumbled and I swung around to face front. My fists tightened around the reins and my arms stiffened with the strain of holding him steady. Ocean Avenue twisted and turned, its surface pitted and scarred from the constant bombardment of storms. The drive required my utmost attention, especially now.

Jarred by movement to my right, I jumped in my seat. The other horse had inched up between my buggy and the swale along the roadside. Was the driver drunk? My heart pounded at the thought, and then the front of other carriage smacked my rear right panel, sending me skidding sideways. Barney stumbled again and let go a whinny. My heart now in my throat, I tightened my fingers around the reins until they ached, and attempted to keep Barney on the road.

My pursuer came relentlessly along my right side, forcing me farther and farther to the left. Into the middle of the road I swerved . . . then into the left lane. If anyone came now from the opposite direction, we'd hit head-on. My carriage lanterns swung wildly, making the road appear to toss and buck around me. We reached a bend, the other carriage beside me now, and though I could look over directly at the driver, all I could make out were his silhouette and the edges of his hood.

But this much I could surmise: He was not drunk. Even in my brief glimpse I saw that he sat too steadily and drove his horse in too determined a manner.

No, definitely not drunk.

"Why are you doing this?" I shouted as my left wheels struck the rocks separating the road from a drop of about four or five yards, and then more rocks, jagged and spiky, that met the ocean waves. The jolt shook my bones and rattled my teeth together. Barney felt the impact and neighed, a high-pitched screech nearly drowned out by the grinding wheels and the thrashing ocean that was close now . . . too close.

The other vehicle hit mine again and the shove sent me sliding across the seat. Reaching up, I caught myself on the spokes that supported the canvas roof and stopped my momentum before I might have tumbled out. The offending carriage fell slightly behind and then struck again . . . and again. My arms were shaking now, my hands throbbing, my lungs burning and ragged. My buggy shuddered and skidded; a splintering crack rent the air. Both carriage lanterns flew off their hooks and shattered on the road. In the sudden darkness the world seemed to teeter. Ocean and sky and boulders tumbled in my vision. I sucked in a breath and waited for the impact, thinking of poor, loyal Barney, who might be fatally injured, who didn't deserve such a fate.

And then . . .

Everything stopped. My buggy came to a tilted halt. I was wedged in the corner of the seat, and to my left I could see nothing but the coal gray gleam of the darkening ocean. All that separated me from the water were the sharp boulders and a narrow spit of sand. I didn't move, didn't dare for fear the carriage would continue tipping, falling onto those rocks, taking me and dear Barney along with it.

In my shock I'd nearly forgotten we weren't alone. The stamp of a pair of boots hitting the ground sent my fears to clog my throat again. What did this person want? I'd never carried a weapon before, but how I wished I'd stored Aunt Sadie's revolver beneath the seat, as she used to do. Through the gathering twilight the individual strode toward me. Frantically, I looked about for anything I could use as a weapon. If I reached out of the carriage, could I grasp a rock from the ground without sending us over the brink? Holding my breath, fingers shaking violently, I stretched out my arm.

To my dumbfounded astonishment, my pursuer suddenly about-faced and scampered back to his carriage. Only then did I become aware of a new set of carriage wheels approaching from behind. Narrowing my eyes, I tried to make out what I could of the carriage that had run me off the road. I saw plain black panels with no distinguishing marks except . . . there, on the left rear corner, were numbers stenciled in white. I struggled to make them out. . . .

The vehicle was well out of sight around the next bend by the time the police wagon pulled up beside me, its lanterns illuminating the road and my lopsided buggy. A familiar voice hailed.

"Emma? Good God, are you all right?"

"Jesse . . ." My voice came out as reedy and frail as a newborn kitten's.

"Don't move or you could tip the balance. I'll get you dislodged from those rocks."

"I think my left wheel is broken," I offered unnecessarily, for the damage to the leaning rig must have been obvious. "See to Barney first, please . . ."

I needn't have bothered. Jesse Whyte already had a hand wrapped around Barney's harness and was making soothing sounds in the animal's ear.

"It's all right, now. There's a good boy."

"Is he hurt?" I called out.

"I can't tell for sure until we get more light on him, but he seems calm enough. Are *you* hurt, Emma?"

I took a quick survey. Twinges in my neck and shoulder promised to ache in earnest come tomorrow, but there didn't seem to be anything wrong that wouldn't heal. "I don't think so. Can you get us back upright?"

His answer was to coax Barney into taking a few careful steps. The carriage creaked in resistance before it lurched and rolled a foot or two forward. I held my breath and clenched my teeth. The damaged left wheel wobbled beneath me as it cleared the rocks, but luckily held beneath the rig's weight. I was back on solid, flat ground, and damned happy about it.

"Go after him, Jesse," I urged. "He tried to run me off the road!" I bit back one of Aunt Sadie's favorite swear words, then let out a sigh. "He's gotten away, hasn't he? While you were helping me, he put enough distance between us—"

"Who?"

"I don't know. He had his hood up and in the dusk . . ."

"Did you see where he came from?"

I struggled with my thoughts a moment, then remembered. "Yes! He turned on from Hazard Road. Which means he might have cut over from Bellevue. Jesse, I was just on Bellevue. Whoever it was might have been following me for the past . . . who knows how long." The notion sent chills up and down my back. "If only you could have followed him."

"It's not like I would have left you hanging half out over the ocean. If I hadn't come along when I did—" He broke off with a shudder. "A lucky thing I happened by."

"What are you doing all the way out here? Were you coming to see me at home?"

"I was. I had a few more questions for your uncle and—"

"Was it about the dent in his balcony doorway? Have you learned something new?"

"It was just a couple of questions concerning the guests, Emma, nothing more.

"Oh . . ."

"Anyway, I thought I'd swing by and check in on you on my way back to town."

I reached across the buggy seat to touch his shoulder. "Thank you, Jesse. That was very kind of you. Not to mention providential. Good heavens, when I think what might have happened." I glanced over at the edge of the road and the ocean beyond.

He offered his hand to help me down. "If you're sure you're all right, we'll get your rig onto the other side of the road, and then I'll unhitch your horse and tie him behind my wagon. Once I get you both home, you can tell me exactly what happened."

"It all went by in a blur. I'm not even sure what I remember." I sighed again as my feet touched the road. "I guess the buggy stays here tonight?"

"It'll have to wait until morning, I'm afraid. I'll send the wheelwright out first thing."

Need I describe how Nanny fussed over me when I arrived home and explained what had happened? I'd almost rather have kept my brush with the Atlantic Ocean to myself, but how else to explain not only my lack of buggy, but my police escort and the fact that Barney was tied to the back of his wagon? There was nothing for it but to grit my teeth and accept blanket, pillows, footstool, hot-water bottle, and a strong cup of tea—with a wee splash of brandy.

To be honest, Nanny's attentions helped sooth away my remaining jitters. Anger soon replaced fear, and determination outweighed any temptation to stay safely at home from now on. As I related each terrifying moment to both Jesse and Nanny, my gumption grew.

"I can't help but think this has something to do with Brady and your going around asking questions," Jesse said when I'd finished.

"I think that's fairly obvious."

Standing behind me, Nanny nudged the back of my shoulder. "Don't get sassy."

"Still, I haven't questioned very many people at all," I

pointed out. "And when I think of who I have questioned, I can't believe any one of them would try to silence me like this."

"Whom have you spoken to?" Jesse held up his empty teacup as Katie approached with the teapot. She filled it and slipped quietly away.

"No one who would try to kill me, I'm sure of it." When he scowled his impatience, I began ticking off names, beginning with the most recent. "Jack Parsons, Theodore Mason, my cousin Neily, Grace Wilson—"

"Who?"

Oops. There was no good reason to drag Miss Wilson into this; all I would accomplish would be to possibly shed guilt on Neily and further aggravate the tension between him and his parents. But Jesse would not be deterred.

"Did you say Grace Wilson?"

"You've heard of her?" I asked evasively. "Stunning, isn't she?"

"I've heard of her family. What does she have to do with any of this?"

"Oh, well . . . she's a friend of the family . . ."

He was already shaking his head. "I doubt that very much, based on what I know about Alice Vanderbilt's standards when it comes to whom she allows into her social circle. The Wilsons may be swimming in it, but they aren't 'old money' like the Vanderbilts or the Astors. So what's her connection?"

"She's, uh, a friend of Neily's," I tried.

Again, he shook his head. "The heirs of great fortunes do not have female friends, Emma. They have debutants determined to marry them."

Nanny came around and resumed her seat on the sofa. Her eyes narrowing to crescents, she smirked at me. Obviously I had greatly underestimated Jesse Whyte's powers of observation. "All right," I conceded, "she's more than a friend. But the matter is a personal one and I really don't think—"

"Everything to do with your family right now holds significance in Brady's case."

My pulse thumped. "Are you saying you believe Brady's innocent?"

He hesitated, looking as though he regretted what he'd just all but admitted. He exchanged a glance with Nanny, who was still smirking like she knew a secret, and sighed. "I took a good look at that dent in the frame of Mr. Vanderbilt's balcony door. I think you're right, the candelabrum couldn't have made a depression of that size. That doesn't absolve Brady, mind you, and the prosecutor would be easily dissuaded. However . . ."

"Yes?" My teacup rattled in its saucer.

"I just can't make myself believe Brady Gale could actually commit murder." He shook his head, the lamplight playing on his hair. "Not good old Brady."

In all the danger and upset that night, I forgot to give Jesse one vital piece of information. I'd seen a number stenciled on the rear bumper of the carriage that tried to run me off the road. I wasn't able to make out the exact digits, but the fact of its being there constituted what could prove a valuable detail in discovering the driver's identity.

That morning I awakened with a stiff neck and a bruise on my shoulder that prevented me from being able to reach around and button up the back of my dress. Katie helped me, dressed my hair, and even worked a bit of magic across my nape with a light-fingered massage. I'd just finished a breakfast of toast and scrambled eggs when noises from the driveway sent me to the front of the house. From the parlor window I recognized Hank Davis, the wheelwright from Stevenson's Livery in town, driving his mule and work cart toward the house while towing my buggy behind. I went out to meet him on the drive.

"Good morning, Mr. Davis. How bad is the damage?" I also wondered with no small trepidation at how much it would cost.

"Axel was busted. I replaced it with a new one and stuck on a temporary wheel to get the thing home, but don't recommend driving on it." The man tipped his hat, then jumped down from the seat. He hitched up his overalls once his feet hit the ground. "I should have a new wheel for you by tomorrow afternoon."

"No sooner, I guess?"

"Sorry. If I coulda fixed the old wheel, I woulda, but it's just too bent, Miss Cross. You don't want to be shimmying around on the road, now, do ya?"

After what I'd experienced last night, the answer to that was a resounding *no.* "Thanks for bringing the rig home, Mr. Davis."

"No trouble a 'tall. How 'bout I tow it 'round back and put her in your barn?"

"I'd appreciate that, thank you." He climbed back onto his cart, but before he set the mule in motion, I placed a hand on the traces. "Mr. Davis, would you know if anyone . . . peculiar . . . leased a carriage last night?"

He frowned and tugged at his hat brim. "Peculiar how, Miss Cross?"

"Well . . . either peculiar in that they might not normally need to lease a vehicle, say, one of the quality here for the summer who already has a carriage house filled with vehicles. Or may be someone who didn't seem to want to be . . . recognized?" Realizing how ridiculous that sounded, I wanted to cringe.

"Now, that's a funny notion, especially in a town the size of Newport. But you'd have to ask Stevenson about that. I don't take much notice of the folks leasing carriages."

"No, I don't suppose you do," I mumbled. Well, then, I'd just have to go into town and ask Mr. Stevenson myself. No, I amended, I'd tell Jesse about the numbers, and he would speak with Mr. Stevenson. Yes, that was safer and made more sense. But then again, when did I ever listen to my better sense?

I had another reason to go into town today anyway. I wanted to question the landlady at Theodore Mason's boardinghouse. He'd claimed to be in his room during the night of the ball, reading. I hoped the landlady might be able to corroborate his alibi, at least enough to confirm that she never saw him go out.

The question was, how would I get to town? How would I get anywhere in the next day and a half?

A plan presented itself to my mind, but it wasn't one I relished. If I asked my relatives for the use of one of their carriages, they would inevitably ask questions. Aunt Alice would be more than happy to supply me with a buggy and driver— *after* I explained why I couldn't use my own . . . and *after* I told her what I intended doing in town. Not to mention *after* she insisted on accompanying me.

It was either borrow a carriage or wait. I didn't dare call Jesse on the telephone to tell him about the leasing numbers because one never knew who might be on the line, just listening. . . . Besides, my baser instincts were getting the better of me. I wanted to snoop around the livery and see what I could find out for myself. Ducking into the alcove beneath the stairs, I lifted the telephone's ear trumpet from its cradle and cranked the call box.

"Morning, Gayla," I said when the operator came on the line after a jangle and a few electrical pops.

"That you, Emma? How you doing today? How's your brother?" I heard the sympathy in her voice even over the static in my ear. Like Adelaide, Gayla had been a longtime school friend of mine.

"He's holding up, thanks for asking."

"Are your parents coming home?" This time a clear note of censure laced her tone.

"I wired them the other day. Still waiting to hear back. Listen, Gayla, could you connect me to The Breakers?"

"Sure thing, dearie. One sec."

I heard a series of clicks, and then Bateman, the acting head butler at The Breakers, bid me good morning.

"Hello, Bateman, it's Miss Emma. I wonder if you might do me a favor." Would I be so lucky as to bypass having to speak with my aunt or uncle and have Bateman grant my wish? "My buggy needs repairs and I need a vehicle today—"

"Please hold, Miss Emmaline."

My stomach sank. A moment later, a second voice came keening over the line. "Emmaline? Good morning, dear!"

I jerked the ear trumpet away from my head. Aunt Alice never did quite get the hang of speaking on the telephone. She seemed to think one needed to shout as if across a great distance. Gingerly, I brought the trumpet back up to my ear and spoke—much more quietly—into the mouthpiece. "Hello, Aunt Alice. I don't mean to disturb your morning. I just wondered if I might borrow one of the smaller buggies. I don't need a driver . . . just going into town . . ."

"Gladys and I can be along to collect you in half an hour. Will that do?"

"Oh, but . . ." My protest died on my tongue. I knew better than to argue. It would only waste time and in the end the results would be the same. Instead, I agreed, hung up, and raced upstairs to smarten up my appearance. I'd dressed in a rather plain brown carriage outfit that morning, but now I switched it for the sapphire blue with the velvet braid and jet buttons. As I smoothed the jacket's flounced peplum and straightened the collar, I was once again grateful for Nanny's talents in keeping my wardrobe presentable. I'd neither shame my wealthy relatives nor prompt Aunt Alice to feel obligated to purchase new clothing for me—or send over Gertrude's castoffs. While I valued my cousins' kinship, I never wanted their charity. We Crosses—and Gales—took care of ourselves.

And each other. That last thought sent me down the stairs at a run, just in time to see the black victoria carriage with the swooping *V*'s emblazoned in its sides rolling up the driveway. I yelled my good-byes to Nanny and Katie, and bounded out the door.

"My goodness, you're in a hurry this morning," Aunt Alice

called from inside the posh vehicle. Her window was open and Gladys leaned over her mother to peer out.

My frustration in having unwanted company for my errand was immediately tempered by the excitement shining in the girl's eyes. I saw she had dressed her hair with extra care that morning, eschewing her usual spiraling curls for a more subdued—and grown-up—coif that left only a few tendrils to dance beneath her wide, beribboned hat.

"Goodness, Gladys, don't you look mature," I exclaimed as the footman handed me into the carriage. "If I didn't know better, I'd say you were eighteen at the least."

Aunt Alice harrumphed her disapproval, leading me to imagine the debate that had preceded Gladys's new hairstyle. But Gladys herself could not have looked more pleased.

"Don't you remember, May Goelet wore her hair this way at the luncheon on the afternoon before her coming-out ball. I was allowed to go to the luncheon," she added with a proud lift of her chin.

Aunt Alice rolled her eyes and harrumphed again. "I wasn't at the luncheon," I gently reminded Gladys. "It was in New York, and I was here."

"Oh, yes, I forgot. Well, I've wanted to wear my hair this way ever since."

"And very becoming on you, it is," I said enthusiastically. To my great surprise, Aunt Alice didn't ask me any questions, not even about why I needed transportation that day. My cousin continued to chatter on, though I noticed she avoided any references to the most recent social event—her sister's coming-out ball. I wondered how much had been explained to her. Once I caught Aunt Alice's eye over the bobbing flowers on Gladys's hat. Her eyebrows twitched closer and she gave a slight shrug. And as the girl's voice continued to fill the vehicle, I found myself longing to be her age again . . . to be free of all responsibilities. Suddenly the weight of seeing Brady exonerated seemed impossible to bear. I wanted to shrink beneath the burden, simply let my knees give way and allow the cards to fall where they may.

"We're almost to town," Aunt Alice said with a glance out the open window. "Where to, Emmaline?"

In the echo of her no-nonsense voice, I knew I had to answer her. I had to make a plan. I had to save my brother. There would be no sinking beneath any burden, no matter how weighty. No challenge was too great for a Vanderbilt, and I was a Vanderbilt, after all.

"The livery first," I said decisively. "Then the police station."

"Oh. Yes, yes, of course." Aunt Alice's lips turned down as if she had a bad taste in her mouth. I can't imagine that she had ever tread in either sort of place. "I suppose it can't be helped. But why the livery?"

I raised my eyebrows in innocence. "One of my buggy's wheels went wobbly on my way home last night, which is why I needed a vehicle today. I need to . . . check with Mr. Davis if the new one is ready yet and pay him." I knew very well the new wheel wouldn't be ready yet, and beneath a fold of my skirt I crossed my fingers as children do to ward off the transgression of a lie.

"Mr. Davis?"

"The wheelwright, Aunt Alice."

"Ah. You know, Emmaline, this is one more reason you shouldn't be driving your own buggy. You might have swerved off the road and gone straight into the ocean."

She didn't know the half of it.

Aunt Alice rapped on the roof, and when her driver opened the trap to peer in at her, she said, "Take us to the livery, please. . . ." She paused and looked over at me. "Is there more than one in town?"

I clarified which establishment I needed to visit and minutes later we arrived, my relatives looking puzzled but vaguely interested in the workings of such a mundane business. I wondered what to do next, how I might evade their curiosity for a few minutes at least. Then an unexpected miracle occurred.

"Great thundering Zeus, is that who I think it is?" the owner, Percy Stevenson, exclaimed from inside the shack that housed his office. I heard a chair scrape, something solid, like a book, hit the floor, and through the window I saw Mr. Stevenson scrambling to button his coat, slick his hair down, and cover it with his derby. In another moment he came hurrying outside. "Mrs. Vanderbilt! A pleasure, madam. A very great pleasure, indeed. And such an honor. What . . . what can I do for you on this lovely morning?" His expression turning to horror, he reached up and snatched the hat he'd just placed on his head. He whisked it to his side, nervously patted his thinning hair, and sputtered something about excusing his manners.

"We're here on behalf of my niece," my venerable aunt all but barked, her lips curving downward. The footman helped us out. As we arrived Aunt Alice had told Gladys to wait in the carriage, but now the girl climbed out anyway. She peered all around her, looking like a cheerful flower amid the dust and clutter of the stable yard.

"Is that a forge?" she asked, pointing into the shadows of a lean-to. "Is that where the horses are shod?"

"It is, Miss Vanderbilt." Mr. Stevenson tipped a bow. "Would you like to see?"

"She most certainly would not." Aunt Alice clasped her hands together, her purse dangling from between them. "We're here about a new wheel for my niece's buggy. Is it ready?"

"Oh, I . . . I'll have to check . . ." The proprietor scratched at his chin and looked uncertain as to what he should do next.

"Then I suggest you do just that."

Aunt Alice's terse command set his feet in motion. He disappeared between the farrier's lean-to and the shed that housed the carriages for lease.

"I want to see the horses," Gladys announced, and without pausing scurried through the stables' open doors.

"Gladys! Gladys, come back here this instant!" Aunt Alice bustled after her, her high-heeled boots raising a small cloud at her hems that the laundry maid would have a terrible time with later. "They aren't like our horses at home," she called after her daughter. "These are dirty creatures...."

Did I mention a miracle? It occurred in that moment, for I suddenly found myself all alone. Wasting no time, I strode into the shack and slipped behind the counter where Stevenson did business. There were several ledger books resting on the rough oaken surface, along with a padlocked cashbox that appeared bolted to the counter itself. My attention went to the largest leather-bound book; it sat open with a pen resting in the crease of its pages.

My fingers trembling, I cast a glance out the window, then through the open door. I listened, hearing voices that were too far-off to herald anyone's imminent approach. Looking down at the page, I began scanning the entries scribbled along each printed line. Names, followed by dates and carriage numbers. Quickly enough I saw that there hadn't been any rentals so far that morning. I flipped the page to yesterday's entries but saw no familiar names, nothing that struck a warning bell. My gaze swept to the left, to the page from two days ago. My heart began to pound.

Chapter 10

Jack Parsons's name wavered in my vision as my temple began to throb. Then my eye landed on another that caused me to suck in a breath: Derrick Anderson. I went utterly still, my gaze darting back and forth between the two. And then a third name caught my eye, vaguely familiar . . . In the next instant recognition leaped from the page to virtually grab me around the throat.

It was not a name I would have known even a few short weeks ago, but at the beginning of the summer, Neily had hired a new valet—a man named Owen Darville. His signature stared up at me from the page.

There were other familiar names, of course, some belonging to summer visitors who moved in my relatives' social circle. Leasing vehicles wasn't unusual. Newport was part of Aquidneck Island, and since most of the quality arrived by steamer, the expense of bringing a carriage along for a mere week or two often outweighed the benefits, even for wealthy individuals.

Yet, the coincidences in this case were piling up too high to be innocuous. All right, Jack Parsons had every reason in the world to lease rather than bring his own carriage; after all, he was also renting the house he was staying in and had no permanent ties to Newport. The same could be said about Derrick Anderson, who claimed to be here researching an article about powerful businessmen. Although when I'd met him outside Adelaide's house the other day, he'd been on foot.

Could he have leased a carriage for one specific purpose . . . say, to run me off the road? Far-fetched? Perhaps, but despite his denial, I still felt he'd been following me that day, for reasons that somehow had to do with the charges against Brady.

But staring up at me was also that third name, Owen Darville. Had the servant himself needed a carriage—which seemed unlikely—or had my cousin sent him to obtain transportation that would be unrecognizable to anyone who knew him? Maybe to visit Grace Wilson without setting her neighbors' tongues wagging. Or maybe to send me a not-very-subtle message last night—to mind my own business and stop investigating.

I restored the pages to their original positions and hurried back outside. Aunt Alice and Gladys were just then stepping out from the stables, the former looking none too happy.

"Really, Gladys, that's no way for a lady to behave. I should lock you in your room when we get home."

"Oh, I just wanted to see the horses, Mama. I wanted to see if they were happy or not."

Her mother waved a dismissive hand in the air. "What a ridiculous notion. Horses happy! What nonsense have you been reading lately?"

"Neily told me that most hacks lead unhappy lives, and that our horses are very lucky to be privately owned and taken such good care of." The girl looked back at the stables over her shoulder. "But these horses didn't look terribly miserable. I suppose Mr. Stevenson is nice to them."

"Oh, hurry along, child. Emmaline? Emmaline, where are you?" Alice's voice rose an octave as she singsonged my name. "Now where did that girl disappear to?"

A few feet outside the shack, I halted and stood with my hands clasped behind my back as though idly biding my time for Mr. Stevenson's return. "Here I am, Aunt. Still waiting to discover if my wheel is ready."

At that moment the proprietor came loping into the stable yard. "Hank says your wheel won't be ready till tomorrow, Miss Cross. Said he told you that this morning."

Indeed, he had, but I pretended surprise. "Dear me, I must have misunderstood. Tomorrow you say?"

"Sorry, but it's been a busy week here. Lots of repairs lately. I hope you understand."

I started to assure him I did, but Aunt Alice spoke over me. "We most certainly do not. However, if it can't be helped, tell us what we owe you and have the wheel sent out to my niece's residence tomorrow the very moment it is ready." She started to open her purse.

"Oh, Aunt Alice, that isn't necessary. I can—"

"Bah, Emmaline. You're as poor as a church mouse; don't try telling me you're not. If you won't let me supplement your income, at least allow me to lift the occasional unexpected financial burden from your shoulders." She raised an eyebrow and pinned Mr. Stevenson with a sharp gaze. "Well, sir, how much?"

"Oh, er, that's very kind of you, Aunt Alice. Thank you. . . ." She briskly waved away my gratitude. Gladys and I left them to settle the bill, and I fervently hoped Aunt Alice wouldn't bargain the man down so low he couldn't make a profit. As we climbed back into the carriage Gladys began telling me about the horses she'd seen, but my mind drifted to what I'd learned and what I needed to do next, if only I could manage a few hours without Aunt Alice chaperoning my every move.

Since I couldn't count on a second miracle in the same day, for my next stop I wagered on what I knew about Aunt Alice. Through the little window that slid open to allow the passengers to speak to the driver, I told the man where to head next.

Aunt Alice's lips thinned with distaste as the carriage came to a stop outside the Harbor Hill Boarding House.

"Good heavens, Emmaline, what are we doing *here?*"

"Who lives here?" Gladys interjected merrily, straining to see past her mother and me.

"This won't take but a moment." I opened the door and started to slide out. From the rear of the vehicle the footman hopped down, ran to my side, and held out a hand to help me down.

Aunt Alice, only inches away in her effort to follow me, deepened her frown. "This isn't the sort of place folk like us typically visit, Emmaline."

"Well, it's the sort of place folk like *me* visit, Aunt Alice." My hand secure in the footman's, I paused to explain, "I'm a Cross, don't forget, and a Newporter to boot. And I'm here to deliver a message from Nanny O'Neal—you remember Nanny—to Theodore Mason. They're old friends, you know."

"Theodore Mason!" She slid back to the middle of the seat, drawing upright against the squabs. "That thief!"

Beside her, Gladys let out a nervous giggle. I caught the gleam in her eye; the child probably hadn't had this much fun on an outing with her mother in . . . forever.

"I know circumstances shed a certain amount of guilt on Mr. Mason, but he may not be the culprit you think he is. Besides, I promised Nanny I'd stop by."

"Couldn't she call on the telephone?" Aunt Alice mumbled between clenched teeth, but I'd already stepped down from the carriage and was marching up the front pathway to the front door.

A disheveled young boy answered my knock, and before I could get a word out he about-faced and shouted into the depths of the hallway behind him. The German lady I'd met previously came shuffling in from a doorway off to the side.

"Yah? Ah, it's you again. Have you not found Herr Mason?"

"As a matter of fact, I have, but I have a question I'd like to ask you, if you don't mind."

Her eyes narrowed slightly. "Depends upon the question."

"Do you know what happened at The Breakers the other night?"

"Yah, everybody knows. A man died."

"That's right. And I believe Mr. Mason was still living here at the time."

"Yah, he was."

"Would you happen to remember if he went out that night?" My heart pounded at the magnitude of my boldness. For Brady, I reminded myself.

A lengthy pause ensued. Just when I thought she'd decided to slam the door in my face, she tilted her head. "I think I don't like to answer that question. Herr Mason is my tenant. He pays me to keep his room even when he is not living here. You do not."

She'd called my bluff. Or had she? I drew myself up as tall as I could and arranged my features in my best imitation of Aunt Alice's scowl—which I'd perfected after years of practice. "Do you know who I am?"

The woman shrugged as if to say she didn't care.

"I am Emmaline Vanderbilt Cross. Do you see that carriage waiting for me?" I gestured behind me without taking my eyes off her. "Do you see the *V* on the crest?"

"Yah . . ." She seemed less certain of herself than a moment ago.

"Do you know who is *inside* that carriage?"

She shook her head almost imperceptibly, a smidgeon of fear flashing in her eyes.

"That is Mrs. Cornelius Vanderbilt II. Mr. Mason's employer." All right, so I stretched the truth a little, since the family no longer employed Theodore Mason. The landlady drew a gasp, and I decided to stretch even more. "These questions I'm asking are on Mrs. Vanderbilt's behalf. And believe you me, when she wants answers, she does not relent until she has them."

Yes, when it suited me, I knew good and well how to be a Vanderbilt.

"Ah, well . . . that . . . that is another story. Why did you not say so?" The woman's eyes were wide, and she tried to glimpse the figures inside the carriage from over my shoulder. "Herr Mason . . . ah . . ." Her eyebrows knitting tight, she paused and thought a moment. "Yah, he went out. I remember he had his supper and went out the back door."

"What time?"

"I . . . er . . ." I noticed she'd balled the edges of her apron in her fists, much like Katie had done when I'd asked her questions she didn't want to answer. To speed things along, I glanced at the locket watch hanging around my neck. She released the next bits of information in a torrent. "It was late. He had a late supper . . . nine, ten? I don't remember exactly. He often eats late. A lot of my boarders do. They work long hours," she added rather defensively.

I didn't bother asking her if she knew where Mr. Mason had gone that night, for I could think of no good reason why he would have told her and then lied to me about going out at all. I thanked her and made my way back to the carriage, to Aunt Alice's disapproving looks and Gladys's bubbly desire to know what the lady and I had talked about.

"Never you mind," her mother chastised.

Whatever other tensions played out between mother and daughter were lost on me; I was too busy thinking about what I'd seen in that ledger book and what Mason's landlady had told me—troubling revelations all—and once again figuring out what to do next.

Sometimes Aunt Alice was entirely predictable, and that morning I managed to use it to my advantage. But at other times she surprised me . . . and made me love her all the more.

"Aunt Alice," I said as we entered town once more, "why don't you and Gladys go and have lunch at the Casino or the country club while I visit with Brady."

"Don't be silly. We'll all go."

"All of us?" I stole a peek over at Gladys, who was practically bouncing up and down on the seat. "Aunt Alice, you didn't want Gladys going into the livery stables."

"We're going to the jailhouse?" my young cousin squealed.

Her mother briefly took on a pained expression. "Gladys, hush." She turned back to me. "Yes, we are going to visit Brady. Horses are one thing, but family is quite another." Raising a fist, she rapped on the ceiling and, without waiting for the coachman to open his little window, called out, "The police station next, please."

"But what will Uncle Cornelius say?" I fretted.

"Leave that to me."

When we arrived, she insisted Gladys and I wait in the carriage while she disappeared into the building, accompanied by the footman. My stomach twisted into knots of impatience and a fear akin to that of a child caught breaking a particularly hard and fast rule. I couldn't imagine Uncle Cornelius being amenable to our visit here, not by any stretch.

And then a thought I hadn't considered struck me an even more fearsome blow. What if Jesse was there and happened to mention last night's incident to Aunt Alice? If she found out from him, the shock of my almost being run off the road would be compounded by my having concealed it from her. And then I wouldn't have a moment's peace, or a moment's independence, for the rest of the summer at least, if not well beyond that.

"I can't believe I'm going inside a jail," Gladys happily chatted, craning her neck for glimpses of the white building with its peaked roof and columned front porch. While the structure didn't exactly inspire fear or foreboding, Gladys apparently had other ideas.

"I'll wager the cells are pitch-black," she said half-breathlessly, "with only slim shafts of light coming through the bars high up on the windows. Do you think the walls are covered in moss and dripping with gook, and . . . oh!" She turned a scandalized gaze on me. "Will there be rats scurrying about?"

"What?" I shook my worries away as her words registered. "Gladys Vanderbilt, don't let your mother hear you talk like that or you won't be leaving the house for the rest of the summer." I twisted the strings of my purse in tight little nooses around my fingers. What *was* Aunt Alice doing? Dared I hope Jesse wasn't here? I turned back to Gladys. "And it's *no* to all of your questions, by the way. Brady is being held in a jail, not a dungeon." Though it might as well be the latter, I silently admitted, remembering the forlorn look on his face the last time I'd seen him.

Some fifteen minutes later, I heard the clatter of high-heeled footsteps ricocheting down the walkway. I sucked in a breath. The footman swung my door open and Aunt Alice leaned in, one hand on the wide brim of her silk-flowered chapeau. "It's all arranged. Come along, both of you."

When she didn't shoot me a reproving stare, I breathed a sigh of relief. Inside, we were led through a door marked *Captain Edward Rogers, Chief of Police.* The man was nowhere in sight, but Jesse stood beside the desk, one hand resting on the holster of his sidearm; seated to his left was Brady. At the sight of us he came to his feet, all smiles.

Gladys launched herself into his arms, and I found myself blinking away a tear or two as he lifted her off her feet and she planted a big kiss on his cheek. I noticed even Jesse shuffling his feet and staring hard down at the floor. I tried to catch his eye. When he finally glanced up, I nodded toward Aunt Alice and mouthed, *Please don't tell.*

I didn't have to elaborate. He set my fears to rest with a reluctant nod. I let go a breath.

Brady placed Gladys back on her feet and leaned over her to right her bonnet, which had slipped askew. "Good to see you, cupcake."

"I don't believe a word they're saying about you, Brady," she declared in a stage whisper. "I know they'll have to free you soon. And then will you take me for a trolley ride down to Easton's Beach and buy me an ice cream?"

"You can count on it, sweetie pie." He chucked her chin. Coming up behind Gladys, Aunt Alice nudged the girl aside and tipped her cheek for Brady to kiss, which he did a good deal more sedately than he'd kissed her daughter, but with no less of a smile. "Thanks, Auntie. This sure is a nice break from the back rooms."

By back rooms I knew he meant the jail cells. My turn came next, and as Brady's arms went around me I realized this was the first time I'd been able to hug my brother since this nightmare had begun, and since even before that. Tightening my hold on him, I silently vowed to hug him each and every day once he was free.

"You've only got ten minutes," Jesse informed us. "Then Captain Rogers wants his office back. I'll wait outside." He flicked a glance at Brady. "Right outside the door, so don't get any stupid ideas."

"Excuse me one moment," I said quickly, and before Aunt Alice or Brady could ask me any questions, I slipped out behind Jesse.

Grasping his arm, I walked him a few paces away from the door. He glared at me suspiciously, prompting me to roll my eyes. "Don't worry, I'm not planning to distract you while Aunt Alice and Gladys spring Brady. I just don't want them to overhear what I have to say."

He chuckled at that and gestured for me to continue.

"I remembered something about last night that might be important."

"Can you identify the driver of the other carriage?"

"No, but it was definitely a leased carriage. There were numbers stenciled on the rear bumper."

"And what were they?"

"Well, it was too dark to see them clearly . . ."

"Then I fail to see how that will help, Emma."

"I went down to Stevenson's livery today and had a peek at his registration ledger."

"Emma!" Though whispered, the admonishment made me flinch nonetheless. "How many times do I have to tell you to leave the investigation to the police? This isn't a game. It's dangerous, and last night should have taught you—"

"I know, I know. But what harm could come of peeking into a ledger. Besides, there were a couple of names that might be of interest. Jack Parsons and Owen Darville—who happens to be Neily Vanderbilt's new valet. He might have leased the vehicle for Neily and—"

"Emma, are you telling me you think Jack Parsons or Neily Vanderbilt might have run you off the road last night? And possibly killed Alvin Goddard?" His voice held a note of alarm.

The wind immediately left my sails. Was I truly ready to incriminate Neily or Jack without more evidence? "No," I said to the floor at my feet. "It's just . . ."

His arm went around my shoulders. "I know. It's Brady, and you want to see him exonerated. But I need more than the fact that Mr. Parsons and your cousin's valet leased vehicles. For all you know, Emma, the carriage that followed you last night might have been leased in Middletown or Portsmouth."

"I hadn't thought of that . . ." I blew out a breath laden with defeat.

"I'll look into it, though," he assured me in that kindly tone I'd heard from him numerous times since this nightmare had begun. "It could be a lead, however small."

"Thank you," I said, and went back into the office.

Brady and Aunt Alice cast me curious looks but didn't ask questions. Gladys did most of the talking, and Brady seemed more than content to sit back and listen to her banter about a book she was reading and other small matters that tend to occupy a thirteen-year-old girl's mind. I stole the opportunity to observe him closely. He looked tired and drawn, the shadows beneath his eyes a worrying shade of blue. I noticed his fingertips trembled when they weren't clutching the arms of his chair. I wished I could have offered him a sip of brandy, because he looked like he could dearly use it.

Finally, a soft knock at the door and then Jesse sticking his head into the room signaled it was time to leave. As we headed back out to the carriage, I let Gladys skip a few paces ahead before leaning closer to Aunt Alice. "Do you believe in Brady's innocence?"

She didn't hesitate a beat. "I believe in innocent until proven guilty, and I'll let the police determine the matter."

"But Uncle Cornelius seemed so . . ." So convinced of Brady's guilt, or at least convinced Brady must take the fall for Alvin Goddard's murder. But I couldn't bring myself to utter either possibility.

"Cornelius tends to see things in black and white. And granted, he's correct about a lot of things, but he's wrong about a lot of things, too." With that, Aunt Alice continued on to the carriage, imperiously holding out a hand for the footman to assist her inside.

On the way to the sprawling lawns and stately proportions of the Newport Country Club, I saw something that made me want to order the driver to an immediate halt. Of course, I couldn't; I had to clench my teeth and continue on to a four-course luncheon that seemed interminable. But as Gladys exclaimed over the family of foraging rabbits visible through the floor-to-ceiling windows and Aunt Alice attempted to fill me in on the impending nuptials of Consuelo, another Vanderbilt cousin, I could think of nothing else but the sight that had caught my eye as we'd driven past Waite's Wharf. It might not have anything to do with Brady's case, but it occupied my mind nonetheless.

I tried to think of a way to backtrack without involving my relatives. I didn't relish the idea I came up with, but there didn't seem to be any other option.

They dropped me off at home nearly two hours later. With brief greetings to Nanny and a call to Katie to come help me, I changed into a riding habit—a rather threadbare one with frayed hems and a veil with more holes than actual netting, but it would have to do. By far my greatest concern awaited me in the barn.

"Help me saddle him, Katie." Gesturing, I directed my young maid toward the corner cupboard that held blankets and tack. With a huffing breath, I lifted the saddle from its rack. "I know it's been a good long time, Barney, and I promise not to push you too hard."

The roan gelding regarded me, then the saddle, and me once more, the expression in his large, velvety eyes approaching indignant disbelief.

"I'm sorry, Barney, but it can't be helped. We won't have the new buggy wheel until tomorrow, and if I wait that long I might not get my answer."

"Are ya talkin' to me, miss?" Katie appeared at my shoulder, the tack snaking from her arms.

"Uh, no. Let's just get him suited up to go." I took the bridle and bit, and slipped them over Barney's head, muttering more apologies to him as I went, especially when I coaxed him into opening his mouth so I could set the unfamiliar metal bar between his teeth, poor thing. When all was done, Katie and I stepped back to appraise our handiwork.

"Do ya think he'll do, miss?"

"He'll have to. Besides, I'm not taking him far. Just to Waite's Wharf, off lower Thames Street. Will you help me up?"

Katie threaded her fingers and boosted me up. I clucked my tongue and tapped lightly with my heels. Barney let out a long, snuffling breath and went nowhere.

"Hold his bridle and walk him outside," I suggested. Katie tugged to coax him to move. Finally, he seemed content to put one foot in front of the other. I signaled Katie to release him, proceeded to the end of the drive, and turned onto Ocean Avenue.

About an hour later and after nonstop encouragement from me, Barney plodded onto Waite's Wharf. The sight that had brought me back was still there, no longer on the wharf itself but occupying a spot on the freight steamer that just then fired up its engines with a great, roaring hiss.

I was happy to see the very men I wished to question were still there as well.

"Mr. Manuel!" I called as I slid from my sidesaddle to the ground. "Mr. Manuel, there appears to have been a mistake."

"Miss Emma?" Elton Manuel, the shorter and younger of the two, removed his hat and wiped his brow with his sleeve. "What brings you here, and what kinda mistake?"

I pointed to a crate that stood some four feet high, the front panel open and leaning off to the side. Next to the crate sat stack of gray packing blankets. "That's Adelaide Halstock's spinet. And that is *not* the Halstocks' steamer. It would say *Halstock Industries* across the side if it were." I strode closer to the boat and scanned the contents in the stern, protected from the elements by a broad stretch of canvas overhead. I saw more than one familiar shape. "Those other crates—don't they belong to the Halstocks as well? You've delivered their things to the wrong ship."

He was shaking his head at me and chuckling. "You're the

one's got it wrong, Miss Emma. I mean, you're right that this is the Halstocks' freight shipment, but wrong about where we were supposed to deliver the load."

"But isn't this all supposed to go to their house in New York? And their steamer is docked at Brown & Howard, so . . ."

"This stuff's going to New York, all right, and then on to London."

"London!"

"Sure. It's all going to Christie's."

"Christie's?" I was beginning to sound like a parrot. "The auction house? You mean it's all for sale?"

"I suppose." He gave a shrug. "Guess it's stuff they got tired of. Mrs. Halstock probably wants to buy all new. You know how rich folks are."

At that moment, Edwin Manuel stepped out from the steamer's main cabin and sauntered down the gangplank. He held what appeared to be a bill of lading, which he stuffed in the breast pocket of his coat. "All right, Elton, let's pack that spinet up right this time and get her loaded. . . . Hey there, Miss Emma. Out for a ride on that old hack of yours, eh?"

It was Elton who turned to him to say, "Miss Emma thought we'd delivered the Halstocks' things to the wrong steamer."

"Well, never you worry, Miss Emma. We've got things under control even if that old spinet nearly did come bursting out of its crate. Phew, close call that was, but no harm done."

"Glad to hear it, gentlemen," I said, though my own words barely registered in my brain.

Elton boosted me back into my saddle and I headed Barney for home. After all, there was nothing more I could ask them, and I didn't want to ride home after sunset and run the risk of repeating the events of last night.

But I'd certainly learned something. Adelaide had lied to me, and it didn't take a genius to figure out why. People sold their belongings on the sly for one reason—because they didn't want anyone to know about their money troubles. If I had any doubts, this freight shipment to London quelled them. Obviously, sending their possessions to auction here in the United States posed the risk of being found out. Who but members of the Four Hundred could afford to bid on European spinets and other valuable items from a house the likes of Redwing Cottage? The Four Hundred was a small and closed society, and how many of them would have recognized those items from visits with the Halstocks?

No, there was only one possibility that made sense, and might even explain Rupert Halstock's strange illness: They'd experienced a downturn in their finances, a serious one.

I felt awful—awful for poor Adelaide, who had only ever wanted to be a rich man's wife and reclaim the social standing her own family once held. That wish had once earned my secret disdain, but who was I to have judged her? I'd never been wealthy, but I've always had the security of knowing my Vanderbilt relatives would never let me starve or be thrown out on the streets. Adelaide had never had that reassurance. She had known some hard times growing up, so who could blame her for the decisions she'd made? Besides, considering everything, I had to admire how well she was holding up, how brave a face she showed the world. She obviously had more mettle than I'd given her credit for. And that, too, made me feel ashamed.

"Barney," I murmured, "from now on I'm going to be nicer to her."

The roan's ears twitched as he trudged along.

"I know; I've already been nice to her . . . sort of. But only when I had to, when I couldn't avoid it. From now on I'm going to be more charitable with my time, and show my old friend she's not alone. Of course, I can't ever let on that I know. . . ."

My vow raised my spirits a bit, especially since it had been heeded by a witness, albeit by Aunt Sadie's tired, uninspired hack. But Barney had as valiant a heart as the staunchest Newporter—like me. Like Brady. Like Adelaide. And we Newporters stuck together.

Chapter 11

That night I sat up late at my desk. For a long while I tapped the end of my pen against my bottom lip and stared at my own reflection in the blackened window pane in front of me. Beyond, I could hear the ocean kicking up a bit of a fuss, the water churning against the rocks even as my mind churned with everything I'd learned up to now, the facts colliding with what I knew and with what I wanted to believe.

Finally, I picked up the ruler I'd set beside me, inked my pen, and set the nib to paper. I started by drawing columns, four of them, and at the top of each I wrote a name. The first was Neily.

Beneath it I wrote what I knew so far. Neily was carrying on a courtship with a woman of whom his parents highly disapproved, so much so Uncle Cornelius had sent Alvin Goddard to spy on them and report back. As his father's eldest heir, Neily had a lot to lose—a massive fortune should his father disinherit him. Doing away with Alvin Goddard might have been a move on Neily's part to buy himself more time to reconcile his parents to the notion of a possible marriage between him and Grace. Neily had been missing from the ballroom immediately following Mr. Goddard's death, and while Grace had corroborated his alibi of being with her below stairs, could I necessarily believe her?

I wrote a second name but almost crossed it out. Reggie. I had no specific motive for the boy to have harmed anyone. There was only that bottle of Tennessee bourbon beside Brady's elbow that night, the lingering odor of spirits, and the fact that Reggie himself had been lately drinking on the sly. Then there had been his interest in my maid, Katie, who had come to me in a delicate condition. Had Reggie fathered her miscarried child—had he forced himself on her? If so, he might have done anything to prevent his parents from finding out. Society might turn a blind eye to such matters, but Uncle Cornelius and Aunt Alice would not. And if Mr. Goddard had a nose for ferreting out secrets . . .

I moved on to my next suspect, Jack Parsons, an investor in the New Haven-Hartford-Providence railroad line. Yes, he was my father's longtime friend, but a simple motive presented itself: anger over the plans designed by Alvin Goddard allowing Uncle Cornelius to take over the line and restructure it from the bottom up. Brady had said the line had been losing money because of corrupt business practices. If Uncle Cornelius managed the takeover, the identities of those responsible might come to light. Was Jack Parsons one of them? I might be stretching things, but the pocket watch I'd found in Uncle Cornelius's safe, with the *P* engraved on its cover, suggested . . . what? A bribe? A kind of promissory note? A payment? Maybe Uncle Cornelius had already uncovered secrets from the New Haven-Hartford-Providence line, and Jack Parsons had given him the watch as collateral for the money he'd be forced to pay back.

Then why kill Alvin Goddard? I tapped my pen to my lip again. Murdering a man like Cornelius Vanderbilt would have dire ramifications, would even bring the attention of President Cleveland himself to the investigation. But murdering a mere financial secretary would be a matter left to the local police. Perhaps Jack hoped murdering Alvin Goddard would delay the buyout proceedings and give him enough time to cover up his financial shenanigans.

Sighing, I shook my head and wondered if all of these motives and scenarios were being supplied by my overactive writer's imagination, rather than the actual facts.

But the basic facts continued to niggle. Theodore Mason's name occupied the top of the final column. Just prior to the ball, the Vanderbilts' head butler had been accused of the worst thing a head butler can be accused of—theft from the very house in which he worked. Such a charge meant never serving in any great house again, in any capacity, and the position of head butler generally took years, often decades of dedicated effort to achieve. Once again, here was a suspect with much to lose, at least from his perspective. And Alvin Goddard had been his accuser.

Added to that, I now knew Mr. Mason had lied to me when he claimed he hadn't strayed from his boardinghouse the night Alvin Goddard was murdered. Lies usually meant one thing: that the liar had something to hide. The question was what?

Sitting back in my chair, I stared down at my notes and realized I was no closer to an answer than when I'd started. The niggling hadn't stopped either; in fact, the hairs at the back of my neck continued to prickle. I couldn't banish today's revelations from my mind. Jack and Neily—or rather his valet—had leased carriages from Stevenson's Livery. So had that reporter, Derrick Anderson, and while I saw no reason to suspect him of murder, his behavior had been nonetheless suspicious. It occurred to me he could easily be lying about his reasons for being in Newport; for all I knew, he had been hired by the murderer to keep an eye on things and make sure no one came too close to the truth.

My pen fell from my fingers and clattered to the desk. I was certain Derrick Anderson had followed me on more than one occasion. Who was to say he hadn't followed me yesterday from Adelaide's house to Jack's, and then out along Ocean Avenue?

Not surprisingly, I tossed and turned that night and slept in the next morning. I found Katie bustling around the morning room, but when I greeted her, she dipped a quick curtsy and scampered out through the baize-covered service door. The door swung inward and this time Nanny shouldered her way in with the coffeepot.

"What's gotten into her?" I asked with a nod toward the passageway. My query sounded halfhearted and no wonder, because I was pretty certain I knew the answer. The problem was me.

When Katie had first arrived on my doorstep, I'd asked precious few questions. The girl had needed time to heal, to recover from her ordeal. She had needed time to gather the courage that seemed to have been frightened out of her during her time at The Breakers. So while I'd privately turned my anger on Neily, I'd given Katie the respite I thought she'd needed, and it seemed to have helped. The color had returned to her cheeks, the light to her pale blue eyes. But ever since I tried questioning her the other day, she'd become a jittery bundle of nerves and given me a wide, wary berth.

For a moment I didn't notice that Nanny hadn't answered, hadn't said anything. She'd silently filled my coffee cup and turned away to fuss with one of the platters on the sideboard.

"Did I do something . . ." I trailed off as a yellow envelope beside my place setting caught my attention. I rushed closer and snatched it up. "This is from Western Union. When did this come?"

Nanny turned slowly back around, her kindly face tightened into a severe mass of wrinkles. "Earlier."

"Earlier . . . why didn't you tell me? It must be from Mother and Dad. They must be on their way home from Paris. . . ." I turned the missive over to break the seal, only to discover the paper hallmark bearing the initials *WU* had already been torn. I glanced over at Nanny, raising an eyebrow.

"It came like that," she said defensively.

"Did you read it?"

Her lips pursed. "I might have peeked . . . a little."

"Nanny, how could you? This is private correspondence from my parents. . . ." My indignation melted away when she pouted up at me, her spectacles magnifying her wounded expression. "Never mind . . . So when will they be here?" I spread open the page.

As I read the message, Nanny spoke, her words as sharp and cold as icicles. "They're not."

My heart thumped in my throat. The short note read:

DEAREST EMMALINE, HAVE RECEIVED
YOUR NEWS. IMPOSSIBLE FOR US TO
GET AWAY RIGHT NOW. HAVE WIRED
MONEY TO HELP WITH BRADY'S
EXPENSES. NOT MUCH, BUT THE BEST
WE CAN DO. HAVE FAITH. ALL WILL BE
WELL. BE THERE WHEN WE CAN. LOVE
TO YOU BOTH.

I reread the words several times; surely they couldn't mean what they appeared to mean.

"Oh, Nanny, how can they not come? How can Mother not be here for her son?" I slapped the telegram onto the table so hard Nanny flinched. My voice reached a crescendo. "Her only son, Nanny. How can she stay away?"

Nanny glared back at me, the wrinkles around her pursed lips deepening. "Because . . . Oh, sweetie, I know what I'd like to say, but they're still your parents, so I'd better keep my mouth shut."

I knew what she would have said. It spoke volumes that she and I were sitting at the breakfast table together, not as house-keeper and employer, but as close to grandmother and grand-daughter as two unrelated people could possibly be. It's not that my parents had been neglectful of Brady and me when we were young. They'd shared their world with us, taught us more about the literature and music and art than we ever learned in our respective schools.

Our cultural education hadn't come to us in a series of class-room lessons learned by rote, but in always having people in our house—poetry readings, musical soirées, friends of my fa-ther's setting up their easels in our backyard. I grew up around artists like Frederic Edwin Church and James McDougal Hart, writers like Oliver Wendell Holmes, Sr., and Edith Wharton, and I thought nothing of it. Why would I? There were always people about, debating, philosophizing, dreaming. . . . Brady and I grew up in an enlightened environment where creativity and independent thinking had always been encouraged, valued.

But sometimes a child just wants to be held. Just wants a mother's or father's whole attention, not as a reward for any particular achievement, but simply *because.* I was seven years old when I realized my parents were caught up in a world that certainly included me, but didn't revolve around me. Edith Wharton had come to visit that afternoon, and as Mother had welcomed her new friend into our home, I'd seen a joy in her eyes that had never been there before. That I'd never put there myself.

And while Mother and Mrs. Wharton had taken tea on our small patio, I'd run to Nanny, who held me and stroked my hair and sang softly in my ear, and never once asked me what had made me sad. She knew what made me sad, but in the end it hadn't mattered, really. What had mattered was that I was a child who needed to be held, and so she held me.

Somehow the two of us muddled through the rest of the morning without speaking the thoughts on both our minds. My parents were who they were, and no amount of wishing would change them. Did I even want to change them, need them to change? Even now, I couldn't answer that question.

Hank Davis arrived around noon with my new buggy wheel, but although I was once more independent, I made no plans to go anywhere—not just yet, anyway. Earlier, I'd taken my coffee cup and crossed the narrow peninsula that formed the rear of my property and gone to sit on the boulders that overlooked the sea. Mother and Dad weren't coming—the reality hadn't quite sunk in, not in my heart, but my logical mind accepted the fact for what it was. Our parents would be of little or no help. Nor would Uncle Cornelius, who refused to so much as hire a lawyer for Brady. Since yesterday I'd formed a notion that perhaps Aunt Alice might convince him otherwise, but I knew better than to hold out too much hope there. Once Uncle Cornelius made up his mind, very little could change it, not even his wife.

I might have won over Jesse to our side, but if the prosecutor insisted on bringing charges, there was little Jesse could do to stop him, not without hard evidence. I even wondered if Uncle Cornelius had used his influence and his considerable resources to persuade the authorities—not Jesse, of course, but others—to ignore any leads that led away from Brady . . . and perhaps to one of his own sons. Would he go that far? Betray me that way?

I didn't like to admit it, but yes. To save one of his own, he very well might.

Balancing my cup on the boulder where I sat, I spread out the piece of paper I'd brought outside with me—not the telegram, but the list I'd made the night before. As I studied it, new plans formed in my mind, my resolve bolstered as never before by the anger and indignation burning inside me.

I had four suspects: Neily, Reggie, Jack Parsons, and Theodore Mason. All right then, I would systematically investigate each of them. And I intended to start that evening, when people would least expect a woman to be out alone. True, I'd been followed at dusk by someone threatening my very life . . . but two could play at that game. Retreating into the house, I put a call through to Peterson's Livery to reserve a hired carriage.

A bright moon hung over the island that night, a good thing for me as it meant I wouldn't have to light the carriage lamps hanging from the corners of my vehicle. On Victoria Avenue, some twenty yards or so away from The Breakers' wrought-iron gates, I sat parked in my rented carriage, looking like a hackney driver waiting for his charge to exit the mansion to my right.

Earlier, I'd collected the horse and buggy from Stevenson's, telling the man a little white lie to prevent his tongue from wagging. "Nanny is mending the seat on my own buggy," I'd confided, "and I don't want my relatives to know or they'll feel obligated to pay the leasing fee on this carriage. And they do so much for me already . . ."

In truth, it was money I could ill afford to spend, and I cringed a little as I handed the bills over, but I couldn't risk being seen in my own rig tonight. Mr. Stevenson had agreed to silence on the matter, and with Barney tied behind the leased carriage I'd returned home to prepare for my evening outing.

Would I have long to wait here on Victoria Street? Or would I sit here for hours for no good reason. It occurred to me that I was following a rather blind plan when a metallic rattle from down the street snapped me to attention.

The gates opened and a carriage, a sleek, well-sprung curricle, rolled through. A deep voice briefly thanked Shipley, the

Vanderbilts' gatekeeper. Through the darkness I strained my eyes to catch the moon-silvered outlines of the driver, though my rapid heartbeats told me I already knew. I watched Neily turn onto Ochre Point Avenue, waited a few moments, then set off after him, keeping a safe distance behind and maintaining a leisurely pace. Unlike my own dark lanterns, his swung back and forth in bright arcs at the corners of his carriage, lighting my way.

My wager had paid off. I had known that Neily had moved back into The Breakers and attempted to make peace with his parents; I also knew that it was his habit to go out most nights, and that not even his parents would interfere in that. He was a young heir on holiday, a Newport summer dandy, and it was considered his right to sow some wild oats.

I kept well to the side of the road in the shadows cast by the overhanging branches. But even if Neily had looked back, he would only see a smallish young man in denims, corduroy jacket, and a plaid cap, all of which had once belonged to Aunt Sadie. That venerable lady had deemed it ridiculous that women should perform outdoor work—planting, weeding, mucking the barn—in petticoats, dresses, and flowered bonnets. Tonight I thanked goodness for her rebellious spirit.

Neily turned onto Narragansett and proceeded toward town. I tried to anticipate his destination, but he stopped at none of his usual haunts and kept going. The sidewalks grew quieter, the road less congested with evening traffic. A new likelihood occurred to me: a clandestine meeting with Grace Wilson.

Finally, he turned into the Point, the oldest section of town and the neighborhood where Brady and I had grown up. The houses here dated back to the seventeenth century; a few were even older than that. Though most held a colonial charm, these were modest homes and often cramped inside, with small rooms, narrow staircases, and bedrooms whose ceilings sloped beneath the eaves of the roof. In short, not the sort of places one would expect to find a man like Cornelius Vanderbilt III.

The briny scents of the harbor assaulted my nostrils. A buoy bell tolled mournfully, a lonely sound muffled somewhat by the evening mist that swathed the cobbled lanes. The air was warm, heavy with humidity, yet I shivered. A carriage drew up close behind me and the hairs on my nape stood on end. Had I been followed—the hunter now hunted, as I'd been the other night? But, no, the driver turned left and headed down toward Washington Street, which ran along the harbor front. I sighed in relief and returned my full attention to Neily.

On Third and Poplar he pulled his curricle to the side of the road in front of a blue clapboard saltbox. After setting the brake, he jumped down and looked quickly around before bounding to the front steps of the house. With another glance over his shoulder, his eyes lighting on me briefly but obviously dismissing me as inconsequential, he opened the door and slipped inside.

He'd neither knocked nor called out before crossing the threshold. I wondered who owned the house, and who waited for Neily inside. As I passed the structure, I noticed a single glow of lamplight in one of the downstairs rooms. All else lay dark. I kept going all the way to quiet Walnut Street, where I had grown up. Turning onto it, I pulled past the house my parents now rented out, except for the top floor where Brady lived. I didn't spare a glance at the house; I especially didn't want to look up and see the third-floor windows gazing back dark and empty. Instead, I continued to where the road ended at the railroad tracks, set the brake, and hopped down, my feet swallowed by the low-crawling mist.

By the time I returned to the blue saltbox, the downstairs lamp had been extinguished. Neily's curricle still sat outside, his horse dozing lightly. Careful not to wake him and set him snorting, I crossed to the far side of the street, stepped into the shadows between two houses, and waited. . . .

The upstairs windows were open. Suddenly, sounds drifted down—voices, laughter, a high-pitched squeal that was quickly stifled. That last was definitely feminine, counterbalanced by a man's deeper tones. My cheeks began to heat. I couldn't make out the words, but something in the general timbre of the voices suggested intimacy . . . sensuality. A glow filled one of the upper rooms and I glimpsed a pair of entwined shadows against the sloping ceiling, and then a bright flash of Grace's vivid auburn hair being pulled from its pins. A pair of masculine hands shoved the window closed and pulled the curtains together.

I felt like a voyeur standing there, for what had I learned but that Neily and Grace yearned to be together but must always do so on the sly. Though Neily was still a year from his majority, he was a man who obviously knew what he wanted, and Grace, a few years older, was an adult with the right to choose her destiny.

But did that also give them a reason to have murdered Alvin Goddard, who would have interfered in their happiness? I couldn't discount the possibility, yet the voices I'd just heard echoed in my mind. They hadn't sounded like the voices of co-conspirators. They'd sounded simply like the voices of lovers, joyful at finding a stolen moment together.

Feeling ashamed for spying, I started to move out of my shadow when the sound of another carriage held me in place. My disguise was a good one, but why take chances?

An enclosed brougham, its curtains drawn, pulled up behind Neily's curricle. The driver sat stiffly in the box, facing straight ahead. I waited, watching to see who would descend from inside, but the vehicle's doors remained closed.

With a start I spotted the outlines of stenciled numbers on the rear bumper, indistinct in the mist. I squinted to make them out, but smears of mud further obscured the identification numbers. I inched out from my hiding place, craning my neck and straining my eyes. Was that a three or an eight? A nine or a seven? Had the carriage been leased from Stevenson's Livery?

Suddenly the front door of the house opened and a figure in sweeping skirts, cape, and a concealing bonnet came down the steps and moved toward the carriage. The feminine figure was almost to the vehicle when she paused, gazing over her shoulder at the front door that stood open still. She blew a kiss to someone I couldn't see from my angle. The coachman made no move to come down and assist the woman, nor did she seem to expect him to as she reached her hand for the door latch. A gust of salt-tinged wind thrust back her bonnet back from her face. A few blond curls spilled forward and the moonlight caught her features.

I gasped. "Adelaide?"

I whisked a hand to my mouth. My surprise at seeing her there was so great, her name had tumbled out before I could stop it. Had she heard me? Would she attribute the sound to the breeze or the lapping of the water against the nearby docks?

Righting her bonnet, she stared in my direction, and for a fleeting instant I could have sworn she looked right in my eyes, that a trace of recognition flared her nostrils. But her gaze swept quickly past me; then she disappeared into the carriage.

I waited for the sounds of hooves and grinding wheels to fade before stepping out from my hiding place. The front door of the house now stood closed. Pulling my cap low over my brow, I hugged my sides and began making my way back toward Walnut Street. Exactly what sort of house was this unassuming blue saltbox? Even I, in my naiveté, recognized a tryst when I saw one. But Neily and Adelaide? Could it be?

I shook my head. I'd distinctly seen Grace Wilson's vibrant red hair in the lamplight. And anyway, it wouldn't have made sense. Neily risked his entire future by courting Grace; why on earth would he compound his difficulties by being untrue to her . . . and with Adelaide, no less?

No, Adelaide and Neily could not have stolen to the Point tonight to see each other. But they obviously knew of each other's activities and were in collusion together, sharing this modest house for their illicit affairs. Who owned the place, I wondered, and who had Adelaide come to see?

My throat tightened around a lump. I don't know why it should make me sad that my old friend might be having an affair, but I kept thinking of the girl she'd once been, and all the dreams she'd had. And I thought of her husband, alone in that big house of theirs, ailing and confused. . . .

A noise behind me drew me to a halt. I turned and scanned the dimly lit street. I saw nothing but low swirls of fog. A dog began to bark, a high-pitched, erratic sound that grated on my nerves. I continued walking. I'd no sooner taken three steps when I heard it again, what sounded like a crunching footfall. I whirled about, arms ready at my sides, fists curled.

"Who's there?"

Only a sharp breeze, the barking dog, and another clang of the buoy answered. That last reminded me that the sound I'd heard could be a line slapping against a mast or the creaking of a hull. Sounds carried strangely along the harbor, seemingly close by when they might be a quarter mile out on the bay.

Hurrying my pace, I made it to Walnut Street and turned the corner. My buggy loomed not far away, a black hulk amid the surrounding darkness. I wanted only to be up on the seat and heading for home.

From behind me a hand clamped my shoulder in a grip that sent instant pain speeding down my arm and across my chest. A solid weight slammed my back and sent me face-first onto the walkway. I might have cried out; I don't know. I landed half on the bricks and half on a bed of grass and flowers. My shoul-

der struck a rock, fresh pain zigzagging through me with nau-
seating sharpness.

I tried to rise, tried to pry myself from beneath the weight
pinning me down. And then something cool slid across my
throat . . . and pressed. An icy edge cut against my flesh until I
couldn't breathe.

Didn't dare breath.

"You can't save your brother," a voice rasped in my ear. "So
save yourself and leave well enough alone."

Chapter 12

From somewhere behind me, running footsteps echoed off the houses, and a shout pierced the muffling fog.

"What's going on here?"

The dagger yanked away from my throat. My attacker pushed off me and scrambled onto his feet. A corner of heavy fabric slapped my cheek, and I managed to raise my face off the ground in time to see nothing more than a billowing black shadow racing away, the misty darkness swallowing him as he disappeared between the houses across the street.

A distant clatter of overturned trash cans accompanied the urgency of a new voice in my ear.

"Miss Cross! Emma! Are you hurt?"

Hands gripped my shoulders, trying to turn me, but the past several seconds of being thrown to the ground with my face in the dirt and a knife threatening my very life's breath came crashing down on me. I fought the hands, tried to claw my way to my feet, to my carriage, to freedom.

"Emma, I'm not going to hurt you. It's me, Derrick Anderson. You remember me, don't you?" The reporter from the

Providence *Sun* rolled me over and pinned me down, his hands clamping my shoulders almost painfully. "Please calm yourself!"

As I continued to struggle, he knelt over me, straddling my legs. His face hovered over mine, his features shadowed, eyes fiercely catching glints from the streetlamps. My heart pounded as if to escape my chest, and my breath came in ragged gasps. But as I stared up at him without blinking, I detected a softening of his expression, a relaxing of his features, and somehow this set me at ease.

His hands came away and he sat up on his haunches. "Are you all right?" Before I could form an answer, he turned his head to stare in the direction the attacker had gone. "I should have gone after him. Might have been able to catch him, too, but . . ." His jaws clenched. He stared a few moments longer, ears obviously pricked. I listened as well, but the cloaked assailant gave no further hints to his whereabouts. He could be anywhere by now, either hiding in a dark yard or walking calmly down a street back in town.

Mr. Anderson looked down at me again, his face determined and set, but his mouth once more softening. "I couldn't just leave you here, not without seeing if you'd been hurt."

I nodded, spitting bits of grass and dirt out from between my lips. He offered me a hand. I hesitated as the half-cloudy, half-starry sky above me slowly spun in my vision. I shut my eyes and laid my hand in his. His palm was warm and smooth, his fingers strong and lengthy as they enveloped my own. I felt immediately safe, yet suddenly shaky again. I opened my eyes and clamped my teeth over my bottom lip.

As he helped me sit up, my hair fell around my shoulders and down my back. My cap sat some few feet away, in the gutter. After helping me to my feet, Mr. Anderson held on to my hand until I assured him I wouldn't fall over. Then he bent to retrieve the plaid fabric hat that had held my hair in place.

"Did you see who it was?" he asked me.

"No, he came up behind me. I never saw anything until he ran away, and then only his cloak. What about you?"

"Pretty much the same." He let out a sigh. "Damn, but I wish I'd gotten here sooner."

"Sooner or not, I owe you a great debt, Mr. Anderson. Thank you. If not for you happening along when you did . . ." A shudder traveled my shoulders as I considered the alternative. "But . . . you called me Miss Cross even before you saw my face. How did you know it was me?" Stiffening, I backed up a step. "You were following me again, weren't you?"

"Actually, no. Not you. But when I saw you drive your carriage by and then return on foot . . . well, Miss Cross, it didn't take much observation to see that you're no boy."

Something in his voice, some slapdash note of . . . appreciation . . . made me cross my arms and hug my cap against my bosom. I narrowed my eyes at him and gritted my teeth. "If not me, then who were you following?"

"Who were *you* following, in your elaborate disguise?"

"That's none of your business—"

"Let's not argue here." He cupped my elbow in his hand and turned me toward the railroad tracks. "Is that your carriage up ahead?"

When I nodded, he wasted no time in herding me toward it. He helped me onto the seat, climbed up beside me, and took up the reins. We drove in silence for some minutes, leaving the Point taking Thames Street along the waterfront.

"Where are we going?"

"Home, Miss Cross."

As before, I stiffened my back. "I will not go home with you, Mr. Anderson, wherever that may be."

"Not my home. Yours."

"Oh." Silence descended again as the horse trotted a few more paces. "Don't you want directions?"

He merely shook his head. Was that a slight smile curling his lips?

"You know where I live?"

"More or less."

Yes, that was definitely a smile. My insides began to boil. "Stop the carriage. Stop right here and not an inch further."

We were at King Park, just after the turn where Thames Street turned onto Wellington Avenue. Mr. Anderson directed the carriage off the road and onto the grassy verge that marked the edge of the small, waterside park. "Yes, Miss Cross?"

"I want to know why you always seem to turn up in odd places. And why you seem to know so much about me. And I want to know whom you were following tonight. And why."

He shifted to face me and slung an arm across the top of the seat, which brought his large hand unsettlingly close to my cheek. I tried to create more distance between us, but as I was already on the end of the seat there was little room to maneuver.

"As far as turning up in odd places, Miss Cross, one could say the same for you."

I huffed in denial, but he kept talking.

"I was at the jailhouse that first day because upon arriving in town I'd heard there'd been a death the night before. Any reporter worth his ink would inquire about that."

"But you followed me out of the jailhouse and around town, until I spotted you on Spring Street."

"I confess I did. But it had nothing to do with your brother."

I shook my head. "That doesn't make sense."

"Miss Cross, I'm not here to investigate your brother or you, or the death of Alvin Goddard."

I quirked an eyebrow at him. "And you're not here to research an article about America's wealthy industrialists either, are you, Mr. Anderson?"

"No, I'm not." He drew a breath, looked out over the silver-tipped waves, then back at me. "Since we literally keep running into each other, maybe you and I can find a way to work together."

"Maybe," I agreed, "assuming you can find a way to tell me one thing that's true."

"Touché." He laughed softly, his eyes crinkling pleasantly at the corners. "All right, then. I'm not here on behalf of the *Sun*. I took on this assignment privately."

"And what assignment would that be?" I couldn't help smiling. I wasn't sure why, but I was suddenly enjoying the little game we seemed to be playing. That is, until Derrick Anderson spoke his next words.

"I'm investigating Adelaide Halstock."

"Adelaide?" I sat up straighter, all amusement gone from my thoughts. "Why on earth?"

But even as I asked the question, Adelaide's mysterious errand on the Point formed images in my mind. I sank back against the squabs.

"There is someone, whose identity I can't divulge, who mistrusts your old friend's intentions when it comes to her husband. That's why I followed her to the Point tonight. It isn't the first time she's slipped out of that mausoleum she shares with Rupert Halstock, only to return home in the wee hours of the morning."

"You think she's having an affair?" The question came out more like a statement and I immediately regretted my words. I believed exactly that, but who was I to judge Adelaide? It certainly wasn't my business to see her punished for what might be the desperate actions of a young woman who found herself trapped in a loveless marriage to an aged, ailing husband.

"It goes beyond questions of fidelity, Miss Cross, and involves more than wounded family pride. I can't tell you much else, but your old friend might be in the middle of something that promises to barrel out of her control."

"My old friend . . ." My mouth dropped open. "That's why

you've followed me, because I'm Adelaide's friend. But how did you know that?"

He smiled that enigmatic, infuriating smile of his. "I'm an investigative reporter, Miss Cross."

I remembered the kiss Adelaide had blown over her shoulder after leaving the saltbox, prompting me to ask a bit too eagerly, "So did you see who it was Adelaide came to visit?"

"Unfortunately, no. The individual was obviously already inside before she or I arrived. I'd hoped he might exit after her, but then I heard your shout."

"Yes . . . I'm sorry about that."

"Sorry I was there to ward off your attacker? I'm not." His voice deepened with quiet conviction, melding like a caress with the breeze and raising goose bumps across my back. A nervous sensation fluttered in my stomach.

Needing to escape his scrutiny, I stared out over the water. I cleared my throat. Shoved my hands in the pockets of my corduroy jacket. When I glanced back at him it was to catch the ghost of his smile just before it vanished.

"What can you tell me about Mrs. Halstock?" he asked.

The sudden shift back to Adelaide came as a welcome distraction. "Not much." At his skeptical expression, my chin came up defensively. "It's true we've known each other all our lives, but we were never particularly close. We're only now just reacquainting ourselves, perhaps as better friends; but if she's having an affair, she hasn't told me anything about it. I was surprised to see her tonight. You can believe it or not, Mr. Anderson, but that is the truth."

"Oh, I'll take you at your word, Miss Cross. Something tells me nothing but the truth ever leaves those pretty lips of yours." He paused and a blush climbed up my neck—partly from unexpected pleasure that he should mention my lips, partly with shock that he should do so . . . and partly with a smidgeon of guilt because, truthfully, I wasn't above a little white lie if I deemed one necessary.

His hand moved, the forefinger lightly tapping the brim of my boyish cap. The backs of his knuckles grazed my cheek. My lower lip trembled in response, but other than that I held myself immobile. What would he do next? My pulse raced as I waited.

"It's your turn." He returned his hand to the back of the seat, and the smudge of dirt across his knuckles made me realize the point of his gesture—to remove said dirt from my cheek, a reminder of my attack. "What brought you to the Point tonight?" he asked.

I worked through a sense of schoolgirl-like disappointment. "I was following my cousin."

"Cornelius the third?"

"Yes . . . we call him Neily."

"I thought that's who arrived right before Mrs. Halstock left the house." He studied me a moment. "This has to do with your half brother, Stuart Gale?"

"Brady," I corrected him, but didn't answer the question. After all, I didn't know what he might do with the information.

"Who else is on your list of suspects for the murder of Alvin Goddard?"

The question startled me. "How do you know I have a list—"

"Miss Cross, there is always more than one suspect. Besides, from what I've heard around town, you have a good relationship with your Vanderbilt cousins, especially Neily. You can't want him to be Alvin Goddard's murderer any more than you want your brother to be guilty."

"That may be so," I conceded, "but I'm not about to shed guilt on anyone until I have proof."

"Until," he repeated, smiling again, "not *if.* I like your spirit, Miss Cross."

The heat of another blush surged into my cheeks. I diverted

his attention from it with a suggestion. "I suppose we could try asking Neily who else was there tonight . . ." I trailed off, already realizing the flaw in that plan.

"But then he'd know you were following him." Mr. Anderson frowned. "Then again, maybe he was on to you."

I shook my head vigorously. "It can't have been Neily who attacked me, if that's what you're implying."

"You sure about that?"

No. I wasn't sure about anything—not even about the possibility that as I'd followed Neily to the Point, someone else had followed me. Nor was I sure about how much I should be trusting Derrick Anderson.

"All right, we'll leave that for now," he said when I didn't reply. "I have a proposition for you, Miss Cross."

I studied him through narrowed eyes. "What sort of proposition?"

"You don't have to look so cynical." His hand moved toward my face again, then stopped suddenly as if he thought twice about touching me. "What I propose is that we work together from now on. Pool our resources. Share information."

I sat back and studied the play of moonlight on his even, yet somehow rugged features. "Why would you want to do that? You yourself said I was Adelaide's friend. How do you know I'm not involved in whatever it is you're investigating?"

"Because I saw your reaction when Mrs. Halstock exited the house, and I believe you were utterly taken aback. I realized then you were no confidante of hers."

My mouth fell open. "Where were you?"

"A few feet away, just on the other side of the garden wall of the house to your right. I could see over well enough, while the lilac bushes provided ample camouflage."

"And you watched me . . ."

"Watching them—your cousin, his sweetheart, and Mrs.

Halstock. Yes." He shrugged, a careless gesture that should have infuriated me, yet somehow didn't. "Sorry," he added.

I blew out a breath, trying to sound exasperated, but the truth was I realized his proposition might turn out to be a godsend—if I could trust him. "All right. What do you have in mind?"

He hesitated just long enough for the silence to become heavy with unspoken innuendoes, and for my cheeks to blaze again; thank goodness the breeze had blown a cloud across the moon. "First we need to find out who owns that house on the Point," he said. "We'll proceed from there."

He stuck out his hand. "Partners . . . Emma?"

Every instinct and every notion of propriety ever instilled in me roared out a warning. I knew nothing about this man, had no reason to trust him. And I knew what happened to young women who put their faith in dashing, charming gentlemen. Yet for reasons I still can't explain, I placed my hand in his and gave a firm shake.

It was all I could do the next day not to drive straight over to The Breakers and confront Neily about being on the Point the previous night. Adelaide as well. Between the two of them, I would certainly be able to identify the fourth person in the blue saltbox. But besides not wanting to reveal my having followed Neily, I realized questioning either one of them could potentially put them in danger—and me in even greater danger than I already was. If that fourth person had been my attacker, it might also mean he murdered Alvin Goddard. Better to let my assailant believe he'd frightened me away from investigating any further, while at the same time leaving Neily and Adelaide ignorant of any information that could make them targets as well.

Of course, I hadn't been frightened off, and another possibility existed. Considering that a carriage had entered the Point behind me, it was possible my attacker hadn't emerged from the house at all, but from one of the side streets. And if the individual took the trouble of following me and running me down with a knife, it must mean I was getting closer—uncomfortably close—to the truth.

Besides the names I'd read in Stevenson's ledger, I'd learned something else the day I went into town with Aunt Alice and Gladys. Theodore Mason had lied about his whereabouts the night of the murder. He told me he never left his room but had sat reading *Great Expectations* until turning in. His landlady had a different story: Mr. Mason had indeed gone out that night.

At midmorning, then, I stood in front of Jack Parsons's front door. From somewhere in the house drifted a deep drone of voices, far off and indistinct, but suggesting Jack was at home. I clanked the knocker until it raised resounding echoes in the hallway inside. A moment later the door opened and Theodore Mason peered out at me with fatigue-ridden eyes.

Surprise instantly replaced his tired look. "Good morning, Miss Emma."

"Good morning, Mr. Mason." I started to step over the threshold, but he blocked my way.

"Er, I'm afraid this isn't the best time, Miss Emma. Mr. Parsons is otherwise engaged." He moved as if to close the door.

"That's quite all right, Mr. Mason." I held my ground and smiled. "It's you I've come to see."

"Me?"

"Indeed. May I step inside for a moment, or would you rather I ask my question here on the stoop, where the gardener might overhear?" Fortunately for me, the gardener at that moment walked around the corner of the house, hedge clippers in hand.

"It's really not a good time, Miss Emma." But he widened the door all the same.

He led me into the small receiving parlor at the front of the house. The voices I'd heard persisted, and I thought I detected a note of hostility, though I still couldn't make out the words. Mr. Mason closed the door behind us, enveloping us in silence. He took several paces into the center of the room before pivoting soldier-style to regard me.

I saw no reason to vacillate. "You lied to me the other day. You were not in your boardinghouse room reading the night Alvin Goddard died."

His shoulders sagged as the breath breezed out of him. "No, I wasn't, at least not all night. I did go out for a short time."

"How short?"

"I don't know . . . not long."

"Where did you go?"

He scowled at the floor, only just managing to smooth his brow before looking back up at me. "Nowhere in particular. For a walk. As people will do of an evening, Miss Cross."

I tilted my chin at him. "Then why lie about it?"

"Why?" He held up his arms. "Why lie when someone practically accuses you of murder?"

"I did no such thing, Mr. Mason. I only asked you some questions."

"Yes, about a murder. One I did not commit."

"Neither did my brother. But someone did, and we'll never get at the truth if people persist in lying about that night. So I'll ask you again. Where did you go, and can anyone verify your story?"

He stared at me a good long moment, his eyes burning with indecision. His nose became pinched, and his brows cinched tightly enough to appear painful. Finally, he sighed. "Yes, someone can verify where I went that night. That is, I visited someone, but . . . I cannot tell you whom."

"Why on earth not?"

"Because . . . I can't. I promised. It's a matter of . . . well . . ."

Again he pinned me with a gaze that blazed with uncertainty. "I promised and I can't break that promise unless . . . it becomes a matter of life and death."

"You do realize, Mr. Mason, that I might have to go to the police with the information I have . . . tell them you lied, that you were not at home that night. I don't wish to, but you're not giving me much choice."

His inner debate cleared from his expression, leaving his face a blank. "You do what you must, Miss Emma. And I will do what I must, when and if I must."

I wanted to shake him. But I had one last question. "Where were you last night?" I inquired in a deadly quiet voice.

He seemed to take the query in stride. "I was here."

"Can Mr. Parsons corroborate that?"

A corner of his mouth quirked with irony. "Mr. Parsons wasn't home last night."

Damn. But why would I expect a man like Jack Parsons to be sitting at home on a summer evening in Newport? Of course he was out, at the Casino or the Newport Country Club—or any of a dozen other places where music, good food, and pleasant conversation could be found.

I drew myself up, readying to leave. "I'm sorry to have upset you, Mr. Mason."

His long-suffering look unexpectedly melted into something resembling sympathy. "I hope you clear your brother, Miss Emma. I always did like Mr. Brady. I always did," he repeated absently, more to himself.

He walked past me to open the door, and angry voices spilled into the room. Familiar voices, both of them.

"You said you would, Jack. You can't back out now."

"Are you crazy? If you know what's good for you, you'll change your ways and keep your mouth shut in the bargain."

"It's too late, and you're gonna get me killed."

"Don't be melodramatic."

Forcing my unhinged mouth to close, I strode into the hall, effectively silencing Jack and my young cousin Reggie. "What is going on here?"

Jack's back was to me, but now he whirled about. The two of them stared at me like a pair of raccoons caught rummaging through the garbage. "Emma . . ." Jack said weakly and trailed off.

"What are you doing here, Em?" My young cousin shoved his hands in his trouser pockets and scowled. I'd thought Mr. Mason looked tired, but Reggie looked downright . . . damaged. Worn out, defeated, and much, much too cynical for a boy of sixteen. At the sight of him, all I wanted to do was wrap my arms around him, rock him back and forth, and assure him everything would be all right.

Not that I knew what that "everything" entailed. Not that my embraces or reassurances would make a difference. Reggie had set out on a road that threatened to consume him whole— the circles beneath his eyes and the untimely brackets around his mouth attested to that—and it broke my heart.

"Reggie," I said gently, "what's going on? What will get you killed?" I shot a glance at Jack and demanded, "Who is going to hurt my cousin, and why?"

Chapter 13

"See here, Emma, it's not as bad as all that. Why don't we all have a seat and discuss this calmly." Jack gestured toward the room I'd just vacated, and the three of us went in while Mr. Mason stole the opportunity to disappear down the hallway.

I didn't point out that they had hardly been discussing anything calmly moments ago. Still, I hoped I might learn something in the next few moments that would ease my rising concerns for Reggie.

"Would you like some tea, Emma?" Jack asked me once we'd settled ourselves in the rather uncomfortable chairs the receiving parlor had to offer.

Tempted to snap in reply, I gritted my teeth. "What I'd like is for one of you to come clean, and fast or . . . I'll go straight to Uncle Cornelius."

I doubt I'd have done any such thing, but the threat certainly had its effect on Reggie; his eyes bulged and his cheeks flushed. "It's just the summer sporting scene, Em. Happens every Season. Being a girl, you wouldn't understand."

I opened my mouth to protest the nature of that statement

when Jack held up a hand. "He's talking about yacht races, Emma."

Settling back in my chair, I pondered that for all of about three ticks of the mantel clock. "Dishonest ones, I presume."

"I told him it was a bad idea—"

"Not at first you didn't," Reggie interrupted, sliding forward to perch at the end of his seat. "You were going to place hefty wagers . . . you promised."

"That was before I realized what was going to happen," Jack shot back.

"Which is what?" I tossed up my hands. "One of you had better explain—or else."

The implied threat worked its magic. Jack let out a breath. "Reggie's mixed up in a plan to fix next week's unofficial tournament at the Yacht Club."

"Shut up, Jack!"

Jack ignored Reggie and went on. "The trick is to get everyone betting heavily on the favorite, and then for said favorite to encounter a problem that prevents them from finishing the race. A snapped rigging, a broken rudder."

This wasn't exactly a new concept for me. I was Brady's sister, after all. Newport in the summer was all about wagering—on anything and everything. Our wealthy vacationers thought up all sorts of imaginative means of making—and losing—great sums of money. This wouldn't be the first time someone had tampered with the outcome.

"And you were in on this with him?" I asked in a calm voice that belied my rising anger.

"I pretended to be. Reggie came to me asking for a loan, a big one, and when I questioned him as to why, he let drop enough information for me to realize he was getting himself eyeballs deep in a huge mess."

"You were all for it a few weeks ago," Reggie said with a hiss. "You helped plan the thing."

Jack shook his head. "Only to put myself in a position where I could stop you and stop the illegal betting. My advice to you, Reggie, is to step back, stay home, and pretend you know nothing."

"Can you?" I asked my cousin. My stomach clenched. "Or are you in too deep?"

He shrugged, staring at the floor. "Don't tell Father. It won't help anything." With that, Reggie sprang to his feet. "Without your money, Jack, I'm out of it whether I want to be or not. So go ahead and stop the tournament or whatever the hell you feel like doing. I'm going home."

He strode out of the parlor. Jack and I stood as well, and I held out my hand to him. "Thank you for not letting him do this thing. For looking out for him. He's . . ." I shook my head.

"As a family friend it was the least I could do." Jack smiled his brilliant smile, showing nearly all of his even, white teeth. "It's what your father would have done if he were here."

"I don't know about that. Do you realize neither Mother nor Dad is coming home to support Brady? They're staying in Paris, Jack."

His smile faded. "I'm sorry to hear that, Emma. I'm sure they'd come if they could. You know how the art world is . . . there's never enough money for necessities, much less trips across the ocean."

I nodded, swallowing against a growing lump in my throat. Brady, Reggie, Neily . . . I felt myself up against far more than I could handle, and for the first time I questioned my ability to go on fighting for my brother's life. Nothing I'd done so far seemed to have helped, had brought me no closer to discovering who murdered Alvin Goddard. I was tired and frustrated and . . .

I wanted my parents. There, I said it. I wanted them here to help shoulder the burden. To talk to. To tell me everything would be all right . . .

Bitterness rose up so suddenly I nearly choked on it. How dared Mother and Dad leave this to me? Did they believe me to be strong enough for this? And even if I was, how could they possibly believe I should have to be?

If it had been me in Europe, I'd have sold my last belonging in order to book passage home to help my brother. That my parents hadn't done so only reinforced what I'd known for a long time, since childhood, though I couldn't have verbalized it then: On some deep, yet indecipherable level they simply didn't grasp what it meant to be parents. And they never would. Life to them was a series of artistic adventures, an intellectual fairy world that might or might not include Brady and me at any particular time.

"I'm here, Emma." Had Jack read my mind? Or did he simply understand my situation? After all, he'd been my father's friend since their university days. He knew Arthur Cross better than anyone, and knew my mother, too. His arms went around me and he pressed my cheek to his shoulder. "Whenever you need anything, Emma, I'm here."

"Thank you." I stepped away to give myself a shake and gather my composure. My falling apart due to unfulfilled parental obligations wouldn't help Brady. I needed to remain levelheaded and focused.

A new thought prompted me to ask, "Is Reggie walking home?"

Jack seemed a little taken aback at my abrupt shift. "I presume so."

"Then I need to go. Thanks for everything, Jack."

Outside, I climbed into my buggy and steered Barney toward The Breakers. Sure enough, within a minute or two I came upon my cousin trudging along, his head down and his hands shoved into his coat pockets. I pulled alongside him. "Get in."

He looked up at me but continued walking.

"I mean it, Reggie. Get in. I have more questions for you and if you won't answer them now, I'll be forced to follow you home and interrogate you there."

He plowed to a halt. "When did you become such a tyrant?"

"I'm a Vanderbilt. Now climb up." Once he had, I turned to face him rather than set Barney to a walk again. "You went to Jack for money."

He frowned at me like I'd gone daft. "Didn't we just establish that a few minutes ago? And it didn't happen exactly the way he tells it, Emma. He was hot for the deal."

"Yes, all right, but before you thought of asking Jack, did you maybe think of another way of getting the money?"

"Like what?"

I pursed my lips, then said, "You tell me."

"I have no idea what you're talking about."

I leaned closer and lowered my voice. "Reggie, did you steal the items that went missing from the house? The ones Mason was accused of taking? The ones he was fired for?"

"What?" His mouth dropped open and he fell back against the squabs as if I'd shoved him. "You'd accuse me of . . . No! Absolutely not. I like Mason. I wouldn't . . . I can't believe you'd even suggest such a thing."

"Someone stole from the house, Reggie. Someone who obviously needed money." I raised my eyebrows at him.

"Look. I wanted money, sure. I still do. I want my own money so I don't have to rely on the paltry allowance Father gives me. But I didn't need it enough to ruin Mason's life."

Anger fueled his protest, but it was the hurt gleam hovering behind the ire that won me over. "I believe you."

He blew out a deep breath. His fingers trembled where they lay spread on his knees. "Thanks. I think."

"Sorry." I patted his shoulder. "But can I ask you one more question?"

"Can I stop you?"

I suppressed a smile, but it faded quickly enough anyway when I turned my thoughts to another serious matter. "It's about Katie. Reggie, I need to know . . . did you . . . were you . . . um . . ." This turned out to be much harder to say than I'd realized.

"Are you talking about her being . . . in the family way?"

I expected him to protest as hotly as he'd done moments ago, and I braced myself to watch him closely, to detect whether he'd tell the truth or not. His quiet reply surprised me—shocked me. "No, it wasn't me, Em. It maybe could have been, but it wasn't."

"What do you mean?"

He met my gaze. "Will you swear to secrecy?"

"Reggie . . ."

"Swear, Em, or I won't tell you a thing."

I didn't like the terms, didn't like promising to something before I knew what it entailed. Even so, I held up my hand. "I swear."

He nodded. "You remember when we all came up in the spring to view the finished house? I brought Justin Reynolds with me—he was my roommate at school last term. Justin and I . . . well, Katie's pretty, you know, and outgoing and all, and we . . . we thought she wanted . . ."

It didn't take a genius to comprehend what two teenaged, youthfully arrogant boys believed Katie wanted, and the notion made me queasy. Reggie's gaze darted away. He sucked his lips between his teeth, cracked a couple of knuckles. "You can't tell anyone, Em. You swore."

Part of me dearly wished I hadn't. But I'd met Justin, the son of yet another powerful industrialist. The realistic part of me guessed that even if I went to the authorities and persuaded Katie to testify against him, Justin Reynolds wouldn't receive more than a slap on the wrist. It would change nothing. Maybe if Katie's baby had lived . . .

"What happened between them, Reggie?"

"Well, one night Justin arranged to meet Katie in the play-house." His eyes went fierce and his chin jerked to a defensive angle. "She went of her own free will, I swear it, Em."

"She might have gone of her own free will, but that doesn't mean she wanted what happened to her when she arrived." My stomach threatened to turn over; bile rose in my throat. "You knew at the time this was happening?"

He offered me that shrug of his and said, "Didn't think it was any of my business. She never looked at me, only Justin. I was in my room at the time."

"Poor Katie . . ."

"Look, Em." Reggie's sharpened tone cut through my thoughts. "You've been asking a lot of questions lately, and not just of me."

As I briefly wondered how he knew that, he went on, "You should quit playing sleuth and prying into other people's business. Running around poking your nose into things isn't a child's game. It won't help Brady, and it could get you hurt, or worse."

The words echoed through me, producing tremors that ran up and down my arms as I flapped Barney's reins. Last night someone had breathed nearly those same words in my ear while pressing a knife to my throat. I glanced over at the boy at my side. Could Reggie have attacked me? Could he have run me off the road along Ocean Avenue? I'd suspected him before, true, but only because of his penchant for the same bourbon found next to Brady after the murder. Now I had a motive— Reggie's involvement in illicit gambling, and the possibility that Alvin Goddard had found out.

A few minutes later we drove up The Breakers' long drive and came to a stop. Reggie swung down and stood looking up at me.

"So are you going to tell Father?"

"I should," I said woodenly, staring straight ahead. Relenting, I returned his gaze. "But if you promise me you're out of this yachting scheme, I won't."

"Don't have much choice now, do I?"

I studied his youthful face, already showing hints of a hardened lifestyle. Were those patrician, even features those of a murderer? I couldn't bring myself to believe it. And yet, Reggie was no innocent.

"Don't you know how easy it is to end up like Brady?" I asked him in a whisper. "Is that what you want? To be in the wrong place at the wrong time, and have no one believe in you because of wrongs you've committed in your past?"

With a grin as brilliant as pure sunlight, he reached up and clasped my hand. "You'd believe in me, Em. I know you would."

I watched Reggie enter the house, but I didn't leave The Breakers. Within all the turmoil of these past days, something tugged at me, a sentiment instilled in me long ago that connected me to this place, to the property if not the newly reconstructed house. I'd spent the larger share of my summers here as a child, playing with my cousins and feeling part of a large brood whose roots extended back well over a century. Though I often liked to pretend otherwise, a significant portion of who I am had formed on these lawns, in the shared laughter of my cousins, in the admonishments and, yes, the wisdom of their parents, and in the order and ritual of life on an estate of this magnitude.

I liked to pretend I was independent and self-sufficient and unconventional, but the truth—yes, the *truth*—was that I only possessed the strength to be those things because of this place and these people; because of the Vanderbilt steel running in my veins. I needed them, and I realized I wasn't just fighting for Brady anymore. I was fighting for all of us. For Brady and Neily and Reggie and even Mason—for the entire family. A family that suddenly seemed to be slipping away, breaking apart.

I set off with long strides away from the house. I headed first toward the playhouse, empty now but ringing with memories. I stood on the porch for long minutes, remembering how Neily had always insisted he be in charge of our make-believe household because he was the oldest, and how Gertrude always shot him down, telling him in no uncertain terms that ridiculous notions of primogeniture had no place in our games.

My strides brought me next across the back gardens, my gaze sweeping the lawns as I remembered picnics, ballgames, kite flying. . . . Gladys always wanted to hold the string. Reggie always ran faster than any of us. Neily always maintained a slight reserve, in keeping with his position as his father's heir, I suppose.

I was nearly running by the time I reached the base of the property. My hat flew off, the ribbons having pulled free, and I let it sail behind me to land somewhere in the grass. The ocean stretched out in front of and below me, an ever-moving carpet of deepest sapphire glittering with sunlight. I found the gate separating the property from the Cliff Walk unlocked, as it usually was during the day. I opened it and pushed through, considering the possibility that someone had done the reverse the night of Gertrude's ball. Come through the gate and stolen into the house . . . someone who wasn't Brady or Neily or Reggie or Mason.

What about Jack? If what I'd learned today shed incriminating light on Reggie, I had to admit the same held true for Jack. He'd pled innocence in the yachting scheme, but Reggie certainly believed Jack had been a willing partner, at least at first. Did Jack need money? Was he in debt? Not for the first time, I admitted he might have given Uncle Cornelius his pocket watch as collateral, then entered into the illegal gambling plan to raise the cash to pay him back.

The possibilities made my head swim—not a good thing when one walked along a cliff-side path. Yet onward I went, needing the bracing wind in my face, my hair, fanning my skirts against my legs. I almost felt capable of taking flight. Light, airy, free. I rounded the bend at the corner of The Breakers' property—and drew up sharp with a yelp.

Chapter 14

"Neily!"

My cousin and I nearly collided. He had come around the bend from the opposite direction, his steps as determined as my own, his head down and shoulders bunched. With the crunching of my own boots on the sand and rocks, as well as the preoccupation of my thoughts, I hadn't heard him coming. Now we both stood ramrod straight like rabbits caught nibbling carrots by the kitchen maid. My heart nearly pounded its way out of my stays, and Neily, too, pressed a hand to his chest.

"You gave me quite a fright, Emmaline. What are you doing down here?"

"I guess I could ask you the same. I needed a brisk walk, I guess."

"Same here." He looked apologetic. "Things have been . . . hectic lately. Unsettled." His rueful expression deepened and he quirked an eyebrow at me. "To the say the least."

I nodded my agreement, at the same time wondering how I might work in a question or two about last night without giving myself away.

"You, er, look tired, Neily," I ventured. "Is everything all right?"

"Well, let's see. A man I've known most of my life is dead, my step-cousin is in jail on murder charges, and my father is threatening to disinherit me if I don't do as he says."

"Over Grace," I said more than asked.

He shrugged and looked miserable. "Emmaline, what am I going to do?"

"I don't know, Neily. Maybe in time he'll come around. What about your mother?"

"She's as adamant as Father. They don't even know Grace, yet they loathe her."

"Still, it's all new to them, and you're so young. Maybe in a year or two . . ."

"Maybe," he conceded, but the hard line of his jaw spoke of impatience and stubborn resolve. The wind swirled around us, and Neily thrust up a hand to shove back a shock of hair blown into his eyes.

I swallowed a gasp. A slash of raw flesh scored Neily's right hand across the palm and into the corner of his thumb. My throat convulsed with the biting memory of the knife pressed against it last night. Dear God . . . could it have been Neily holding that knife? My attacker and I had struggled—his hand could easily have slipped down onto the blade.

Oh, God . . . Neily? The waves and the wind and a crunching echoed in my ears. I realized I'd begun to back away from him. He reached out to grasp my shoulder and I flinched.

"Jeez, Emmaline, are you trying to fall? What's wrong with you all of a sudden? Why are you looking at me like that?"

He tightened his grip on my shoulder and I went utterly still, afraid to move, afraid to look away from him for even a second. And desperate to form a reply that would placate him. Was he intending to push me over the edge?

"I . . . I've just got a lot on my mind." I struggled to come up with a plausible excuse for my behavior. "Wh-when I said 'maybe in a year or two,' it made me think of Brady. Oh, Neily, what if he has to spend the rest of his life in prison?"

That seemed to work, for although he raised a hand to grasp my other shoulder as well, his grip loosened as he gave me a gentle shake. Relief weakened my knees, but I fought not to show it.

"That won't happen, Emmaline," he said. "I know it won't. If you can be optimistic about Grace and me, then I can surely be as optimistic about Brady being exonerated. It'll happen, and soon."

My eyes filled with tears, dangerously obscuring my vision. If Neily had wished to push me to my death, nothing could have stopped him. Were his words sincere? Or meant to soothe me into dropping my guard? A second passed, then several, and Neily only smiled down at me and patted my shoulders until he finally released me.

"What a pair we are, huh?" He laughed weakly. "One would think we'd both come out here to jump."

My heart skipped a beat. "Don't say that!"

"Well, even if we were, at least we have each other to talk us out of it." He shook his head. "Not sure that made sense, but you know what I mean." He held out his hand. "What say we go up to the house for a stiff brandy?"

I took his offered hand—the left one, without the cut—and casually gestured toward his right. "That looks painful. What happened there?"

He didn't miss a beat. "Oh, that. Cut it trying to open a tin of caviar."

"Silly Neily," I joked, keeping my voice light, "that's what servants are for." Though I guessed there hadn't been any servants in the little harbor-side saltbox last night.

"Yeah, I learned that the hard way."

Laughing, we made our way back through the gate, though

I'm a bit ashamed to say I breathed a clandestine sigh of relief as we stepped onto the safety of the lawn.

"A gentleman to see you, Miss Emma," Katie announced when she poked her head into the morning room early the next day. Her cornflower blue eyes twinkled and her freckles stood out against rosy cheeks. "A right handsome one, I daresay."

Her cheerfulness led me instantly to know it wasn't Neily or any other Vanderbilt calling on me, for Katie hadn't lost her skittishness when it came to my family. Across the table from me, Nanny peeked over the latest edition of the Newport *Daily News*. "Who's this, Emma?"

"Am I psychic?" I shot them both an impatient look. "Did he give a name, Katie?"

"Aye, Mr. Anderson."

I was on my feet in an instant. "Show him into the conservatory, please."

"Hmm, you seem awfully eager. He must be someone interesting." Nanny rustled her newspaper. "Do I get to meet him?"

"No." Hearing the brusqueness of my tone, I stopped halfway to the door. "Sorry, Nanny. This isn't a social call. Mr. Anderson is helping me with Brady's case, so whatever he's come to tell me, I'm sure he won't want to talk in front of others."

"Well, whatever it is," she said sweetly, "I'm sure you'll be telling me before too long."

I continued walking. "Always so sure of yourself, aren't you, Nanny?"

"Right enough," she murmured to my back as she noisily turned a page.

Quickly I ran up the back stairs to smooth my hair, remove the carriage jacket I'd donned in preparation of leaving the house, and replace it with an embroidered shawl. On impulse I slipped on my best diamond teardrop earrings, the same ones

I'd worn to Gertrude's coming-out ball. A quick check in the mirror brought me to a rueful halt.

"Not a social call," I reminded myself. "So stop primping like a giddy debutant."

Yet the earrings remained in place as I made my way back downstairs and to the conservatory. I found Derrick Anderson near the ocean-facing windows, leaning over to examine one of Aunt Sadie's exotic statues. This one was a bronze casting of a scantily clad female, her body curvaceous, her expression stern, and her six arms snaking out from her sides. I'd always found something oddly sensual about the lines of those arms, and I found myself blushing now at how intently he was studying the piece.

"The Hindu goddess Kali," he said, turning his head to peer at me but not quite straightening. "Gentle mother, fierce warrior."

I shivered slightly as I watched his fingertips trace the curve of a shoulder. Foolishly I envied the statue for a moment, imagining that broad palm on my own shoulder. Then I tightened my shawl and looked past him, through the windows. "Yes, well, that describes my Aunt Sadie to a tee, I should think."

"Aunt Sadie?"

"My great-aunt. Not a Vanderbilt," I added for no good reason, or was it perhaps to let this man know I was of hardier stuff than even my obvious heritage suggested. Of course, the significance would be lost on him, since he never knew Aunt Sadie. "This was her house," I explained. "Her things. Her life, actually."

"Funny, because I'd say this house and these furnishing fit you to a tee." He stood upright, looking almost ridiculously tall and broad in this feminine room. A certain quality, an elegance about him sometimes made me suspect a gentleman's upbringing, yet at other times I sensed a raw and rugged energy running right beneath the surface, a vitality that left me unsettled.

My hand drifted to my throat. "And how would you know that, Mr. Anderson?"

"Too late to go back to being formal, wouldn't you say? I wish you'd call me Derrick. I already think of you as Emma. I hope that's all right."

His cheekiness wasn't lost on me. And yet . . . "After the other night . . . yes, it's all right." I smiled. "So what brings you here? Have you learned something?"

His hand trailed over one of the statue's smooth arms in a parting gesture. He came toward me, and I resisted an involuntary urge to retreat a step or two. Was it because it suddenly struck me that other than Brady and my Vanderbilt relatives, Derrick was the first man I'd ever entertained in my home? I stood gawking up at him, very much feeling the breach of etiquette, hearing, in my imagination, Aunt Alice's outrage.

He gestured to the wicker settee. "May we?"

"Oh, I'm sorry. Of course. Can I get you anything? I was just having breakfast when you arrived. Nothing fancy, mind you, but Nanny's a wonderful cook. Nanny's my housekeeper and I've known her all my life. . . ." Goodness, I was rambling. I clamped my mouth shut and wondered why this man always managed to fluster me so. I sank onto the sofa and concluded with, "Coffee, perhaps?"

He sat beside me with an indulgent smile. "Nothing, thank you. I have some news about the blue house. I've discovered who the owner is." He paused, perhaps for effect, and I found myself pressing forward to the very edge of the seat cushion. "A part-time Newport resident named John Benjamin Parsons."

"Jack!"

"You know him?"

"Of course I know him. He's a good friend of my father's."

My mouth fell open and I clutched the edges of my shawl in tight fists.

"Emma, are you all right?"

"Jack . . . and Adelaide . . . I never would have guessed . . ."

"Well, it would appear so, unless there's some other reason for their nighttime meetings. She's never indicated anything to you?"

"Not a thing. And neither has Jack." A dull pain pushed at my temple. I couldn't make sense of this latest revelation. "Jack and Adelaide . . ."

"He's quite a bit older than she is," Derrick pointed out.

"Not as old as her husband and besides, Jack doesn't look his age at all. But . . ."

Suddenly I remembered the afternoon I'd spent with Adelaide, when she first told me how Mr. Goddard had been sent to spy on Neily and Grace Wilson. That was my first inkling that Neily might have had a motive to want Alvin Goddard out of the way. Adelaide said she'd overheard Uncle Cornelius and her husband discussing the matter. But if she and Jack were using the same house to meet in as Neily and Grace, then Adelaide had known of the affair firsthand.

Good heavens, had she purposely shed guilt on Neily in order to lift it from Jack?

"Emma?" Derrick nudged my arm. "Where are you? What are you thinking? How well do you know this man?"

I snapped out of my reverie and turned to face him fully. "Not as well as I thought, apparently. Derrick, can you find out . . . things . . . about Jack Parsons? His finances, his debts if he has any. I need to know—"

"Slow down." He pressed a palm to my forearm, the gesture sending tingling heat up to my shoulder and beyond. "Does this man figure into your brother's case?"

I forced myself to focus. "Brady sneaked into Uncle Cornelius's room that night to replace a set of plans he'd pilfered, plans outlining a secret buyout of a New England railroad line. Jack Parsons is a member of the board of directors of the line, so he stands to lose a good bit of money. You see, the line has been losing money and the stocks are down, so the company will sell at a sharp loss instead of a profit. Not only that, but Uncle Cornelius was predicting corruption on the part of the board is going to come to light. According to Brady, the line has lost money more due to skimming off the top than to flagging business."

Derrick looked skeptical. "And you believe that's a motive for Parsons to have murdered Alvin Goddard? Why not Cornelius himself—"

"No one in their right mind would do away with Uncle Cornelius. That would bring the highest authorities here to investigate. But killing Mr. Goddard would halt the plans at least temporarily and give Jack time to cover his tracks."

"Hmm. Possibly." I could see by his frown that Derrick's doubts persisted, so I told him about the pocket watch with its etched *P* and about Reggie's fixed yacht tournament. Halfway through, his expression eased and he began nodding. "But we don't know for certain yet that Jack Parsons is in financial straits. Where is he staying?"

"A house on Lakeview Avenue, just off Bellevue."

"Big house? Servants?"

"Not quite a mansion, not by The Breakers' standards, but big enough. He's got a butler and a cook, a maid as well, I would think."

"So how would he be affording all that if he's got money troubles?"

I eyed him askance. "Credit, of course. He wouldn't be the first to pretend his pockets are deeper than they are."

His hand, still resting on my arm, slid lower until his fingers curled around mine and sent my thoughts for a whirl. He, however, seemed as sharp as ever. "Before we get ahead of ourselves, let me see what I can find out about Mr. John Benjamin Parsons, or Jack as you call him."

He was still holding my hand, his thumb absently tracing

circles around my first knuckle . . . and tying my insides in not altogether unpleasant knots. I tried to focus, but it wasn't easy. "What if you can't find the information? It can't be easy to snoop into a man's finances."

"I'm a reporter, aren't I?" He grinned.

"Seems a tall order for even the most seasoned investigative reporter." A sense I'd had before about this man returned to nudge my curiosity. "My guess is you have a source somewhere within the Four Hundred."

"I might." He regarded me a long moment, his gaze heating my skin, bringing a burn to my cheeks. "But a good reporter never reveals his sources."

He released my hand and slapped his knees in preparation of rising, but hesitated. "Will you do something for me in exchange?"

"That is our bargain," I reminded him.

"I'd like you to visit with Adelaide Halstock and try to get her to confide in you about this affair she might or might not be having. Don't be obvious, just be a good listener. And maybe bring up this Jack Parsons, since you know him, too, and see how she reacts. . . ."

I cleared my throat. "Perhaps you don't know this, but I'm something of a reporter myself, for the Newport *Observer.* I think I know how to coax information out of people."

"I don't doubt that you do, Emma Cross."

"Emma, what an absolutely lovely surprise. To what do I owe the pleasure?"

I stood in the entry hall of Redwing Cottage, gazing up at Adelaide where she stopped on the staircase's half landing. Framed by the stained-glass window behind her, she looked like an angel with streams of colored sunlight filtering all around her.

After Derrick left me earlier, I changed into my prettiest

summer carriage dress, one that hadn't belonged to Aunt Sadie but that I'd splurged on in a moment of weakness the year before. The light jacket and matching flowing skirt were of a soft green moiré dotted with bright yellow and purple flowers, and made me feel young and vibrant and ... well ... part of the happy, carefree summer Newport society.

I'd had many moments of remorse after purchasing that carriage ensemble, but today I knew it suited my purposes perfectly. I'd paired it with a smart little chapeau adorned with silken violets, and if I'd had any doubts about my appearance, Adelaide's obvious delight smoothed them away.

She came rushing down the stairs to wrap her arms around me, then pulled back and held my hands. "And how ravishing you look, my dear. I can't remember ever seeing you look prettier."

"Thank you, Adelaide. I came by to see if you'd like to spend the afternoon shopping and driving around town. Just the two of us. Can you get away?"

Her eyes darted about the hall as if she were checking for eavesdroppers. Leaning closer, she smiled and whispered, "I believe I can. Just give me a few minutes, yes?"

"Take all the time you need," I said, but hoped she wouldn't.

"Make yourself comfortable, do." She practically skipped back up the stairs, reappearing quicker than I would have given her credit for. I might have known her own carriage outfit would outshine my own, being of the very latest Parisian fashion, but that wasn't what mattered. What did matter was that I'd have Adelaide's full attention for the better part of the day.

"We'll take my carriage and have Henderson drive us," she said decisively, nearly causing me to trip over my own feet. The last thing I needed was someone listening in on our conversations.

I recovered quickly. "No, Adelaide, driving is half the fun.

We'll be so much more independent that way. We'll go in my carriage."

"I hadn't thought of it that way. I do believe you're right. Oh, how exciting." She wrapped a white-gloved hand around my wrist. "Thank you, Emma. Thank you so very much."

Her earnestness squeezed a pang of guilt around my heart. "For what?"

"For being my friend." Her eyes darted away and then back. "I don't have very many nowadays."

My throat tightened and I almost dropped my plan then and there. But I rallied my determination for Brady's sake and smiled back at her. "Let's be off."

Her spirits remained high as we drove along the ocean and into town. We talked of fashions and upcoming parties, and the newest mansion going in along Bellevue Avenue. She told me about her Fifth Avenue mansion, thus providing me with my first opportunity to begin subtly questioning her.

"Did your things arrive there safely?"

"Things?" She looked at me blankly.

"You know, the items you moved out of Redwing Cottage. Remember, the Manuel brothers were loading their freight wagon that first day I came to visit."

"Oh . . . those things. Uh . . . yes, I suppose they've all been moved into the New York house by now."

"Why the spinet, though?" I pressed, even as my conscience nudged. "I couldn't help noticing you don't have another instrument at Redwing Cottage. And your husband seemed so attached to it."

She studied her clasped hands, and I felt like a scoundrel because I knew very well the spinet hadn't been moved to her New York home. "That spinet holds particular memories for Rupert. It belonged to his first wife, you see, and I thought perhaps by moving it . . ."

Obviously Adelaide was sticking to her original story and

wasn't going to confess to any financial difficulties, at least not now. I held both reins in my right hand and with my left I patted her forearm. "Never mind. I didn't mean to pry. Forgive me."

She cheered up after that and we returned to lighter matters. Until, that is, Adelaide noticed me urging Barney through town and toward the Point.

"Where on earth are we going?"

I put on a carefree grin. "I thought it might be fun if you and I visited the old neighborhood."

"Oh." Her nose crinkled. "Must we?"

"Surely the place where we were children together holds some good memories for you, Adelaide."

"I suppose . . . Though I'll confess the times you invited me to play with your cousins up at The Breakers are happier memories. Oh, such fun that was."

"And look at you now." I passed an admiring gaze over her. "Now you're living in your own mansion—or mansions, I should say."

"Yes, I am, aren't I?" she agreed with no particular enthusiasm.

As we turned onto Third Street she stiffened beside me. I brought Barney to a slow walk and began pointing out where neighboring families had lived, and mentioning which were still there and which had moved away. We approached the blue saltbox.

"That's a lovely house," I mused aloud. "I always did like it. Didn't Kenneth and Emily Daniels live there?"

"The twins?" Adelaide asked absently.

"Yes, I'd forgotten they were twins. They really didn't look much alike, did they? Was that where they lived?"

"I think it was," she replied after a hesitation.

"It was always a little rundown in the old days, but it certainly looks well taken care of now. I wonder who owns it. . . ."

Adelaide shrugged.

"Does Mr. Halstock own any of these houses?" I asked, and watched her flinch.

"Why do you ask that?"

"Oh, I believe quite a few were bought up as investments, so I just wondered. Anyway, here's Walnut Street coming up."

Adelaide's enthusiasm continued to wane as we paused in front of our former homes. I could barely coax a word out of her, so I concluded our tour quickly and headed back into town. We parked the carriage along Spring Street and proceeded on foot. Or rather, I followed Adelaide about as shop windows beckoned to her. I didn't comment on the fact that, despite her *oohs* and *aahs,* she never strayed inside to make any purchases. I knew the reason.

And then I saw my intended destination: Lily's Tea Emporium—the very same tea shop where Grace Wilson and I had had our intimate chat. I hadn't brought Adelaide to the Point expecting the sight of the blue saltbox to prompt a confession about her affair with Jack. I'd brought her there to evoke a mood, to plunge her into a melancholy state of mind where later, amid the comfortable surroundings of floral chintzes, sweet, steamy teas, and warm, luscious pastries, she might feel inclined to confide.

In me, apparently her only friend.

Guilt clutched at my heart with full-out spiky claws, but I'd promised Derrick I'd try, and I owed it to him—

No. What was I thinking? I owed it to Brady, my brother sitting at that very moment in a jail cell for a crime he didn't commit. And if Derrick would help Brady in exchange for information about Adelaide, then yes, I'd shove my conscience aside.

A few of the tables were occupied; women looked up as we entered the shop, eyed us up and down as they undoubtedly assessed our attire, and returned to their quiet conversations. The hostess brought us to a corner table, flanked on one side by a shelf holding porcelain figurines and on the other by a painted

Oriental screen that concealed the doorway into the kitchen. Away from the front windows, the table sat swathed in comfortable shadows that danced subtly in the glow of the single candle at the center of the table. The location afforded us exactly the privacy I'd hoped for.

"This place is charming," Adelaide said as she placed her embroidered purse on the table beside her. She looked happy again . . . relieved. "I can't believe I've never been here."

"It's popular with locals and with the more modest of our summer visitors, but not a place Aunt Alice and her society friends would tend to patronize."

"No, our sort are consigned to places like the Casino or the country club. And teahouses and private gardens, of course." Adelaide sighed. "It's taxing sometimes, the unspoken rules the wealthy must live by."

"It is what you always wanted, Adelaide," I reminded her gently.

Her reply was quiet, wistful. "I thought it was . . . once."

"And now?"

"Now . . . nothing turned out as I thought it would."

Pushing the candle aside, I reached across the small table and placed a hand over hers. "I'm sorry you're not happy," I said with sincerity.

"Oh, Emma, I don't deserve anyone's sympathy, least of all yours. I wasn't . . ." Her breath trembled in her throat. "I wasn't always the nicest or most loyal of friends, was I?"

"Children are children," I answered lightly, moving my hand away but leaning closer to her over the table. "We had our differences at times, certainly, but we're friends now, and you can confide in me . . . if you ever wish to."

Those words prompted me to grit my teeth and look away. True, Adelaide hadn't always been the warmest of friends. She'd been a rather selfish, vain child, one who'd resented her family's lack of resources, their loss of a once-significant fortune made in the hotel business. And she'd made it no secret that she resented my connection to one of America's wealthiest clans. Sometimes I'd had the feeling she only tolerated me for the occasional invitations to visit my cousins.

But we were adults now, and it was me being disloyal, deceptive, and taking advantage of our friendship for selfish purposes. I wasn't proud of it.

"I've been so lonely, Emma," she suddenly said. "More lonely than you can imagine."

I didn't say anything; I barely breathed, waiting for her to continue.

"At first Rupert doted on me. He was kind and patient, rather like having a second father. But from the first his sister, Suzanne, hated me. She suspected me of being a gold digger—and I suppose she was right. But I'd fully intended being a good wife to Rupert. I never meant him harm."

"Of course not," I quickly agreed.

"But then the society dragons closed forces against me. Invitations never arrived for society teas or ladies' club meetings. Even events where Rupert and I were invited as a couple became fewer and farther between. I believe it got Rupert rethinking our position in society . . . resenting me possibly."

"Oh, Adelaide, you don't really think so."

"I do, Emma. I believe he began to regret marrying me. He became colder, began avoiding me. I began to fear . . ."

"Yes?"

"That Rupert might divorce me."

"No!"

Adelaide nodded vigorously. "Yes, I truly believe he would have. And, oh, Emma, I didn't want a divorce. The shame of it. Why, I'd be more of a social pariah than I already am."

Pausing, she opened her purse, pulled out a handkerchief, and dabbed at her eyes. "And then when he became ill, Rupert literally pushed me away in favor of old memories of his first wife. I've been alone ever since, Emma. I might as well be divorced. I'm all alone in those big, echoing houses, with no friends to speak of. Well, until you came along, that is. And until . . ."

She trailed off and compressed her lips. A torrent of red flooded her face.

"Are you all right?" I reached across the table again.

Before she could answer, the waitress came with our tea and platter of tiny sandwiches. I pulled my hand back, and Adelaide stared down at her lap while plates, cups, and saucers were set before us. The last word she spoke echoed in my ears: *until.* Until what—or who—had come along like I had? Had she been about to confide about her affair? Impatiently I willed the waitress away.

When she finally left us, Adelaide let out a mirthless chuckle. "I don't feel so hungry anymore." Her eyes glimmered in the candlelight. "Poor Emma, you wanted an afternoon of fun and I've spoiled everything."

"You haven't spoiled anything. I wanted an afternoon with my friend, and that is exactly what I have. You can speak freely with me, Adelaide." My conscience struck with particular fierceness at that, for I knew if she confessed anything incriminating, I'd promised to share the information with Derrick.

But she didn't. After sipping her tea, she picked up a chopped salmon sandwich and nibbled. "Hmm . . . good. Try one, Emma. This reminds me of the delightful little meals Mason used to bring us when we played at The Breakers' playhouse."

Her lack of appetite forgotten, Adelaide tucked into our repast with enthusiasm, and I learned nothing more about her current troubles.

Chapter 15

That night, I sprang upright from my pillows, instantly awake. Reggie's words from the other day, child's play, coupled with Adelaide's innocent observation at the tea shop yesterday, echoed in my ears while an image flashed in my mind's eye.

The playhouse—where my cousins and I had enjoyed countless games of make believe when we were children. Good heavens, I'd stood on the porch a day ago and hadn't even thought to go inside. . . .

We *always hide our treasures in the playhouse; no one ever thinks to look there. . . .*

So had Gertrude confided in me so many years ago. Two loose flagstones, a hole hollowed out beneath. It was the one secret the Vanderbilt children shared that none of them had ever betrayed to the adults. At least not as far as I knew. As young children we'd stashed shells and stones gathered at the beach to keep the governess from tossing them away. Gertrude had once secreted a stack of letters from a beau there to guard against her mother finding them. I had hidden my earliest efforts at article writing. If any of my cousins had ever read them, they'd never let on, and I'd always believed they respected the sanctity of our shared cache.

Did any of them even remember about it now? Did they still hide things away? I wondered about the bottle I'd caught Reggie drinking in the playhouse. What else might he . . . or Neily . . . have concealed beneath the floor near the big stone fireplace? The candlestick found near Brady could not have killed Alvin Goddard . . . at least, it could not have caused that dent beside the balcony door in Uncle Cornelius's room. So what had, and where was it?

Didn't it make sense that the guilty party would have wanted a convenient place to hide his weapon? The cliff was too far a walk across the back lawns; he might have been seen. But the playhouse sat at the front of the property, along the service drive halfway between the house and Ochre Point Avenue. And that night, both the main and the service driveways had been lined with posh vehicles. No one would have thought twice about someone strolling in the direction of the playhouse.

It crossed my mind that Theodore Mason might very well know about our hiding place, for there was little the man hadn't known or suspected about us children. For the most part, he never betrayed us to the adults as long as we hadn't been about to hurt ourselves.

But, yes, Mr. Mason might also know about the hole beneath the flagstones.

Tomorrow, I vowed as I stretched out and rested my cheek against my pillow. Tomorrow first thing, I would return to The Breakers and see what, if anything, lay hidden beneath the playhouse floor.

As it turned out, I didn't go anywhere first thing in the morning.

"He's nearly broke, Emma," Derrick Anderson said without

preamble when we stepped beyond the kitchen garden and approached the dampened edges of my property.

He'd arrived just as I'd finished breakfast, causing a good deal of eyebrow raising and lip pursing from Nanny when Katie announced him. I ignored Nanny's pointed stares, met Derrick in the parlor, and promptly ushered him through the house and out the kitchen door. After his last visit here I hesitated to be alone with him in the privacy of a closed room. Derrick Anderson . . . did things to me . . . distracting things . . . things I might come to regret. I wanted open air and the vastness of the ocean surrounding us; maybe then that compelling energy of his wouldn't seem so overwhelming.

We reached the boulders that separated my yard from the Atlantic Ocean and halted. "Jack is nearly destitute?" I asked, not because there was any question in my mind as to whom he referred, but to give myself time to think. Jack broke and possibly involved in the corrupt business practices that had been driving the New Haven-Hartford-Providence line into bankruptcy—could it be true?

"But that doesn't make sense," I said with a burst of hope. "How can he be nearly out of money, yet have been skimming off the railroad's finances?"

"His bank accounts are so empty, they're all but echoing, and he's sold off a good deal of stock lately. As to where the money might be . . ." Derrick was silent a moment, staring out at the tossing waves. "Either he's damn bad at finance or he's got a stash hidden away somewhere, probably in the hopes of fooling his creditors into thinking he's a stone."

"A stone?"

"As in 'you can't make a stone bleed.' " When I continued to stare at him blankly, he clarified, "They can't squeeze payments out of someone with no money to give."

"Oh." I gathered my skirts and perched on the flattest boulder, my *thinking rock* as I liked to call it. Drops of ocean spray splattered my dress, but I didn't care. I drew my legs up and hugged them, and let my chin fall to my knees. Jack was in financial trouble. He was connected to the New Haven-Hartford-Providence line. And he might very well be the owner of the pocket watch I'd found in Uncle Cornelius's safe.

My stomach churned, and my heart ached.

I felt rather than saw Derrick arrange himself beside me, not quite touching but somehow imbuing my limbs with the steadiness of his own. "It doesn't mean he's guilty, Emma. We need more information."

"But he might be." I swallowed around the lump in my throat. "He certainly had a motive, just as much as Brady did. And . . ." I swung my head upward. "Oh, Derrick, his affair with Adelaide. Do you think he initiated it to try to coax money out of her?"

"Are we sure they're even having an affair? Have you spoken with her?"

"We had tea yesterday. She didn't come right out and say it, but at one point she told me she believed her husband had decided to divorce her before he became ill. She said she'd felt all alone until I came into her life, and until . . . until something else happened, but she never said what. But she could have meant her affair with Jack."

"That might be stretching things. She thinks Halstock was going to divorce her?" It wasn't a question so much as Derrick thinking aloud and processing the information. His forehead pulled into a tight frown and he reached over, absently tracing a pattern of moist splotches on the hems pooled around my feet. "If he did, I have no doubt she'd have been left virtually penniless. Men like Halstock protect their fortunes. It's unlikely he'd have been willing to give her much of a settlement, especially after only a year of marriage. I don't suppose your friend would have liked that very much."

Sudden anger rose up and I tugged my skirt out from beneath his trailing finger. "Now you sound like Mr. Halstock's sister, Suzanne. I'll have you know Adelaide is more than some greedy monster looking to cheat an old man out of his fortune. Much more. That sort of judgment is unfair and I won't tolerate it, not here in my home."

I swung my feet around and, placing them on the grass, stood up to make my way back to the house. Derrick stood and caught me by the wrist, stopping me, and as he gently turned me back around I'd already begun to wonder why I'd taken him to task like that. Hadn't I suspected Adelaide of un-praiseworthy motives not all that long ago?

"I'm sorry," we both said at once. Then we both let out a nervous laugh and looked away self-consciously. And then looked back, our gazes meeting, and for a time that might have been seconds or several long minutes, we stared at each other, that strange energy of his coursing around and through me until my insides heated. Derrick's hand slid downward and our fingers twined. The next thing I knew, he tugged me closer. We stood toe-to-toe, our bodies touching, mine trembling, his steady and hard against me. He dipped his head; I tilted mine upward, and the next moments were a blur of sensation as the ocean and my own heart roared in my ears.

The kiss ended with the curving of Derrick's lips against my own; his smile persisted as he raised his face and looked down at me. "Sorry. Again."

"I'm not," I whispered, but I stepped away. He didn't try to pursue me, but let me open a respectful distance between us. Unspoken words hung in the salt-laden air. Now was not a time for ourselves or for each other; we had too many important things left to do.

"I have some errands to run back in town," he said, suddenly all business. "If you need me, call my hotel and leave a message. It's the Atlantic House on Pelham. I check in periodically. For now, stay away from Jack Parsons."

I nodded, not entirely trusting my voice.

*   *   *

As soon as Derrick left me, I hurried to change into my carriage jacket. Katie harnessed Barney to the buggy, and as I readied to leave I pondered why I hadn't told Derrick about my intended trip this morning. Was it because I didn't expect to find anything, and because searching an old childhood hidey hole seemed ridiculously far-fetched? It might have been, but I intended to leave no stone unturned—literally.

Some ten minutes later I approached The Breakers' main gates. They already stood open, and a carriage came barreling out from the drive. As it veered onto Ochre Point Avenue it nearly rose onto its two right wheels and kept going, without so much as pausing to see if there might be other carriages traveling the road. If I'd come along a minute or two earlier, he might have broadsided me.

Shipley, the gatekeeper, swore under his breath and watched the vehicle recede—a vehicle that bore a leasing number on its rear bumper. The flash of blond hair I'd seen from beneath a black derby left me gaping as well.

I proceeded to the gate and brought Barney to a halt. "Was that Mr. Parsons?" I asked the servant.

"It was, Miss Emmaline. Don't know what's got into him. Seemed calm enough when he arrived a little while ago."

"How strange." Ignoring a warning sensation at the nape of my neck, I drove on toward the house, but I didn't go inside. Instead, I turned down the service drive and stopped in front of the children's playhouse. The door was closed, but I found it unlocked as it usually was.

I pushed it open. "Anyone here?"
Silence.
Cautiously, I stepped inside. "Hello?"
Not a sound came in response. I closed the door behind me.
A gasp spilled through my lips. I'd been right. There had been something hidden beneath the floor, and Jack hadn't even attempted to cover his tracks; the flagstones had been hastily

shoved back into their approximate places, but where they met their edges overlapped and protruded from the surrounding tiles. I bent and dragged them aside, and my stomach fell. The hidey hole lay empty.

My first thought was to take off after Jack, but I didn't want to be overhasty and go running off blindly. I returned to the main house, where I found my uncle lounging in his smoking room.

"Just a social call," Cornelius replied to my query about what Jack had been doing there. Jack hadn't sneaked onto the property, but had come on the pretense of visiting. Uncle Cornelius studied me from over the book he'd been reading. "Invited me to tennis tomorrow. Nice fellow, that Jack Parsons."

"And he didn't mention anything else? Any other business here?"

"Didn't have time to. Didn't stay but a few minutes. Wouldn't even sit down and have a brandy."

"He was in a hurry," I said, more to myself than Uncle Cornelius. He only shrugged. "Sorry to bother you, Uncle Cornelius. Oh," I added suddenly, "is Reggie at home?"

"Of course he's home. Somewhere. Keeps to himself quite a bit these days. Quite the brooder, that boy is. It's a stage I'll be glad to see him grow out of." His eyes returned to his book.

A warning sat at the tip of my tongue that Reggie's *phase* might not be grown out of but could dog him the rest of his life if his family didn't pay attention and straighten him out. But now wasn't the time. I needed to find out if indeed Jack had gone into the playhouse and taken—what? And why? Was he protecting someone? I'd asked about Reggie because it had suddenly occurred to me that if Jack had tried to protect my cousin from falling into an illegal gambling scheme, he might also be trying to protect him from something far worse.

And right that moment, Jack could be disposing of evidence—against Reggie . . . against himself . . . against Neily . . .

or even Mr. Mason. What would he do with it? Throw it into the ocean? But, no, he couldn't risk being seen, and in Newport on a summer's day, that risk loomed all too large.

The Point. He could hide whatever it was in his little blue colonial and toss it into the harbor tonight, with the darkness and the inevitable mist to conceal him.

I headed down Bellevue Avenue toward town before coming to a halt and turning Barney in an abrupt half circle that headed us back toward home. What was I going to do—track down Jack and force him to answer my questions? When he might have the murder weapon in his possession? If he was the murderer, chances were good he was the person who had attacked me the other night. I'd foolishly placed myself in danger twice and didn't need to be warned a third time. No, what I needed were reinforcements.

Barney achieved a brisk trot along Ocean Avenue, and when we reached the end of my drive I practically jumped down from the buggy before it had rolled to a stop. I raced inside and headed straight for the telephone.

"Gayla," I brusquely greeted the operator when she came on the line, "connect me with the Atlantic House Hotel. Please."

"Sounds like an emergency," she said with no particular urgency. I distinctly heard the sound of chewing over the wire. "Everything all right, Emma?"

"Yes, Gayla, everything's fine."

"Ooh, are you booking a room for your parents? Are they in town?"

"No, Gayla, they're not. Please, I just need you to—"

"Don't get your knickers in a knot, dearie. The Atlantic House coming right up."

The concierge picked up after a few crackles and shouted in my ear. "Atlantic House Hotel. How may I help you?"

I whisked the ear trumpet away from my head before speaking much more quietly than he had and hoping he got the message that one didn't need to shout for one's voice to carry over the distance. "Is Mr. Derrick Anderson in, please?"

More crackles and pops, a buzzing sound, and then the concierge came back on the line. "Mr. Anderson does not appear to be in the hotel at present, ma'am. I don't see his key here." I once more had to jerk my head away from the earpiece. "May I take a message?"

"Um . . . yes. When he comes in, please tell him . . ." I paused, wondering how best to phrase the message without creating a scandal. For all I knew, Gayla and a dozen other people between here and town might be listening in. "Please tell him the, ah, luncheon is being held on the Point today, at the blue saltbox."

The concierge repeated the message back, his puzzlement evident in his tone. He certainly wasn't going to get an explanation from me. We disconnected and I cranked the call box again. "Gayla, it's Emma again. Would you please connect me to the police station?"

"Checking on Brady, are you?"

"Yes, Gayla. Just seeing if I can visit today."

"Well, if you do, tell him I send my best."

I tapped my foot in impatience. "I will, Gayla. Thanks."

"Hold on while I connect you."

"Newport police," a gruff voice answered next.

"Hello, this is Emma Cross. May I speak to Officer Whyte?"

"He's not here. You wanna leave a message?"

Before I could reply, footsteps thumped down the staircase over my head. I peeked around the alcove to see Nanny descend into the hallway. When she caught sight of me, an animated expression claimed her features and she began waving both hands at me.

"Is there a message?" the officer on the line repeated tersely.

"Emma!" Nanny's whisper carried through the hallway.

"I've been waiting for you." I held a finger to my lips, but that didn't deter her. "I've got news you'll want to hear. You won't believe it."

"Miss?" the officer barked in my ear.

"Er, no. No message, thank you."

The line clicked off, leaving a buzzing in my ear. I replaced the trumpet in its cradle as Nanny reached me. She grasped my elbow and spun me about to face her.

"Nanny, what on earth is wrong?"

"Come into the parlor." She seized my hand to pull me across the hall and through the doorway into the front parlor. Once there, she practically tossed me onto the sofa and then plunked down beside me, her hefty frame sending up a hiss from the down-stuffed cushions. "I found something out today and you need to hear it."

She was frightening me, but I said, "Go on."

"You know my friend Ruth, who works for Mrs. Astor . . ."

When Nanny paused, I nodded to indicate that yes, I knew Ruth. She was the housekeeper at the Beechwood estate.

"Well, Ruth was talking to Connie Lewis . . ."

When she paused again, I supplied, "Mrs. Stuyvesant Fish's head maid, right?"

"That's right. Well, Connie heard from Edith Wetmore's under butler that—"

"Nanny, please!"

"I'm getting to it," she said with wounded dignity. "I just wanted to relay my sources so you knew there was some credibility to the story."

I bit back a sigh. "Sorry. Please go on."

"The Wetmores' under butler has a brother who works for Mrs. Arnold Rockport in Providence. . . ."

"Rockport . . . Why do I know that name?" A memory nudged. I'd heard the name recently, I was sure of it.

Nanny smiled. She was obviously enjoying this. "Probably because she's Rupert Halstock's sister."

"Suzanne!" I exclaimed. "His sister in Providence. The one who refuses to acknowledge Adelaide."

"That's right. And the Wetmores' under butler's brother—he's a footman in her home—overheard some very interesting news. Seems Suzanne Rockport is so worried about her brother's health, she's hired a private detective to investigate that friend of yours."

"Yes, I know Adelaide's being investigated. Although I didn't know it was Mr. Halstock's sister who hired Der—er, the detective."

If I expected Nanny's enthusiasm to wane, she proved me thoroughly wrong. She puffed up like a pheasant in springtime. "I'll bet you didn't know this: Mrs. Rockport suspects Adelaide of intentionally making her husband ill so she can inherit his money."

"What? No, Nanny, that's not right. Mrs. Rockport suspects Adelaide of having an affair and wants to expose her to her husband. You know the Halstock family doesn't approve of the marriage."

"But don't you see, the affair itself might be what's making Rupert Halstock so ill," Nanny insisted. She used a forefinger to adjust her spectacles. "I'll bet you anything she's been leaving hints so he'd know and make himself sick with jealousy."

"That's ridiculous. What kind of plan would that be? Why, if Rupert Halstock knew his wife was having an affair, he'd simply divorce her." I didn't add that Adelaide suspected him of wanting to do so before the affair ever started. Nanny opened her mouth to protest, but I didn't give her a chance. "What's more," I said firmly, "I've been with Adelaide during one of her husband's bad days. She was utterly distraught."

"Hmm, I'll bet she was," Nanny murmured under her breath.

"And who can blame her for having an affair—if she even is," I added. After all, as Derrick had pointed out, we still didn't know for certain the nature of Adelaide's connection to Jack. Perhaps she'd only gone to him for comfort or . . . who knew.

Did I believe that? Not really. But I wasn't about to add fruit to the servants' gossip vine. I leaned to wrap a hand around Nanny's wrist and gently said, "If she is having an affair, who are we to judge? She's married to an old man, and no one in society, including his own family, will acknowledge her beyond the coldest of civilities."

Nanny's jaw squared. "She made her bed . . ."

With an earnest promise to Barney that when this was all over he'd enjoy a nice long vacation and a hefty sack of his favorite oats, I climbed back into my buggy. I'd left Nanny with explicit instructions on what to tell Derrick if he called, and to try the police station every ten minutes or so in hopes of reaching Jesse.

I headed back to Lakeview Avenue, hoping to find Jack at home, hoping I was completely wrong in my assumptions. Yes, I knew Derrick had told me to stay away from Jack; but first of all, it was broad daylight and Mr. Mason along with the other domestic staff would be at the house. Secondly, it was possible that nothing more menacing than the recollection of a previous appointment had been what sent Jack racing helter-skelter from The Breakers. In the meantime, I hoped Derrick and Jesse would receive my messages.

Turning from Ocean Avenue onto Bellevue, Nanny's revelation about the Halstocks crept into my thoughts. I'd pooh-poohed the story, but now I wondered . . . Of course it came as no surprise that the family believed Adelaide might be cuckolding her husband; Derrick had confided as much. He had neglected to add, however, that the accusations didn't stop there. Did Suzanne Rockport truly suspect Adelaide of intentionally making Rupert ill through infidelity? Was such a thing even possible?

What motive could Adelaide have? If her affair—if it was an affair—came to light, I felt certain Rupert would manage to divorce her well before the stress sent him to meet his maker. And with Adelaide at fault, she'd receive next to nothing in the proceedings.

No, it simply didn't make sense.

But it did bring me to another delay in pursuing Jack. If he did have something to hide, I needed to warn Adelaide.

When her butler opened the door, I stormed in. "I need to see Mrs. Halstock immediately."

The man blinked and stuttered in response, but stopped when Adelaide's face appeared in the curtained alcove that led to a more private region of the house.

"Emma? I'm right here, dear. What is it?" She came toward me with both hands extended and gripped mine warmly, strongly.

"We need to talk, Adelaide. I don't have long, but—"

She shushed me softly. "Come, we'll talk inside."

Leading me back through the crimson velvet curtain, we entered a large, sunny room situated with an informal table and chairs, sideboard, and hutch. The morning room.

The remnants of a solitary meal sat on the table beside a letter Adelaide had apparently been writing; a couple of platters occupied the sideboard. "Shall I ring for another plate?" she asked as she bade me take a seat. She moved to the corner and hovered beside the bell pull.

I shook my head. "No, thank you, there isn't time. I need to tell you something. Something that will no doubt shock you."

"My dear, what is it? My goodness, you're in quite a state, aren't you?" Sitting in the seat beside my own, she leaned to press her palm to my cheek. "You look pale. Are you ill?"

"No, Adelaide, please listen. It's about Jack." I'd lowered my voice as I made that second statement. Her eyes widened and her hand fell to the table. "It's all right," I assured her quickly. "I'm not here to judge and I couldn't give a fig what the Halstocks or anyone else thinks about you. But Jack ... he's ... or ... he might be ... "

Adelaide sat stiffly, her head making little side-to-side jerky motions, as if she already knew what I might say but didn't wish to hear it. But she couldn't know, could she? I'd shocked her badly by blurting Jack's name, but I hadn't time for niceties. I looked away to give her a moment to collect herself and my eyes fell on the half-written letter across the table. The stationary bore Adelaide's initials across the top in bold, swooping letters. Something about the monogram seized my attention for a fraction of an instant, before I shook it away as irrelevant.

Drawing a deep breath, I turned back to my friend and covered her hand with my own. "Adelaide, I have reason to believe Jack might be the man I've been looking for." Good heavens, even now I found it almost impossible to speak the truth aloud. But what other choice did I have if I wanted to keep my friend safe? I steeled my resolve and gave her fingers a squeeze. "I think Jack Parsons might have murdered Alvin Goddard."

Her gasp pierced me through. She whisked her hand out from beneath mine and lurched to her feet. Her knees hit the back of her chair, sending it toppling with a bang that further rattled my nerves.

She stared wildly back at me. "How can you say such a thing?"

I came to my feet. "Adelaide, please listen to me. You know I'd never accuse an old family friend lightly. It's not easy to explain, but I arrived at The Breakers today just as Jack sped away from the property and ... do you remember the hidey hole Neily made in the playhouse floor, where we used to secret all manner of things?"

Her expression clouded, became confused. "I don't think I do. . . ."

"Well, never mind. Just please promise me you'll stay away

from Jack for now, until I say otherwise. Promise me, Adelaide."

"Yes." She nodded, that vague, confused look persisting, almost as if she'd gone into some kind of trance. One of shock, of course. "I'll wait till I hear from you, but..." Her lovely eyes cleared. "Emma, I know you're wrong."

"I hope so." I turned and walked toward the doorway.

She called me back. "Emma."

"Yes?"

"I..." She looked down at the floor. "Please understand. Jack and I..."

I returned to her long enough to set a hand on her shoulder. "I told you, I'm not here to judge."

Some three or four minutes later, I turned onto Jack's rented property. Even before I approached the front door I could sense the emptiness of the house, the utter lack of life inside. An eerie sense of abandonment crept over me, sending goose bumps down my back.

I tapped the knocker twice against its brass plate. Moments later the door opened and a maid leaned out. "Yes?"

"I'm Emma Cross, here to see Mr. Parsons. Is he at home?"

Her answer didn't surprise me, however much I'd hoped for another. "No, ma'am. He left about ten minutes ago and I'm afraid I don't know when he's expected back."

Ten minutes. I wanted to berate myself for wasting precious time in coming after him.

"Did you happen to notice if he was carrying..." How could I ask if I didn't know exactly what I was looking for? "A package of any sort?"

"A package? No, ma'am. Odd, though. He was carrying a valise but didn't say if he'd be home tonight or not."

I just managed not to gasp. He'd rushed home for something to put the murder weapon in.

"Thank you." I turned to go, but something occurred to me. "Excuse me another moment." I gripped the edge of the door before she could close it. "But why are you opening the door? Isn't Mr. Mason here?"

"No, ma'am, he's not here either. He left with Mr. Parsons."

Once more she started to close the door, and once more I stopped her. "Is there a telephone in the house?"

"Why, yes, ma'am, two. One in the kitchen and one upstairs."

"May I use the one in the kitchen, please? It's an emergency."

She hesitated only long enough to peruse me up and down, conclude that I appeared neither insane nor dangerous, and gestured me inside with a curtsy. "It's this way, ma'am," she said, leading me across the entry hall and down a corridor that led to the back of the house.

Moments later, Gayla, disgruntled that I cut her pleasantries abruptly short, connected me with the police station. Upon being told yet again that Jesse wasn't in, I gritted my teeth and admitted I no longer had any other choice.

"May I speak to Officer Dobbs, then?"

"Hold on." I heard the rub of a palm being held to the mouthpiece and then a shout of, "Hey, Tony. There's a dame here wants to talk to you."

"Yeah," a gruff voice said next.

I steeled myself to continue. Unlike Jesse Whyte, Officer Anthony Dobbs was no friend of mine or of Brady's. I shuddered to count how many times Dobbs had taken discreet slaps and punches at my brother when Brady had been apprehended for drunken and disorderly conduct, and I couldn't help but remember how eager Dobbs had been to condemn Brady for Alvin Goddard's murder.

But Anthony Dobbs knew who I was, and more importantly who my relatives were, and he didn't dare snub me. Besides, I reminded myself, as hardheaded and arrogant as he might be, he had a reputation for being an honest if rough-hewn policeman.

"Officer Dobbs," I said decisively, "this is Emma Cross. I have good reason to believe Alvin Goddard's murderer is on his way to the Point. He's probably there already, as a matter of fact, and I need you and your men to apprehend him."

"Now, Miss Cross . . ." I heard a barely restrained chuckle. "You know good and well where Alvin Goddard's murderer is, and it's not on the Point. He's in a cell in this very building."

I tightened my grip on the ear trumpet and wrapped my other hand around the mouthpiece for good measure. "You listen to me, Tony Dobbs. You've had it in for my brother for years, but even a bully like you can't want to send an innocent man to the gallows. Now, I have reason to believe Jack Parsons retrieved the murder weapon from The Breakers less than twenty minutes ago. He owns a small house on Third Street between Poplar and Walnut, a blue clapboard saltbox, and I believe that's where he was headed. It's where I'm headed now, and where I dearly hope you'll be headed in the next few minutes."

His words of protest died as I closed the call.

Vehicles clogged Third Street when I arrived, and a warning gripped my nape. Police mounts and wagons lined the street, forcing me to leave Barney and the buggy half in the middle of the road. I jumped down to the ground and proceeded on foot. That warning pinched at the sight of several officers striding in and out of Jack's open front door.

Good heavens, had they apprehended him so quickly? Had I been right?

I was almost to the front step when a hand seized my arm from behind. "Emma. Don't go in there."

I turned to see Derrick Anderson's dark eyes filled with concern . . . and something more. "Did Jack put up a huge fuss? Did they have to restrain him?"

That something more defined itself as regret and reluctance as Derrick slowly shook his head. "We all arrived too late. . . ."

"So you got my message."

He nodded, but repeated, "Too late, I'm afraid."

"I don't understand." I tried to tug free. "I want to go inside, Derrick. I have a right to confront him after what he's done. Brady . . . Mr. Goddard . . ."

He wouldn't release me, his hold stubbornly firm. Then he drew me closer. "He's gone, Emma." Seeing my puzzlement, he clarified his meaning. "He'd dead. When I arrived, the door was ajar and Jack Parsons lay dead on his parlor floor, a bullet through his chest."

Chapter 16

Derrick's grip on my arm relaxed. I suppose he thought the shock would immobilize me, but, in fact, it had the exact opposite reaction. Surprising him by whisking free, I hefted my skirts and bulldozed my way past the swarm of police officers and into the house. Vaguely I heard my name being called; from the corner of my eye I saw Jesse beckoning, but I didn't pause to acknowledge him. My boots clattered loudly on the wide floorboards of the tiny front hall, their echoes clashing with my pounding heartbeat.

Through the parlor doorway, I saw his feet first, toes pointing upward, the tips of his ankle boots reflecting the glow of the many gaslights burning around the room. The heat of all those lamps struck my cheeks and burned my eyes. Or were those tears swimming in my vision and rendering that familiar, handsome face watery and indistinct, as though he floated beneath several inches of water?

"Back away . . . give her a moment."

Jesse's quiet order scattered the handful of officials who had been leaning over the body and examining the room. I fell to my knees beside that silent, too-still form, one hand braced on the floor to support my weight while with the other I swept a shock of bright, golden hair off his brow. A brow still so smooth and youthful for a man in his forties. . . .

"Oh, Jack . . . I'm so sorry." I was sorry for not trusting him, sorry to have played at being a detective. I had thought to save Brady, and all too willingly I would have condemned an innocent man based on . . . what? The fancies of my faulty imagination, fueled, obviously, by pseudo-evidence I was all too eager to credit. Obviously Jack had done no wrong and the killer was still out there.

It struck me a stinging blow that in his final moments, Jack had known who the killer was, and must have confronted him with whatever weapon or evidence he'd found secreted in our playhouse hidey hole. I trembled to consider the terror Jack had faced in those moments, how he might have struggled, wishing he could convey what he knew. . . .

And then I felt it—moisture seeping through the rug and into my palm, enveloping my fingers as they sank into the woven pile of the floral design. I lifted my hand, and the sight of the blood, clotting and matted with rug lint, made my stomach pitch.

His suit coat was closed but not buttoned, I now realized. One of the authorities must have discreetly covered him when I barreled in. Instinct urged me to look away, to stand up and let the police get on with their work. I couldn't. If Jack had confronted the murderer, then I owed it to him, to my father, and to Brady, to know exactly what happened to him.

From somewhere behind me someone had pressed a dish towel into my bloodied hand. Dully I used it to wipe away the mess, or most of it, because try as I might, I couldn't erase the rusty traces staining my fingers and caking in the creases of my palm. Would I ever erase those stains? Maybe not.

Still, I set the rag aside and reached for the placket of Jack's coat.

"Emma, don't," I heard from behind me, and realized it was Derrick, down on his haunches, hovering close.

I shook my head and opened Jack's coat. At first what appeared to be a giant, vibrant rose blossom formed in my gaze—nothing sinister, just a rose! But, no, that couldn't be right, and as I stared the *petals* rearranged themselves into angry blotches and splatters, with a vicious entry wound torn at its center.

Quickly I replaced the edges of his coat and turned away . . . to be caught up in Derrick Anderson's arms.

"Emma, how could any of this be your fault? You need to listen to reason."

Derrick and I sat at the little round table in the cramped kitchen at the back of Jack's house. Cups of tea steamed before us, yet neither of us did much drinking. I hunched with my head in my hands while Derrick alternated between rubbing my back and slipping his arm around my shoulders and hugging me close.

His firm touch came as a great comfort to me, which only heightened the guilt coursing through me. How could I possibly be enjoying a man's embrace when my family's dearest friend lay dead only two rooms away?

"But don't you see," I said without much feeling, "if I hadn't been running around asking questions, Jack wouldn't have gotten involved, and he wouldn't be dead. . . ."

"Nonsense. We don't even know for sure yet that Jack's death is related to Alvin Goddard's—"

"Oh, don't be obtuse. Of course it's related. Coincidences like this don't happen in a town like Newport. Everything here is connected." My chin sank to the table. "Why didn't I leave it all to the police?"

That last came out as nearly a wail, and Derrick's arm went around me again. Softly he shushed and soothed me, or tried to, with whispered words against my ear. His large palm rubbed up and down my arm, and our sides pressed together as he shuffled his chair closer to mine.

"And what's worst of all, Derrick, is that I suspected him. That's why I called you today. I was certain Jack was a murderer. Instead . . ." It was then I saw the bloodstains smeared across the folds of my skirt. Jack's blood. A man who had been as much an uncle to me as Cornelius Vanderbilt. "Oh . . . Jack!"

I hadn't wanted to cry. I hadn't thought I deserved to cry. I deserved to suffer my guilt and endure the ache in my heart for as long as it lasted. But as Derrick pressed my face to his neck, I cried and cried, soaking his shirt collar, until a small portion of my pain receded. In the circle of those sturdy arms, I began to feel safer, stronger, more myself.

I lifted my face, no doubt blotchy and swollen, and instantly found a handkerchief pressed into my palm. "It's clean," Derrick whispered.

I used it to dab at my eyes. "I'm so sorry—" I tried to apologize, but as I glanced up I found Derrick's face disconcertingly close to my own. His lips touched mine, and any thoughts I might have expressed flew straight out of my head.

The kiss started gently, as this morning's kiss had: a cool brush of his lips across mine. He pulled away slightly and our cheeks touched; the surprising softness of his skin felt heavenly against my own. Deeply I inhaled his scent—shaving soap and starch and a clean, outdoorsy essence. He pressed his lips to mine again, and I tasted coffee and mint and a dark promise of excitement, of a passion I could only partly understand.

But as gently as he'd begun, he ended the kiss, pulled an inch or two away, and rubbed his nose across mine. "I like you, Emma Cross."

My stomach tightened and my heart flipped into my throat. Before I could respond, or even decide how I wanted to respond, there came a throat clearing and a shuffling of feet in the kitchen doorway.

Good heavens, how long had Jesse been standing there? I blushed to the roots of my hair, but Derrick only sat back in his chair and cast an even gaze at the other man. "Do you need something, Officer Whyte?"

Jesse nodded and stepped into the room. "I hate to do this to you, Emma, but I need to ask you some questions. Do you feel up to it?"

I swiped away a remaining tear or two and clutched my trembling hands together. "Of course, Jesse." I gestured for him to sit at the table with us. He took a seat opposite me, taking out a writing tablet and pencil.

"When was the last time you saw Jack?"

"This morning, at The Breakers. I'd gone to—" I stopped and shook my head to clear it. "Jesse, this is a bit of a long story."

"Tell me everything, from the beginning."

And so I retraced my steps for Jesse—the questions I'd asked, the theories I'd formed, the suspects I'd accumulated. With each revelation his frown deepened. He had told me from the first to leave the investigation to the police, and now he knew his warnings had fallen on deaf ears. Though I found myself unable to look him in the eye as I continued my story, I gleaned unexpected courage from the large hand holding my own beneath the table.

"And then I remembered what Reggie said about murder investigations not being child's play—"

"He was right," Jesse interrupted pointedly.

"Yes, well, that was when it occurred to me to check the playhouse at The Breakers. You see, when my cousins and I were children, we used to hide things under the floor. Neily made the hole beneath the flagstones and I thought anyone needing a convenient hiding place the night of the ball might go there, because with all the carriages parked on the front property no one would notice and . . ."

Jesse had been scribbling madly in his tablet. Now he stopped and held the pencil up. "Slow down, Emma. Who knew about this hiding place?"

"All the children, of course. Neily, Gertrude, Reggie . . ."

"So you and your cousins. Anyone else?"

"I suspect Mr. Mason might have known as well. He always seemed to have a sixth sense when it came to us children and—" I gasped and my eyes opened wide.

"Emma? What's wrong?" Jesse asked at the same time Derrick tightened his hold on my hand and leaned closer.

"Mr. Mason. Good Lord, how can I have forgotten? According to Jack's maid, he accompanied Jack from home today. He should be here." I began looking wildly about as if I might find him standing in a corner. "Where is he? Is he anywhere in the house?"

Jesse's expression became alarmed. He instantly came to his feet and strode from the kitchen; his stern orders to search the entire house drifted in from the other room. Then he returned to the kitchen table.

"I'm still confused, Emma. What does all this have to do with Jack Parsons?"

"When I went to check the playhouse this morning, Jack was speeding out the gates—in a leased carriage. He might have collided with me, he was in such a hurry. Still, I didn't think much of it until I reached the playhouse and discovered the flagstones had been moved and the hidey hole was empty."

"And?" Jesse waited, obviously expecting more.

"So whatever was in there, Jack must have taken it."

"How do you know whatever—if anything—had been in there wasn't removed before Jack got there?"

This question came from Derrick and I swung my head in his direction. "I . . . he must have . . ."

"Not necessarily," Derrick said gently. He gave my hand a squeeze. "If Jack knew about the hiding place, one of the Vanderbilt siblings must have told him about it. Who would that most likely have been?"

I started shaking my head, but the sad light in Derrick's eyes forced me to acknowledge the obvious. "Neily," I whispered. "He might have told Jack about the hiding place, but that doesn't mean—"

"Why Neily?" Jesse asked abruptly. "I wasn't aware that Neily Vanderbilt and Jack Parsons were particularly well acquainted, much less confidents."

"I didn't either," I replied, once more setting my chin in hand. "Not until the other night when . . ." I glanced at Derrick. He nodded. "Not until I discovered that Neily and Jack were both using this house for . . . personal purposes."

"Such as . . . ?"

"Oh, Jesse, what does it matter?" I almost shouted. "Neily certainly didn't murder anyone. In fact, is there a telephone in this house? Someone should call The Breakers and find out where Neily is. That would clear him once and for all."

Without a word Jesse once more left the room. When he returned, another officer trailed him. "Theodore Mason isn't in the house, sir."

"Then I want him found. Immediately."

"Try his boardinghouse," I suggested. "The Harbor Hill on Broadway."

Jesse sat back down and picked up his tablet. "Do you have anything else to add, Emma?" When I shook my head, his gaze swerved to Derrick. "And how do you figure into all of this?"

By the time Jesse had finished with us, the body—Jack's body—had been removed. The police were finishing up gathering the evidence when I went to stand in the parlor doorway. Derrick came up behind him and set a palm on my shoulder.

"We should go, Emma."

I shook my head and stepped into the room—this room

where a part of my own life seemed to have died, vanished. Oh, but not without a trace, for in the middle of the carpet, almost mocking the vital, dynamic man Jack Parsons had been, sat the ugly, rusty stains from the blood that had seeped out of him. There had been two shots, the police determined. One had struck him in the back. Then, as he'd turned toward his assassin, he'd been shot again, this time to the side of his chest, the wound I'd seen when I opened his coat.

Two shots, two moments in time that could never be taken back, done over, changed. The finality of it pressed in upon me until I could barely drag my feet one after the other. And yet I did. Careful not to step into the way of the policemen, I entered the room, walked over to the stains, and looked down, trying, somehow, to disassociate those hideous splotches from the vibrant man I'd known.

"Miss Cross, maybe you shouldn't be here anymore." One of the policeman, though who I couldn't say because I never looked up, gave my arm a pat as he paused before walking by.

No, I didn't look up, nor was I still staring at the drying remnants of Jack's life's blood. My gaze had drifted a few feet away to a long, low cabinet against the wall beside the fireplace. I moved closer to it, stood studying the piece a good long while before I realized what had captured my attention.

"Derrick!"

He was at my side in an instant. "What is it?"

I stretched out a finger. "There, along the edge."

Before he could respond, I nearly pounced at the cabinet and fell to my knees in front of it. I ran my hand along the gilded edge and quite clearly felt the sharp indentation of the wood, my fingers catching on fine splinters left by whatever hard, wide object had caused the dent.

"Get Jesse," I said frantically. Less than a minute later he and Derrick stood frowning down at this latest evidence. "It's a match, I know it is," I announced adamantly. "This dent and the one in Uncle Cornelius's bedroom were made by the same blunt instrument. The murder weapon. And it proves Brady's innocence."

"Now, wait a minute, Emma," Jesse said with a shake of his head. "The murder weapon in this instance was a gun. Alvin Goddard wasn't shot."

"No, but the weapon used to kill him was here in this room. Don't you see? Whoever killed Alvin Goddard retrieved the murder weapon from the playhouse, came here to confront Jack, but brought added protection."

"Or," Derrick put in, "Jack somehow found out about the murder weapon, retrieved it from the playhouse, and confronted the killer here with it. Someone who knew he owned this house, who maybe wouldn't have thought twice about being invited here."

Both men regarded me, their silence all but shouting the words that went unsaid.

"Neily," I whispered. "But if he thought nothing of being invited here, why would he have brought a gun?"

"For all we know, Emma, Neily might have taken to bringing a gun with him everywhere these days." Derrick shrugged apologetically. "Maybe he's feeling penned in and desperate."

I realized Jesse had turned away to speak to two other officers. Upon hearing my cousin's name mentioned, I grasped Jesse's forearm. "Wait one minute. What about Theodore Mason? He had a motive to kill Alvin Goddard, who accused him of stealing from The Breakers. And he should have been here with Jack. Someone needs to find him."

Jesse agreed. "We need to find both your cousin Neily and Mr. Mason. Right now. Neither one can be overlooked as a suspect. In the meantime, I want you both out of this." His face became stern. "Understand, Emma? No more investigating. You leave this to me and my men."

I nodded, and Derrick said, "I'll see she gets home."

"I can't go home yet," I objected. When Jesse's expression became exasperated, I quickly said, "I have to see Brady, tell him what happened. He deserves to know, Jesse. Jack Parsons has been as much a part of his life as mine. And my parents . . . I'll need to wire them the news. . . ."

"I don't believe it, Em. Not Neily and not Mason."

I reached through the cell bars to take my brother's hand. "I don't want to believe it either, but don't you see what this means? You'll be exonerated."

"Maybe . . . maybe not."

"But once they have the real murderer—"

Brady shook his head. "That's just it. Mason? Neily? Come on, Em. You know as well as I do that neither is capable of harming a fly. This will be just one more distraction to keep the police busy while the real murderer gets away. Maybe he's already away. Might have left the island right after killing Jack on one of those fancy steamers the Four Hundred are so enamored of. No, Em, Jack's death won't help me at all. It only makes everything that much grimmer. . . ."

"It's not like you to give up hope, Brady." My voice trembled. Tears burned my eyes.

"Well, I didn't so much give it up as run out of it, along with my luck." He smiled bleakly, a gesture that had become so familiar I'd all but forgotten how brightly his genuine smile could shine. "And you have to admit, I've had more than my fair share of that. More than I deserve."

I left the jail feeling so defeated I could hardly gather two words to say to Derrick as he walked me to my buggy. All I managed was a shaky, "Thank you," before expecting to go our separate ways.

"I'll follow you home." He gestured to his own rented carriage parked behind my own.

"Oh, no. You've done enough. I'll be fine."

"I think not. Until this investigation ends with the guilty party behind bars, you're not safe. I said I'm following you, and follow you I will."

I couldn't help a smile, albeit a weak one. "Thank you, Derrick. Thank you for believing me when I say my brother is innocent."

"Yes, well, you seem to have a good nose when it comes to people. If you trust that he didn't do it, that's good enough for me."

He smiled down at me, and for an instant I thought—half hoped—he might kiss me again. But the moment stretched too long, and I saw my own self-consciousness reflected in his eyes. He stepped back, offered me an arm, and helped me up into my buggy. As good as his word, he followed me all the way home, up the drive, and through the front door. But if I'd thought we might share a private moment before he left, I was greatly mistaken.

At a speed of which I hadn't believed her capable, Nanny waddled out from the kitchen. "Well? What happened?" She stopped, drawing her bulk up straighter, a hand pressed to her bosom. Behind her half-moon spectacles, her eyes went wide. "Good heavens, Emma, is that blood?"

Chapter 17

"Here, Nanny, have another sip of tea." Leaning beside her chair in the morning room, where Katie had set out refreshments for the three of us, I lifted Nanny's cup and tried to press it into her hands. Derrick sat to her right, letting his tea grow cold while patiently answering all of her questions, sometimes three and four times. Despite all my assurances to the contrary, Nanny continued to fret.

"If either of you had gotten to the house earlier than you did . . . you might have walked in on a murder . . . Oh, God, Emma, you might have been killed!" The last word dissolved into a hiccupping sob.

I rubbed a hand soothingly up and down her broad back. "We didn't, Nanny. We're both perfectly fine."

It was as if she didn't hear a word I said. "Oh, I should never have let you become involved. I shouldn't have helped you. We both should have left well enough alone."

"Well, I'm out of it now." Straightening, I set her tea back down and resumed my seat to her left. I covered her softly wrinkled hand with my own. "The police have narrowed it down to two suspects and they'll be questioning both to see if either has an alibi. I won't have any more to do with it."

"Neily or Teddy . . ." Nanny dashed her knuckles beneath her eye and shook her head. "I can't believe either could possibly be guilty.

Derrick lifted a shoulder in a half shrug. "Based on everything I've learned since coming to Newport, my money's on Theodore Mason as the guilty party."

"Under the circumstances, I agree," I said. "Neily could never hurt anyone, not for any reason. I believe he'll have a solid alibi. But still, the idea of Mr. Mason—"

As I spoke, the service door swung inward and Katie shouldered her way through carrying a tray of toast and biscuits. She froze, gaping, framed by the doorway; her astonished gaze traveled to each of us around the table in turn.

"Wh-what is that you're sayin', miss?"

"We're discussing Alvin Goddard's murder, Katie," I said calmly, knowing it took little to upset the girl.

"And Jack Parsons," Nanny added with a heavy sigh. "Poor Mr. Parsons. Your father will be crushed when he hears, Emma."

I wondered, not very nicely, whether Jack's death would manage to elicit the response from my parents that Brady's arrest hadn't. No sooner had the thought formed, however, when I tried to push it out of my mind. Now was not the time for resentment or recriminations. Any further thoughts I might have had on the subject were abruptly cut off when Katie all but slammed the tray onto the table, sending the biscuits bouncing and a few crumbs flying.

"But what about Mr. Mason?" she cried, ruddy color climbing from her neck to her hairline.

I ignored the mess she'd made of the table and met her eyes, fever bright against her blush. "I'm sorry to tell you that Mr. Mason is the foremost suspect now, Katie."

She began shaking her head, slowly at first, then quicker, adamant. "No, he can't have. He can't."

Her obvious distress sent me to my feet. "None of us want to believe it, Katie, but Mr. Mason was the last person to be with Jack Parsons, and now he's gone missing. And he had a motive. Alvin Goddard accused him of theft, leading to his being fired from his position at The Breakers."

"No, no! He didn't do it! He didn't. Please, Miss Emma, you've got to believe me. You have to tell the police! You have to . . . he's an innocent man . . ."

Tear ran down her cheeks. I exchanged a glance with Derrick, who looked mystified. Circling the table to her, I set a hand on her shoulder, pulled out a chair, and pressed her down into it. She slumped forward, her face falling into her hands

What could she possibly know about Alvin Goddard's murder? My hand still on her shoulder, I sat in the chair beside hers and spoke close to her ear. "Katie, listen to me. We need you to explain. How do you know Mr. Mason is innocent?"

"I can't say . . . I can't . . ."

"You have to, Katie. If he's innocent, you have to help him. You can't let him be accused of a crime he didn't commit."

Her head slowly came up and she turned toward me. Her palms were wet, her cheeks flaming and tearstained. "I know where Mr. Mason was when Mr. Goddard died."

"Well, where?" This came from Nanny, and I glared an admonishment across the table for her to hold her tongue and let me handle things.

"Don't be afraid, Katie. You're among friends here." I felt her trembling beneath my hand; her shivers traveled up my arm and tugged at my heart. Katie herself had been through a horrendous ordeal only that spring, including losing her own employment at The Breakers for something that wasn't her fault. Trusting her employer couldn't be easy, even now. "You have nothing to be afraid of," I said quietly, as one might soothe a frightened child. "Didn't I help you when you needed it? Haven't you found a good home here with me?"

Her tears only fell harder. "Oh, that's just it, Miss Emma. Once you know the truth, you'll cast me out . . . and I've nowhere else to go!" That last ended on a wail, so loud Nanny and Derrick flinched. I, however, held steady.

"That won't happen, not if you tell the truth. Now, Katie, I want you to take a deep breath and simply tell me what you know. For Mr. Mason's sake." And yet even as I coaxed her, my stomach tightened around a growing dread. Exonerating Mr. Mason might very well transfer the guilt to Neily. But the truth, whatever it was, needed to come out. "Where was Theodore Mason when Alvin Goddard died?"

"Here," she whispered, so low it might have been a hiss of steam from the teapot. But the tea had surely turned tepid by now.

"What did you say?" Nanny frowned in puzzlement. She and Theodore Mason were old friends, but if he visited that night, she obviously knew nothing about it.

Katie raised her hands to wipe at both cheeks. "Mr. Mason came here that night . . . to see me." She flicked a glance at Nanny. "Mrs. O'Neal was already in bed. . . ."

"But why did Teddy come here?" Nanny demanded.

I waited, suddenly unable to speak, to move. Instinctively, I sensed a piece of the mystery, an elusive piece I never could have envisioned, about to fall into place.

"He came because he figured out"—she drew in a deep breath, the air trembling through her lips—"it was me."

I snapped back as if she'd struck me across the face. "You? You . . . murdered . . ."

"No, miss! I don't know who killed Mr. Goddard . . . but I do know who stole the figurines from Mrs. Vanderbilt's parlor." Her fingers clenched into fists in her lap. And then the gates broke to release the torrent. "It was me, miss. Not Mr. Mason. Oh, he never stole a thing. He couldn't, he's an honorable man. I did it. I stole them because I knew I'd lose my job. Once my condition showed, I'd be sacked without a reference. No one would believe it wasn't my fault, and I'd be out on the street with nowhere to go, no one to help me . . . I'd need money for a place to stay, to feed my child . . . I didn't think anyone would notice those tiny figurines missing—that house is so filled with riches."

She turned her face toward me. "And then you took me in, miss, and I couldn't tell you. I couldn't tell anyone. I wanted to return the figurines, I swear I did, but I didn't know how without gettin' caught. I didn't want to go to jail, I didn't . . ." Her sobs overcame her and she wept into her hands, her shoulders shaking violently.

"Where are the figurines?" I removed my hand from her shoulder. She raised her eyes toward the ceiling and I realized Aunt Alice's missing bronze pieces were hidden away in Katie's attic bedroom. "How did Mr. Mason discover that you had them?"

"He said it started as a hunch." Her gaze drifted around the room while she avoided eye contact with each of us. "He'd suspected, and one day he met Lucy in town."

Lucy was another young housemaid in the Vanderbilt's employ. She and Katie had shared a room in the servants' quarters.

"He asked Lucy a bunch of questions about who had access to Mrs. Vanderbilt's parlor once the decorators were done. You see, only she was supposed to have been cleanin' in there. I was a kitchen maid, and I wasn't allowed to be in the family's private rooms on the second floor. But Lucy, I suppose fearin' she might be held to blame for the missing figurines, admitted to havin' me help her on a few occasions. The family was away at the time, so we didn't think anyone would mind. But Lucy, she didn't know . . ."

When she hesitated, staring down at her hands again, I prompted, "Lucy didn't know what, Katie?"

"She didn't know then I was in the family way. She didn't know I'd be losin' my job soon. She left me alone in the parlor and I pocketed some of the figurines, and moved others into their place so maybe no one would notice."

Silence filled the room. I gazed across at Nanny, whose features had pulled into a tight scowl.

"You let Teddy take the blame," she began, but I held up a hand to shush her.

"Please, Nanny. Now isn't the time for recriminations. It isn't easy for Katie to come clean, but she's doing it for Mr. Mason despite the potential risk to her own future."

"But why would Teddy keep her secret? He lost his job because of her."

Nanny's question sent our attention back to the quietly weeping Katie. With an effort, she pulled herself up straighter. "Mr. Mason took pity on me when I told him why I did what I did. And he knows I send money home to my family in Killarney every month. Mr. Parsons had already given him a new job, he said, and he had no desire to go back and work for the Vanderbilts after the way they accused him. He felt betrayed, don't you see. So he said he'd keep my secret if he could."

"He can't keep it any longer, Katie," I said firmly. "If he says he was here that night, the police will want to know why."

"Oh, please, miss, don't send me to jail. . . ." The plea came as a whisper that stabbed clean through to my heart. If there was one thing I understood about Katie, it was that she came to this country after a childhood defined by the kind of poverty the poorest American could scarcely imagine.

"I have no intention of sending you to jail," I told her. "We'll return Aunt Alice's figurines, of course, but Uncle Cornelius won't press charges once I've had a chance to speak with him. But that's for later. Right now we need to get this information to Jesse before he and his men arrest the wrong man." I looked up. "That's if they haven't already."

Derrick was already on his feet. "I'll go. There's no reason for you to go traipsing back into town. You have enough to take care of here."

I had started to rise, but his words sent me back into my chair. "Thank you, Derrick." Across the table, our gazes locked. "But there's still a murderer out there. Please be careful."

"I will. And you're very welcome," he said, his quiet sincerity resonating deeply inside me.

"Are you sure you two will be all right for a little while, Nanny?" I asked about a half an hour later. She and I stood in the front hallway as I readied myself for a short trip to Bellevue Avenue.

Nanny gave a confident nod. "I have no doubt the girl will sleep the rest of the afternoon. That confession of hers took a lot out of her." Her lips pursed in a show of disapproval.

"Don't be so hard on Katie. Put yourself in her place. All alone in a strange country, her family so far away. What was she to do?" It occurred to me that I'd never told Nanny what I'd found out from Reggie. "Her pregnancy . . . oh, Nanny, it wasn't her fault at all."

Her expression remained unyielding. "Did she tell you that?"

"No, Reggie did. It was one of his school friends who visited last spring. He forced her, Nanny."

Her arms, until now crossed in front of her, dropped to her sides. Her mouth lost its severity. "She never said anything. . . ."

"No, why would she? The woman is always blamed no matter what."

"Damn," she whispered. And then louder, "Damn. That changes everything. It's still not right letting Teddy take the blame for the theft, but . . . I guess I understand now."

"And you'll be nice to her if she wakes up and I'm not here?"

"Don't worry, I'll be nice." But her frown returned. She raised a hand and pressed it to my cheek. "Are you sure you want to go out alone? As you said to Mr. Anderson—"

"Yes, I know a murderer is still at large, but I'm not going far and it's still broad daylight."

"Well, all right." Her hand moved to pat my hair, then adjust the ribbon of my hat. "And you don't think you'll need moral support while you talk to her?"

My gaze dropped to the floor and I shook my head. "No, this is something I need to do alone. Friend to friend. I want Adelaide to hear it from me before the rumors start flying."

"And what if her husband is around to overhear?"

"Highly doubtful. But if he is, I'll suggest Adelaide and I take a walk in their garden."

I was halfway through the door when the telephone jangled. Nanny shuffled to the alcove to answer it and I waited, hoping it might be news from Jesse or Derrick.

"Yes, she's here," Nanny said loudly into the mouthpiece, at the same time waving a frantic hand at me. I hurried back inside. She practically shoved the ear trumpet into my hand when I reached her. "It's Mr. Anderson."

"Derrick?" I, too, practically shouted across the wire. "Have you found Mr. Mason?"

"Emma, listen to me," he said briskly, ignoring my question. "Theodore Mason wasn't the last person to be with Jack Parsons. Rupert Halstock was."

"What? But that's impossible. He's too ill."

"Is he? Mason didn't think much of it at the time, but as he left the Point to run his own errands, he plainly saw old Halstock's carriage pull up at Jack's house. I questioned Mason myself after the police finished with him. I fancy myself a pretty good judge of people and I really didn't get the sense that he was lying. Besides, why would he, now that Katie supplied him with an alibi?"

"Then that means—"

"We're not sure what it means yet. They're looking for Halstock now. Apparently he's not at home yet. Jesse sent out a couple of officers to check, and they found his wife there but not the old man."

"Oh, God, Derrick. Did they tell her what was happening? What happened to Jack?"

"No, I don't think they told her anything. One of the officers stayed to keep watch while the other reported back. Jesse's hoping Halstock's still somewhere in town."

"Tell him to check Long Wharf. That's where the Halstocks dock their steamer."

"I believe he knows. I heard him mention something about Long Wharf. We can only hope Halstock hasn't already left Newport."

"That won't be hard to tell. Either the steamer will be there or it won't."

"Right. I've got to go, Emma. I'll check back soon."

The line went dead before I could respond.

"What was that all about?" Nanny prompted. "What's impossible?" Before I could answer, she gasped. "You said he's too ill. Did you mean Rupert Halstock?"

"Nanny, please, let me get a word in edgewise."

"Go ahead."

I made my way around to the staircase and sank onto the first step. The front door was still open, and I gazed outside at the sunlight spilling across my weed-ridden front lawn. "According to Mr. Mason, the last person to see Jack Parsons alive was Rupert Halstock. He pulled up to Jack's house on the Point just as Mason was walking back into town."

"Why that phony! Pretending to be sick all this while . . ."

My head shot up. "Nanny, what if it wasn't Mr. Halstock? What if it was Adelaide, arriving to meet with Jack again?"

She looked like she'd been about to continue her tirade, but her mouth snapped shut. She stood for another moment biting her bottom lip before she lowered herself onto the step beside me. "You think Adelaide could have killed Mr. Parsons?"

I immediately shook my head. "No, that's not what I meant at all. It couldn't have been . . . could it? No, that's ridiculous."

"Is it? Rupert's own sister thinks . . ."

"Oh, bother Rupert's sister. Besides, the one time I saw Adelaide on the Point she came in a rented vehicle so no casual observer would recognize her. Mr. Mason specifically said he saw the Halstocks' carriage. Does it make sense that Adelaide would use a rented carriage for a tryst, but her own to commit murder?"

"No, I don't suppose that makes a lick of sense. But why would Rupert use his own carriage then?"

We both thought about that a moment, our shoulders touching, the parlor clock ticking off the minutes. "Because," I finally said, "he must have found out about Adelaide and Jack. He found out, and in his rage he rushed off to confront Jack and . . ." I reached for Nanny's hand and clutched it tight. She returned the pressure. But I just as quickly slid my fingers free. "I have to go. Adelaide needs me."

I got to my feet. In defiance to her age and bulk, Nanny sprang up beside me. "You can't go traipsing over there now! What if Rupert comes home?"

"He probably won't."

"Probably? Probably does not a certainty make! Emma, I forbid you to go."

I pressed a hand to her shoulder. "It's all right. Derrick told me there's an officer there watching in case Rupert does come home. I'll be fine. I just can't let Adelaide face all of this alone."

I leaned closer to Nanny and kissed her soft cheek. Then I strode out the door.

Ten minutes later, I pulled my rig up in front of Redwing Cottage. A police officer I vaguely recognized walked slowly between the drive and the hedge-lined wrought-iron fence that separated the property from Bellevue Avenue. He stopped when I did and approached my carriage.

"This isn't a good day for visiting, miss," he said with a tip of his high-domed hat. "You might want to come back another day."

"Nonsense. I'm a good friend of Mrs. Halstock. In fact, her closest friend, and she needs me right now." I secured the brake on my rig and set the reins down. "Have you seen any trace of Mr. Halstock?"

"None at all, miss, and to be honest, I don't expect to. But just in case, my partner will be returning to join me just as soon as he's done reporting back in town."

"There, then," I proclaimed with a nod, "with the pair of you here, I'll be safe as can be."

He shook his head doubtfully but didn't order me off the property. He helped me down and I went to the front door. I used the knocker, the *clank clank* echoing deeply inside the house. A minute or two passed and I tried again. A glance over my shoulder revealed that the officer had lost interest in me. He stood at the fence peering through a gap in the hedge, his hand resting on his sidearm.

I knocked once more, the hollow sound rattling my nerves. Finally, I tried the latch and the door opened inward with a light whine of its hinges.

"Hello? Anyone here?"

Had Adelaide given all the servants a holiday? Or had money troubles forced her to fire most of them? The stillness reminded me of my very first visit here, except on that occasion the red velvet curtain that hid the passage to the morning room had fluttered and Rupert Halstock had shuffled through. This time there were no such stirrings of the curtain. I walked several paces into the center of the hall and peeked into the front parlor. "Adelaide?"

An unnatural pall hung over the room; the furnishings and

the grand piano seemed poised as if waiting . . . for what, I couldn't say. The hair at my nape bristled to attention.

Turning, I glanced up the stairs. Afternoon sun poured through the stained-glass window at the half landing, bathing the steps in a rainbow of light. I made my way up, gripping the banister and walking practically on my toes. When a floorboard beneath the stair-runner squeaked, I nearly yelped.

I found the upstairs to be as lifeless as the lower level. Adelaide's bright and feminine private parlor, where she and I had first reestablished our friendship, seemed faded somehow; an inexplicable aura of sadness sent me hurrying back downstairs.

Back in the hall again, I thought I heard a faint hum of voices. Quickly I ran into the parlor and peered out the bay window. Had Rupert shown up? But, no, the policeman was now lingering near the gate at one end of the circular drive, where a sculpted azalea bush hid him from anyone approaching from town.

A wide doorway opened onto a second, rear-facing parlor. I walked through, practically jumping out of my skin when from the corner of my eye I caught my own reflection in the glass-fronted bookcases. I pressed a hand to my heart and kept going. This room opened onto the formal dining room. Here I paused to listen, and once again a low drone reached my ears. I could make out neither the gender of the voices nor the words they spoke, but I determined their direction to be from somewhere near the far rear corner of the house.

Something held me in place, very nearly sent me retreating out the front door seeking the officer's assistance, until a reasonable thought calmed me. Why, Adelaide could be in the kitchens discussing the week's menu with her cook. Or she could be outside in the garden, giving instructions to her groundskeeper. I remembered, too, that sometimes The Breakers felt as lifeless as a tomb, while in actuality its servants and inhabitants were simply going about their business quietly.

Reassured, I made my way from the dining room into a paneled hallway. I passed a small, masculine study, a game room, and what looked to be a cloak room. Finally, the richly woven hall runner disappeared from beneath my feet. I stepped onto wide, white-washed floorboards, the equally white walls to either side of me lined with cupboards and counters. A moment later I turned a corner and stepped down into the main kitchen.

"Is anyone—"

The voices I'd heard rose up again, still muffled through walls but much louder now. Beyond a doubt I heard both feminine and masculine tones raised in unmistakable anger, though I still couldn't make out the words.

I ran to the back counter and craned my neck to see out the window above the sink. A few feet below me and off to my left, I spied a black-clad shoulder, nothing more. But where the counter ended another doorway opened onto what must be a mudroom and an outside door. I hurried over to it.

And slid to a stop, heart in my throat, hands pressed to my mouth in horror.

Had I kept going I'd have tripped over the body of Rupert Halstock's valet, a man I recognized from my first visit here. He lay sprawled across the floor, faceup, a wound to his forehead clotted with blood. More blood matted his hair and soaked the floorboards beneath his head. Rivulets of red filled the thin gaps between the wooden planks on either side of him.

The wound . . . so like the one that had killed Alvin Goddard . . .

Through the roaring in my ears and the pounding in my temples, I heard the voices clearly now. Adelaide . . . and Rupert!

I started to turn. I needed to alert the officer . . . the officer so close at hand, yet. . . .

"Damn you, Adelaide. I trusted you. I loved you. I stood by you when everyone told me I was crazy."

"You are crazy, old man. God help me, why did I ever marry you?" Her words were interrupted by the sounds of a scuffle. And then, "Stop it, stop it, Rupert!"

Alarm drove me to the door, where I could see, through the small curtained window, the two of them struggling on the pathway between the stoop and the kitchen garden. Their hands waved back and forth together above their heads, their fingers locked around the blue-and-red-striped handle of—

A gasp tore from my throat.

In their combined grip, a cricket bat swung wildly back and forth. A bat whose width I didn't doubt exactly matched the dent in Uncle Cornelius's balcony doorway and in the cabinet at Jack's house on the Point.

In that instant I knew Rupert Halstock had indeed been faking his illness. And I knew beyond a doubt if I didn't act immediately, his next victim would be Adelaide.

I wanted to scream, wanted to tear back through the house and seek the officer's help, but how much longer could Adelaide hold off her madman of a husband? I retreated into the kitchen, searching—oh, God—searching for something, anything, to use as a weapon. My gaze lighted on the copper pans hanging from pegs along one wall. Grabbing a solid-looking fry pan with a good long handle, I spun about and returned to the back door.

Turning the knob as far as I could, I managed to open the door without a sound. A few feet below me Rupert and Adelaide continued their tussle; his curses and her yelps of fear filled the air. Couldn't the officer hear them? But the distance was too great, I realized—the house too big, the grounds too sprawling.

As I made my way down the steps, my shadow fell across the thrashing pair. Adelaide saw it, then looked up and saw me. Her eyes jolted wide. They were glassy, gleaming. Her arms were trembling fiercely as she continued trying to wrestle the cricket bat from her husband's hands. Rupert held on obdurately. I raised the frying pan.

And brought it crashing down on the back of his head with a resounding *thwack*. The metal rang out melodiously. Rupert froze, and for a moment I thought I'd missed my mark, feared he'd turn around and accost me, as he had the night he nearly ran me off the ocean drive . . . as he had the night I'd followed Neily to the Point while Rupert had followed me.

In the next instant his legs buckled, his arms dropped away from the cricket bat, and he collapsed to the ground on his back. For the next several moments neither Adelaide nor I moved, but I stood looking down at Rupert, studying the rise and fall of his chest. Great swells of relief rolled through me. I'd wanted to stop the man from committing another murder, but I certainly hadn't wanted to commit one myself.

"Good heavens, Adelaide. Are you all right?" Suddenly more weary than I've ever been in my life, I bent to set the copper pan on the bottom step. I straightened and turned back to Adelaide. She stood panting, the cricket bat gripped at her side, her gaze pinned to the sprawled man at her feet. A frown marred the smoothness of her brow.

"Adelaide? It's all right, it's over. He can't hurt you anymore."

Still she didn't move, didn't utter a word. She kept staring, her scowl deepening as if she were silently raining all her resentment and recriminations down on the man she had once pinned all her hopes on.

"I should go and get the officer," I said, more out of a hope of getting some kind of response from her. Had the shock been too much?

"No," she said, a single flat note. She continued glaring down at her husband.

"What?"

I glanced down at Rupert again, and something occurred to

me. How could he have gotten home without being caught by the policeman? A simple answer formed: He had already been at home when the police came inquiring. Adelaide had lied about the whereabouts of her husband.

But why would she do that?

The second answer followed swiftly on the first as I saw what I hadn't noticed a moment ago: a bruise on Rupert's forehead and a cut along his receding hairline. I could not have caused either with the frying pan. Adelaide's skirts rustled and my gaze shot to her. She had bent down to retrieve something from the ground, and now straightened and squared her shoulders.

I knew then for certain I'd made a mistake.

Chapter 18

I stared down the barrel of the pistol in Adelaide's hand, until a drop of blood rolled off the cricket bat at her side and fell with a plop into the grass at her feet. The sound seemed impossibly loud, echoing in my ears. My stomach roiled at the sight of that glistening red blob sinking into the blades of grass.

"Adelaide . . ." My voice breezed between my lips like a gust billowing off the ocean.

Yes, Adelaide, my friend . . . my childhood chum. . . . The schoolyard athlete, the tennis and archery champion. . . . She had always been a tall girl, solid and sturdy.

And she had been the captain of the girls' cricket team.

Realization solidified along my spine, forcing me ramrod straight. "Peabody. Your maiden name . . . Adelaide Peabody. The pocket watch in Uncle Cornelius's safe . . ."

"My great grandfather's," she snarled with scathing contempt. "The only scrap of his wealth to make its paltry way to me."

"Why did you give it away?"

"Collateral on a loan. But *I* didn't give it to Cornelius, that idiot husband of mine did. Used the money for an investment—another one of his doomed-to-fail schemes. And it did, of course. And to think Rupert had the nerve to bellyache about the loss of his first wife's precious spinet. 'What about Great-Grandpapa's watch?' I asked him. Not that I really cared, mind you. What's a pocket watch to a woman? But tit for tat, you know."

This casual little speech of hers rattled through me, leaving me clenching my teeth, fisting my hands. "It's been you all along," I said tonelessly. I uncurled one hand and raised an accusing finger as if to duel against her gun. I shouldn't have goaded her, but I was shocked beyond caution. "You killed Alvin Goddard. And Jack. And now . . ." I started to glance over my shoulder at the mudroom door, then just as quickly turned back to her. "Why, Adelaide? Why would you do such hellish things?"

She scowled and pursed her lips in a way that made me think she was going to spit. She stopped short of that but, her upper lip curled in a sneer that chilled me. "Why do you think, you stupid girl? I had the perfect plan before your damned uncle Cornelius spoiled everything."

"The railroad. The New Haven-Hartford-Providence Line. Your husband was an investor."

"Yes, and before your uncle became involved, the stock was still worth something. Rupert's holdings were in the millions. And if he'd died on schedule, I'd have inherited those millions."

"Died on schedule," I repeated. "His illness. You've been poisoning him."

"What a brilliant deduction, Emma." She smirked, that spiteful curl of her lip reminding me of the petulant child she had been. "With him gone I'd no longer be dependent on anyone. Not on some doddering old fool of a man, and certainly not on the society dragons like your fat Aunt Alice who've been turning their noses up at me." She swung the cricket bat against the side of her calf, first a light tap, then harder, making a *thwap, thwap* sound against her skirts. "Oh, wouldn't I like to turn my nose up at all of them—and I will, Emma, just as soon as I'm a wealthy widow."

"That's not going to happen, Adelaide," I said steadily. "You know it can't. Information about the misdealings in the railroad management is already coming out. The stock value has plummeted—"

"And whose fault is that?" she all but screamed. A wild spark lit her eyes, and suddenly I saw her for the insane killer she had become. Before I could answer her, she continued more calmly, but with an underlying tremor in her voice. "Your uncle ruined everything. He's a hateful, greedy, horrible excuse for a man and he deserves to die. He would have died—should have . . ."

"Then why kill Alvin Goddard?" I could guess at the answer, but as long as I had her talking, I wanted to keep her doing just that. Keep her from remembering to finish off Rupert . . . and me. Meanwhile, I hoped, prayed, someone would come. With all my might I willed the officer at the front of the house to decide to walk around back.

"The idiot!" Adelaide's voice rose again. Please, I thought, let the policeman hear her. "What was he doing in Cornelius's bedroom? It was dark—especially after I dispatched your stupid brother and extinguished his candle. How was I to know the wrong man entered the room? It's not like I could have said, 'Oh, excuse me, are you Cornelius?' before I whacked him across the back of his head."

As she blurted those sarcastic words she came at me, the pistol pointed at my chest and violence flashing in her eyes. Instinctively I cringed in anticipation of the shot, but when I looked up, she stood frozen in place, her features twisted with fury. Her hand slowly lowered, yet the gun now remained trained on my stomach.

I let out a breath. "And in the confusion afterward you smuggled your weapon out to the playhouse."

"Of course I did. You and your meddling ways. What on earth brought you outside Cornelius's window at just the wrong moment?"

I ignored her question and asked one of my own. "Why the bat? The house was full of potential weapons." I thought briefly of The Breakers' many marble busts, ornamental swords, and, yes, candelabras.

"Oh, because the irony was too sweet to resist," she said. "Don't you remember how your uncle funded our school cricket team? I suppose his charity made him feel magnanimous. To me it was a reminder of how much I didn't have as a child." She shook her head. "My plan was perfect—*perfect*, Emma, if not for you. If you hadn't alerted Neily and then the police, I'd have had time to quietly leave the ball with this cricket bat safely stored in my carriage. But, no, the police were searching all the vehicles and everyone's bags. I had no choice but to hide it away where the authorities would never think to look."

"And where it stayed until Jack found it today." I almost didn't want to ask my next question. "How did he know it was there?"

Please, I thought—I prayed—don't let him have been involved, part of her sinister plans.

Her lips curved, this time in a cunning little smile. "Jack proved most useful. Most sympathetic to my cause. And his own, of course. He stood to profit nicely from helping me." The grin vanished as quickly as it had come. "Until today, that is, when his conscience overruled his common sense and his ambition."

His ambition . . .

"Oh, God. Brady," I murmured as additional pieces fell into place. "Brady originally stole the railroad plans to show Jack.

Brady said it was his own idea . . ." I shook my head sadly. "But it wasn't, was it?"

Her smile burgeoned again. "I've never met a more biddable fool than Brady Gale. Jack hoodwinked him into stealing those plans and making him think it was his own idea with less effort than . . . than I made you believe I was your friend, Emma. It would seem pitiful gullibility runs in your family."

She went on to utter more mockery, but I didn't hear her, didn't care. A pain grew in my chest; my heart squeezed, turned over, squeezed again as I processed Jack Parsons's betrayal. Adelaide's, well, that was my own fault, my own gullibility as she had said. But Jack's . . . oh, I knew that from then on . . . if I lived beyond that day . . . I would never bestow my trust as freely as I had in the first twenty-one years of my life.

"Why did you kill Jack?"

"Because he was going to turn me in!" she cried savagely, spittle flying from her lips. "Because he put it all together and realized it was me—that I killed Alvin Goddard." She swung the cricket bat in the air, making me recoil. "He'd actually suspected Rupert, even remembered about Rupert's collection of cricket bats. Last night he announced his intentions of going to the police and suggesting one of those bats might be the murder weapon, that Rupert was merely faking his illness."

"So why didn't you let him?" I wondered aloud.

"Oh, I applauded his astuteness and encouraged him to go. But then this morning . . . he sent a message asking me to meet him on the Point. I thought we were going celebrate finally getting Rupert out of the way." She laughed, a sardonic cackle.

"And you brought along a gun?"

She shrugged. "I'd taken to bringing it everywhere I went. A girl can't be too careful, you know."

I let that go. "What happened between you and Jack on the Point this morning, Adelaide?"

"He confronted me! He remembered seeing Rupert make his

way downstairs after their meeting in Cornelius's office, right at the time the murder would have been committed. It got him thinking . . . and that's when he remembered me telling him about playing at The Breakers when we were little, how we used to hide our little treasures under the floor in the playhouse. Damn him, Emma! I'd told him that months ago. Why on earth did he have to go and remember about it today?"

I ignored her vehemence, thinking instead about how Jack's carriage had raced down the The Breakers' drive this morning. My father's old friend redeemed himself today, if only fractionally. "What you did horrified him, didn't it?"

She grimaced. "He said the money was one thing, but he never signed on for murder. He blamed me for—"

"Why shouldn't he have blamed you?" A ball of rage that had been steadily growing inside me suddenly burst free. "Don't you understand what havoc you've created? Don't you care how many lives you've destroyed? You're a monster, Adelaide. You've become exactly what you accused Uncle Cornelius of being, only a hundred thousand times worse. And for what? For—"

"Shut up!" She jabbed the pistol in the air toward me. My heart seized, but I stood tall, shut my eyes, and waited. A prayer raced through my mind.

A second passed. Two. I braved opening my eyes and saw, shining in her eyes—what? Indecision? Regret? Fear? Or simply the murky abyss of insanity? Suddenly, I'd had enough.

"Well, Adelaide?" I said. "Are you going to shoot me or beat me to a pulp with your cricket bat?"

Looking the prim society lady once more, Adelaide swung the bat still clutched in her left hand, pointing it toward the back lawns that sloped gently down to the ocean-facing cliffs. Ignoring my question, she said, "Start walking, Emma."

She stood aside to let me pass, then fell into step behind me. "Yes, that's right, around the kitchen garden," she ordered.

"Where are we going?"

"You'll see."

The chuckle that accompanied those words did little to reassure me. As we left first the vegetable garden and then the formal flowerbeds behind, my stomach twisted into tighter and tighter knots. The ocean, heretofore a distant murmur, rose to a hiss and then a downright mocking jeer, or so it seemed to me. Good-bye, Emma, the waves seemed to intone as they crashed around the boulders below. Partway across the lawn, Adelaide tossed the bat down into the grass.

"So then you're going to shoot me and throw me off the cliff?"

"Oh, dearest Emma, I'm not going to shoot you. That would be far too messy. Not to mention loud." I'd slowed my steps, and now she poked the barrel of the pistol between my shoulder blades to encourage me to pick up my pace. "Unless, of course, you force my hand. Keep moving."

"Adelaide, you can't hope to get away with this. But . . . maybe I can help you. Uncle Cornelius is a powerful man, and he likes me—very much. I could talk to him, persuade him—"

"Do shut up, Emma. I won't need Cornelius's help. All I'll need are a few bruises, which I'll inflict on myself with my trusty bat, and enough crocodile tears to persuade the police my husband shot Jack, beat his valet to death, and then turned his rage on me. Luckily, however, I was able to wrench the bat away and knock him unconscious. The gun and the bat both belong to Rupert. It'll my word against his, so who do you think they'll believe?"

What she didn't say weighed heavily in the air between us. It was that I, the only other person who knew the truth, would not be around to contest her story. When the police arrived, they'd find things exactly as Adelaide described, and since they now already suspected Rupert had murdered Jack in a fit of jealousy, she wouldn't need to do a lot of persuading.

Soon the grass grew thin and gravely. A few yards ahead of

us, a line of low hedges separated the lawn from the Cliff Walk. Adelaide nudged me toward a break in the foliage. The sea was a constant roar below us; the wind plastered our skirts against our legs, strained the ribbons that secured our hats on our heads, and plucked strands of hair from beneath the brims to whip our shoulders and the backs of our necks.

We reached the gap and were about to step through. I was seconds away from being pushed to my death. Frantically I searched about me for a weapon, something I could grab without Adelaide realizing until it was too late. But there was nothing. I couldn't very well tear branches from the shrubbery and . . . do what with it? My heart pounded, my pulse points throbbed. I felt dizzy, sick, horribly afraid. I felt hope torn from my grasp like leaves born on that relentless wind. I dragged my feet, my mind scrambling to find a way to forestall death.

If I tried reaching down for a rock, Adelaide would shoot me or send me tumbling with a good shove. Besides, there were no rocks in sight large enough to serve as a weapon.

No, maybe not one large enough, but there were small ones aplenty. Not to mention the loose, sandy soil. My heels were sinking into it.

"Move to your right, Emma."

I'd stepped out onto the Cliff Walk, and I realized why Adelaide had given me this last direction. Squinting from where she stood between the hedges, she gazed out over the water, searching, no doubt, for any boats that might be sailing by. She couldn't afford witnesses. The seas were empty—just my luck. Where were the amateur sailors when you needed them?

Yet it was the moment I'd waited and prayed for. With the sparkling water momentarily dazzling Adelaide, I dug my boot tip into the soil, raised my hems, and for all I was worth kicked up a rocky cloud—straight into her face.

I didn't hesitate long enough to gauge the damage I'd done. At the sound of her yelp, I lunged with both hands outstretched. If her gun went off—well, with nothing to lose, I

shoved her back through the hedge and onto the lawn. Together we toppled to the ground, rolled this way and that, our
skirts tangling. The ribbon beneath my chin tore and my hat
flew off. Hers was somewhere beneath us, smashed against the
ground. Her solid weight crushed me at intervals, knocking the
wind out of me. We rolled again and I sucked in a dusty breath.
A thud told me she had likely dropped the pistol, but her fists
rained down on me, on my shoulders and chest, and though I
squirmed and wriggled to avoid her, the edges of her knuckles
grazed my cheek.

The blows stopped, bringing all too temporary relief, for in
the next instant her hands clamped my throat and squeezed.
Gasping, I clawed at her wrists, a futile effort as Adelaide was
far stronger than me. Her golden curls fell wildly into my face
and her weight pinned me to the ground, immobilizing me . . .
though not quite all of me.

Instinctively I thrust my arms outward and groped through
the grass, hoping against hope to find the fallen pistol. Adelaide's shrieks reverberated in my ears. My breath rattled and
scraped in my throat. My senses swarmed dizzily; a dull blackness began to envelop my vision. My body growing numb and
my mind fading into oblivion, I used the last of my strength to
stretch my hands out farther still. . . .

The fingers of my right hand closed around smooth, cylindrical
metal, warmed slightly by the sun. I tightened my fist, raised my
hand high, and brought the butt of the weapon crashing down on
the back of her head.

"Emma!"

The cry drifted across the lawn, so faint surely I'd imagined
it. Adelaide's body crumpled and she slumped heavily on top of
me. I couldn't breathe, couldn't see past the tangles of her hair.
My throat seized against my efforts to drag air into my lungs. I
tried pushing Adelaide off me, frantic to be free, feeling as
though I was entombed in a fragrant, silken grave.

"Emma!" the shout came again, this time closer, convincing

me it wasn't wishful thinking. I tried to call out, but I couldn't seem to open my throat. Instead, I lay gasping, wheezing, my throat searing with ragged pain.

I heard them before I saw them, a rumbling procession barreling across the lawn. Then all at once Adelaide's weight came off me as she was hauled away by two officers in dark blue uniforms. The next thing I knew, I was sitting up, still gasping for breath, but little by little the air reached my lungs. Someone I couldn't see supported me from behind.

As I coughed and sputtered, Adelaide groaned, then seemed to spring back to life with startling speed. Bolting upright from her prone position on the grass, she first looked about her. The two policemen each gripped an upper arm, one on either side of her. She tugged and kicked and screamed, and I vaguely wondered how she found the energy. I certainly couldn't form a word around the arduous task of drawing breaths in and out, and trying to gain control over my trembling limbs.

She fought on, though, even tried to come to her feet. She almost made it, but stumbled and sank back to the grass. The officers didn't relax their hold on her until a third policeman snapped a handcuff on one of her wrists. She tugged for freedom even as they wrestled her hands behind her and secured the other wrist.

They eased their hold slightly, and only then did the furor drain from her limbs and torso. As I looked on she seemed to sag into the ground, the furious sparks fading from her eyes.

"It was her," she said weakly. She raised her chin in my direction. Tears streamed from the eyes I'd once admired. "It was Emma. She did it. She did it all. . . ."

Her accusation made no impact on me other than to rouse a wave of pity. Nor did it faze the officers, except to make them roll their eyes at her ridiculous claim. With a hand at each elbow they raised her to her feet. I attempted to stand up, too, but my knees refused to cooperate.

Those hands that had been supporting me, that I'd all but forgotten about, moved away from my shoulders and then strong arms encircled me from behind. A familiar voice rumbled quietly in my ear. He'd been speaking all along, but I only now became aware of the words. "Emma, Emma, my God . . . did she hurt you? Are you injured, sweetheart? Can you speak?"

I turned my face until warm lips met my cheek. "I'm all right . . . I think."

"You were so brave." Something between a laugh and a sob caught in Derrick's throat. "And here I was thinking I needed to come rescue you."

My stomach flipped pleasantly at those words. "How did you know I'd be here?"

I shuddered against his chest and his arms tightened around me. "I'm not even sure why I decided to check in on you from town, but when I called your house, Mrs. O'Neal told me where you'd gone. And I thought . . ." Releasing me, he scrambled around to face me, his hands once more gripping my shoulders, no longer quite so gently. "What were you thinking? Have you learned nothing in all of this?" His voice boomed in my ears, making me flinch. "How could you be so reckless?"

On any other day I'd have scowled and told him he wasn't my keeper, that he had no right to speak to me like that and I could take care of myself. And I *had* taken care of myself, hadn't I? But I'd stumbled over two dead bodies that day, had almost been thrown from a cliff, shot, and strangled, not to mention learning I'd been betrayed by not one, but two old friends. I'd more than reached the limits of my fortitude. Tears filled my eyes. Derrick's face blurred.

Before I could get out a word, his hands left my shoulders, this time to cup my cheeks. "I'm sorry. I'm so sorry, Emma. Please don't cry. I didn't mean to sound so angry. It's just . . . you're so damned headstrong."

His fingers grazed the swelling left by Adelaide's knuckles. His brows drawn in a scowl, he pressed my good cheek to his shoulder. I sighed and leaned a moment against him as I gathered what I could of my composure. Finally, I lifted my head, frowning. "How did you know Adelaide would be a danger to me?"

"The coroner found a clue the police had overlooked earlier." He rocked back on his heels a little and reached into his pocket. In his palm lay a shiny brass button. "See the *A* embossed on the surface? What the police suspect is that after Adelaide shot Jack at close range, he stumbled into her. They must have struggled before the wound overcame him, and he managed to tear it from her carriage jacket and hide it away in his coat pocket before he died. We brought it to compare with the buttons on the jacket she's wearing now."

"You mean Jack deliberately left a clue behind?"

"Looks like it." The officers had begun half walking, half dragging Adelaide toward the house. Derrick called to them. "Did you check her jacket?"

They came to a halt, one of the examining the front of her fashionable, peplum jacket, now stained, dusty, and hanging askew from her shoulders. He nodded back at us with a grim expression. "Missing," he confirmed.

They continued toward the house as another dark-clad figure rushed past them in Derrick's and my direction. In another moment I recognized Jesse. When he reached us he practically skidded to a halt on the grass and fell into a crouch. "Emma. Why on earth are you here?"

"Jesse, please," I began.

Derrick spoke over me. "Don't. You'll just feel like a cad for scolding her. Take my word for it."

Jesse's hand came up to gently touch my cheek. "That's going to hurt. Are you all right otherwise?"

"As right as I can be at the moment." I shook my head and tugged at my collar. "I don't think she did any permanent damage. Oh, but what about Mr. Halstock?"

"Alive, conscious now, but dazed." Jesse shielded his eyes from the sun as he glanced back up at the house. "My men have him resting inside now. I sent one of them for a doctor."

"Jesse, Adelaide admitted she's been poisoning him," I said. "Trying to kill him so she could inherit his millions."

Neither Jesse nor Derrick looked at all surprised. "He doesn't have quite so many millions these days, apparently," Derrick said. "That's the only reason he's still alive. He'd have been dead weeks ago, except that Cornelius initiated the buyout of the New Haven-Hartford Providence line. She was trying to halt the sale and salvage what was left of her husband's fortune by selling off the stock while it was still worth something. Only then would she have killed him."

"How do you know all that?" My question came out sounding like an accusation.

"Halstock's sister, Suzanne Rockport, suspected Adelaide was mixed up in her husband's finances and in this railroad deal in particular. She didn't realize Adelaide was poisoning the man, but she feared Adelaide would take advantage of Rupert's illness to either manipulate him or have him declared incompetent. That's why she asked me to investigate."

Something about his explanation niggled, but I couldn't put my finger on what it was that didn't sit quite right. My thoughts tossed in logic-blurring chaos. I shook out my skirts and began to shift my feet underneath me. "Help me up."

Both men made a grab for the hand I extended; Derrick clasped it first. Jesse moved out of the way as he rose, but not without a little slant of his eyebrow aimed at Derrick.

I swayed and Derrick's arm slid around my waist.

"I'm all right," I insisted. "Just give me a minute."

"I could carry you," he offered.

"Don't you dare," I retorted, but with a smile to soften the admonishment.

Jesse smirked and flanked my other side. "Emma, I guess it's high time to head back to the station and set Brady free."

My heart did a little dance. "Goodness, in all this turmoil I'd nearly forgotten the reason I became involved in the first place. Can we go right now? Derrick, will you come, too? Brady will want to thank you once I tell him everything you did to help."

"I wouldn't want to intrude. Besides, in all honesty, my help was for you, Emma." He averted his face in a rare show of modesty. "Although I'm glad everything worked out for your brother."

"Don't be silly," I said with a laugh in my voice. "Brady will want to meet you. Once he hears all you've done, he'll be your friend for life. And while that prospect does have its hazards, as Jesse and I can both attest, Brady's a good soul and I do so want you both to meet."

"Well . . ." His arm retreated from around my waist as we reached the rear gardens and the view of the half-dozen or so policemen milling about, taking notes and examining the crime scene. Any attention they might have paid us, however, was diverted by the arrival of the coroner's wagon, which just now jostled over the lawn around the corner of the house. One of the officers climbed the steps to the kitchen door, and I looked away, realizing they were about to remove the body of Rupert's valet from the mudroom. Of Adelaide I saw no sign.

I reached for Derrick's hand and gave it a squeeze. "Oh, just say you'll come and let's be off. I can't wait to see Brady's face when he learns this nightmare is over."

Chapter 19

I waited alone for Brady in the police chief's office; the man was kind enough to once again vacate as he had done the day of Aunt Alice's unprecedented visit. This time his eye twinkled as he congratulated me on the turn of events. In fact, quite a few smiles had greeted me as I'd entered the building. Only Officer Dobbs sported his usual surly expression, now mixed with obvious disappointment that my brother wouldn't be hanged after all.

Humph. Knowing well enough this probably wouldn't be Brady's last run-in with the law, I resisted shooting his nemesis any triumphant looks.

I could barely keep from bouncing up and down in my excitement to see Brady. Jesse had agreed to tell him only that I was here to see him; I would get to break the news of his release to him myself. Still, I wished Derrick hadn't insisted on waiting in the lobby. He repeated his reluctance to intrude on the reunion of our little family, but he was as responsible for Brady's being exonerated as I was, not to mention having saved my life on more than one occasion. He certainly deserved to share in this happy moment.

The door opened quietly and Brady stepped into the room. "Em? What's going on?" Furrows gathered on his brow as his gaze swept the office. "Is Aunt Alice here?"

"It's just me this time, Brady." I hurried the few feet to him and threw my arms around him. "Oh, Brady . . ."

Before I could get any coherent words out, I dissolved into tears. Brady just stood there supporting my limp weight against him while I dampened his shirtfront. He patted my back and rested his chin on my hair.

"It's all right, Em. I knew it was a long shot. Hey, I've had a pretty good run all in all, so no regrets. Just tell Mother—"

I picked my head up. "What are you talking about?"

"I'm done for, right? They're taking me to Providence for the trial, and then—"

"No, no! It's over, Brady! You're free. We did it. We did it!"

"We did?" His hands found my shoulders and he set me at arm's length.

I could hardly contain my peals of laughter. Anyone on the other side of the door must have been certain I'd lost my mind. Brady surely was, judging by his baffled expression. "It was Adelaide. She killed Alvin Goddard . . . and Jack and . . ."

"My God . . ."

My mirth abruptly ceased. "Oh, Brady . . . I can hardly believe it, either. I have so much to tell you. Sit down."

We pulled two chairs close and sat facing each other, our shoulders huddled, hands gripped tight, as I plotted out Adelaide's trail of mayhem. The murders, the attempts on my life. When I finally stopped talking a thick silence fell over us. Brady's face had gone sickly pale. His hands trembled in mine.

Finally, his colorless lips parted. "I don't want you ever taking risks like that again, Em. Nothing is worth all that. Not even me."

I sat back a little and shook my head. "If you weren't looking so ghastly, I'd smack you right in the head for that comment. As it is, you *are* worth it, Brady. You're my brother—"

"Half brother," he corrected me with the faintest beginnings of a grin.

"Brother," I insisted. "You and I hail from the same hardy old Newport stock. We stick together."

He nodded, made a fist, and tapped it gently against my chin. "Even so. Next time—"

"Are you planning a next time?"

"God, no! The only thing I'm planning is some decent food and a good long sleep in my own bed." He wagged his eyebrows and cocked his head. "And to start searching for new employment."

"Maybe not. I'll speak with Uncle Cornelius—"

"There's no way he'll take me back."

"Aunt Alice might be able to sway him."

"Not after what I did. Forget it, Em."

"Well, there are more Vanderbilts where they came from." I thought for a moment. "You know, Alva Vanderbilt might need a secretary or a steward to help her run Marble House. She'd probably hire you just to stick a thorn in Aunt Alice's side."

It was true. Alva Vanderbilt was married to, yet soon to be divorced from, Uncle Cornelius's brother, William. She and Aunt Alice had always maintained a fierce rivalry. Why, if it hadn't been for Alva building Marble House, Aunt Alice would never have had The Breakers rebuilt on such a monumental scale. With resentments already running high, the divorce proceedings had relegated Alva to the position of persona non grata among the rest of the family.

"Yes," I said with a nod, "I do believe Alva might be willing to help us out, Brady. But, come on. Not only can you walk out of here a free man, there's someone I want you to meet."

I flung the office door wide, grasped his hand, and practically hauled him out behind me. In the entrance to the lobby, however, I pulled up short and Brady collided softly with my back. "Where is he?"

"Who?"

"The man who helped me uncover the truth, of course. Derrick Anderson."

"Oh, you mean *Andrews*." Brady came up beside me and viewed the empty lobby. "I saw him through the doorway as they brought me in from the cells. He was more or less hovering by the street door. I waved, but he didn't seem to see me. Anyway, looks like he's gone now."

I turned to him in surprise. "You know Derrick Anderson?"

"It's *Andrews*, and sure, we've met. He's all right. So how'd *you* meet him, Em?" He smiled a bit devilishly.

Whatever innuendo that look conveyed was lost on me as I processed what I'd just learned. "Andrews . . . ? Not Anderson? Are you sure, Brady? Quite sure?"

"Of course I'm sure. Remember when I went with Uncle Cornelius to that regatta in Boston two summers ago? Derrick Andrews was there." Brady grinned at the memory. "Hell of a sailor. And he can toss down a good bourbon with the best of 'em. Man after my own heart, that Andrews is."

"He lied about his name . . . and what else?" I murmured. Then, louder and angrily, "Does he even work for the Providence *Sun*?"

"Work for them? Oh, Em, that's rich. Derrick is Lionel Andrews's son and heir. He'll *own* the *Sun* someday."

And then it hit me. Just a little while ago, when Derrick explained his involvement in this mess, he's said Suzanne Rockport had *asked* him to investigate Adelaide. Not hired him—*asked* him. As in one friend asking a favor of another.

He *knew* Mrs. Rockport, was probably a family friend. Because Derrick Anderson—no, Andrews—hailed from the same societal stratosphere. Was probably even one of the Four Hundred.

"That's why he left. He knew you'd give him away and end his little charade."

Brady just gave me a puzzled look.

Oh, what wouldn't I tell that man when I saw him again. I straightened my spine. "Let's ask Jesse for a ride to your place, Brady. You'll gather a few things and come home with me to Gull Manor. I'm sure Nanny will love to cook for you."

"Now that's the best offer I've had in the longest time," he replied with a burst of his former enthusiasm. "And no doubt the dear old peach'll brew me a spot of tea with a wee splash of brandy.

"Now who could that be?" Nanny muttered as the telephone jangled yet again. It had been ringing all morning for the same reason: friends calling to congratulate Brady on his release.

Never mind that many of those friends not only hadn't visited him in jail, but had remained silent rather than stand up for Brady's innocence. Luckily for them my brother had a forgiving nature and a short memory.

"I'll get it," he said quite needlessly, as neither Nanny nor I had made a move to rise from our chairs in the front parlor. Quickly he crossed into the hall and ducked under the staircase.

Jesse, sitting on Aunt Sadie's favorite overstuffed, camelback sofa across from me, grinned. "It's good to see him out and his old self again." His smile vanished and he shook his head. "I wish I could have brought you better news today, though."

He had come to tell us of Adelaide's fate. Nanny hadn't stopped scowling since he arrived. "Convalescent home, bah! There should be a trial, after which she should spend the rest of her miserable days in a dark, dank cell where she belongs. Where our Brady would have ended up—or worse—if Emma hadn't cracked the case."

" 'Cracked the case'?" I couldn't help smirking at her. "Nanny, have you been reading Sherlock Holmes again?"

She shrugged, but the twinkle in her eye spoke of guilty pleasures.

"I agree with you, Mrs. O'Neal," Jesse put in, "and this is officially off the record. But her husband and his sister apparently offered a hefty . . . shall we say . . . donation . . . to just the right political campaign to have the affair neatly tied up as quickly and quietly as possible. Adelaide has been declared incompetent due to a nervous condition and bundled away to an isolated asylum on the Maine coast. They're calling it a convalescent home, but trust me, Mrs. Halstock won't be strolling any gardens or soaking in any hot springs anytime soon."

"Well, that's something, I guess." I lifted the teapot from the low table in front of me. "More tea?"

Jesse set his cup down and pushed to his feet. "Thanks, but I've got to be getting back."

I walked him to the front door; Brady's hearty voice echoed at our backs from the alcove as he continued his jabbering over the line. Jesse waved a salute to him and Brady saluted back.

Jesse turned to me in the open doorway. "I should yell at you, you know. I told you to keep out of it and look what almost happened."

"I hear a bit of hesitancy, though," I teased.

He pursed his lips ruefully. "The truth is, you'd have made a fine detective, Emma. Just . . . just don't make a habit out of it."

He looked about to say something else, and his expression made some instinct inside me clench. His thought went unspoken, however. An open rig, its top down, rumbled up the drive. Even from the distance I could make out the wide-shouldered figure of Derrick Anderson—make that Andrews—perched behind a dapple gray hack.

"I'll see you soon, Emma," Jesse said, and made his way stiffly to his own buggy.

As Derrick climbed down I considered shutting the door

and locking it. This man had lied to me for no good reason that I could see, except possibly to make a fool of me, to have something to snigger about behind my back. I'd been nothing but honest with him, and the betrayal stung. Probably always would.

He approached with his bowler in his hands, head slightly bowed. Perhaps his conscience niggled, or perhaps he correctly read the less-than-welcoming expression on my face. "Good morning, Emma."

"Mr. Andrews."

"Ah, yes."

I drew up rigidly. "Is that all you have to say for yourself?"

Brady's voice had gone quiet in the ensuing moments, but now the telephone jingled again. Derrick gazed past me into the house, then looked off to his left. "Will you walk with me?"

I glared at him for a full five or six seconds. "All right."

Our steps crunching on the drive, we circled the house in silence and headed toward the spit of land that jutted out into the ocean. Once there he turned to face me and reached for my hand, but I grasped it primly at my waist with my other.

"I don't appreciate being lied to," I said.

"I'm sorry, Emma. But surely you can understand my need for discretion. I couldn't exactly arrive in Newport as Derrick Andrews, investigating a man at the request of a family friend. Mrs. Rockport was trying to protect her brother while at the same time avoiding a scandal—"

"No," I said.

"No?"

"No. Oh, I'll concede the validity of your argument up to a point, but are you forgetting that you confided in me about your reasons for being in Newport the night I was attacked on the Point? *That* was the time to tell me the truth—the whole truth of who you are. And yet you continued to lie. Why is that?"

He started to crush his bowler between his hands, then stilled them. "Because I'd begun to like you," he murmured.

"And that's a reason to deceive me? Why, you ki—" I broke off just before blurting the word *kissed*. And maybe that was the reason his deception appalled me as much as it did. The man had kissed me, toyed with my emotions, while playing me false. I compressed my lips and stared at the rocky ground between us."

"It was stupid of me. But, Emma, the more I learned about you, the more I realized Derrick Andrews was not a man you'd ever think twice about. At least not in the way I'd come to think about you. Derrick Andrews is too rich, too much a part of society, too much like your Vanderbilt relatives. Why, one look at you and a man can see you don't want to be a society matron like your aunt. You're too independent, too headstrong. Too daring and full of adventure."

I held his gaze and said nothing, challenging him with my silence to change my mind about him; good heavens, hoping in spite of myself he *could* change my mind.

"But Derrick Anderson, investigative reporter, is like you, Emma," he went on after a moment. A plea for understanding turned his deep voice husky. "He works for a living, and he's as adventurous and daring as you are. He can find pleasure in small moments, in experiences that have nothing to do with capital gains." He stepped closer, making my peninsula suddenly feel far too small for the two of us. "He's like you. *I'm* like you, Emma. I swear it."

The sea breezes and briny spray shut out the world around us. Like rocks that are slowly broken down by the tides, I felt my anger ebbing, breaking apart, scattering. He spoke the truth. He had been listening to me all those times we'd spent together—listening well. Getting to know me, and to like me for who I was. The power of that swayed any resolve I'd made to stand strong against him.

My pride, however, held like the strongest mortar. My Vanderbilt heritage again, I suppose, a legacy I could never quite escape.

"I suppose I should forgive you after everything you've done. It wouldn't be very sporting of me to hold a grudge, would it?" I smiled good-naturedly and held my right hand out vertically, an offer to shake hands and reconcile. "We can, of course, be friends."

"No, Emma, more than that."

I shook my head. "Don't you see? You aren't Derrick Anderson. You're Derrick Andrews, and you always will be."

"I can offer you so much."

"Did you not listen to your own words? What you can offer, I don't want. You can't escape your society obligations, and I can't consign myself to a life of balls and soirées. I want to be a newspaper reporter, not the wife of a newspaper owner. I'd much rather live at Gull Manor than an estate like The Breakers. At Gull Manor I can hear the ocean spray against my bedroom windows. The Breakers is set too high and far away from the water's edge. I want to feel the spray in life, Derrick. I need that."

"What makes you think you couldn't have that with me?"

"Because of who you are. Right now I'm a novelty to you. Different from all the other girls you've known. But novelty wears off. Deny it all you want, but society is persuasive. I'd always be that poor, obscure little Vanderbilt relation, and dear Derrick could have done so much better than her."

"To hell with everyone else. I'd never think that way."

He believed it. Oh, yes, his certainty shouted from the tension of his fists around his hat brim, the flexing of the muscles in his cheek, the intensity of determination in his eyes. For the briefest moment Adelaide stole into my thoughts. Not the murdering, devious Adelaide, but the defeated, isolated wife who'd been shunned by the society dragons; the Adelaide who, for brief moments at least, had reached out to me as a friend.

That Adelaide whispered the truth in my ear, that Derrick Andrews and I were simply not for each other.

I smiled sadly. "Good-bye, Derrick. Thank you ever so much. But good-bye."

I turned away and started toward the house at a brisk stride, damnable tears filling my eyes and blurring the garden around me. Then Derrick brushed past me, and on a lick of breeze I could have sworn I heard, "Good-bye for now, Emma Cross. But mark my words, I'll be back."

Afterword

The events in this book are purely fiction. However, the story is centered around a key social event of the summer of 1895, that of the reopening of The Breakers after the original, much more modest "summer cottage" had burned to the ground three years previously. The extravagant affair also celebrated the coming out of young Gertrude Vanderbilt, a quiet, introspective girl who felt awkward in her finery and in finding herself at the center of so much attention. She might have much preferred a quiet evening spent with her closest friend, Esther Hunt, whose father, Richard Morris Hunt, had designed her palatial Newport home, as well as many of the other "cottages" lining exclusive Bellevue Avenue.

Gertrude's brother, Neily Vanderbilt, did, in fact, dance with Grace Wilson that evening, beginning a courtship that both enraged and dismayed his parents, who didn't believe the stunningly beautiful Grace, or her family, to be good enough for their son. He would, however, remain undaunted in his intentions toward Grace, even under the threat of being disinherited. Although Cornelius's brother, William K. Vanderbilt, was a welcome guest at the ball that night, due to his recent divorce, his ex-wife, Alva, was excluded from the festivities as the Vanderbilt family closed ranks against her.

Beyond this, the story and characters are the product of my imagination, though I've done my best to keep true to the nature of the times and the people who lived in them. The name Vanderbilt had always had iconic connotations for me, more a symbol of the extravagancies and waste of a bygone age than flesh-and-blood people. What I discovered in my research, however, was a family that was in many ways much like any other, with all of the hopes and disappointments, loyalties and betrayals, love and resentments that arise whenever individuals of differing dispositions and aspirations endeavor to form a cohesive unit. In the end, money and power didn't make the Vanderbilts any happier, healthier, or more indestructible than anyone else. But as more and more of their faults and frailties, as well as their strengths and talents, came to light, my understanding and my fondness for them grew, until I've almost come to think of them as old, dependable friends, who, for a short, glittering time in history, shared the same island home as my husband's own Newport family.

Please turn the page for an exciting sneak peek of
Alyssa Maxwell's next Gilded Newport mystery

MURDER AT MARBLE HOUSE

coming in October 2014!

Chapter 1

Newport, Rhode Island
August 1895

The tide splashed against the boulders at the tip of my property, the spray pattering my face to mingle with the single tear I could not prevent from rolling down my cheek. I stared out over the ocean in an attempt to channel all that great strength and make it my own. The waves, however forceful, didn't quite drown out the footsteps receding through the grass behind me, and I wrapped my arms tightly around my middle to keep from calling out, from turning and running and speaking the truth that crashed like a thunderous sea inside me.

I stood immobile, buffeted by the briny winds while Derrick Anderson—no, I now knew he was Derrick *Andrews*—strode away. He had lied to me about his identity for days on end, and the sting of his deceit had left me feeling like a naïve fool. But that wasn't the only reason I'd sent him away, or why, however much I yearned to recall my cold words, I could not. Not if I wished to remain true to myself, to continue to be the woman I had struggled, and would continue to struggle, to be.

Finally, when I deemed him far enough away that I would be safe from temptation, I turned and glimpsed his retreating back—his dark hair and tall figure and the sturdy shoulders I'd come to depend on so much in the previous days. Shoulders I'd cried against. Shoulders with the power to make me lose all sense of myself, and that even at this distance proved an enticement I very nearly could not resist.

And wasn't that but one more reason to deny his suit? How long had we known each other? Days? A couple of weeks? In that time, we'd lived through more than most people did in a lifetime. Our emotions, sensibilities—indeed, our very lives— had been thrust into turmoil as fierce as any ocean storm. We had survived. We had triumphed. Is it any wonder, then, that we might be caught up in an attachment to each other . . . but one that might not last once the final currents of upheaval had settled.

Despite the blustery winds, the sun shone sharp and bright that morning, the glitter on the water dazzling, while glaringly white clouds scuttled gaily across a brisk blue sky. How dare a morning be so happy? Tears fell like frigid rain on my cheeks as Derrick disappeared around the corner of my rambling, shingle-style house.

I stood for an indeterminate length of time, staring at that space beside the hawthorn hedges where he had disappeared. I wondered which would finally win out: regret or resolve. I allowed myself that much self-indulgence before straightening my spine, dropping my arms to my sides, and giving myself a hard shake. Did I love Derrick Andrews? If this sinking, ill sensation inside me could be interpreted as love, then perhaps. Or then again, perhaps what I felt had more to do with being thrown together into a maelstrom of events over which we had little control other than to form an alliance and pool our resources.

Either way, I'd made my choice. I would not be the wife of a wealthy, influential man and have my life mapped out in a series of balls and regattas that would accomplish nothing of substance in this world. Yes, Vanderbilt blood ran through my veins, but I wanted no part of the gilded prison in which my Aunt Alice and all the other society matrons resided.

I glanced back out at the tossing ocean and realized the brine of Newport, of rocky, resolute Aquidneck Island, also ran through my veins to mingle with the blood of the Commodore, that first stubborn Vanderbilt who had set out to build an empire. So yes, I was a Vanderbilt, but I was also a Newporter born and raised—salty, sturdy, and fiercely independent.

Thus assured, I picked my way over my shaggy lawn—I really needed to purchase a new goat since poor Gerty had died last spring—toward Gull Manor, the house my equally independent Aunt Sadie had left to me in her will. She would be proud of me today. She would approve.

Yes. There. I wished Derrick Andrews well, always, but I'd made the right decision. For me, and in all likelihood for him as well.

The jangling of the telephone startled me as I neared the open windows. Knowing there were others at home, I didn't run to answer the device, installed months earlier at my Uncle Cornelius's generous insistence. I sighed. As independent as I liked to be, sometimes it was easier to accept my relatives' largess rather than argue a case I'd likely lose in the end anyway. If my illustrious extended family was happy to provide little luxuries I couldn't afford, who was I to deprive them of that satisfaction?

As I said, I didn't run to answer the ringing summons. It had been reverberating all morning, not for me but for my half brother, who was temporarily staying with me. Friends and acquaintances—some of them barely known to us—had been calling almost nonstop to congratulate Brady on being released from jail the day before. He'd been accused of murdering Uncle Cornelius's financial secretary on the night of our cousin Gertrude's coming-out ball at The Breakers, but Derrick and I had discovered the true culprit even as the police had been preparing to ship Brady off to Providence for trial. That is what had brought Derrick and me together. But that, friends, is not a story I care to revisit.

I was surprised, therefore, when Brady held the ear trumpet out to me the moment I entered the house. He raised a hand to cover the ebony mouthpiece protruding from the oaken call box.

"There you are, Em. Thought you'd run off to elope with Derrick." He waggled his pale eyebrows at me. Less than twenty-four hours out of his prison cell and the color had already returned to his cheeks, the mischievous sparkle to his eye. His sandy blond hair fell in rakish disarray across his brow, and he wore neither suit coat nor collar, his shirtsleeves rolled up to his elbows. Somehow Brady managed to wear his dishabille with a relaxed, thoughtless style that men often envied and women found delightful. It seemed no matter what happened to Brady—the good, the bad, and the drunkenly disastrous—he somehow emerged unscathed and unjaded; unchanged from the boy I'd grown up adoring.

But on this particular day, I was in no mood for his teasing.

"I don't wish to talk to anyone," I answered wearily. "Whoever it is, tell them I'll return their call later." I dragged myself toward the parlor, where Nanny O'Neal, my housekeeper and surrogate grandmother, would embrace me briefly in her pudgy arms and pour me a cup of tea.

Brady extended the earpiece as far as the wire would allow. "It's Cousin Consuelo. And she sounds a bit frantic."

I frowned, but didn't question him. Instead, I moved to switch places with him in the alcove beneath the stairs, waited for Brady to make his way back to the parlor, and spoke into the mouthpiece. "Consuelo? It's lovely to hear from you, dearest. We missed you at Gertrude's ball—"

"Emmaline. I don't have much time. I need you. Can you come over right away?"

"What is it? Is something wrong?" I cringed at my stupid

question. Consuelo's parents, William and Alva Vanderbilt, were recently divorced—quite the scandal of the moment. They'd been bickering for years, and there were rumors of lovers on both their parts. The two younger sons had been at boarding school and were now with relatives on Long Island, so they missed the worst of it. But poor Consuelo had been caught in the middle like a doll fought over by two recalcitrant children, each tugging on an arm until the seams threatened to split.

"No time to explain," she said in a breathless rush. "You're my only hope, Emma. Please, can you come? Now?"

"I . . ." Frankly, after some very close scrapes in the past several days and now this morning's emotional trial, I very badly needed one of Nanny's strong cups of tea . . . with the wee splash of brandy she often added on the sly. But Consuelo's sense of urgency all but made the ear trumpet tremble against my palm. Besides, she had deepened her appeal by calling me Emma. My Vanderbilt relatives almost always insisted on Emmaline, as if that could somehow raise me up to the status of the rest of them. Only Consuelo, and my young cousin Reggie, seemed able to take me as I was.

I glanced with longing through the parlor doorway, where I could just see the rather threadbare edges of Nanny's velveteen house slippers propped on a footstool. Brady's and her quiet voices called to me like a soothing aria. With a sigh I leaned to speak into the mouthpiece. "Yes, all right. I just need time to hitch Barney to the buggy. . . ."

Consuelo gasped. "I have to go!"

The line went dead.

Some twenty minutes later Barney and I rumbled up Bellevue Avenue. Our pace didn't exactly match the urgency of my cousin's summons, but I didn't dare push my aging hack any faster than a sedate walk. And even if I had pushed, it's doubtful he'd have deigned to oblige.

Gravel sputtered beneath the carriage wheels as we turned through a pair of broad marble columns onto a raised circular drive bordered with stone railings that cut like gleaming ivory arcs across the manicured front lawn. Marble House, with its Corinthian-columned entry flanked by two massively solid wings, represented, both to me and the world at large, the fierce competition between the William K. Vanderbilts and the Cornelius Vanderbilts, who lived nearby at The Breakers. Or, perhaps more accurately, the two houses embodied the intense rivalry between my aunts Alva and Alice, who each vied to stand supreme as the queen of all society.

From some unseen door off to one side, a liveried footman ran out to help me down and relieve me of my rig. He blushed to the roots of his slicked-back hair as I bade him good morning, thanked him, and asked after his grandmother, who was a longtime friend of Nanny's. I always made a point of greeting servants as though they were human beings. Some appreciated the gesture; others, like this young man, were left flustered by my familiarity.

Morning sunlight glittered on the house's pristine façade. I paused before approaching the front door, blinking in the glare and remembering how, after nearly four years of construction behind high, concealing walls, it had been the unveiling of Marble House that had spurred Aunt Alice to have The Breakers rebuilt on such a dizzying scale. Alice Vanderbilt simply could not live in a house smaller and humbler than Alva's. If Aunt Alice's one-upmanship had infuriated her sister-in-law, however, Alva never once allowed Alice the satisfaction of seeing her haughty smile slip, not even a notch.

I wondered what role Alva had played in Consuelo's frantic call this morning. I'd heard rumors—we all had, that summer—but I would save judgment until I had the facts from my cousin.

"A good morning to you, Miss Cross," a youthful voice hailed from the corner of the eastern wing. A young man wearing a tweed cap tugged low over a riot of golden red curls sauntered closer, a pair of trimming shears held out in front of him like a divining rod. He nodded in that deferential way servants had, yet in his case the gesture brought a genuine sparkle to those bright blue eyes of his.

"Good morning, Jamie. How are things going? Are you liking it here at Marble House?" This I inquired in an undertone, for if Aunt Alva caught us conversing I'd receive an admonishing *tsk,* while her newest gardener could very well find himself sacked. Had I been an expected guest, he would not have been permitted anywhere near the front drive until everyone had arrived and been brought safely into the house, lest the sight of a workman offend their sensibilities. In houses such as Marble House, servants learned to perform their duties at both the whim and convenience of their employers.

"Why, 'tis going splendid, it is, and I've got you to thank for that, miss." His earnest reply, with its lovely Irish cadence, acknowledged my role in securing his present employment; Jamie was a friend of my Irish housemaid, Katie, and I'd intervened at her hearty request.

I waved his thanks away. "I'm glad it worked out."

With that, I proceeded between two massive, Corinthian-topped marble columns, which always made me feel impossibly small. The front entryway presented an equally intimidating prospect with its grillwork of elaborately wrought bronze. Lifting the knocker that was several sizes larger and a good deal heavier than my hand, I let it fall once, cringing at the echoes resounding on the other side of that forbidding door.

As if I'd been expected—indeed, looked for—the door opened immediately. Instead of the porter, however, Grafton, Marble House's head butler, greeted me with a frown. "Miss Cross, good morning. Are you come to see Mrs. Vanderbilt?"

Did I imagine wariness in those sharply aquiline features? "Good morning, Grafton, and no. I'm here to see Miss Consuelo."

"I'm afraid she is not at home, miss. Would you care to leave your card?"

"My card?" I narrowed my eyes at the man, at his intimidating six-foot frame, his thick but silvered hair, the arced nose with its resolutely flaring nostrils. He eased backward from the doorway as if about to shut me out. What was going on here? "I don't typically carry cards when I visit my relatives, Grafton, especially when I'm arriving at the request of my cousin who called me not a half hour ago."

"Perhaps she called you from the country club, miss."

"She most certainly did not. Miss Consuelo was quite clear when I spoke to her. Now, may I please come in, Mr. Grafton?"

His peppered eyebrows went up in an unspoken admonishment: Was I calling him a liar? Good heavens, I might be able to make a footman blush with no more than a gentle good morning, but it seemed Grafton would not be budged by my persistence.

Well, I wasn't about to turn tail and run, either. "Is my aunt at home, then?"

The lines above his nose deepened. "She is . . . however she is not quite at liberty at the moment—"

Clattering footsteps echoed in the entry hall. "Grafton, who's at the door?"

I recognized the voice. Not giving the servant the chance to block me from view, claim I was a vagrant, and shut the door in my face, I quickly ducked my head around his shoulder. "It's me, Aunt Alva."

"Emmaline! Oh, Grafton, don't be a goose, and let my darling niece inside."

Like Cornelius and Alice Vanderbilt, William and Alva were not my aunt and uncle, but rather cousins several times removed. But with a generation separating me from them, I fell naturally into the role of niece. In all honesty, I'd never been Alva's "darling" anything until recently, when she'd realized how much of a favorite I was of Aunt Alice's. From then on, Alva became determined to flood me with affection and bestow little favors on me, especially if word of it might reach Alice's ears.

Still, I smiled and greeted her warmly, letting her enfold me in her sturdy arms and returning her kiss.

"I'm so glad you're here, Emmaline," she sang out gaily, her voice bouncing on the cold Sienna marble of the floor and walls. I'd been told the house had been fashioned after the great palace of Versailles, on a smaller but no less grand scale. "I have special company this weekend and I'd love for them to meet you."

She would? She'd never been that eager to introduce me to her society cronies before. "That would be lovely, Aunt Alva. Is, er . . ." I assumed my most innocent, nonchalant expression. "Is Consuelo here, too?"

"Well, of course she is. Where else would Consuelo be? Surely not with her father out on that ostentatious yacht of his."

Funny, Alva hadn't considered the yacht ostentatious when she'd taken Consuelo on an exhausting European tour all last summer and autumn. Her sudden scowl drew me from the memory, and my stomach clenched in anticipation of one of her quick, wildfire tirades outlining the many sins of her newly exhusband. She surprised me, however, when her smile returned and her voice dipped lower on a conspiratorial note. "Did Grafton tell you she wasn't at home?"

I cast a glance over my shoulder to discover the man had shuffled quietly away, probably through the grand dining hall and to the servants' domains. "He did. Why would he lie?"

"Consuelo . . . hasn't been feeling at all well lately."

A surge of alarm went through me. "She's been ill?"

"Oh, not ill exactly . . . Come with me." She grasped my wrist and whisked me through a doorway into the Gold Room, a sumptuously gilded, Louis XIV–style ballroom whose ornate décor rivaled that of The Breakers' Great Hall. The Gold Room was situated at the front of the house. Her guests couldn't glimpse us through the windows here, which essentially belied her reason for overstepping Grafton and admitting me to the house. Here, amid rich carvings and chiseled marble, French silks, Italian brocades, and vibrant porcelain from ancient Chinese dynasties—riches enough to feed several orphanages for several years—she told me of a plan that raised bile to my throat and urged me to rush to Consuelo's side.

"He should be here in about a week, Emmaline, so you see the urgency."

I nodded absently, not truly hearing her question as my mind spun with a dozen contrary thoughts. The "he" she spoke of was Charles Richard John Spencer-Churchill, recently dubbed ninth Duke of Marlborough—or Sunny, as his friends apparently called him. Even now his transatlantic steamer headed toward New York, where he would turn north for Newport and officially become engaged to the eighteen-year-old Consuelo.

Aunt Alva hadn't counted on one small problem: Consuelo was having none of it.

"If anyone can convince her, Emmaline," Alva said, "it's you."

I stepped back as though she'd struck me. "Me? I'm sorry, Aunt Alva, but you can't imagine I'd approve of a forced marriage. Or that I'd ever step into the middle of a family matter. You know me better than that."

She took an ominous stride closer, forcing me back another step, and then another. Alva followed my backward course until my calves struck a thronelike side chair. She loomed mere inches away. Her features hardened; her eyes turned icy. A lethal finger rose to point squarely at my heart. "Make no mistake, Emmaline. Consuelo *will* marry the Duke of Marlborough. There *is* no other choice in the matter. The only question that remains is, will she do so willingly, or will I have to drag her by her hair to the church?"

The breath froze in my lungs, and chills traveled my spine. Yet this was nothing new. Alva wasn't acting out of character with her threats or her sudden vehemence, nor with her desire to live vicariously through her daughter. Alva had *always* intended for Consuelo to marry into minor European nobility, landed gentry at the very least; hence last year's European cruise. But a duke! I could already hear her, announcing to all of society: *Oh, yes, my daughter the duchess . . .* What a triumph: every society mother's fondest ambition. Here was a prize this bull terrier of a woman had sunk her teeth into and would never, ever, *ever* let go of.

With Alva standing so close, all but threatening to sink her teeth into me as well, I became very afraid, not for myself, but for Consuelo. Because I knew that no matter what I or anyone else did, in the end, her mother would prevail. She always had; she always would.

With or without a handful of her daughter's hair.

In a perverse way, then, Alva was right. The best thing I could do for my cousin was comfort her and help her face her impending marriage bravely. But to do it I would have to disavow everything I believed in, such as a woman's right to choose her own fate, as I had chosen to do only that morning. To help Consuelo, I'd have to lie to her and do so with a smile.

How I dreaded the role I must play.

"Is she upstairs?" I asked in quiet resignation.

With a victorious spark in her eye, Alva nodded. Her smile returned, but her chin lifted and her nostrils flared in a way no doubt intended to remind me of my place—my lowly place—in the family. "She respects you, Emmaline. Even has a silly notion that you're better off than any of the rest of us Vanderbilt women. That's why if you, of all people, tell her this marriage is in her best interests, she'll believe you."

As she spoke those last words she took in my carriage dress, the dark blue one formerly belonging to my Aunt Sadie, but which Nanny had freshened with new velvet trim and shiny jet buttons. Her assessing gaze didn't stop until it reached my hemline, where Nanny had done a splendid job of concealing the slight fraying of the fabric where it skimmed the floor.

"Remember, Emmaline, as a duchess, Consuelo will never want for anything. And if it's a bit of independence she's after, between her new title and her inheritance, no doors will be closed to her. Good grief, think of the good she'll be able to do, if that's what she wants. She'll have the means to fund charities, form scholarships—whatever strikes her fancy, as long as the cause is a suitable one and her husband is agreeable."

Yes, independence. Aunt Alva's definition of the word dripped its bitter irony on my already sagging spirits.

She reached out and gave my shoulder a little nudge. "Go on. She'll be delighted to see you." Her eyes narrowed. "Don't think I'm not aware that she called you earlier. The little sneak. Why, I should have—oh, but we'll work it to our advantage, won't we?"

"*Our* advantage?"

She nudged me again. "Just talk to her. She adores you. And make her come downstairs. Tell her I have a surprise for her."

"What is it?"

Alva rolled her eyes. "A surprise. Now go."

I turned and began walking, wondering how much Consuelo would adore me—or respect me—once she discerned my part in this debacle. Somehow the task ahead seemed even more difficult than tracking down a murderer, nearly being murdered myself, and clearing my brother of false charges. Gripping the cold, wrought-iron banister until my knuckles whitened, I started up the staircase.

Alva's parting words drifted from the doorway of the Gold Room. "I'm counting on you, Emmaline. Do not let me down."

The *or else* hovered in the air between us.